# BLOOD
# SHADOWS

# BLOOD
## SHADOWS

### BLACKTHORN

### BOOK ONE

# LINDSAY J. PRYOR

*bookouture*

Published by Bookouture

An imprint of StoryFire Ltd.
23 Sussex Road, Ickenham, UB10 8PN
United Kingdom

www.bookouture.com

ISBN: 978-1-909490-01-7

*For Moth*

*With special thanks to:*

*Anita*

*You've done more for me than you'll ever know*

*Those who have been there whenever I've needed you:*

*Christine, Tracey, Michelle, Charlotte, Katie and Michele.*

*The person responsible for making this dream come true:*

*Oliver Rhodes*

*For your faith in these stories and me as a writer.*

*Team Bookouture are amazing.*

# CHAPTER ONE

Something was wrong.

Partially shielded behind her umbrella, Caitlin watched Kane Malloy from across the street, her fingers loosely entwined in her colleague Morgan's as they feigned a lovers' kiss goodnight.

'We're going to lose him,' she whispered into her earpiece. 'If we don't move now, he's going to be gone.'

'Hold your position,' Max replied. 'Not all exits are secure. We still have too many unmarked alleys behind those buildings.'

Max had promised her he wouldn't interfere, had assured her it was her case, damn it. Since he'd realised it might actually happen, she might actually succeed, it had all changed. If she lost this one opportunity…

'How much longer?' she asked.

'Eight minutes.'

Caitlin's eyes narrowed on her target as he stood outside the club. Both of the honey-trap girls with him were trying to outdo each other with suggestive body language so shameless she was starting to question just how focused on the job they actually were. But if Kane was falling for it, he would have had them by now. Instead he was stalling, using them as a shield to check out the street. And that meant one thing: the vampire was on to them.

'Max, I'm telling you—'

'And I'm telling you to hang back, Parish. You don't have enough backup.'

Caitlin exhaled tersely. She glanced at Morgan frowning down at her before turning her attention back across the street. Caitlin Parish knew everything possible for any human being to know about Kane Malloy. In the six years she'd been with the Vampire Control Unit, the latter four had been tracking him. But it wasn't only the countless unsubstantiated offences that frustrated her, or the inconclusiveness of some of his most heinous crimes – it was the fact that everyone knew his name and feared it, everyone knew his reputation and so reported nothing and, above all, everyone believed him untouchable.

Everyone except her.

Ever since her first day, when she'd seen the picture of him in prime position on the 'Wanted' board, she knew she had to take the case – even more so when she saw the smirks around the table when she'd requested it. From old and experienced to talented and ruthless, they'd all had a go at bringing down Kane Malloy. And she'd seen it in their eyes – no twenty-three-year-old slip of a girl newly in position was going to outdo them, seventh sense or no seventh sense.

She'd had everything to prove in the years since then, not least that she wasn't as vulnerable and fragile as her physical appearance portrayed. Despite her extensive qualifications, she knew she'd never have landed the job if it hadn't been for her gift. The VCU was the dark, murky corner of law enforcement where life experience was more defensible than any piece of academic paper. Penetrating the deadly streets of vampire-infested Blackthorn required a physical, intellectual and emotional mindset reserved only for the elite. Over half the district's less fearful population were openly expressive of their views about VCU interference. To them, her unit was just another in a long line responsible for keeping vampires in their place – contained and forgotten in the over-populated, over-polluted, dense urban mass that humankind had abandoned along with its promises of better provision one day. Resentment was rife. So was retaliation.

History dictated she should never have passed the application stage. But lucky for her, shadow readers were too invaluable for them to turn her down. Her innate ability to delve into the soul-substituted shadow of the vampire, lycan or any of the other third species was too vital to her unit. Her sensitivity to the pulse of the detainees – an open door to every act, thought and emotion – secured a conviction every time, another case closed. The fact it could all be done in the relatively safe confines of the interrogation room was the step in she needed.

But Caitlin never had any intention of playing safe. Ever since she'd been a young girl, she had wanted only one thing – to be a tracker, out there on the field, in the thick of it, just like her father. And being the one to finally capture Kane Malloy would not only seal her career and silence every critic who had underestimated her, capturing Kane would at long last get her up close and personal with the vampire himself. Then she'd get what she really wanted: truths hidden deep in his master-vampire shadow – not least what had slaughtered her parents.

Kane was core to her vengeance and, moreover, core to her survival.

Either that or she was about to make the biggest mistake of what could be the last night of her life.

'Time's ticking, Max.'

'Six more minutes, Parish.'

She closed her eyes for a moment before staring back across the rain-soaked street, compelling herself to obey her boss's order. But when Kane exhaled one final steady stream of smoke into the night air, when he smiled assuredly to himself as he threw his cigarette to the ground, Caitlin knew he may as well have flipped up his middle finger and slid her perfectly manicured plan down onto it.

'No,' she hissed.

Before Max had time to question her exclamation, before Morgan had time to restrain her, she'd stepped off the kerb. She pounded through the puddles, Kane already disappearing back into the club.

'Parish, get back into position!' Max warned. 'Do not go in there. I repeat, do not go in there.'

'We lose him now, we lose him for good,' Caitlin declared. 'And I am not going to let that happen.'

'You have insufficient backup. I repeat: insufficient backup.'

But Caitlin ignored his warnings as she followed every gut instinct she had, every moment of tracking experience she had gained hunting vampires over the years.

'Damn it, Caitlin, that's an order!' Max barked. 'There are too many people in there, too much interference. I'll lose you.'

'But I'm not going to lose him,' she said, flashing her badge to ward off the bouncer who stepped in front of her.

She couldn't lose him, not now.

'He will have worked out the side exits are manned,' she added. 'He's going to head up to the roof. Focus the team up there. I'll drive him up or take him out before then.' She reached inside her jacket to flick the latch off the tranquiliser gun.

'Parish, you are in contempt of my orders. Get out of there now or face suspension!'

But the adrenaline took over, her heart pounding, her throat dry.

Two years of proving herself more than capable as a tracker, two further years compiling the Malloy case before finally taking over as lead, twenty months of intense planning and it was finally coming to this – a last-minute, poorly executed scuffle to detain him. But there was no way she was going to let him slip through her fingers, because if she did, it would be over. Now he knew they were on to him he'd be gone into the ether – gone from her jurisdiction, gone from her life.

And she wasn't going to let that happen.

Couldn't let that happen.

Tonight she would finally look Kane Malloy in those painfully cruel yet enticingly seductive navy-blue eyes and tonight he would look right back into hers. The thought terrified and exhilarated her, both emotions exacerbated by the buzz of the club. The pounding of the trance music evoked her blood to pump, the mass of milling, gyrating bodies making the room surge, the air thick with the scent of dry ice, smoke, alcohol, sweat.

Too many times she'd gazed into those penetrating eyes on paper, eyes framed with thick lashes as dark as his cropped hair. Too many times she'd dwelled on that sensual, masculine mouth as she pored over files at her desk until the early hours, paperwork spread across the lounge of her tiny apartment – yet another night alone in front of the TV.

And on too many occasions, when the darkness was all-encompassing, when the rain tapped lightly against the windowpanes, she'd find her mind wandering to what their first encounter would be like. Sometimes he would visit her in her dreams when her subconscious took over, when the deep dark fantasies she suppressed were allowed free reign. She would wake at times beaded in perspiration, other times soaked in sensual heat.

Caitlin refocused and pressed on through the crowds, knowing there were three exits he could choose from but only one that led up to the roof.

Senses overwhelmed, ears ringing, she burst through the doors and into the corridor. The volume of the music evaporated slowly with the increased distance as she marched ahead through the stragglers, turning left down a dimmer, more isolated corridor.

'Caitlin, listen to me, damn it!' Max commanded, a faint crackle telling her the depth of the building was already causing connection problems. 'You cannot face him alone. Do not face him alone.'

'This is my case, Max,' she said, every sense on full alert as she glanced warily over her shoulder before assessing the corridor ahead again. Reaching into her jacket pocket, she pulled out her gun, holding it poised and ready, loaded with enough sedatives to knock out four Great Whites if she let off enough rounds. 'I know what I'm doing.'

'You sure as hell better, Caitlin,' Max warned, his stepfather tone finally overriding his role as her boss. 'Brovin and Morgan are coming in behind you. Be careful. You know how…' The crackle developed to a buzz so piercing she was forced to pull the earpiece out, lower her guard and strike position for a split second.

That was all it took.

He appeared from behind her.

His movements were swift and accurate: snatching the gun from her hand, in the same instant he forced her face-first up against the wall, her earpiece hitting the ground.

She caught her breath, pressed her palms and knee to the wall in preparation to push back but his hard body was already against hers, his power reminding her that the strength she had in spirit was absolutely no match for the supposedly three hundred-year-old six-foot vampire who had her pinned to the wall as easily as he would a sheet of paper. And as she felt the tip of her own gun press below her ribs, she knew all four shots of the potent sedative, too powerful for the human body, would end it all for her.

Just like that.

But instead of firing, his soft lips brushed her ear, the arrogant upward curl of those enticing bow lips as clear in her mind as if he were facing her. He tutted playfully, his low rasp raking beneath her skin. 'A little girl doing a man's job – bound to end in tears.'

Caitlin clenched her fists. Brovin and Morgan had to be less than a minute away. She had to stall him. Her instinct was to try to reach back and catch his wrist. All she needed was her fingers on his pulse point and she'd finally know those dark recesses that no expert could reach – information she so desperately needed. But she knew she wouldn't have enough time to wait for that painfully slow vampire heartbeat, even if she was in a position to get to him. There was only one way she was going to get the time with him that she wanted and needed.

'Kane Malloy, I'm detaining you under section 3.4 of the Vampire Disciplinary Clause…'

He laughed, deep, guttural, terse. 'You're detaining me?'

'On twenty-one alleged accounts of crimes against members of the third species including your own, thirty-two against humans…'

'Delusional as well as reckless. Are you seriously the best they've got?'

'It's over, Kane.'

'You breathe too fast to be convincing,' he goaded.

'You don't breathe enough to judge me.'

He exhaled curtly. Panic jolted through her as he deftly unclasped the belt threaded through her jeans. To her disgust, for the first time on any tracking operation, she froze.

Kill her? Yes, of course the thought had crossed her mind. No matter how unbelievable or surreal it seemed, she had known it was a possibility. But rape? With her colleagues closing in there was no way even Kane would have the arrogance to attempt it in the minutes, maybe even seconds he had left.

But this was Kane. And if he wanted to leave a message for the VCU, a dead and violated tracker would ring loud and clear.

The fact she'd even got this close would be insult too much for his ego.

She snapped back a breath as he yanked her belt through the loops. And as his heel cracked the buckle, destroying the only way the VCU could locate her, she knew it was about to get worse.

Her phone followed next, removed from her back pocket by his stealthy fingers.

'You're lucky you serve a purpose,' he said, combing her hair back over her shoulder.

Her heart pounded painfully. 'What's that supposed to mean?'

'You're the one who's obsessed with me – what do you think?'

As he traced the back of his cool fingers tenderly down her exposed neck, a caress more sensual than she would have thought possible for someone with such renowned brutality, Caitlin held her breath. She was stunned by her own involuntary arousal, suppressing it with every iota of conviction she had.

'I think you'd better walk away,' she said, battling to get her focus back on the job. 'Or give yourself up.'

'Not going to happen, Caitlin.' Pressing the tranquiliser gun tighter into her side, Kane made her wince, his reputation restored. 'Question is, are you going to walk out of here co-operatively or am I going to have to carry you?'

The girl may have flinched when he'd pushed the gun deeper into her flesh, but she hadn't made a sound. He'd already seen her in action enough, heard enough to know she was used to keeping a brave face. She wasn't about to let that slip now. Instead, Caitlin's fingers coiled against the wall, her knuckles pale, her body tensed in anticipation of the shot.

'I'm flattered you're giving me an option,' she said, turning her head towards him, 'considering your usual tack.'

Kane couldn't help but smile. Controlling her body had been easy, but controlling her mind was going to be a whole other challenge.

This was worth the lingering moment.

He leaned closer, one arm above her head as he slid the gun slowly and coaxingly over the inward curve of her waist and down her hip. 'Is that what keeps you warm at night in that empty bed of yours, Caitlin – thinking you know me?'

She frowned, clearly using all her willpower not to flinch. 'I know this is where it ends for you.'

Easing her jacket aside to assess the outward curve of the small of her back, the pertness of her behind, he whispered against her ear, 'Tell me, what's it like being the token psychic on the big boys' team? Someone have an equal opportunities box to tick, did they? Or was someone promised the prising open of those slender thighs?'

She scowled. 'You can go to hell, Kane. And I'm going to put you there.'

Cornered and still fighting. He could almost like her if she wasn't a tracker, if she wasn't who she was. But the VCU and their sanctimonious ways irritated the hell out him, interfering in things that were none of their concern whilst they hid behind their masks of respectability. And with her mind admirably but insultingly still focused on the job, coupled with her naivety, Caitlin Parish was already presenting a lethal concoction that was threatening his self-control. Self-control that was brittle enough from finally being able to touch her, let alone sensing her potency. Her years of abstinence had clearly made her precious shadow-reader soul as untouchable as if she'd been celibate all her life. Still, challenge was good.

'Now that sounded like you meant it,' he said.

'There's no way out, Kane. Just pull the trigger or give yourself up.'

Releasing the gun from her side, he flipped her around and pinned both her hands above her head with one of his.

Her eyes flared as she snapped back a breath, their eyes meeting for the first time.

Hers were captivatingly bright, their milky-coffee colour beautifully offset by her flawless pale skin. Her shoulder-length sandy-brown hair was still damp and tousled from the rain, its unruliness suiting her. From a distance she could be mistaken for unassuming, but up close she was pretty. Her features were delicate, her full lips enticing – lips that under any other circumstance he would already have been tasting. And from the sudden dilation of her pupils, the flush in her cheeks, he wasn't alone in liking what he saw.

It was a shame. Another place, another time, she had enough feistiness to keep it interesting until he chose to exhaust her, playfully and cruelly manipulating the resilience indicative of her kind. Because the more self-controlled they were, the more pleasurable it was. And this girl oozed restraint.

But this was no time to play. This was about preserving her until it was time to drain her body, mind and spirit. This was about toying with her slowly and excruciatingly until she made that fatal choice of letting him in, allowing him access to that otherwise inaccessible soul.

He raked the tranquilizer gun teasingly down her chest, along the top of her jeans, now sitting loose on her slender hips, over the inviting hint of bare flesh, the subtle curve of her toned stomach. Hitching the waistband down just a little further, his gaze lingered tauntingly on the cream lace band of her underwear before meeting her eyes again. 'Are you calling my bluff, Caitlin?'

Her chest heaved beneath her T-shirt, her defiant gaze fixed with steely determination on his. Her curt breaths were enticingly sexy, her pulse racing, her warm body trembling.

'Or maybe you're just stalling until the real agents show up?' he added.

Caitlin's eyes narrowed in indignation. 'I'll repeat: Kane Malloy, I'm detaining you on twenty-one alleged accounts of crimes against members of the third species, including your own, thirty-two against humans, crimes of the third, second and first degree. You will be detained until further notice whereon you will undertake questioning through which a confession is recommended. Should you elect not to confess, your shadow will be read. If you are subsequently found guilty of any charges, your reticence will automatically qualify you for a more severe sentence.'

The girl was unbelievable. Hauled up against a wall and still reading him his rights. Taming her for the sheer pleasure of it really would have made for an interesting couple of nights.

'You don't do submissive well, do you, Caitlin?'

'I don't do submissive at all.'

He leaned closer, his mouth hovering less than an inch from hers, her erratic breath evocative against his lips. She recoiled tight against the wall, forging whatever distance she could. To taunt her further, he nudged her thighs apart, keeping them that way with one of his. The panic in her eyes was further confirmation of what he'd guessed from her reaction when he'd unclasped her belt: Caitlin was way out of her depth coming after him. And if the stakes hadn't been so high, he'd already be proving it.

'Tell me you've never fantasised about this moment,' he said, revealing just enough of his incisors to goad her.

Her pulse raced as she floundered under his scrutiny. 'I have,' she said breathily. 'Only I'd already lodged a stake in your dysfunctional heart. Now are you going to pull that trigger or am I supposed to stand here all night until you work out how to use it?'

He laughed tersely, but then he saw something in her eyes. There was uneasiness there – an uneasiness that wasn't attributed to VCU agents used to staring into the eyes of vampires for a living. She clearly knew he wasn't an ordinary vampire. And if she'd known that before-hand, her actions in pursuing him were far more than just reckless, they were insulting.

But restraint was a necessity, and the echoes of two sets of footsteps fast approaching from the main corridor told him time was short.

Taking both her hands in one of his, he turned her around again, tucking her against him as he raised the tranquiliser gun to the brighter light of the main corridor ahead. 'Looks like we have company,' he whispered against her ear. 'Make a noise and I'll do more than send them to sleep.'

As soon as they appeared, Kane let off a single shot.

Neither agent saw it coming.

His shot pierced the first agent cleanly in the chest.

But something also pierced Kane. Pierced him in the palm of his shooting hand. Something that threw him off balance, weakening his hold on the gun as paralytic pins and needles swarmed his fingers, his wrist and his elbow.

The second agent took the opportunity and shot Kane twice in the shoulder.

But Kane's world was already turning black.

He didn't even have time to curse.

# CHAPTER TWO

Caitlin's breath misted the office window as she gazed out across the headquarters' floodlit grounds. The smattering of rain obscured Lowtown's cityscape, Blackthorn nothing more than a blackened mass beyond the distant border.

The radiator warmed her thigh through her jeans, as she nervously bit the thumbnail she had jammed between her teeth. Vampires hunted more in the rain. Rain meant hoods up, umbrellas up, deficiency of sound, lowered eyes. Rain disorientated and distracted people, making the kill or capture so much easier. Even there in Lowtown, rainy nights were busy nights. Busy nights when you weren't suspended pending a full investigation.

She mindlessly rubbed her neck where he'd caressed her. All those years studying him and none of it had prepared her for the lethal spark behind those navy-blue eyes. Eyes that only seven hours before had confirmed her deepest fears, her deepest hopes. The truth of what he was had glimmered through that compelling self-assured gaze. Kane Malloy was indeed a dual feeder, a master vampire: a rare archaic strain of vampirism believed to have slipped into extinction in place of the weaker but more prevalent singular-blood feeders. And deep in the shadowy recess of his absent soul, every last remaining truth about his species lay concealed.

Or at least it would be concealed until she got into that interrogation room, which is exactly where she needed to be instead of wasting time waiting on others to decide her fate.

She pulled away herself from the window, glanced down at her watch for the ninth time in ten minutes and wandered over to her desk to find the last of her caffeine tablets.

'Caitlin,' Mark called from behind, 'you're wanted.' He looked as sullen and tired as the rest of the team but there was something more. He cocked his head towards the corridor. 'Max's office. Now.'

Her stomach flipped. With leaden legs, Caitlin walked past the disdainful looks of her male colleagues and headed a few doors down the corridor. She steadied her breathing and composed herself before opening the door.

Her stepfather stood in front of the floor-to-ceiling window, his hands cradled behind his back. As he turned to face her, his lips were taut, his eyes grave.

And behind the dominating conference table, folder neatly opened in front of him, sat Xavier Carter, chief of both the Third Species Control Division, of which the VCU was a component, and the Third Species Intervention Division. His (usually elusive) presence was enough to tell her something had gone horribly wrong.

Xavier stood, indicated for her to move to the seat opposite his, his wrinkled grey eyes observant, intrigued. 'Agent Parish. It's nice to meet you. I've heard much about you.' He held out a hand across the table.

'Just in the last few hours I bet.'

Xavier smiled as he shook her hand once, firm, businesslike, and indicated for her to sit. 'On the contrary. Your work hasn't gone unnoticed. Your name has been put forward for some rather significant achievement awards at next year's ceremony.'

'I don't do this for personal accolade, Mr Carter.'

He smiled again but just a hint this time. 'Your dedication hasn't gone unnoticed.'

She eased her chair under the table, perched on the edge, her hands concealed in her lap so they couldn't see the tremor.

'Which is why I'm sure your temporary suspension has come as quite a shock to you,' he added. 'I can see it has caused you some distress.'

She glimpsed across at Max as he took his seat beside Xavier, in full official role mode. She wouldn't expect anything less. Wouldn't want anything less. In this room, under these circumstances, Max wasn't her stepfather, he was her boss.

'Max warned me of the consequence if I proceeded with my course of action,' she responded. 'I chose to ignore it.'

'So you agree with the suspension?'

'Absolutely not.'

Max shot her a warning glare as Xavier lifted his eyes from the paperwork. 'You appear very resolute in your conviction,' Xavier remarked.

'I have a job to do, Mr Carter. My job is to track and detain vampires who breach the code of conduct established by the Global Council. Kane Malloy has proven elusive for far too long. As soon as I sensed that he was going to abscond, I proceeded to locate him and detain him. That's what I'm paid to do.'

'You are also part of a team, Agent Parish. You moved directly against my orders,' Max reminded her. 'You went in there unprepared and unsupported. You put yourself at risk as well as Morgan and Brovin. You're lucky they turned up when they did.'

'I hear Morgan's doing fine.'

'You're fortunate Malloy only got one round in him.'

'I was handling it.'

'And if they hadn't intervened when they did?' Max asked.

'Morgan wouldn't have got shot,' she finished. 'Just me.'

Max opened the package in front of him, took out the plastic bag, placing the gun it contained on the table between them.

Her gun.

Her heart thudded uncomfortably as Max slid it towards her, displeasure clear in his eyes.

'Who made this for you?' he asked.

'Does it matter?'

'Illegal customisation of VCU property? Yes, Agent Parish, it matters. The lab tells me the release pin was not only loaded with sedative but also a hefty dose of hemlock – an illegal weapon and an illegal substance. Who designed it?'

Caitlin lowered her gaze.

'Agent Parish?' Max persisted.

She sighed and reluctantly looked back at him. 'I did.'

'You?'

'I wanted a backup plan.'

He picked the gun up, held it by the barrel and squeezed the trigger. The pin sprang through the back of the grip with a powerful stab, hitting the air instead of the flesh of his palm as it was designed to – what it had succeeded in doing with Kane. 'So anyone with pressure different to yours activates this and that goes straight into their bloodstream.'

She shrugged. 'Worked didn't it?'

Max placed the gun back on the table, unable to mask the disapproval and disappointment in his eyes as he leaned back in his chair.

'Tell me again what happened,' Xavier said, drawing her attention back to him.

'Like I said in my statement and in every interview since then, when I saw Kane Malloy re-enter the building, I pursued him. I worked out that he was most likely to head up to the roof where he would be able to cross several buildings and enter any one of them to escape. There is a single corridor leading to the roof so I chose that one. I proceeded several metres and turned down a darker corridor when interference in my earpiece caused me to momentarily lower my guard. He came up behind me, took my gun and pinned me up against the wall. I advised him of his rights and suggested he give himself up. As I was disarmed, but knew Brovin and Morgan were not far behind, I resolved to keep him occupied for as long as possible. Malloy heard Brovin and Morgan approach, shot Morgan, thus activating the pin in my gun, releasing the hemlock and sedative, the former temporarily paralysing his hand and arm. Brovin immediately counter-shot Malloy twice in the shoulder. Malloy was unconscious within seconds.'

There was a momentary silence. Max and Xavier exchanged glances, adding to Caitlin's unease. She clenched her hands to stop herself from demanding they just spit it out. If they had a point, she wished they'd just make it.

Max leaned forward again. 'I last spoke to you at 10:27 p.m.'

'Okay.'

'Brovin reported having taken Malloy down at 10:31.'

'So?'

Max's eyes were riddled with suspicion. 'Four minutes to read him his rights?'

'If you say so.'

'And what did Kane say to you?'

'Very little.'

'In four minutes?'

'Time flew.'

'Agent Parish,' Xavier cut in. 'You're the only member of this division, let alone this unit, who has ever got that close to Malloy and survived. I'm sure you understand we want to know why.'

Because he had a purpose for her and one that clearly required her to be alive for the time being. 'He was interrupted.'

'Four minutes later, yes. It would have taken him a split second to kill you,' Max said.

'I'd have been no use as a hostage then, would I?'

Max narrowed his eyes. 'Why would he need a hostage when he could have outrun you? All of you? Instead he held back, followed you down that corridor, subsequently increasing his risk of getting caught.'

'What do you want me to say? I took a chance and it paid off.'

'A chance that could have got you killed,' Max reminded her.

'It was a snap decision.'

'No, Caitlin. You knew before you started last night that you weren't going to let him go. Your gun is proof of that.'

'This is my case,' she said, meeting his accusatory gaze. 'It's me who got us to this point. Four years it's taken me. So, no, I wasn't going to just let him walk out of there. It was then or never.'

'You do know that your action meant he was apprehended illegally?' Max continued.

'If he hadn't shot Morgan, the gun wouldn't have activated. He was an active aggressor trying to escape. I did my job and I will stick by my decision.'

'Are you attracted to him, Agent Parish?'

Caitlin's gaze snapped to Xavier, the question almost winding her. 'Excuse me?'

'It's a simple question. Are you attracted to him?'

'I don't see what that has to do with any of this.'

'It has everything to do with this.'

She frowned. 'Are you accusing me of being unprofessional in my intentions, Mr Carter?'

'It's merely a question,' Xavier said.

'I acted fully within the code. I read him his rights word for word.'

'You wanted him to pull the trigger.'

'I was willing to take a shot to bring him down.'

'Did you try to provoke him?'

She kept her gaze solemnly on Xavier. 'Where is this going?'

'I'll ask you again: What prevented him from shooting you?'

'I don't know. Why don't you ask him? Or can I assume that he's saying nothing? Just as I'm guessing he's refused a voluntary confession. Which is why I should be in there shadow-reading him and not sat here wasting time.'

'We brought in Isla,' Max declared.

Caitlin's heart leapt at the treachery. But not just that. If Isla, a much weaker shadow reader though she was, got even an inkling of what Kane was, then suspension would be the least of her worries. But then again, if they got so much as a hint that her going after Kane had been far more than just professional, her life wouldn't be worth living anyway. 'And?'

Max hesitated for what felt like a lifetime. 'Nothing.'

Her heart lunged with relief. 'What do you mean, "Nothing"?'

'He blocked her. She couldn't even read his mood.'

He had to be a master. It was the only explanation. She stared from Max to Xavier and back again. 'Did she retry?'

'Three times,' Max said. 'No reading. No confession. All topped off with an illegal apprehension. Still sure we've won, Caitlin?'

Discomfort squeezed the pit of her stomach, a light perspiration sweeping over her. 'You'd better not be saying what I think you are.'

'We have no choice,' Max declared sullenly.

'Yes, we do,' Caitlin said, standing. 'You need to reinstate me.'

'Sit down.'

'No third species can block shadow readers. It's just a trick. Isla has half of my seventh sense. Let's see how much of me he can block.'

Max glowered up at her with the warning of a protective parent. 'Sit down, Caitlin.'

But she couldn't. She needed him contained. She needed him confined. It was the only way she'd ever have him long enough, and be safe enough, to extract the information she needed. 'He's only been here seven hours. We can keep him for another seventeen. Let me in there and I will sort this out. You know I'm stronger than Isla—'

'I said sit down!'

Reluctantly she did so, perching on the edge of the chair. 'He is not slipping through our fingers because you've suspended me over some technicality. Just give me an hour with him and I'll get everything we need—'

Max showed her the palm of his hand, the cue for her to stop talking and start listening. She pressed her lips together in resentment.

'You've been suspended. Even if you were able to read him, it would be thrown out of court.'

'So that's it? He walks free? After all this?'

Free and with clear intentions for her.

Max held her gaze, his eyes sober, his lips terse. 'He's requested you be the one to take the release papers to him.'

Her stomach flipped. 'I bet he did.'

Xavier leaned forward, his fingers interlinked as he rested them on the table. 'He wants it done in private. He knows we'll insist on watching, but he has demanded no audio. They're his terms for not pursuing the illegal apprehension. Caitlin, he wants something from you. If he has given you any indication of what that is, you have to tell us.'

And let them yank her off the case and wrap her in cotton wool in some distant locale? Make her fight her way back to the top of some other control unit in some other vampire-infested district? No. She had come too far. Invested too much. More than that, this was the only way. 'I told you – he didn't say anything.'

Xavier leaned back in his seat, the disconcertment in Max's eyes telling her she wasn't the only one holding information back.

'I'll be upfront with you, Caitlin,' Xavier said. 'Kane Malloy has been involved in some cross-species activity. Regular contact has been established between him and Jask Tao. Were you aware of that?'

Another fact she'd have to avoid disclosing – ammunition she'd held on to for when she finally got Kane inside. Revelations of furtive meetings with the lycan leader would have allowed her to detain him for longer should her initial readings prove less fruitful than planned. 'I had heard rumours but nothing anywhere near confirmation.' She glanced at Max to see him silently berating her for her lack of disclosure.

'Well, the Lycan Control Unit has noted several reports of their meetings,' Xavier continued.

'What does that have to do with me?'

'I'll get to the point,' Xavier said. 'A young woman like you gets the better of Kane Malloy, especially as underhandedly as you did, and he's going to want to reinstate his control. Unfortunate, yes, but maybe your hastiness tonight has given us the biggest advantage we've ever had of convicting him. We all know there are only two ways we're going to do it. We either get him shadow-read when his defences are down, or we catch him in the act. Something big. Something indisputable.'

She knew exactly where Xavier was going with this. 'Something involving collaboration with other third-species deviants?'

'Kane is going to walk free in the next couple of hours. We need to know what he's planning. And we need someone on the inside to do that.'

Caitlin frowned. 'You mean me.'

'You never discussed this with me,' Max cut in, shooting Xavier a glare contemptuous enough to have placed him on conduct procedures himself.

'I am here to advise this unit on the best course of action,' Xavier reminded him. 'Taking everything into account, I believe this is it.'

'By offering my best agent, my stepdaughter, as bait in a situation we have no control over with a vampire none of us can even begin to comprehend?'

'A risk but, based on the fact Kane clearly wants her alive, a calculated one. I'm asking her to do her job,' Xavier said, squarely meeting his glare. 'But if your family connection is going to be a problem...'

'It's never been a problem,' Caitlin said, avoiding eye contact with Max. 'I make my own choices.'

'Good. Because I'm offering you the biggest opportunity of your career, Caitlin, one that I have no doubt is well within your capabilities. I'm sure I don't have to spell out what this will mean for that career if you're successful.'

'A career I've been suspended from, remember?'

'Something else that has worked to our advantage. You're out of the loop as far as anyone is concerned. Officially, I can get you reinstated in the next twenty-four hours on undercover work. No one else in the team need know. And I think it best we keep it that way.'

'Caitlin, you don't have to do this,' Max said. 'We can move you to a safe house. Get you the security you need.'

'For the rest of my life?' She could see from the discontent in her stepfather's eyes that he already knew what she was going to say. 'This is my case. I'm not backing out now.' She looked back at Xavier. 'I want to hear what Kane's got to say for himself.'

It took three double doors, each under a security code, to get to the containment quarters. At the fourth, the security guard keyed her in.

'You know the procedure,' Hadrian said. 'Stay on your side of the table. Pass all things across the top of the table. We'll be watching you from behind the mirror. If you're in distress, bite your lip and we'll intervene.'

Caitlin nodded. 'Kane touches me and he knows he's not going anywhere. I think he'll keep his distance.'

Hadrian indicated for her to make her way through the next set of doors into the interrogation area. 'Room one.'

Turning her back on him, she passed two rooms on her right before stopping at the third.

She took a steady breath, her pulse racing, reached for the handle but let go.

You can do this, she insisted, her hands clenched by her sides. She closed her eyes for a moment then opened them with renewed determination. She reached for the handle again and pushed the door open.

Kane Malloy sat back on the metal chair as relaxed as he would be if knocking back shots in a club, legs casually apart beneath the table, his jeans cuffing his chunky lace-up boots. He didn't flinch as she entered, his elbows remaining lax on the armrests. His self-assurance exacerbated her unease, not helped by his position emphasising the taut muscles of his biceps, revealing glimpses of his honed chest through the fabric of his dark grey T-shirt.

Caitlin instinctively lowered her gaze, her stomach tightening as she recalled how that hard, powerful body had felt pressed against hers.

But it was too late to turn back now.

She closed the door, the twenty-by-twenty-foot room suddenly feeling claustrophobic, the throbbing silence adding to the tension as she felt him unashamedly assessing every inch of her. She cursed silently as tingles swept up her spine, berating herself for letting him affect her.

The intimidation was clever, dangerously low key.

The games had already begun.

Clutching the release papers tight to her chest, she'd never had so much difficulty putting one foot in front of the other. Grateful to reach the table quickly, she stopped at the far side and placed the papers on the corner, the pen on top.

'You need to gain more confidence in those sexy hips,' he said, that low rasp making every hair rise on the back of her neck. 'Learn to make the most of them.'

Sitting in the bolted-down chair opposite him, she interlaced her hands on the table. She used every reserve to meet his gaze, keeping her expression impassive despite her pounding heart. 'Very clever, Kane. How did you do it?'

'Do what?'

'Block her.'

Satisfaction danced behind those captivating navy eyes. 'It's an old vampire secret.' If he knew she'd worked out what he was, he wasn't letting on.

At this stage it was safer to play along. 'Not one that I've ever heard of.'

'Because you're the authority on all things vampiric, right?'

'I know enough to know what you did is impossible.'

'Don't be a sore loser, Caitlin. I'm sure you enjoyed the chase while it lasted.'

'It's not over yet, Kane.'

'Unsubstantiated accusations. No forensic proof. Hearsay. Alleged crimes. Failed shadow- reading. Not looking good, is it?'

His self-possession was intoxicating, infuriating.

'Still got you here, didn't I?' she retorted.

'You cheated,' he said, an unnerving glimmer of rebuke behind his eyes.

'I thought you had to have rules to cheat. I don't remember agreeing to any.'

He flashed her that fatally charming smile. An effective predator at work. A master predator. 'Now that sounds like a fun precedent to set.'

'You were waiting for me, weren't you?' she said, desperate to break the tension.

'You're not the only hunter around here, Caitlin.'

'What do you want with me?'

'If you hadn't upped the ante, you would have known by now. But don't worry, you will soon enough.'

Her stomach lurched at the candour in his tone, the darkness in those eyes. 'Is that a threat?'

'I prefer to call it foreplay. But whatever works for you.' He leaned forward, rested his hands on the table – strong, masculine hands that had pinned her to the wall with such competent ease. 'You upped the ante with the wrong vampire, Caitlin.'

She leaned forward to mirror him. She had to do something to goad him. She needed him to snap, needed him to do something to justify keeping him in for a few more hours. 'I thought you would have noticed I don't play the helpless-female card very well, so you can quit with the power games.'

'Easy to say when you're surrounded by people to protect you. How convincing will those pretty brown eyes be when I've got you alone again?'

'You touch me and I will convict you.'

'Like you have this time?'

She held his gaze defiantly. 'It's okay, Kane. Your ego is having trouble dealing with the fact that I outsmarted you. I can take it.'

He smiled again, albeit briefly, revealing an alluring hint of those even white teeth, those slightly extended incisors, purposefully drawing her attention to those sexy masculine lips. 'So, tell me, has your pulse raced that fast with every vampire you've caught?'

It was a cruel but clever change of tack. One he clearly sensed would make her falter.

'I thrive on the chase,' she said.

'Not as much as you thrive on fear. Or maybe it's me that's the potent aphrodisiac for you.'

She exhaled curtly, felt herself flush. 'Believe me, this is purely business, Kane. Much as I'm sure that's another blow to your ego.'

He smiled again, his gaze unfalteringly intrusive. 'I heard those shallow breaths when I had you pinned to that wall. I felt you shudder when I unfastened your belt.'

'Repulsion does that to me.'

'You are so unconvincing,' he said, raking her slowly with his gaze. 'But I guess for someone like you, denial is the safe option.' His eyes rested squarely on hers again, their intensity making her stomach flip. 'Much safer than letting me in.'

'Well, you know all about denial, don't you, Kane? Why don't you be a big boy and confess to what you've done? Unless you're scared of the consequences?'

'Such vehemence. I'm going to put that to good use. I think too many nights alone in front of the TV has left Caitlin a very tense and frustrated girl. A pretty girl like you, I'd have expected a few male friends. At least one or two one-night stands.'

The 'empty bed' remark back in the corridor had been unsettling enough but she'd managed to dismiss it as a random jibe. These remarks were too close to the truth to be random. He'd been into Lowtown. He'd found where she lived. Or he wanted her to believe that. Her heart pounded at the prospect of him watching her – thuds of fear, thuds of unforgivable excitement as she tried not to waver under the practised seductiveness of his eyes. 'My love life of interest to you is it, Kane?'

'You probe around in someone's business long enough and they're going to start to notice you, Caitlin.'

'Did you know we were coming for you?'

'I know a lot of things.'

'Except about hemlock pins in gun handles.'

'Like I said, you cheated. But I'll give you that one.'

'And I'll give you some advice: don't underestimate me, Kane. Whatever trick you used tonight with Isla, I'll work it out. And next time I bring you in, I'll be the one to read you. We'll see how clever you are at blocking then.'

'Now who's making threats?' Warning flashed in his eyes. 'Do it again, Caitlin, and I'm going to stop being nice to you.'

She pushed the papers towards him, slid him the pen. 'I'm not scared of you, Kane.'

He picked up the pen, a self-satisfied smile curling the corners of those seductive bow lips. 'Lie all you want, Caitlin,' he said, signing the papers, sliding them back across to her. 'But we both know you know what I am. Just as we both know you're never going to get me back in here again. So if you want to read me,' he said, leaning back, lifting his wrists, his gaze locked challengingly on hers, 'let's see what you've got.'

Panic and shock whipped through her. If he was calling her bluff, he was playing a very dangerous game.

Kane Malloy was many things, but stupid and careless were definitely not on the list. He was either one hundred per cent convinced she would fail or one hundred per cent convinced she would refuse. Because they both knew if she saw anything, even claimed to have seen anything, the fact he had volunteered would mean they could reinstate detainment.

Her instinct was to throw that compelling self-assurance right off balance. But it wasn't that simple. Shadow-reading was an intimate act – the proximity it required, the length of touch it necessitated, the sustained penetrative eye contact. Even if she could get inside him, overpower those barriers he'd used with Isla, it wasn't going to be quick and it wasn't going to be easy. And the absence of the containment chair, the protocol, others in the room, would only exacerbate the intimacy.

The very thought of it terrified her.

Back in the corridor, she at least had adrenaline to blame for her reaction to him. How her body had ignited at his closeness, relishing his intoxicating scent of musk and spices. How when he'd held her against that wall, his lips temptingly close to hers, all she could think of was how his kiss would feel – whether he'd tease her lips apart sensually or overpower her with force.

But now, as his gaze lingered on her, she knew it was nothing to do with adrenaline. And putting herself in that position again wouldn't only be a test of her self-control, it could show him just how vulnerable she was.

But those beyond the two-way mirror didn't know that. Nor could she allow them to know. If she turned Kane down, turned down the unexpected but perfect opportunity, they'd want to know why.

Caitlin had no choice.

'If I find something, Kane, I can keep you in for another seventeen hours. Be warned – I'm stronger than you think.'

'Maybe. But nowhere near as strong as me.'

She glanced across at the mirror. She knew Xavier would want her to take any opportunity she could. She also knew if she did, Max would be watching, cursing her stupidity, demanding she sat back down again or have someone intervene.

But there was an agreement: no interference unless she bit her lip.

And there was no looking into the void unless you got dangerously close to the edge.

After a few more moments of hesitation, she grasped the arms of the chair and stood. She stepped up to his end of the table, stopping at the corner, inches from his thigh.

His gaze didn't falter as he moved his leg out a little, enough to let her slip between him and the table before closing the gap again.

She felt the compulsion to lean back and grip the table's edge for support, but that would have given too much away. 'Last chance, Kane.'

His eyes sparkled coaxingly as he held up his wrists.

She hesitated for a moment longer before reaching out, her finger-tips already tingling at the prospect.

But he was quick. He snatched hold of her wrist and was instanta-neously on his feet.

A split second later, she was flat on her back on the table, his thighs forcing hers apart.

Caitlin snapped back a breath. Panic surged through her as, in the swift skilful move, he had trapped her beneath him, his hips meld-ing against hers like they were two parts of the same piece. And as he slammed her hands either side of her head, gazed deep into her eyes, Caitlin shuddered.

Because even in its wrongness it felt unnervingly right. Even in her alarm, the power of his cool hard body was painfully evocative, his un-wavering self-control rousing her further, the provocative playfulness in his gaze doing nothing to help abate her arousal.

'You're not the only one who can cheat, Caitlin.'

'Big mistake,' she hissed.

He looked at the mirror and then back at her. 'No one's come run-ning yet.' He dragged his gaze appreciatively down her throat, her cleav-age. 'Just how much can I get away with before they come to the rescue, huh?' His eyes glinted with mischief as he looked back into hers. 'I bet Max is poised and ready. I'm sure he wasn't happy you coming in here all alone. I know how protective he is towards you after all you've been through. Not that you talk about it. Not that anyone ever talks about it. How fitting he made a move on your mother so soon after his best friend became ashes.'

Caitlin glowered at him, stunned by his knowledge. 'You don't know what you're talking about.'

He leaned closer, his lips dangerously near hers, his eyes terrifyingly beautiful in their menace. 'Struck a nerve, Caitlin? Not nice having people pry into your personal business, is it?'

She turned her head to the side to break from the intensity, anger, fear, resentment searing through her. And she tensed as his lips brushed intimately against her ear, just as he had done in the corridor. Only this time she knew he was doing it to avoid being lip-read.

'I know your mission to read me isn't just about convicting me, or uncovering vampire secrets, Caitlin. So, if it makes you feel better, yes, I do know what killed your father and yes, it is the same thing that came after your mother. And you're right – it is some ancient species you've never heard of. Yes, I do know how to find it and yes, I am one of the few capable of killing it. And maybe, one day, just for the hell of it, I will. But in the meantime, I have my own revenge to fulfil.'

She held her breath as he lifted her wrist to his mouth, brushed his soft lips along one of the most tender, receptive parts of her body. And as he let it go and gently used the back of his hand to turn her head towards him, she almost conceded and raised the alarm.

'Unfortunately, for what I have planned,' he said, lowering his mouth to hers. 'I'm going to need that precious glowing soul of yours.'

She knew she should have stopped it then and signalled for reinforcements. But the shock of the revelation distracted her, her need to hear more overwhelming any self-defence. She stared at him in horror. 'That's why you want me?'

'Why else?'

Heat consumed her body as their lips almost touched.

'Fight it all you want, Caitlin. But you're no match for me. And by the time I've finished with you, I won't need to seduce your soul out of that impenetrable astral body – you're going to give it to me willingly.'

# CHAPTER THREE

With a triumphant glimmer in his eyes, Kane pulled back, releasing her wrists. But Caitlin caught hold of his T-shirt. Her trembling fingers clutched the soft cotton as she kept him above her, her fingers tense against his hard chest.

'What's it called?' she asked, hating the urgency in her voice.

'The question that's been burning those lips for the past fourteen years, right?' he said, his arms braced either side of the table, his biceps taut.

'Tell me,' she demanded quietly.

He glanced down at her fist then back into her eyes with a hint of a coaxing smile. 'That's a tight grip. I could make good use of that.'

'How do you know all this stuff, Kane?'

'Later,' he said with a playful wink as he pressed his thumb down over her knuckles, forcing her to release him before lifting her hand to his lips, tauntingly kissing the back of it.

As he relaxed back in his chair, she wanted to grab him again but suppressed her exasperation. Kane wasn't going to tell her anything between these four walls, no matter what she did. He had no intention of putting his release at risk. She had to be satisfied with knowing that it wasn't the last she'd be seeing of Kane Malloy, that she'd achieved at least one goal tonight.

But as Caitlin pulled herself off the table, she still couldn't suppress her indignation enough to prevent her glaring at him on her way to the door. A look that told him it most definitely wasn't over. He might be coming for her but she'd be ready. And judging by his smirk, he was thriving on her silent defiance, their secret unspoken exchange of understanding concealed from those behind the glass.

Exiting the interrogation room, Caitlin slammed the door behind her and leaned up against the corridor wall. Resting her head back against it, she clenched the papers to her chest as the shock hit her for the second time.

Kane had at last confirmed it. Whatever others had denied, she had been right – there was a link between her parents' deaths.

She took a few steady breaths. Her throat tightened, her heart pounding.

Seven years to the day. Seven years to the hour.

Everyone else might have insisted on it being a coincidence, but Caitlin had never believed it. And never less so than when she'd risked her new job to break into the department's secret archives – a furtive endeavour that led to her uncovering her only clue. The psychics' independent reports had specified both her parents had had their astral bodies torn out and, with them, their souls – souls that were subsequently trapped and not at rest. It was information that never made it onto the official database, information that had instead been shoved away in some dusty old filing box at the back of a disused storeroom never to see the light of day.

But her findings had only reinforced her logic that whatever had killed them was coming for her next.

Coming for her in less than five days' time – the anniversary of their deaths.

Those who denied it were just protecting a scared young woman but Caitlin didn't want protecting. Caitlin had wanted the truth. And nearly fourteen years later, Kane had been the only one to give it to her. It might have been hard, fast and cruel but it was the truth at least.

She raked her trembling fingers back through her hair. She'd been right; if anyone was going to know of the species, it had to be a master vampire. It had to be something archaic if no one else could identify it, if even the most learned of the third species from whom she had begged for information over the years had come up with nothing.

More to the point, she believed every word when Kane told her he could kill it. Whatever it was.

Though it wrenched at her stomach, tore at her dignity, her self-respect, she now knew for sure that Kane was integral to her survival, her vengeance – all he knew, all he was, all he was capable of. It was going to take something lethal to bring that creature down, and there was nothing more lethal than Kane Malloy.

Damn him that she needed him. And damn it that her wrists still tingled from his touch, heat still lingering in her cheeks. She lifted the back of her hand to her mouth so her lips could touch where his had been, but she flinched, dropping her hand away again as the doors to her left flew open.

Max stopped abruptly as their eyes met, an uncharacteristic panic in his.

'I'm fine,' she said, pre-empting his question.

He marched up to her and shoved open the door opposite, stepping inside. Caitlin reluctantly took her cue and followed him in.

'What the hell was that?' he demanded, spinning to face her, his finger thrust in the direction of the interrogation room.

'What?'

'Stay on your side of the table. Do not approach the assailant. Stick to the line of questioning. At what point did you decide all of the above were inapplicable?'

She leaned back against the table and placed the signed papers beside her. 'He offered to let me read him.'

'Which you fell for.'

'I knew he wasn't going to do anything to risk being able to get out of here.'

'I just sat behind two-way glass and watched that bastard pin you to a table. Which bit of this are you not getting?'

'He caught me off guard.'

'Like he did in the corridor? He was toying with you, Caitlin. With all of us. He is a game player.'

'He had his little Neanderthal routine – and so what? I've been pinned down by uglier and more vicious vampires than him.'

He sighed in exasperation. 'He played you like a puppet in there all for our benefit and you let him. Just like he was planning to snatch you from right under our noses earlier. You should never have approached him. You know what he is capable of.'

'But he hasn't fully worked out what I'm capable of, has he? He wanted to prove a point and he did. Let him keep thinking that way and he'll be more pliable. By lowering my guard, he'll lower his. I know what I'm doing, Max. And I can do this, I promise you.'

Max took a step closer. 'I have spoken to you as your boss, but now I'm telling you as your stepfather that this is over, Caitlin. You are not getting involved. You are ending this now.'

'I can't do that.'

'Yes, you can. And you will. Xavier's going to join us in a few minutes, and you're going to tell him you've changed your mind.'

'Nothing has changed, Max.'

Max frowned as he studied her warily. 'He said something in your ear when he had you on the table. What was it?'

It sickened her to lie to him, but telling him the truth would have him locking her in a safe house whether she chose it or not. It had to be between her and Kane. She needed it to be between just her and Kane if she was going to get what she wanted. And she would get what she wanted. She wasn't sure how yet, but she would. 'Nothing of importance.'

'It didn't look that way from the expression on your face, or from the way you grabbed him.'

'Like you said, he's a game player. He likes a reaction. I decided to give him one to play with.'

Max's eyes flashed with suspicion but there was also an unease behind them that, if she hadn't so desperately wanted to get out of there, break from the scrutiny of his gaze, she may have been tempted to probe. 'So he gave you no clue as to why you're still alive? Or why he summoned you?'

'We both know him better than that.'

'Why didn't you bite your lip, Caitlin?'

'Like he wanted me to? He knew you were watching. He was waiting for me to call in the reinforcements. I wanted to show him I wasn't scared of him.'

'And are you scared of him?'

'What kind of question is that?'

'Too many people have been reeled in by him, Caitlin. Behind those looks and that charm he is dangerous and he is vicious and he will do whatever it takes to get what he wants.'

'I'm the one who contributed to that profile, remember? So don't talk to me like I'm some rookie, Max. Not you, of all people. You know I know my stuff. And I know that vampire better than anyone else in this unit. I know you have this need to protect me because of Mum, because of Dad, but I'm a grown woman. And this is well within my ability. And reluctant though you are to admit it, you know it.'

'What you are doing is insane. It's suicide.'

'It's hard to think of it as suicide when the clock's already ticking.'

His eyes flared. 'No. Please don't tell me that's what this is about.'

'I'm just saying I see things differently to you.'

He stepped up to her. 'Nothing is coming for you, Caitlin. What happened to your parents is totally unrelated – a mind-screwing coincidence and nothing more. You cannot put your life on the line for some delusional belief.'

But now she knew it wasn't delusional. No matter how much everyone had tried to convince her otherwise. 'I have a job to do, Max,' Caitlin said firmly. 'Kane is my case. I'm going to bring him back in and this time, I promise, I'll do it legit.'

'You are stepping beyond the boundaries of your job. I've suspected it for months and now that performance in there just confirmed it.'

The door handle turned, and Xavier's frame soon dominated the open doorway. He looked first to Max then Caitlin. 'Are you all right, Caitlin? Max was worried you'd be shaken up.'

'I'm fine,' Caitlin declared, shooting Max a glower at even suggesting the possibility. She handed Xavier the papers. 'When will he be released?'

'Now that he's signed, within the next couple of hours.' He looked across at Max. 'I'd like a few moments alone with Agent Parish please, Max.'

Max glanced from Xavier to Caitlin, his frustration clear as he reluctantly conceded, closing the door sharply on his way out.

Xavier indicated for her to take a seat. 'I must say, I'm impressed. That was quite the performance in there. That whole helpless-female-on-the-table routine must have had Kane's pulse reaching almost human rates. You nearly got us a conviction in one simple move.' He pulled a chair from the wall so he could sit adjacent to her. 'If I had any doubt you could do this, it's well and truly quashed. I think you made the best decision of your career tonight.'

'I wish Max would see it that way.'

'You said the family connection wouldn't be a problem.'

'It's not. But he's still my boss. And I'd still like my job back at the end of this.'

'Don't you worry about that.' He paused. 'I know you've not had it easy in the unit, Caitlin. I know you've had a lot to prove both in living up to your father's reputation and proving you're not just here because of Max. You're the only shadow reader to get out of the interrogation room. You should be very proud of yourself as I'm sure your father would be.'

'My father never wanted me to come into this line of work, Mr Carter. He didn't want me to use my shadow-reading at all.'

'I think he might have changed his mind after tonight. You're an exceptionally talented young woman. We're lucky to have recruited you.'

'I appreciate you saying so.'

'And clearly I'm not the only one to have noticed. Did Kane give you any more clues as to what he might want with you?'

Caitlin held his gaze as steadily as she could. 'No. Nothing.'

Xavier contemplated her in the silence for a moment. 'Are you sure, Caitlin? It's very important I know before I send you in on this case. If there is anything I should be aware of, now is the time to tell me.'

'If he does want me for something, he's not going to let it slip until he's ready. You know that.'

'Indeed I do.' He leaned back in his chair. 'For over forty years I've been trying to get my hands on him. I'm not ashamed to say I will have a lot of personal satisfaction when he's finally brought to justice.'

'I read some of your early reports on him. They're very damning.'

'He's done some damnable things. Some of the worst crimes I've ever come across. Sadistic. Cruel. Twisted. I've seen some vicious cases of torture over the years but I've never seen the process seemingly enjoyed as much. Some of those people, those vampires, he'd kept alive for days. One of them – an agent who couldn't have been much older than you when you started – he'd torn a tooth out every hour before starting on the fingernails, then the toenails. The mess he made of his face, I...' He lowered his gaze for a moment before looking back at her. 'Sometimes you see it – the anger, the hatred. Then other times he's so terrifyingly detached. I don't know which I despise more.'

She'd read every one of those reports. Every one she'd managed to get her hands on. Some substantiated. Many not. Witnesses were in short supply. So were survivors. 'They got worse after Arana died, didn't they? The incidents. As if what happened to her was a catalyst. '

He frowned a little, a hint of disapproval in his eyes at the suggestion. 'It's more likely he just stopped caring about covering his tracks when he didn't have her to protect anymore.'

'From what I managed to find out over the years, she was the only thing he ever cared about.'

Xavier raised his eyebrows slightly. 'I read the insightful piece you wrote about that in his profile. It was quite brilliant. But the death of a loved one is never an excuse to inflict the kind of pain he has.'

Death was the kindest part of what Kane's sister had been subjected to. Caitlin remembered having thrown up after reading the details of her murder. She remembered the sleepless nights. It was the only time she'd had second thoughts about being an agent.

'When you've lost someone you care about under such brutal circumstances, excuses are irrelevant.'

'Your empathy is admirable. But Kane is Kane. He's done far worse than those lycans did to Arana. The only difference is someone he cared about was the victim that time. He's never spared a thought for his victim's loved ones – wives, husbands, sons, daughters. The only difference is those lycans had no control over what they were doing. Kane knows what he is doing every step of the way. And he enjoys it.'

'Really? I still think a lot of those crimes were committed when he was looking for answers.'

'And if we'd told him, he would have torn every one of the lycans in Blackthorn apart. We would have had lycans from every other locale inciting revenge and had an inter-species war on our hands within days. I don't need to explain how many human lives could be lost in the crossfire in Blackthorn and Lowtown alone. Shared vampire and lycan communities like ours would implode and we don't have the resources to deal with it. We bring him in and we guarantee safeguarding this community. We need to protect human lives first and foremost, Caitlin. That is why we exist.'

'I understand that. And I appreciate your faith in me.'

'Faith I don't give out freely. He's up to something and I'm not afraid to admit to you that I'm worried.'

'Do you think he's found out lycans were responsible for Arana?'

'There's no way for him to know.'

'But his conversations with Jask have you worried, right?'

'The fact Jask is still alive is reassurance enough. But nothing good can come out of communications between them. The vampire and lycan communities in Blackthorn may have to share the same district, but ensuring they maintain separate areas sustains the peace. We can't let anything jeopardise that.'

'So what now?'

'You get yourself home,' Xavier said. 'You get a good meal in you. You sleep. You rest and you wait until he comes to you. Keep to your normal routine. Make yourself available. My guess is he'll lie low for a couple of days. I suggest you reserve as much strength as you can in the interim.'

'Maybe I should go to him. I can go to some of his more popular haunts. If I put word out I'm looking for him, he'll have to come. He won't be able to abide people thinking he won't face up to me.'

'I think more provocation would be a bad idea. You've already humiliated him enough. I don't want him making this personal. As much as it goes against your nature, I would acquiesce at this stage. As far as he's concerned, he's got the upper hand. And we need to keep it that way.'

'And when I come into contact with him again?'

'It's going to be purely down to your intuition. Obviously we can't wire you or set you up with a tracking device. If he gets a hint of an inside job, there's no saying what he'll do, whether he needs you or not. Provoke him as little as possible, but ascertain whatever you can as quickly as you can and then you do what you can to get the hell out of there.'

She frowned. 'You do know that my chances of finding anything out are minimal, sir?'

'Minimal is better than impossible, because that's the alternative we're facing. The only reason I am letting you do this is because you've survived already. The only conclusion I can make is that he's hand-picked you because he needs a shadow reader for something. If you can defer whatever that is until you can find out more, that's what you need to do. Keep yourself useful to him. Do not aggravate him. Do not challenge him. I want you back alive and intact.' He took a card from his inside pocket and slid it across to her. 'That's my personal number. Memorize it. Use it and we'll find you wherever you are.'

She nodded as she examined the card.

'Caitlin.'

She looked back up at him.

'I would not ask you to do this if I had any other option,' he said. 'There are huge risks involved, and I won't deny it. If you are having second thoughts, I would rather you say now.'

'If I wanted easy options, I wouldn't have taken this job, Mr Carter. I want to do this.'

He nodded, stood and held out his hand for her to shake. 'I admire your tenacity and your bravery. And I look forward to your success.'

Caitlin accepted his handshake, before stepping over to the door. Her hand hovered on the handle before she turned to face him again. 'Do you think my father was killed by a rogue vampire, Mr Carter?'

He kept his gaze squarely on hers. 'The evidence certainly pointed that way, Caitlin.'

'And my mother?'

'I wish we could have found out more.'

'You personally oversaw the two cases, didn't you?'

'I had a lot of time for your father. Rick was my best VCU agent. But things happen, Caitlin. Things beyond our control. Agents like you stop things like that happening to other people the way it did to your family. Many would run and hide after what you've been through. And that's why I can say, in no uncertain terms, that your father would be proud. Vampires like Kane Malloy, with the damage they do, need to be brought down. Brought to justice. And agents like you are just the ones to do it.'

Max paced the corridor, stopping abruptly to spin on his heels and face the opening door behind him.

Caitlin stepped out, her gaze immediately meeting his. Standing under the stark light, she didn't just look tired, she looked exhausted. He wasn't sure the last time she would have slept properly. He'd spent enough time kicking her out of the office the last month, and even then he knew she was going home and working.

She was tenacious and stubborn – always had been. But he'd never seen determination like he had these past few months when she had believed, convinced herself that Kane was finally within her grasp. And she'd been the only one to believe it. Because, as effective as she was, as proficient, he had believed alongside everyone else that her pursuing Kane was just a continuing waste of resources.

He'd hoped that night would have finally convinced her to fuel her energy elsewhere. Instead, the worst scenario had occurred, and he had been a party to it. He had always sworn to Caitlin's mother he'd protect her precious girl. If she'd still been alive, if she knew what he was letting her do, Kathleen would never forgive him. But the power was out of his hands. With Xavier Carter involved, the power was always out of his hands. At least Caitlin's father would have understood that, though he wondered if even Rick would forgive him for this.

'I'm still doing it,' Caitlin said, determination brimming in her eyes, tension in her hands –hands he had first held when she was only two years old. The same hands that had clenched and trembled when he'd told her about her mother seven years before. It was news that he thought would break her, but instead it had filled her with a muted determination that she was going to join the unit.

She was a success in the interrogation room and a success on her assessments, and had subsequently gained agent status. But those first few months in the field had been tough. They had all been waiting for her to fall. They'd goaded her, belittled her, but never once had he seen that composure break. She could catch and convict a hundred more vampires and each time they'd say it was a fluke, or luck, or down to the team. It was an all-boys' club and they were waiting for her to mess up.

Now, as far as they were concerned, with Kane being let free and her partner under medical care, she finally had. But those reserves were still coming. And he knew, more than anyone else, that they kept coming because she had nothing else. Nowhere else to go. Nothing else to live for.

But this had to stop. And he'd do whatever it would take. And she'd hate him for it.

'I know,' he said, with a gentle nod. 'Then you go home and get some rest. You hear me?'

Caitlin nodded. And as she stepped past, she didn't need to meet his gaze again for his heart to ache any more than it already did. He still had that one option, one more chance to convince her otherwise – and he was going to use it whether she liked it or not. He'd let her get some sleep, and then he'd do the only thing he had left to do to get her to change her mind.

He watched her walk away before stepping back into the room with Xavier.

Xavier stood at the table, flicking through the papers, no doubt checking the validity of the signature.

'This is wrong, Xavier. And you know it,' Max said from the doorway.

Xavier turned to face him. 'What is, Max? Using the best agent you've got to do the job the rest of your team has failed on year after year? I'm telling you, that girl's got talent. She reminds me of her father.'

'And he'll be turning in his grave over how you're manipulating her. Just like you manipulated him.'

'What's made you so righteous all of a sudden, Max? You put her on the case, remember?'

'She's my best agent. I had no legit reason to justify declining. Or, believe me, I would have.'

'Are you saying we made a mistake in appointing her?'

'Of course not.'

'Good, because I'd hate to have to convert her suspension to dismissal.'

Max glowered at him. 'This job is all she has. And you know it.'

'And that's what makes her so effective.'

'But not effective enough to go up against Kane single-handedly.'

Xavier smiled. 'You didn't think she'd catch him tonight, did you? When she took off like that, your heart must have been in your throat.'

Max held his gaze steadily on Xavier's. 'Have you thought for one minute that sending Caitlin in on this mission might have sealed all our fates?'

'That's a little over-dramatic of you, Max.'

'Then why the hell does he want her?'

'My guess is he has a need for her shadow-reading.'

'Why her?'

'Because she's the best, Max. So let her get on with her job,' Xavier said. 'She looked like she was holding her own in there.'

Max narrowed his eyes. 'You don't believe that for one minute. He knew exactly what he was doing.' He paused. 'What if he knows the truth?'

'You're being paranoid.'

'I'm not just asking you, Xavier, I'm pleading with you – pull her off the case. Tell her you've reconsidered.'

'She is the only one who can do this, and I am not going to let him slip through my fingers again.'

'And if I can get her to change her mind, will you accept it?'

Xavier almost smiled. 'I saw the way she was looking at him in there. She's not going to want to quit.'

Max stepped up to him, his eyes narrowed as he used every iota of self-control. 'You're both as bad as each other, you and Kane. Using people. Manipulating people. Getting what you want in the end. But I'm telling you, if he hurts her, your no-kill policy on him is going to mean nothing to me.'

Xavier didn't flinch. 'Just you remember who you're talking to. And you just remember what you've got to lose, what we've all got to lose, if we don't bring Kane down. Alive.'

Max held Xavier's gaze as he tried to glare him down. 'And what if it's bigger than this? What if it's bigger than all of us? What if by sending her in there you're giving Kane exactly what he wants, what he needs? What if he's the one, Xavier? Has that crossed your mind? What if Caitlin is the key to unleashing the prophecy? What if that's why he wants her?'

'That prophecy has nothing to do with a shadow reader. Or Kane.'

'Because your source is so reliable and trustworthy?'

'Because I would not be sending Caitlin in there if I thought for one moment that is what he wanted.'

'Thought – exactly. But you don't know, do you? We know only what they've told us. I know only what you've told me. You are second-guessing Kane, Xavier. You know how dangerous that is.'

'Humankind is at no immediate risk. That is why the divisions are in place. That is why the Global Council works with the vampire ambassadors to maintain peace.'

'And what if those vampires have lied? Or what if they're wrong? If you're wrong? We are talking about hundreds of thousands of lives if they come to rule. We're talking about the world as we know it coming to an end. All from one decision made in this locale here today. So excuse me for questioning your authority.'

Xavier didn't flinch as he studied him in the silence for a few moments. 'If you want me to help Caitlin four days from now, you leave her to do this. Because I can promise you – if you interfere, you're on your own. We both know there are worse things out there than Kane. Much worse fates. You need me. She needs me. And don't you forget it.'

# CHAPTER FOUR

Caitlin stood in the doorway of her tiny second-floor apartment, surveying the clutter and chaos that was indicative of her work-life balance: the stacked-up sink and draining board; the overstuffed bin full of empty take-outs; paperwork and mugs strewn everywhere.

She closed the door and dropped her work satchel to the floor, slipped off her coat and discarded it over the kitchen worktop on her way across to the sofa. She sank down onto the edge, elbows on her knees as she gazed down at Kane's case folders still spread across the coffee table. She slid out the half-exposed photo. It had been taken during one of his night dealings. He wasn't looking directly at the camera but there was a noticeable hint of a smile on his lips, the smile that in animation had been even more compelling. She lingered on the slight glimpse of incisor that now sent a familiar warm flush through her body.

Hell, she was playing a dangerous game. She knew it. Max knew it. Xavier knew it. And if they knew the full story, they'd tear the case from her in a split second.

The professional in her knew it was time to pull out. The professional in her would have never got involved in the case in the first place knowing the instant physical attraction she'd felt on first seeing his picture. That kind of attraction was dangerous, though not unusual in any of the units when dealing with the more sensual species. Detachment was a skill all good agents developed – a skill Caitlin had never really had to work on either professionally or personally, except with Kane. A part of her had hoped it would all instantly dispel on their first encounter. She'd needed it to dispel to make her true purpose easier. Shadow-reading was hard enough but attraction to the subject caused all sorts of problems, not least blocks.

But having stared deep into those lethal navy eyes, having felt the potential of his cool hard body against hers, those sensuous lips against her neck and wrist, heard the caress of his whispers, she knew her job had only got harder. He was already embedded in her bloodstream, her every thought. After that last encounter, he may as well have been the oxygen she breathed. And that threat of seduction, whispered like a lover's promise, still lingered forefront in her thoughts. Thoughts that terrified her but also excited her, somewhere deep, somewhere dark, somewhere she wasn't quite ready to confront yet.

But he truly was arrogant if he thought she could feel anything for him, anything anywhere near powerful enough to give him access to her soul. Attraction was one thing, but what he was suggesting was completely another. What he was suggesting was impossible. There was no way he was going to succeed. She just needed to make sure she did before he realised that.

She'd play the master vampire at his own game.

Somehow.

But for that she'd need to know why he wanted her soul. He'd said he wanted it for revenge. That was his only clue. And despite Xavier's reassurances, she had the nagging feeling it was something to do with Arana's death. Why he needed her in particular remained a mystery. Removing her soul, even if it was possible, would render it useless – render her useless. Unless that was what he wanted.

Caitlin pushed the folders aside and sank back in the sofa. She needed to think.

As a master vampire, he would have come across countless shadow readers. It was nothing unusual for her kind to be held captive by area rulers on account of their seventh sense. Where there was a master of any third species ruling a territory, whether a vampire, lycan, demon or witch, having a shadow reader was a sure way to have the rest of the species in the vicinity fearful of acting against their ruler. Kane, if her research about him had been right, would have doubtlessly had shadow readers of his own.

She leaned forward and flicked through the paperwork. She had to get inside of him and fast. Four days wasn't long. Not to break inside the mind of the solitary vampire notorious for keeping himself to himself. She needed to keep her head clear and focused. She needed to prepare herself.

She rubbed her wrists mindlessly where he'd held her, her stomach leaping at the memory. The way her body had involuntarily responded to him had shocked even her. She wondered if he'd seen it in her, if he'd sensed it. He'd mocked her about it but that could have just been his arrogance. She wasn't going to let herself be yet another in a long line of conquests. She wouldn't give him the satisfaction.

Picking herself up from the sofa, she headed over to her bedroom. She lowered to her knees at her bed and reached underneath for her suitcase. She dragged it out and unzipped it. She took a moment before flipping the lid back, exposing the contents. A small knot formed at the back of her throat and in her stomach.

She hadn't kept much of theirs. Her mother had sorted through her father's things a couple of years after he'd gone. Most of it had been donated to charity, but she had given Caitlin the choice of a few keep-sakes. She'd opted to keep one of his shirts, a couple of pens, a notebook that still had his doodles on, his watch and his VCU badge.

She picked up the badge and rubbed her thumb over the silver emblem.

The official line had always been that he had been killed by a rogue vampire – it was the most likely conclusion. It was a hazard of the job. You didn't spend fifteen years immersed in the vampiric underworld without piquing the interest and resentment of a few unsavoury vampires. Her father had been exceptional at his job and everyone knew it, not least the vampires he dragged kicking and screaming into conviction. Revenge against VCU agents was not uncommon, especially if a vampire had a grudge to bear. And plenty had grudges against super-agent Rick Parish.

Caitlin reached for her worn, dog-eared Companion to English Literature she had carried home from school the day her mother had broken the news. She'd sat her on the sofa on that bright, sunny Thursday afternoon. Her father hadn't been at the breakfast table that morning but that was nothing unusual. Working until dawn was routine. But Caitlin had known something was wrong. She had known when she'd left for school that morning – satchel hanging heavy across her chest, coat loose on her slight frame, scuffing her shoes against the pavement as she ambled to school alone. She'd known something had changed. She'd felt it in her sleep. She'd woken with that unsettling feeling that something ominous had happened. But nothing had prepared her for the look in her mother's large hazel eyes, the clench Caitlin had felt in her stomach as she'd sat on that sofa. Thirty-five was no age to be widowed. Fifteen, only days away from being sixteen, was no age to lose a father.

That afternoon, the cool winter sunshine had brought with it a chill, not just of death, but of the pending horror of life after her father.

She'd hated the sunshine ever since. Hated the way its glow ignited all the pleasures of the world, brought out the best in people's hopes and dreams, when inside that house that afternoon, Caitlin had seen all her mother's dreams ripped away.

Caitlin remembered holding in her tears, knowing it would make it worse. Instead she'd remembered nodding and listening to what her mother had to say, hugging and comforting her as best she could. She'd kept her own tears for private times, times alone when her mother wouldn't hear and be distressed by them.

She'd done the same thing seven years later when it had been Max's turn to break the news about her mother. Max, her father's best friend. Max, their rock since Rick's murder. Max, who, three years after her father's death, inevitably became much more than just a rock to her mother. They'd never concluded what had killed Kathleen Parish, only that it hadn't been a vampire. All the pointers had been towards a demon species, and the Demon Control Unit had worked flat out for six months to work out what. But with demons being the most diverse and intricate of the third species, it remained inconclusive as to whether the attack on her mother had been random or because of Max's work.

Now, after seven years of seeking the truth, Caitlin was finally on the cusp. And want her soul though he may, Kane was going to learn that she needed her vengeance more.

She placed the ID back in the suitcase, moved aside some of her mother's boxes of jewellery and took out the handbook she had been seeking. She closed the lid of the suitcase and shoved it back under the bed.

She knew every archaic page of this notebook, having read it countless times – the shadow readers' guide, which had been given to her over twenty years before when her gift had been diagnosed. Caitlin had always been overly tactile and one of her teachers had seen her trying to read a friend at school during break-time. All such instances were reported. Shadow readers had to be declared to the state. There was no rhyme or reason as to why a child was born with the ability, and many lost the skill by the time they reached their mid-teens. Many more crumbled during assessments, their energy drained too hard and too fast by the darkness contained in third species' shadows. Many were left too traumatised by the images they saw, especially when they were upgraded to reading vampires.

Somehow she'd managed to keep an emotional distance. She'd let the images play like a film in front of her eyes and then, after she reported what she'd seen, she'd switch off. By the time she'd applied to be a VCU agent, she was already top of her game. And somehow, losing her parents, the agony, let alone all else that had happened, had helped with that switching off, no matter how disturbing the images were that she saw. In doing so, she'd convinced the unit assessors that emotionally she was up there with the elite. Intellectually, she was ahead of them. Physically, she was sufficient enough, on nimbleness and speed even if not on strength. They'd had no choice but to accept her application.

She opened the first few pages. She knew it wasn't going to tell her anything she didn't already know and certainly not why Kane wanted her soul. But she needed something to distract her thoughts from him, something to curb her frustration. She needed to at least feel like she was doing something, however futile, because even that felt better than sitting and waiting for the vampire to make his move.

Kane stood outside the VCU headquarters' gates as he lit a cigarette, exhaling a steady stream of smoke to mingle with the fresh morning air. Despite the sunrise, the sky was fortunately still a heavy, tepid grey, the clouds blocking the ferocious UV rays. It wouldn't do him much good to be stood it in for too long, though, and he'd have to sleep it off when he got back to his place. He'd probably lose most of the day recovering from the long walk back in the draining sunlight.

The inhalation of smoke did little to sate his irritation, his frustration. Two encounters with the girl and she was already making him second-guess her. He didn't want to be intrigued by her – something that aggravated him more than the fact she had outsmarted him. Feisty, obstinate, intelligent and brave Caitlin Parish who'd felt as soft, warm and enticing as woodland moss as he'd lain on top of her, pinning her nubile body to the table with ease. A fragile body and eyes even more vulnerable, eyes that had been wary but nonetheless still defiant enough to grate on his nerves. And that was what he had to hold on to – that sense of irritation she had evoked, not the fascination.

But at least he'd fed her enough information to make sure she didn't run and hide. Not that it was in her character to do so. But questions would have been asked: why she was still alive, why he'd confronted her, why he'd allowed himself to be tracked. Questions and complications brought about by her escape. But she'd only get away from him once. Nothing was beyond rectifying and nightfall would come soon enough. It needed to, because losing any more time wasn't an option.

He lifted his cigarette back to his lips. He didn't need to look over his shoulder to know who was there. Despite the clench of fury in his chest, he kept his gaze ahead, exhaled another steady stream of smoke as he took a moment. 'What do you want, Max?'

'I want to know what you're playing at, Kane.'

Kane licked his bottom lip, composing himself before turning to face him.

Max remained rooted to the spot a safe enough distance away and in plain sight of the security cameras and the armed guard in his tower above.

'I could ask you the same question, allowing me to be brought in with nothing conclusive to support your accusations. Still, it got me up close and personal with the VCU's golden girl.' Kane exhaled a taunting, steady stream of smoke. 'So it wasn't a complete waste of my time.'

Max adjusted his position to try to take the authoritative stance, but Kane could see the unease in his eyes; he could sense the fear. Max shouldn't be at the gate talking to him or confronting him. But he had the obvious question that he couldn't manage to contain: 'Why did you let her live?'

'I don't just go around randomly killing anyone, Max.' He glanced to the floor as he flicked ash onto it. He looked back into his eyes. 'Despite what you boys like to claim.'

'Leave her alone, Kane.'

Kane smiled. 'You should have trained her better. Taught her about playing kiss-chase with boys from the wrong side of the track.'

'She was doing her job. She did it and now it's over.'

'Says who?'

Max's eyes exuded dread and resentment despite his efforts to contain it. 'What do you want with her, Kane?'

Kane took a step closer, just enough for Max to lose his stance and take a small but wary step back. 'What would any cold-blooded vampire want with her?'

Max narrowed his eyes. 'Do you want to make a deal over something? Is that what this is about?'

Kane smiled again. 'Maybe I'll get back to you on that one.' He turned away before his instincts got the better of him.

'Is it to do with the prophecy?'

Kane stopped. He exhaled another steady stream of smoke despite the inner jolt at hearing the words slip from human lips. If they'd been alone, Max would have already been pinned face-first against the gate, his swiftly broken arm wrenched up behind his back, his knees cracking against the tarmac as Kane demanded his source. But he knew the rumours were out there, even if they didn't know all the facts. No one but the Higher Order vampires and master vampires knew the precise facts of how it would be brought to fruition. At least it had better be that way or he'd find whoever had decided to the contrary.

He turned to face him again, kept his composure impassive. 'And what prophecy is that, Max?'

The grip of silence was indication enough that Max had clearly said something he shouldn't. Wary hesitation flooded his eyes. His lips and eyebrows twitched. His stance was instantly defensive. 'The one where you win.'

Kane dropped his cigarette hand loose to his side again. 'Someone has been telling tales.'

'It's no secret. Not anymore. And you know it. Just tell me if that's why you want Caitlin.'

The fact that Max seemed to believe a shadow reader could have something to do with it was reassurance enough that he clearly didn't know what he was talking about. Kane lifted the cigarette back to his lips. 'You need to find yourself more accurate sources.'

'Vampires will never rule humans,' Max said firmly. 'We'll see to it.'

Kane suppressed his scowl with a smile. 'Take care of yourself, Max,' he said, turning away again. He sauntered out onto the street. 'And that pretty stepdaughter of yours.'

# CHAPTER FIVE

Caitlin woke up feeling cold, the door's buzzer jolting her back to reality.

Images of Kane were still fresh in her mind, the memories dispersing with her increased consciousness. She'd been back in the corridor, his hard body pressed against hers, his cool, strong hands pinning her wrists to the wall as his lips had lowered to hers.

She wiped the dampness from the corner of her mouth and scanned the darkened lounge to regain her bearings. She lifted her head to check the windows. They had been brimming with the dull light of day the last time she'd looked, but were now opaque with dusk. She twisted her wrist and squinted at her watch. It was just after five in the evening. She'd only been asleep a couple of hours at most and now both her head and body achingly recognised it.

The buzzer rang again.

Her socked feet met carpet as she moved into a seated position and rubbed her neck from where she'd fallen asleep at an awkward angle amongst the sofa cushions. As the buzzer rang for longer this time, more impatiently, she staggered across to the intercom. She pulled her sloppy, oversized sweater back up over her shoulder, the hems of her jeans scuffing on the carpet. By this time she was usually already at work but now HQ felt like nothing more than some distant, alien concept. She took the intercom phone off the hook and held it to her ear. 'Hello?'

'Caitlin, it's me.'

Her knees weakened at the sound of the voice, her grip tightening on the handset as she stood stunned to silence. Rob. The man who'd abandoned her when she'd needed him most.

'Can I come up?' Rob asked.

She rested her palm against the wall, repressing every urge to hang up. 'What do you want?'

'I need to see you.'

She took a deep steady breath, her finger hovering over the door release button.

'Caitlin, please.'

After a few more seconds, she pressed the release. She smoothed down her hair, readjusted her sweater and opened the door. She stood in the doorway waiting, her clenched hands tucked in the sleeves of her sweater as she folded her arms. She hadn't even showered since last night's events. She should have cared, but surprisingly she didn't.

The slow, steady scuff of boots against the stairs filled her with long-suppressed memories. It was an even greater blow to her stomach as he emerged from around the corner. Rob looked at her with those all-too-familiar pale-blue eyes, his sandy hair still as ruffled as it had been when she'd been in love with him all those years ago.

Before he'd left her.

'This is so transparent,' she said, her glare fixed on his as she guarded the threshold to her home. 'I assume you've been talking to Max?'

'Can I come in, or are we going to do this out here?'

She kept her arms folded as she leaned against the doorframe.

He stepped up to her, amusement in his eyes. 'You always were tetchy when you'd just woken up.'

'Don't you dare,' she warned.

'I'm not denying I deserve the cold treatment but you can at least give me ten minutes, Cait.'

'Sounds like ten minutes too long to me.'

He kept his gaze steadily on hers. 'I still care about you no matter what you think. So, yes, Max did send me here to talk some sense into you, but it didn't take a lot of persuading, trust me.'

'Trust you? That's a joke.'

He sighed steadily, squeezing through the doorway and past her.

She closed the door behind them but stayed rooted to the spot. It shouldn't have felt so strange having him in the apartment, but every facet of her slipped into defence mode. She'd once loved this man, adored him, would have done anything to get him back six years before. But now his presence felt oppressive, uncomfortable even. And it irritated her as he appraised the state of her apartment.

'I've had other priorities,' she said in defence of the mess.

'So I hear.' He wandered over to the coffee table to where Kane's picture lay amongst the pile of paperwork. He lifted it up, his eyes cold as he stared down at it. 'The infamous Kane Malloy. You sure know how to pick them, Cait.'

'My job has nothing to do with you. And neither does the VCU anymore, remember?'

He looked across at her. 'You must know what you're contemplating is insane?'

'Max had no right to disclose this to you.'

'He's trying to stop you making the biggest mistake of your life.'

'He's eight years late for that one.'

Rob raised his eyebrows. 'Ouch.' He threw the picture down and reached for one of the folders to flick through the paperwork. 'How long have you been tracking him? Five years?'

'That stuff is confidential.'

'Which is why you've made private copies?' He threw the folder back down and strolled over to the kitchen. 'Make myself a coffee, shall I? Are you still plenty of milk with no sugar?'

She bent over the coffee table, shoving as much paper as she could back into the folders. 'Why the hell is any of this your business? Why are you even making it your business? You still care, yeah, lovely. Thanks for leaving it over six years before letting me know.'

'Don't make it sound like I just left you with no explanation,' he said, turning to face her, the kettle boiling in the background. 'What we had should have always stayed as friendship.'

'My friend wouldn't have walked out on me when I needed him. Three months, Rob. My mother had been dead less than three months and you turned your back on me.'

'Like there was ever a good time.'

'My father would have been ashamed of you.'

'He would have understood.'

She gazed deep into his pale-blue eyes, the creases just beginning to form around them betraying his forty years. 'I was in love with you. From thirteen years of age I idolised you. Whenever Dad did a night shift, I used to set my alarm for dawn and watch through my bedroom window in the hope he would give you a lift home from work and invite you in for a coffee first. I lived for the day I wouldn't have to wear my school uniform anymore. When I could go to college and you would start looking at me like a woman and not just a girl. You were all I wanted.'

'And I tried not to fall in love with you back. But it happened. Those two years were the best of my life. I know you probably don't believe that, but they were. But I needed more than that.'

'A girlfriend who didn't plan to chase vampires for a living, you mean. A nice normal girl who didn't shadow-read third-species criminals.'

'It didn't mean I stopped loving you.'

Months earlier, this would have been a statement that would have changed everything. Would have gone some way to heal the wound of his leaving. Now she felt nothing.

'You knew I couldn't handle it, Cait. You made your choice.'

'And you punished me for it.'

'No, I let you do what you wanted to do.'

'Let me?'

He grabbed two mugs from the drainer, checking they were clean. 'I've not come here to argue with you.'

She folded her arms. 'No, you came here to tell me exactly what I should and shouldn't be doing again.'

He made the coffees and turned back around, handing her a mug.

She unravelled her arms to accept it, wrapping her hands around it. She stared into the contents.

'Max tells me you used hemlock on Malloy.' He took a mouthful of his drink as he leaned back against the counter. 'Into messing with VCU property now, are you?'

'I did what I had to.'

'And just how long had you been planning that?'

'Long enough.'

'This has to stop, Cait. This whole Malloy thing. You're out of your depth.'

'So Max thinks.'

'You don't?'

She took a slow sip of coffee, breaking away from the interrogation of his gaze again.

He strolled past her into the living space. Placing his mug on the coffee table, he slipped off his jacket, throwing it over the back of the sofa. He was still in good shape. Always had been. He had aged well. In fact, seemingly very little had changed other than the way she now felt inside. She should have felt more, knew she should. Maybe relief at least or a pang of something that reminded her why she'd fallen so deeply for him. But still she felt nothing.

'I know what I'm doing, Rob.'

'But do you know what Malloy's doing?' he asked, taking a seat. Different apartment but same sofa and the same seat he'd sat in the last night they'd been together. She doubted he remembered.

She'd never forget.

She'd known something was wrong and she'd asked him a few times during the course of the night until he'd started to get irritable. He'd been getting irritable a lot over the few weeks before. She'd put it down to grief. Losing her mother had hit them all – her, Max and Rob. Max, Rob and her father had always been inseparable. Ever since Rob had been taken on as her father's rookie, they'd got close. Over the two years they'd worked together, he'd become like a substitute son.

Her father hadn't been alive to see them get together. It had been years later. Rob made his move one night after dropping her home from work. She'd been twenty-one and fresh out of college. He was already working his way up the VCU, determined to make her father proud. Max had become the head of the unit by then, a role everyone knew would have gone to her father if tragedy hadn't struck.

It had felt like the most natural thing in the world that they would get together. They'd been friends. Companions. He was the only male she ever let close. The only one good enough to go some way to fill the gap her father had left. He'd made her happy. In many ways. In other ways, nothing ever would, but she'd learned to live with that.

Her mother's death shook him as much as everyone else. Something changed in him after that. She knew he felt guilty – as if he should have done more to protect them. Max had been the same.

At first she'd made excuses for him when he'd left. When he'd told her he needed some time away. She'd felt the weight of responsibility on his shoulders. She'd recognised that he felt he'd let her down. And her father.

And then time away became weeks, months, years. For that, she'd never forgive him. And now he was back, trying to take away the only thing she had left to fight for. The very thing he should have been by her side fighting for too. But he was like Max and the others – telling her she was just imagining it all. How she wished she could throw it all back at him then and there.

'What's that supposed to mean?' she asked as she sat opposite him.

'It means you have no idea what's going through his head. You can read all the files you want, all the psych evaluations, every shred of evidence, but you will never really see what is going on up there. You think you'll ever outsmart him again? All you've done is made him play harder. You're dangerously naïve if you think anything to the contrary.'

'Have you finished?'

'You're as stubborn as ever, Caitlin Parish.'

'And if you seriously believed you could come here and persuade me to give this up, if both you and Max believed that, then I'm not the only one who's naïve.'

'You know what he does to people, Caitlin. To his own kind. To others of the third species. To anyone who doesn't do what he wants, when he wants, how he wants. What he can't have, he takes. Those who cross him get hurt, and so do the people closest to them.'

'Which is why he needs to be brought in. And I'm going to do it.'

'And you believe he's going to let you inside his world? Xavier's plan is ludicrous. Kane will use you up and spit you out. You have to know when to stop. You proved your point. You brought in Kane Malloy. It's not your fault he couldn't be read. Cait, you have to let it go.'

'Did Max tell you he's coming after me?'

'Yes. And that's why I want you to come with me. I'll get you somewhere safe. Somewhere he can't find you.'

Caitlin gazed into his eyes, noting the desperate plea behind them.

'You don't need to live here,' he added. 'Someone with your skills and education. You could be doing something else. Living in Midtown, Summerton even. You're better than this place.'

Come with me.

There was a time when they had been the only words she'd wanted to hear, but now they only evoked irritation and indignation. 'My job's here. Or should I prove what everyone in this district thinks: that they've been abandoned – that even the agents who claim to protect them, who enforce the ideals laid down by the Global Council, don't dare live here? In fact, why am I even justifying myself to you? Do you really think you can just walk back into my life and treat me like some damsel in distress not capable of looking after myself? I've stood on my own two feet for long enough, Rob. I'm not some dewy-eyed twenty-one-year-old flattered by your advances anymore. I sort my own problems. So, no, I'm not going anywhere with you, even though my life might very well depend on it. And you can tell Max the same thing.' She stood up, holding her hand out for his mug, her glare locked on his.

Rob didn't move as his eyes narrowed in resentment and suspicion. 'Is it the job, or is there something more going on here?'

She felt a flutter in her chest at the insinuation. 'Like what?'

That Kane was no longer just a mission? That going after Kane was a compulsion – a necessary compulsion for her own survival? That right there and then, Kane was the only one she knew of who could save her?

'He beds women as a pastime,' Rob said, looking up at her. 'You know that. When he's not murdering and maiming and torturing that is.'

'You think I'm planning to jump into bed with him?' She exhaled curtly, and broke from Rob's probing gaze in case he should read into her defensiveness. 'That's one too many insults for the day.' She snatched the half-empty mug from his hand and marched back across to the kitchen.

'I'm not blind,' Rob said, following her. 'I know the effect he has on females – of all species.'

'You almost sound jealous,' she said, discarding both mugs in the sink. She turned to face him, her arms folded.

He narrowed his eyes. 'Is that what this is about? You pick the biggest, baddest vampire out there to make me jealous?'

'Oh, don't flatter yourself. What I mean is you thinking you can come back in here with any kind of claim over me. I can do what I like, so I will do what I like. And I will go after Kane Malloy and I will bring him in. And I'll do it my way. I'm not that vulnerable, fragile thing anymore. I'm probably nothing like what you remember.'

He held his gaze steadily on hers. 'You're wrong, Caitlin. You're exactly how I remember. You can put up all the front you want, but I can still see behind your eyes better than anyone. And he'll use that. He'll revel in it. He'll turn you inside out and rip you apart because it's what he does. You seriously think you can handle that? You let him in, and he'll tear you to pieces.'

'Like you did? He's got the excuse of being a heartless vampire. What's yours?'

Rob pressed his lips together as he stepped away. He reached into his jacket pocket and pulled out five pastel-coloured envelopes. Returning to join her, he held them across to her.

She saw a glimpse of her address on the top one. The stamp.

She took them from him. She flicked through each. All were addressed in his handwriting. All were to be opened on 16th December.

'I never forgot,' he said. 'I just never thought it right to send them. I didn't want to confuse you any more than I had.'

She swallowed against the tightness in her throat. She discarded the cards on the draining board and moved to step past him, but Rob caught her hand. The warmth of another human being should have felt comforting. The intimacy should have felt right, the familiarity reassuring. Instead it felt shockingly non-intimate. There was no spark and no surge of tension like she'd felt the moment Kane had touched her. It was non-comparable – the way Kane made her catch her breath in her throat, the way her body immediately responded to his. She looked up into Rob's eyes and the barrier was almost palpable. She immediately pulled her hand away. When Kane had let her go, it had felt like a void. When Rob did, it was a relief.

'Please,' Rob said, gazing deep into her eyes. 'Don't do this.'

'You asking me not to shows you've never known me at all. I want you to leave, Rob. I'm tired. And I have things to do.'

Frustration emanated from his eyes, his lips taut. 'You're making a mistake.'

The urge to tell him he was wrong and that she was right was overwhelming. That instead of insisting, like everyone else, that nothing was coming for her, he should have believed her. That instead of denying her claims, he should have been trawling the streets alongside her for answers. But confronting him with the truth now would have given too much away and nothing, absolutely nothing, was jeopardizing her plan to get to Kane.

'We'll see,' she said.

Rob's glower remained fixed, Caitlin's barriers hardening with every second that passed.

'Do you really think you'll survive this?' he said. 'Do you really think he'll let you live? Once you've given him what he wants, or once he's taken it, he'll kill you. You're a willing victim, for fuck's sake. You step over his threshold and you are his. Is that what you want? Am I right? Is it more than just the job? Is it him?'

The look in his eyes unnerved her – the amalgamation of jealously, anger and disappointment. 'I want you to leave, Rob.'

'There are better and safer ways to get your sexual kicks, Caitlin. I've seen enough females firsthand who thought it would be a challenge to slip between his sheets. You don't come out the same person. He's sick. He's twisted. He doesn't have limits. And you will end up doing whatever he wants you to do.' He pressed his forefinger to his temple. 'And he'll get so far in your head, you'll actually believe you want it. Is that who you want to give yourself to?'

She defiantly held his glare. 'You don't know me anymore.'

'Been with anyone since me, have you?'

She exhaled tersely and moved to step past him again but he caught her upper arm, pulling her back against the counter before standing in front of her.

'Have you remembered what it was like?' he asked, standing too close for comfort.

She lowered her gaze, staring at the floor as she clutched the counter.

'But I was patient. I loved you. I understood. I know how hard intimacy is for you. I know how hard it is to break through that barrier that protects you – your heart and your soul – from all those readings you have to do.'

She didn't want to remember how it had been between them. She didn't want to acknowledge it. How quickly it had all become difficult. How loving him like she did had made it all the more painful. The disappointment in his eyes, the failure she'd felt. Wanting to be normal. Wanting to feel something. He'd put the first time down to her inexperience. The second and the third, the few times after that down to stress, her expectations being too high. But she felt nothing. Nothing but shame.

And she wanted so much more.

But it had never got any easier.

And the last time they were together, the month before he'd left, when she'd turned to him as much for comfort as to be sated, should have been the most special of all.

Instead, she'd been left feeling hollow again.

'That's why I never wanted you to go into all this shadow-reading, Caitlin. It wasn't just me being selfish. You were committing yourself to a life that was wrong for you. You deserved better. I knew it. Max knew it. Your parents would never have wanted that for you. Your father would go insane knowing what you're about to do. You can't handle Kane. And deep down you know it. And I can say that because I know you. I know you better than anyone.' He caught her by the jaw, forcing her to look up at him, his blue eyes burning deep into hers. 'Kane won't be patient. He won't be kind. He won't tell you it'll be okay. He is cruel and self-sating. He's not exciting, he's not challenging, not when he's hurting you. Not when he's making you cry. When he's making you bleed.'

Caitlin pushed past him but he caught her by the wrist.

She tried to yank it away but he held tighter.

'It's not nice not being in control, is it?' he said.

She glowered up at him.

'Do you think you'll be in control with Kane?' he asked. 'Do you think you've got him worked out?' His eyes softened. 'Walk away from it. Please. Don't do this to yourself.'

'Let me go,' she said firmly.

The air thickened between them, Caitlin holding her breath as she stared him down.

Eventually he conceded and let her go.

As he stepped away, she sagged against the worktop, not knowing if she wanted to cry or lash out at him.

'Max is worried Kane wants to use you to bring about the prophecy.'

She snatched her gaze back to his. Her heart thudded. It had crossed her mind, too, but she hadn't dared say anything in case it convinced Xavier she was too much of a risk to go undercover after all. 'You seriously think Xavier would let me do this if he had any suspicion that was Kane's intention?'

And if anyone knew, it was Xavier. It was never spoken of officially, but everyone knew he had some kind of inside scoop. The Higher Order, 'vampire royalty' as everyone referred to them, had links with the Third Species Management Divisions across all the locales. Xavier seemed to have closer links than others though, if the rumours were to be believed. If Xavier had had any suspicions a shadow reader had played a role, he wouldn't have supported her place in the field, let alone going after Kane.

And Kane had spoken about vengeance, not fulfilling the prophecies.

Unless he meant vengeance against the whole of humankind.

No. He wouldn't have waited for that. He'd clearly been watching her for a long time and would have had plenty of opportunities to snatch her. His motivations were definitely more personal.

'Xavier will do whatever it takes to bring in Kane. There's no better excuse to lock him up and throw away the key than catching him red-handed trying to incite the prophecy.'

'It could happen decades from now, centuries even. I'm supposed to shy away based on that?'

'You're not shying away. You're saving your life.' He sighed heavily. 'Max told me you still believe all this stuff about Rick's and Kathleen's deaths being linked. That it's coming for you. He thinks that's why you're doing this. That you just don't care.'

She folded her arms and lowered her eyes.

He stepped up to her again and tenderly pushed her hair back from her face, cupping the back of her head as he always used to.

She closed her eyes. Responding, reaching for him, accepting his help, admitting defeat all crossed her mind. But not one of them felt right.

'I'm here for you, Caitlin. I left you once but I'm not going to leave you again.'

She looked up at him, deep into his soft blue eyes, not needing to search for sincerity because it was so apparent.

'Nothing is going to hurt you,' he added. 'Not while I'm with you.'

He leaned in before she had time to respond. His lips were as soft as she remembered. As warm. They met hers with ease. And, consumed by familiarity, she reciprocated.

She wanted to lose herself in the moment. To forget everything. To think of nothing but him.

Maybe if last night hadn't happened, she could have.

But Kane had touched her now. Kane was no longer just a report, a photograph or a moving image on camera. She'd felt his lips against her skin, his hard body against hers, his strength, his resilience, the threat and promise of sensual sexuality. And her body had responded. More dangerously, so had her mind. Or he wouldn't have been so lodged in her thoughts right there and then.

She didn't want Rob. She hadn't wanted Rob for a long time. She wanted Kane. More than that, she needed Kane.

Kane was the only one who could give her what she wanted, even if she was pressing the self-destruct button in the process.

She broke away from Rob's kiss, the tension in his body consuming the gap between them. 'I need you to go,' she said, lowering her eyes again to break any other prospect of intimacy.

He hovered for a moment as if searching for the right thing to say. She could feel his anger. Anger that had never been more apparent.

She looked up warily as he brushed past her to the draining board.

He slid the cards towards him and, grabbing a pen from the counter, wrote a phone number on the envelope of the top one. 'Think carefully, Caitlin.'

He stopped in front of her again, reached to smooth her cheek as he always used to, but she sidestepped away. He retracted his hand, this time impatience, not upset, igniting behind his eyes.

She watched him go. Watched him close the door behind himself.

Feeling sick, she collapsed against the counter again. She stared back down at the cards, urged herself not to open them, but grabbed the one with his phone number on and ripped open the envelope.

The birthday card was simple: white, with a small, shaggy teddy sat amongst some presents. Inside it simply said, Always in my thoughts.

As a tear trickled irritatingly down her cheek, she wiped it away, refusing to break open old wounds that she'd spent long enough trying to stitch.

She threw the card back down and scanned the chaos. She had to do something worthwhile, something to work it all off. And starting with cleaning the apartment seemed as valid a task as any.

The club was awash with people lining the basement entrance, chatting against the graffiti-emblazoned stone walls. It had once been a row of five derelict houses, but Alexander had knocked them all through, albeit illegally. The heavy beat of the music vibrated through the floor. The scent of excitement, of illicit substances, of sex dominated the air.

Kane made his way along the length of the dim corridor, people automatically moving out of his path. He took a right, not into the heart of the club, but down the worn stone steps into the cellar's caverns. The bouncer sent him a polite nod, letting him pass unquestioned into the exclusive area. Taking the second recess on the left, Kane stepped into one of the catacombs.

Alexander glanced across his shoulder from the card table. 'Kane.' He leaned back in his chair and tapped the behind of the woman who was sitting on his lap as a directive for her to move. His dark eyes ignited, his easy grin broad. 'It's good to have you here. Do you want to join us?'

'Not tonight,' he said, fleetingly appraising the woman as she sauntered past him, her large doe-eyes meeting his as she smiled slowly, sensually.

Alexander took Kane's hint. He discarded his cards onto the table and lifted his six-foot-four, lean frame from the table to promptly join Kane in the doorway before leading him out into the private neighbouring catacomb. 'I wasn't expecting you tonight.'

'I hope that's not your way of telling me you haven't got my stuff.'

'Of course not.' Alexander grinned again, his dark eyes flashing. 'When have I ever let you down?'

Kane followed him through to the back of the catacomb and into the makeshift office. He eased back on the sofa as Alexander crossed to the old metal filing cabinet.

He rifled through the top drawer before joining Kane on the sofas. He lay what looked like small plastic evidence bags on the glass tabletop between them, each small enough to hold in the palm of his hand. The first contained a tight-knit green herb, the next a bunch of brown leaves and the last a fine powder. Each was marked with symbols.

'Mix it all together with warm water. They have to drink it all.' He slid over a folded piece of paper. 'They're the words you utter. It should all take less than five minutes.'

'You make it sound simple.'

'It's frighteningly simple, if you have the right ingredients. I've had to call in a lot of favours for these. Some of this stuff I haven't seen for centuries. Trust me, the process is easy but finding the tools is not.' He leaned back in the sofa. 'Who's the lucky victim?'

'No questions, Alexander. That was our agreement.' He sent Alexander an amiable smile, before gathering up the packets and tucking them inside his coat as he stood. 'And you know I'll return the favour. With gratitude.'

'I know you will.' He hesitated. 'Rumour has it you're after the VCU's numero uno. '

Kane smirked. 'Is that right?'

His eyes narrowed with concern. 'Am I?'

'Questions, Alexander.'

'I've never known anyone capable of removing a shadow reader's soul, Kane. Just a friendly warning. Those things are locked down tighter than any other humans'. Either of you could end up damaged in the process.'

'I'll bear that in mind. What do I owe you?'

'Some loyalty is all I ask. Defence if I need it.'

Kane nodded. 'Goes without saying.'

'But Tyler's been causing some trouble again,' he said, following Kane back across to the door. 'And Tay.'

Kane stopped. He took a cigarette out of his top pocket and placed it between his lips. 'What have they done now?'

'Tyler's had three open feeds. Full public view. One wasn't willing. We had a gang of humans come round seeking revenge late last night. You know I don't mind sharing my premises with vampires, but not ones out for trouble.'

'Did you handle it?'

'We sent the humans away with their tails between their legs. But if he keeps pushing it they're going to come back and in greater numbers. We don't need the hassle. And we sure as hell don't need the VCU all over the place.'

'I'll sort him out,' Kane said, stopping at the door. 'What about Tay?'

'Usual. I swear he's in with them. The VCU and stuff, I mean. He's got snitch written all over him. I don't trust him.'

'He's done some work for Caleb hasn't he?'

'Caleb will kill him if he gets word. I know you've never met him, but trust me – Caleb doesn't take any shit. That vampire rules that nightclub and the five blocks around it.'

'So I've heard. Then make sure he knows. And if Caleb doesn't do anything, I'll gut Tay for him.' He turned the handle.

'Hey, Kane.'

Kane looked back across his shoulder at him.

'There's plenty would pay a good price for that shadow reader,' Alexander said. 'If you wanted to rethink.'

'Are you saying you're interested?'

'I could make use of her.'

Kane smiled as he opened the door. 'Trust me, she's more trouble than she's worth.'

'A girl Kane can't tame. Nice to know she's living up to her reputation.'

'Taming is all about letting them run wild first, Alexander. You know that. Let them think they have control.'

'Well, you don't want to be holding on to her too long. Rumour has it that girl's parents were slain by some fourth-species being, and it's coming for her. You might want to be done with her as quick as you can.'

'Concern noted.'

'We need you around here, Kane. I hope you know what you're doing.'

Kane sent him a smile across his shoulder as he stepped back out into the catacomb. 'Always.'

The woman who'd been sat on Alexander's lap stood outside waiting, hovering though trying not to make it look obvious. She was certainly stunning. Tasteful too. She sauntered towards him with an appealing grace, only slightly inhibited by one drink too many. But the look in those doe eyes, framed by the heavy fringe of her bobbed hair, the upward curl of those full sensuous lips, told him she knew exactly what she was doing, the alcohol merely giving her the courage to approach him. Hopefully it had also given her enough courage to let him indulge in ways other than just a feed, especially with that nubile human body offering potential for so much more.

Alexander stepped up alongside his friend. 'I see Mila's caught your eye.'

'Is she not yours?'

Alexander smiled as he handed Kane the key to his office. 'Not for the next couple of hours apparently.' He slapped him on the shoulder as he stepped away. 'Although minimal damage would be appreciated – of her and the room.'

# CHAPTER SIX

Kane stood in the darkness. Her street was always quiet at this time of night. Another few hours and the place would be crawling with Curfew Enforcement Officers doing their rounds in Lowtown – ensuring all the non-residential vampires had crossed the border back into Blackthorn and that the vampires who had earned residence there were back in their homes. Then the district would be deemed safe again for the humans who opted to stay behind their barred windows and reinforced doors whenever nightfall came. Humans who hadn't made it far enough up the social ranks to warrant a home across the closely guarded border into Midtown or the exclusive, elite, vampire-free Summerton.

Every locale was the same. Same principle, different district names. All there to suppress, repress and control. To keep the powerful in power. To keep the third species in their place.

Border control was always stronger at that time of the morning, but it would make no difference. To most it was an urban legend, but Kane knew of the underground tunnel that joined the two districts. And it would prove an asset tonight.

Kane took the back lane. He broke open the locks and bolts that held the shabby metal gate upright, the only rear entry into the courtyard. There was the usual Lowtown household security but the place wasn't even being monitored, let alone guarded.

They may as well have offered her on a platter to him. Which seemingly they were.

Interesting.

He crossed the darkness with ease, the space visible only from a few barred side windows along the five-storey building.

He broke into the back door in three easy moves, despite the residents' clear attempt at security, and made his way up the two dark flights of stairs. It took him no time to conquer the lock of her door and less than a second longer to slip inside.

The small apartment was heavily shadowed, silent apart from the resonance of Caitlin's gentle breathing beyond the ajar door to his left. Her breathing was soft, subtle, melodic. The pace of a woman's sleeping breaths had always enticed him. A perfect reminder of the rhythm of their life.

The open-plan living space had been recently cleaned but there was still a lingering male scent in the air. It was faint enough to tell him that whoever it had been, he'd not been there long. Kane stepped over to the coffee table and picked up one of the folders from the neat pile. He smiled to himself as he looked through the pages upon pages about him. The girl was thorough, he'd give her that.

He placed the folder back down and sauntered around the rest of the living room, past the dining table that she used as a desk. Her DVD collection was sparse, unlike the overflowing bookcase. Her taste in music was hard to determine from the eclectic handful of CDs shoved amongst them. Her choice of pre-Raphaelite pictures adorning the walls looked out of place in the otherwise minimalistic contemporary apartment she called home. There were no photos of friends or family. No ornaments other than the singular Pegasus he picked up from beside the TV. The place was nothing more than an office away from work.

Glancing into the bathroom and then her bedroom, he continued back around to the open-plan kitchen. He took her workbag from the counter and started emptying its contents, until the pile of cards caught his attention. He picked them up from the top of the other post. Each was stamped but had never been posted. Each was in the same writing. The male scent on them matched the one he had picked up on in the room. He slid the card out of the open envelope.

Rob.

He instantly sneered.

Rob and six years of birthday cards, but from the strength of his scent on them, they hadn't long arrived in her apartment.

And Caitlin had only opened one before tucking them aside.

He threw the card back down and returned his attention to her work satchel, quietly emptying the rest of the contents. He gathered up some of the paperwork from the table and shoved it inside. He crossed to the bathroom and took the shampoo and shower gel from the still-damp shower cubicle. He took her hairbrush, comb and toothbrush from beside the sink before lingering over the three perfumes. He selected the one with the delicate, feminine scent of magnolia and cedarwood, the subtle undertones of musk and vanilla – the one she'd been wearing the night before. He tucked it in the bag with everything else.

He stepped through the only other door in the apartment, his boots silent on the deep pile carpet as he crossed the threshold into her bedroom.

She lay facing away from him, lit by the lamp she had fallen asleep to. She lay almost on her stomach, her top leg bent more or less in line with her waist. The position displayed the appealing inward curve of her lower back, enticingly accentuating her behind, her hip.

He silently opened her wardrobe and flicked through the few clothes she had. There were jeans, trousers or shirts – all sensible workwear. But he found three tea dresses near the back. He carefully slid them off the hangers, tucking them in the bag before opening the top drawer of the chest. Her lingerie drawer contained plenty more samples of the pretty lace underwear he'd examined on her in the corridor. Picking out a few delicate items in white and cream, he added them to the bag before leaving it in the doorway.

Kane stepped around to her side of the bed. She lay with one arm beneath her head, her hair partially covering her pretty face. He surveyed the outline of that slender, delicately curved body beneath the sheet, a sheet he slowly and carefully pulled back, revealing the plain delicate silk negligee that only added to her vulnerability. He reached down to move some of the hair from her cheek. She frowned, shifted slightly but didn't wake as he lingered over the soft, flawless skin of her shoulder, her neck. The male in him, let alone the vampire, instantly stirred. He forced himself to look away.

Her bedside table was a mess, crammed with half-read books. Clearly concentration was an issue unless it was in relation to her job and pursuing him. He pushed aside the alarm clock and half-empty mug of coffee to pick up the photo frame of her with her parents. Rick and Kathleen Parish stared back at him. Caitlin had been their only child. She looked about nine, her eyes radiating mischief and happiness. A perfect life waiting to be shattered as she clung on to her parents, particularly her father.

He picked up her mobile phone and scrolled through the messages. They were almost all work related, with a few from Max. There was nothing indicating friends, nothing indicating any other kind of relationship. The girl couldn't have been more alone if she'd tried. It was as if she didn't try. As if she didn't see the point.

He placed the phone back on the bedside table and glanced to check that she was still asleep as he slid open the drawer. He rummaged through silently and found an old picture of her with Rob. She had the same beautiful beaming smile, but this time her eyes didn't radiate the same happiness. Instead they were troubled. Subdued. He slipped the pictures back in the drawer before watching her sleep for a few more moments – the subtle rise and fall of her chest, the tension in her forehead as she dreamed. Shadow readers were notorious for nightmares, even hallucinations. Something told him Caitlin was no different. But this shadow reader carried more weight than others. This one carried a ticking time bomb she was clearly only too aware of, given her recklessness in coming after him.

She shifted and rolled languidly onto her back, one arm loose beside her head, one leg now tucked under the other. She turned her head away from him, fully exposing her slender neck.

The movement was graceful, the opening up of her body arousing. He felt himself harden just looking at her. But he couldn't mess up. This was about self-control – something that had never been an issue for him until Caitlin. Until he'd heard through underworld communications that the VCU's golden girl was now after him. The golden girl who'd had the audacity to take on his case. The golden girl with the gentle eyes and delicate stature who took down vampires as effectively as any man on her team could, if not more so. The girl who went home alone every night or at the crack of dawn. The girl who stepped outside only to go to work, for the occasional movie rental, or food shopping to return with a small bag of meals for one.

The girl whom, under any other circumstances, he would already have had in his bed.

He slipped the tiny bottle from his back pocket and held it under her nose. It would take only seconds for the potent sedative to get into her system. To check it had worked, he placed a trace of the liquid on his thumb and rubbed it gently across her soft, delicate lips before tucking his thumb just a little into the heat of her mouth.

She didn't so much as flinch.

He removed the ring from the index finger on her right hand, the watch from her wrist, freeing her of everything traceable except the negligee she was in.

Pulling the sheet away completely, he gently scooped her up, lifting her soft, warm body against his.

And carried her effortlessly across the threshold.

# CHAPTER SEVEN

Caitlin woke face down on black sheets. She'd never slept on black sheets. And she could hear distant music. Nirvana? And a shower running.

She jerked upright and nearly wrenched her arm from her shoulder in the process. Metal clinked against metal. Blood rushed to her head. She brushed her hair from her eyes and yanked at the handcuff that bound her left wrist to the headboard before clutching her free hand to her throbbing temple.

The room was dim, the window to her left boarded up. A flickering music video featuring Kurt Cobain filled the 42-inch screen up in the distant left-hand corner. Beneath the TV were two parallel sofas, a coffee table between them. To the right of a door recess was a tiny open-plan kitchen. The wall running right of the bed was bare other than the two-pronged wall sconce that was the only other source of light. Between that and a wardrobe, a bathroom door stood ajar.

She was still wearing the silk negligee and underwear she'd gone to bed in – her bed and not the wooden four-poster she was now manacled to. The bastard had swiped her in her sleep and, from the headache and dizziness, she knew how. She checked for bite marks on her thighs, her chest and ran her hand over her neck. Nothing.

Yet.

The minimalism of the furnishings and absence of any personal items told her she was in one of his dens. Had to be. She reached for the beer bottle on the bedside table to her right, her only possibility of a weapon. The cuff bit into her wrist, her shoulder straining in the socket, but she still fell a couple of inches short. She examined the vertical metal bars her cuff was attached to – solid, robust bars embedded in the mahogany headboard. She slumped back against it.

The shower stopped.

The bathroom fell silent.

Heart pounding, she curled her legs under her, pushed her negligee back over her knees and smoothed down her hair. The seconds scraped by like nails down slate as she watched the doorway with baited breath.

When Kane finally emerged, Caitlin snapped back a breath, enraptured, shocked at the warm rush between her legs.

He was naked aside from a towel resting dangerously low on his trim waist. Her attention was drawn immediately to the captivating Cobra tattoo guarding his heart, before being distracted by the droplets of water that slid down the crevice between his pecs – droplets that glided languidly down that honed abdomen towards his belly button. Every trained, taut muscle in his arms and broad shoulders flexed as he wiped the back of his neck with his hand, revealing the symbols up his left side – the protective ward against staking through the most accessible point to a vampire's heart. His cropped dark hair glistened, his compelling navy eyes fixed on her.

She just about stopped herself swearing aloud. Even if she'd been holding a broken bottle, she wasn't sure now if she'd want to use it. He was perfection incarnate, from every sinew of that hard, toned body to his enticingly relaxed composure. Kane Malloy was undoubtedly everything an effective vampire should be. And despite his brief nonchalant assessment of her, that had infuriated her and triggered a painful sense of inadequacy, she still couldn't tear her attention away as he turned to open the wardrobe. She lingered over the sword tattoo stretching the length of his spine, the ornate hilt resting between his shoulder blades. The beauty of its intricacy held her spellbound until he discarded his towel.

Caitlin flushed and immediately snatched her gaze away. Hearing him pull on his jeans she glanced back to catch a glimmer of amusement in his eyes – eyes sinfully dark in the dim light. And as he stepped up to the bedside table and knocked back a mouthful of drink, Caitlin braced herself, her fingers digging into the bed sheet.

This was it. She was finally alone with him. She was finally totally alone with Kane Malloy. And from the amalgamation of contempt and distaste in his eyes, he had no intentions of making this pleasant.

But she reminded herself he wasn't going to hurt her. If he wanted her soul, there was only one way in. Kane needed her on side.

But not as much or as soon as she needed him.

She warily watched him sit back against the footboard, bottle in hand, his legs bent and casually splayed.

She couldn't show she was intimidated. She couldn't risk showing anything of what was going on inside.

'Nice to know I make you nervous,' she said, holding up her wrist, metal clinking against metal again.

He took a mouthful of drink, his sullen gaze not leaving hers.

'I suppose it's too much to ask where we are?' she added.

'Blackthorn.'

'That narrows it down,' she sniped before reminding herself to curb the sarcasm. 'How long have I been out?'

'Two hours.'

'What time is it?'

'Half-four.'

'So is this where you were planning to bring me last night?'

He stretched an arm across the footboard, defining every muscular curve. 'You wanted me alone, right? Preferably in a detainment cell, I know. But this is so much more intimate, don't you think?' His gaze unashamedly raked the length of her body. 'No risk of interruptions,' he added before taking another mouthful of beer.

She felt herself flush again. His toying with her was cruel and intentional and, as she reminded herself, insulting. But she had to be smart.

She had to maintain her composure without provoking him. He was calm, he was controlled, but Caitlin knew only too well of the impulsive side, the reckless and self-sating side. And she knew that, aroused or incensed enough, he could forget the consequences.

He lowered his hand to hold his beer bottle loosely against his bent knee, his legs still casually open, and subtly licked beer from his bottom lip in a way she found painfully provocative. She didn't want to think of sex, but just being in his presence again was enough to spark the usually restrained part of her. Just the thought of it made every nerve ending ignite in panic. The prospect of sex with him had always seemed impossible, despite it splintering her conscience on far too many occasions.

But there, alone with him, on his bed, it suddenly seemed all too feasible – especially as he looked at her like he could devour her just for fun. Unabashed, self-assured, experienced predator Kane was already chipping away at her convictions. Kane who had no qualms about taking whatever he wanted, whenever he wanted and however he wanted – just like Rob had said. Sex with him wouldn't be affectionate – it would be power-driven and brutal. Kane Malloy clearly despised what she was, and he despised her coming after him even more.

'So,' he said. 'Do the rest of your team know just how personal your mission is, coming after me?'

Straight to business. She almost felt relieved. 'I was bringing you in because I had a good lead. Anything more was a bonus.'

'But you must have known I wouldn't confess, which means you must have had everything hanging on being able to read me. That's one hell of a risky strategy.'

'I know about your communications with Jask Tao.'

He almost smiled. 'You were going to blackmail me?'

'If I had to.'

'And you thought it would work?'

'I would have done whatever it took to keep you there long enough to read you.'

'Clearly,' he remarked, before taking another mouthful.

'When I joined the VCU, I searched the archives about my parents' deaths. Two separate psychic reports said the same thing: that their astral bodies were taken with their souls still intact; their souls hadn't passed into the afterlife. But there was only so much I could research without a name to go on. No third species would talk to me because of my job and my links. I was running out of options. And time.'

'So you came looking for me.'

'I knew you were no ordinary vampire. The things people said. The way you conducted yourself. Research I'd done. I was going to bring you in anyway but yes, I was hoping to find something in my shadow-reading.'

'But not one of your colleagues knew what you were up to? Not even Max?'

'No one's ever believed me that my parents' deaths were linked.'

'Well, well, the golden girl's got a devious streak.'

She knew she had no time to waste, that he would have already planned what he was going to do with her, but it still stuck in her throat even as she said it. 'I want to make a deal with you. The thing that slaughtered my parents is coming for me too. Help me kill it and I'll give you what you want.'

His silence, his dismissive smile, riled her.

'It wants my soul, Kane,' she added. 'And obviously so do you.'

'But it's not coming for another three days. I'll be done with you by then.'

Her pulse raced at his nonchalance, as she struggled to suppress her annoyance and panic. 'To get to my soul you need my heart. So far you don't stand a hope in hell. I'm offering you a way in. You'd be a fool not to take it.'

'Such conviction.'

'I mean it, Kane.'

His gaze slid tauntingly over her again. 'So are you advising I'd best take what I want, while I can?'

Her stomach flipped. Her eyes narrowed at the passive threat. 'Why not? Help me hate you more. That'll help your cause.'

And she did hate him. Hated him for discarding her plea like it was nothing. Hated him for being so arrogant as to think he could still seduce her. Hated the fact he had got her there in the first place.

And as he flashed a hint of that sexy smile, those deadly alluring incisors, she hated the way he ignited her inside.

Hated the fact he was so damned sexual. So damned bad. So damned everything that deep inside she craved.

Hated the fact that she wanted him despite knowing he was poison. A poison so deadly that if she let it into her system, it would all be over.

Silence filled the gap between them as Caitlin's defiant eyes locked in indignation on his.

If he hadn't indeed needed her, her belligerence and insolence would have incited him to act on his carnality without hesitation. Nobody looked at him like that. And certainly no VCU agent.

But the stakes were too high.

Besides, hate was less painful than love, and he wasn't going to be that merciful. Because glower though she may, Kane had seen the look in her eyes when he'd strolled out of the shower. He'd seen the transfixed gaze she'd snatched away when he'd dropped his towel. Caitlin who, in that simple momentary act, had given away that she wasn't just inexperienced, but also enticingly shy.

He'd been watching her long enough to know that in work mode she was bold, impetuous and calculated. But only because she had control, where there were boundaries and protocol. Here she was awkward and unsure – and not solely because of the power shift. He'd already seen evidence of it in the corridor and on the table. He incited something painfully uncomfortable in her, something potentially integral to his advantage – a potential worth exploring.

Besides, it was better she learned quickly who was in charge before he was tempted to do something more damaging to prove his point.

Kane moved off the bed and placed his bottle on the bedside table. He cleaned his lips of the remnants of alcohol that would taint the taste of her. He caught her behind her knees, unravelled her legs with ease despite her struggle, and slid her onto her back under him. Caitlin snatched back a breath as he pressed his hips to hers, her hand slamming against his shoulder to forge distance, a hand he pushed away, deftly interlacing his fingers with hers, pinning it down beside her head.

He watched every response as he trailed the back of his free hand slowly down her bound wrist, down the soft, delicate skin of her forearm, past the upward mound of her breast to her throat. As he gently caught hold of her jaw, he revelled in the telling spark in her eyes – a spark that every vampiric instinct incited him to fuel.

But there was a fine line between a spark and an uncontrollable blaze, and never had he needed to wield such self-control. Caitlin's nubile, warm body, the panic and latent desire in those beautiful vulnerable eyes, instantly summoned the depraved side of him. A side he reserved only for the most sexually proficient, not those barely teetering on their awakening. Taking her then would ruin everything, because if she saw what he was capable of, if she learned what he'd wanted to do from the moment he'd first seen her, it'd scare the hell out of her and forge a distance he couldn't afford. Let alone if she knew how even now he fought beneath the surface to suppress the deepest of his desires, his need to feed on her. Humans were one thing, but the energy that shadow readers gave off when they climaxed was as intoxicating as it got, the bite during sex knocking it up a notch – the ultimate dual feed. And Caitlin, with all that finely tuned repression, would be as sating as a shadow reader could be.

This wasn't about satisfying his desires though. Not yet. This was about initiating hers. This was about getting inside her body, then her mind, before unlocking the chastity belt that was her heart, to steal the soul inside.

This was about getting his roots in deep, because they'd have to be deep to get what he wanted. And Kane wanted, needed, to be as deep inside Caitlin as anyone could be.

And he'd do it without the deceit of playing her protector.

He'd do it without the deceit of being her hero.

The satisfaction of Caitlin accepting him for what he was would serve to make his triumph even greater.

Unfortunately there was a delicate balance between arousal and fear, between pleasuring and wounding her. He couldn't go too fast. He had three days to break her. Three days to work out exactly what would tip the balance with the consummately restrained shadow reader.

He held her jaw still as his mouth met hers. He gently prised her lips apart with his, caressing those soft, warm lips, exploring her teeth and tongue slowly and coaxingly with his. Her refusal to reciprocate, despite her arousal, gave him further satisfying clues of her enticing internal struggle. And the flush of her cheeks, the dilation of her pupils revealed too much for him to act the gentleman, especially with the rosy tinge of those tempting lips, her pulse racing invitingly, her tense body compelling him to mercilessly break inside her.

He bit her lip and Caitlin flinched, her fingers tightening in his as he savoured her blood —blood just as sweet and intoxicating as he'd imagined. Her shudder and gasp were temptation enough to release her hand to slide his to the exposed waistband of her underwear, Kane yearning to tear the fragile silk, his self-control teetering as her eyes flared.

'Stop,' she said, blood still seeping invitingly from her lower lip, her trembling hand clutching his wrist, her long, slender fingers unable to meet its circumference. 'Or you've already lost.'

He licked his lips as he coaxingly entwined the band of her knickers around his index finger. He absorbed the heaviness of her breathlessness and the panic in her eyes, because Caitlin didn't panic. She was trained not to show fear. So the rawness of her reaction, let alone the immediacy of her protest, only added to his curiosity.

She was scared of him, yes, but she seemed just as scared of herself – or at least of her responses to him. Caitlin wasn't as confident of her ability to handle him as she liked everyone to believe, nor as she liked to portray.

He tugged the band down just a little further, causing her to tighten her grip. 'Really?' he asked, searching her eyes. 'I'm not so sure.'

She swallowed hard, the quiver of her lower lip showing him she'd reached her limit.

He removed his hand, placing it beside her head, his lips hovering just above hers, her whole body tensing again in a way that enthralled him. 'Then don't goad me, little girl,' he said. 'No rules, remember?'

He could see her assessing him and the risk he posed. The fact he'd stopped when she'd asked had clearly confused her. She already had an established view of him, thought she knew him. And he'd have to start by doing something about that.

A game.

Caitlin's pulse raced painfully as Kane's clever, perceptive eyes assessed her every reaction.

Some kind of twisted test.

He'd toyed with her and she'd fallen for it. He'd wanted to reclaim the balance, remind her who was in charge, and she'd let him. In a moment of weakness, she'd panicked and given him exactly what he'd wanted.

Part of her wanted to retaliate at that point, but common sense told her to keep her mouth shut while the tempestuous vampire still lay above her, still held her confined to his bed.

There was no VCU to back her up now. There was no one to come running when she bit her lip. And there was no guarantee, despite the hint of playfulness in his eyes, that he wouldn't think better of his decision to stop. The vampire in him could so easily decide it was worth the risk.

'I need the bathroom,' she said, the first and only thing she could think of to break away.

He held her gaze for a few torturous moments longer, before partially moving off her as he reached to open the beside table drawer.

She caught a glimpse of the key and, as he looked back down at her, she silently pleaded that he wouldn't humiliate her by making her beg. That he wouldn't keep her there more than a moment longer.

It took all her composure not to heave a sigh of relief as he eased off her completely to sit beside her. His cool hand took hold of her wrist to unlock the cuff before he finally moved off the bed.

Caitlin rubbed her wrist to encourage the circulation back in, watching him warily as he held out his hand towards the door.

'Be my guest,' he said.

She slipped off the bed, her bare feet meeting wooden floorboards then a rug as she tentatively crossed the small space past him and into the bathroom.

Closing the door behind her, she leaned back against it, her eyes closed, her heart pounding. Twenty minutes. That's all it could have been. It had taken all but twenty minutes. There was no way she was going to survive a couple of days of this – not if he kept looking at her like that. Not if he smiled once more in that self-assured, coaxing manner. Not if he pressed his hard, capable body against hers again. He was probably laughing to himself now. Laughing at the awkward, sexually inept VCU agent who panicked the minute he touched her knickers.

She clutched her head, heat flooding her face. She hated herself for being weak. She was never weak. Not when it came to that. Her head was always so screwed on. So why, and how the hell, was he making it spin? It was as if he could see right into her as he cruelly played on her every weakness, her every psychological G spot.

He was so sure of himself. So arrogant. So infuriating.

And her negative, self-deprecating thoughts were not going to help her in either of her causes. She needed to get back into agent mode and fast. This was what she'd wanted for so long – to get up close and personal with the vampire himself. It wasn't in the detainment unit as she'd planned, but it certainly didn't get more up close and personal than being tied to a bed in one of his dens. This was as close as anyone got to Kane Malloy. As close as any VCU agent had ever got. She had a job to do. She had information to get for the VCU and for herself.

But it was pointless getting information if she was trapped here with it. She needed to keep assessing her surroundings and look for weaknesses.

She focused on the three high narrow horizontal windows ahead, mirrored glass from the looks of it, or certainly UV shields. They were ajar, the rain tapping lightly against the angled glass.

She hurried to the three steps leading up to the large, oval sunken bath that stretched the length of the wall to her right. She balanced her feet on the edge of the bath and cocked her head awkwardly to look out. She stared directly out onto steel railings. It was dark and dank beyond, seemingly the back of some alley. At least she knew they were ground level, if not basement level. But there was no way she was getting through those gaps, even as small and nimble as she was. She sighed with frustration and sank onto the middle step, her feet on the tiled floor.

What she needed was to stay smart and to stay focused. He wasn't going to kill her and he wasn't going to rape her. Not yet. He was playing mind games and that was all. But one thing she knew for sure was that hostility would get her nowhere. She had to stay calm. More than that, she had to stop giving him a glimpse of any vulnerability he might use against her. If he thought she was sexually weak, he'd play to his strength and that was one mind game she knew she'd fail at.

She had to keep reminding herself that she had equal advantage because there was one sure impossibility in this world – you couldn't make someone fall in love with you. You could trick your head into thinking you were in love, you could even trick your heart – but you could never trick your soul. All she had to do was keep hers safely locked up to stop him getting what he wanted. Locked up until she convinced him to help her. There was a long and hard road between attraction and love

– especially for shadow readers and especially for her. It seemed even worldly wise Kane had a lot to learn when it came to that.

And she still had three days.

Caitlin used the toilet and washed her hands. She ran her fingers through her hair to tidy it as she checked her reflection in the mirror. She clutched the edge of the basin and stared into her eyes.

She wasn't weak, she was just tired. Tired, drugged and overwrought. And Kane was using that opportunity to test her barriers, watch her reactions and assess her responses just as he had done in the interrogation room. It was what the great manipulators did. And master vampires were the greatest manipulators of all.

Common sense told her she needed to play along. There was always the risk that if she played too hard to get, he could give up on her and select another shadow reader. And if he had no use for her, he could do whatever he wanted to her. She needed to let him think he might stand a chance, at least long enough for her to persuade him to help her.

She ran her hands down over her negligee and turned back towards the bathroom door. She stepped tentatively over the threshold to see Kane leaning with his back to her against the bedpost, watching the TV. He didn't just have a shirt on now but also his jacket.

Her first response was to worry about where he was going, and more so why. Worry that was quickly replaced by realisation that his absence would give her a much-needed opportunity to examine her prison more closely.

But as he turned to face her, cocked his head towards the bed, indicating for her to get back on it, she knew that little glimmer of hope was short lived.

Despite her instinct telling her to comply, her pride kept her rooted to the spot, even with the six-inch height difference suddenly seeming far more intimidating than when he'd had her pressed against the corridor wall.

'Five seconds and counting,' he said.

Her pulse raced. She glanced across at the cuffs still attached to the headboard, then back at him. 'I'm not going to do anything.'

His eyes echoed unnerving sobriety. 'Three, two—'

Reluctantly she conceded. She coiled back against the headboard and lifted her wrist. To limit the intimacy of his proximity, she looked away as he sat beside her, as he secured the cuff into the final notch around her slender wrist before easing back off the bed. She watched him tuck the key in his jeans pocket as he strolled away, reluctantly admiring the confidence of his posture, the broadness of his shoulders, the power behind that body as he disappeared through the door.

She listened to him slide a bolt across in two places – top and bottom. A key turned in two separate locks. This was the place he kept things contained. His very own prison. A prison with a bed – more proof that he had more than one way of getting information, or whatever else it was that he wanted.

There was the rumble of an engine and the faint sound of metal grating against metal, the echo dissipating into a large and hollow space beyond.

Then everything fell to silence again.

Caitlin yanked her wrist in annoyance in its binding and slumped back against the headboard. She tongued the bite on her lower lip, which already felt less painful. His sensual licks had been nothing more than preparing her for the feral, cruel bite to follow.

She reached across for the bottle of water he had left on the edge of the bedside table for her, rested it between her thighs and unscrewed the already loosened cap. The water was cool and refreshing as she took a small mouthful.

If that was how he was going to play it, she needed to toughen up. And fast.

# CHAPTER EIGHT

The old bell tinkled as Kane stepped inside the cluttered store. The room lingered with the aroma of incense sticks, cinnamon and cloves. He strolled past the familiar shelves and glass cabinets over-stuffed with emblems, charms and miscellany – toys for those who liked to tamper with things they didn't understand.

He stopped at the platformed counter, in front of the human goth girl sitting behind it. He surveyed her minor piercings and tattoos – an attempt to fit into the crowd she was hankering after. Working at the store no doubt helped towards the kudos she seemed to be desperately seeking. Her large brown eyes, chocolaty against the thick black kohl defining them, instantly met his. Despite looking like she was somewhere in her late teens, those eyes told him she was more likely approaching mid-twenties. She blushed through her foundation.

'Is Tamara in?' he asked.

A glimmer of disappointment flashed behind her eyes. 'Is she expecting you?'

'Tell her Kane's here.'

Her eyes flared. Seemingly she recognised his name. She reached for the phone, pressing her lips together as it rang. 'Kane to see you.' Placing the phone back in its cradle, she shyly looked down at the talisman she was polishing. She rubbed it even harder before holding it up, closing one eye with feigned expertise to examine if it was a job well done.

'Do you even know what that is?' he asked.

She looked flustered, but shrugged in feigned nonchalance.

He rested both arms on the counter and he leaned forward a little. 'You got a name?'

'Bea,' she said, the increase in her breathing subtle but noticeable.

'Have you got a boyfriend, Bea?'

Her tongue darted out to swiftly lick her bottom lip, her eyes wide as she placed the talisman down next to a long line. She picked up another. 'No.' She glanced back across at him, struggling to suppress a smile. She was trying to be cool. It was almost cute.

'Keep practising rubbing like that and you might get yourself one,' he said, capturing and holding her gaze.

Tamara emerged through the bead curtain, her long velvet dress, the one she wore for the tourists, clinging to every curve. She'd always looked better in leather and lace, but he wasn't going to tell her that. She smiled, her full rouged lips as tempting as they always were, her kohl-lined bright-blue eyes igniting the minute she saw him. She bent over the counter, her heavy breasts, just about contained by the low fabric, having little to help their cause. 'Hey, handsome.'

He smiled. 'I got your message.'

She stood up and cocked her head towards the beads.

He stepped around the side of the desk, took the two steps up, boots clumping against wood as he followed her through into the musty old room, out into the space that she reserved for her more private clientele.

The back room was dim, the thick scent of herbs and incense exacerbating the density of the large but cluttered room. Heavy drapes and tapestries dominated the walls, adding to the claustrophobia of the enclosure.

'Where did you find the goth?'

Tamara smiled. 'Where I always find them,' she said, pouring liquid into two glasses.

'Is she a feeder?'

'Not that I know of. Not yet anyway. She won't take much breaking in, though, from the way she was looking at you.' She handed him the drink, her eyes glinting with mischief. 'But what's wrong with me? My witch blood not good enough for you tonight?'

He took a mouthful. 'I'm after something purer. I need the sustenance. No offence.'

'Some taken.' She rubbed the rim of her glass against her lips as she stepped up to him. 'Then maybe something else?' She ran her hand down his chest, nails scraping against the cotton of his shirt before unfastening two of the buttons, sliding her hand inside before lifting her thick, false eyelashes to meet his gaze. 'It's been a while. How about you remind me what I'm missing?'

'As if I'd be that cruel.'

She laughed seductively. 'You know that's how I like you.' She opened his shirt a little, her eyes flaring in admiration. 'Surely you're not so short of time you can't spare me fifteen minutes to work some of that magic of yours? Especially not after what I've managed to do.'

'You have got it then?'

'Of course. After moving heaven and earth and pulling in more than a few favours these past few months.' She searched his gaze. 'You really do owe me big time for this,' she said, slipping her hand down to his behind.

He caught her hand and pulled her closer. 'How about you show it to me first,' he said, his lips hovering tauntingly over hers.

She smiled, her eyes flashing with arousal, before she stepped away from him.

He knocked back the rest of his drink as he glanced around the room. He stepped up to the round table to lift the crystal ball, tossing it in his hand before placing it back on the stand with an exhale of amusement.

Tamara was back within a few minutes, a cloth-wrapped object clutched in her hands. She knelt at the low coffee table and placed the item in the centre. Kane lowered to his knees opposite her as she carefully unwrapped the cloth. She met his gaze, the excitement sparkling in hers as she slid the hand-sized book towards him. It looked like something that had been shoved to the back of a shelf in a junk shop. Its dull leather cover was smudged and worn, the platinum lock that bound it buckled and tarnished.

But he knew better than anyone that appearances could be deceptive. 'It certainly doesn't look much.'

'That's the whole point. Nothing with that much power ever does.'

He held it up to examine it and thumbed the lock.

'You don't unlock it until the time,' she said, sliding him the tiny key. 'And once it's closed, you don't open it again. Read anything contained within and it will tarnish the soul, preventing any return to its host. If you want it returned.' She looked at him hesitantly. 'That's serious stuff there.'

He wrapped it back in the cloth.

'So whose soul is it for?' she asked. 'More to the point, what did they do to deserve this?'

'That's two too many questions, Tam,' he said, standing.

'You can't blame a woman for being curious.' Tamara mirrored him expectantly. 'You do know you need things to extract the soul. Things I can't get you.'

'All under control,' he said, taking the money from his coat and handing her the wad of notes.

She took it, but didn't check it. She licked her lower lip and met his gaze. 'So how about a thank you?'

'Thank you.' He kissed her lightly on the lips before clipping her chin with his thumb as he stepped past her, back towards the storefront.

'That's it? Where you going?'

'I told you. I'm hungry.'

'But you said...'

'I said what?'

She folded her arms. 'You're a bastard, Kane Malloy, you know that?'

He smiled as he turned to face her. 'I thought you said you liked me cruel.'

She shook her head, pressed her lips together, but couldn't help but smile back. 'I'll have you next time.'

'Whatever keeps those hopes alive, Tam.'

He stepped back through the beads and glanced across at Bea tapping her pen against a pile of paper. She sat upright as he descended the steps, her eyes sparkling with ready compliance.

Easy pickings. As easy as it came. And way too desperate.

Bastard, yes. But not that much of a bastard.

She was too fragile for sex with any vampire, let alone him. Too needy. Too vulnerable. Too susceptible. She had vampire victim stamped all over her. It was only a matter of time before she was found in some alley or in one of the many derelict houses somewhere, her delicate, non-consenting flesh ravaged by fervent bites.

He fought the images that played in front of his mind like disassociated pieces of film – Arana's torn and defiled delicate body lying limp and bloodied on the cold concrete of the abandoned warehouse floor. His throat tightened along with his chest.

And this girl – itching to be a conquest. Clueless of consequence. Clueless of what lay behind the eyes she was staring into.

Her ignorance plunged deep into him and twisted a little, the barbs catching, preventing him from walking away. And that pulse beneath her pale flesh was already far too rapid to ignore.

He was probably about to do her the biggest favour of her young life.

He crossed the room to the nearest glass chest and relaxed back against it, his arms casually braced on the cold surface. He looked directly across at her in the silence.

Her eyes flared, part in arousal, part in shock. Clearly she got the hint. She glanced anxiously over her shoulder towards Tamara's room then returned her full attention to him.

He offered her a hint of a smile to reassure her she'd read the situation right.

She pushed back her chair and stood with an edge of wariness that would be her saving grace. Arrogance on top of ignorance was something he'd never been able to tolerate, and his bite technique had demonstrated that to plenty of first-time donors.

She came to a standstill a foot away from him, clearly having got to him sooner than she'd intended, from the awkwardness of her stance. She smiled. Didn't seem to know what to do with her hands. Resolved to rest them on her slender hips.

He let her stand there as the seconds ticked by, keeping her in the painful position of not knowing whether to make the first move.

'I've heard of you,' she said.

'Have you now?'

She nodded. 'You and a vampire called Caleb. Do you know him?'

'Of him.'

Her eyes narrowed in confusion. 'What?'

'Never mind.' He leaned forward to grab her by the small of the back, yanking her towards him.

She caught her breath and smiled. 'I've always wanted to meet you.'

'And why's that?'

'You're a legend around here.' Her gaze lingered on his mouth and she subtly licked her lips and looked back into his eyes, but clearly found it too intimidating to sustain. 'Can I touch your fangs?'

'They're called incisors.'

She shrugged. 'Can I touch them?'

He curled his upper lip slightly so she could touch the small section of exposed incisor.

Her eyes gleamed. She smiled, gasped and physically trembled as her forefinger made contact with enamel. 'Wow. That's so hot.' She withdrew her hand again. 'I mean, sexy.'

'I'm glad you think so. Because I need to use them. On you.'

She snapped back a breath, her wide eyes wavering with uncertainty. 'Sure. Yeah, I understand. You need to feed, right?'

'Right.'

She nodded as she scraped her hair back from her neck. Her hand was still trembling. 'I've never been bit. But I've had piercings and stuff.' She let out a short, curt, nervous giggle. 'I liked it. I liked the feeling.'

'You think a bite is like a piercing?'

'That's what my friends say.'

'Then your friends have clearly never been bit.'

Her startled gaze met his.

He had her face-first over the counter a split second later, her arm wrenched up her back.

He removed his penknife from his back pocket, flicked it open and laid it on the glass counter so she could see it.

Her eyes widened again, her panting uncontained. 'What the fuck is that for?'

'Dessert,' he whispered in her ear.

She immediately struggled and squirmed, trying to buck beneath him until he wrenched her arm up a little further. She learned quickly to still, the first tear trickling from the corner of her eye. 'Don't hurt me,' she whimpered.

'I'm a vampire,' he said, scraping her hair back from her neck before he ripped her loose black T-shirt down over her shoulder. 'Not your boyfriend. What do you think I'm going to do?'

He looked down at her trembling lips before cupping her mouth with his hand. She'd scream on the first bite, he just knew it.

Sure enough she did – silently against the palm of his hand as he bit deep into the base of her neck with no anaesthetic, no warning.

He felt her shudder as he drank hard and fast, her fragile body shaking, quickly weakening. He bit into her again and again until her sobbing ceased, her body fast becoming lax.

When he'd fed enough, he reached for the knife. The blade slid easily through the pliable flesh of her neck, shoulder, and collarbone – a few superficial engravings just to remind her of the moment – not with any depth to scar her permanently, but probably enough to save her life if she used them for their real purpose: to make her think twice about tempting her kind again. He licked away the trickles of blood seeping from the shallow wounds before letting her go.

She had no idea how lightly he was letting her off.

She collapsed to the floor against the counter, tears damp on her cheeks, her make-up smudged around her glazed eyes so she looked like some badly painted rag doll.

He licked his knife clean and snapped it shut. He slid it back in his pocket just as he looked up to see Tamara watching him from the counter. Arms folded, there was no shock in her eyes but her raised eyebrows told him she wasn't impressed with the pending aftermath.

'I think you'll need yourself a new assistant,' he said.

'No kidding,' she said after him as he strolled back through the store, the bell tinkling as the door closed behind him.

# CHAPTER NINE

Caitlin sat upright as she heard the rumble of an engine beyond the door. The grate of metal against metal told her he was back. Or someone was. A car door slammed. Then there was silence again. The bolts were slid across, the door unlocked.

Her heart leapt as Kane stepped across the threshold. To her relief, he was alone. He closed the door, left his keys in the keyhole, but didn't lock it. He hung up his jacket and placed the bag he was carrying onto the kitchen counter, a bag she recognised as hers. He placed the paper bag he'd also been carrying down beside it, before heading towards her.

She braced herself as he reached into his jeans pocket, taking out the key. He slid it into the lock with calm precision, eyes meeting intimately with hers for a moment. She lowered her gaze from the intimacy again, irritated at the pang in her chest.

He unfastened the cuff and Caitlin clenched her wrist as she watched him turn and stroll back across the room.

'I've brought you something to eat,' he said. 'And there are a few things in your bag that I picked up from your place earlier. Feel free to freshen up.'

He stepped back out through the door, closing and locking it behind him.

She listened out for the sound of the car engine again, but there was nothing. She slipped off the bed and tentatively hurried over to the recess. She pressed her ear up against the door, struggling to hear over the low but insistent music from the TV. He was definitely out there. She could hear clanging and the clink of metal. Footsteps.

She examined the door more closely and ran her fingers over the two locks. Just basic locks. She could handle basic locks – they would be easy enough to pick with the right tool. But the door opened inward and those bolts on the other side were going to prevent any kind of pressure against it. There was only one way she was getting out of there and that was when those bolts were drawn back. And that only happened when he was in there with her. Still, a glimmer of hope was a glimmer of hope all the same.

She turned to face the room again and stepped over to her bag. She found her shampoo and shower gel, her comb and brush. Toothbrush. Perfume. She pulled out the clothes, all three of her patterned button-through knee-length tea dresses, dresses that she hadn't had the occasion to wear in years. She raised her eyebrows. Feminine was obviously his thing. Either that or accessibility. She rooted through to find he'd even packed underwear. She shoved everything back in the bag, uncertain if she felt embarrassed or just indignant at the thought of him rifling through her personal items.

She glanced back at the door behind her. A shower would be good and getting herself into some proper clothes would be even better. She opened the paper bag to find a croissant and a pain au chocolat, some fruit and a bottle of juice. But they could wait.

She hoisted her bag over her shoulder and stepped across to the bathroom. She closed the door behind her, feeling uneasy to see there was no lock. She reminded herself she'd been unconscious with him for over two hours. If he'd wanted to see her naked he already would have. Maybe even had. But something told her that wasn't his style. He'd want her to know. He'd strip her whilst she was conscious. He'd want to see her reaction.

Caitlin ran the shower and pulled off her negligee and knickers. She stepped under the spray, the warm flow making her skin tingle. It felt good to be clean. Good to be fresh. The familiar smell of her shower gel was reassuring even in the strange cubicle where she bathed. She dried off with the warmed towel she plucked off the rail and kept it wrapped around her, its generous size allowing her to simultaneously towel-dry her hair. She combed through her tresses and brushed her teeth, placing her toothbrush next to his. Her hand automatically reached for the brass and amber bottle beside them. She took off the lid. It smelt like him – warm, musky, with notes of spice and amber. The very scent of him sent butterflies soaring in her stomach.

She screwed the lid back on and placed the bottle back on the shelf.

She could do this. It didn't matter how attracted she was to him, just as long as she didn't fall for him. That was all it was – a crush: some besotted, unavailability-induced primal attraction. He was so deep in her psyche, so built up after all the years. The handsome face, the perfect body, the enticing smile. It was all just a mirage for what lay beneath, and she needed to keep that at the forefront of her mind.

Caitlin pulled on her underwear and dress and stood in front of the mirror as she fastened the last couple of buttons at her chest. She reached for her perfume and hesitated.

If she tempted him, she had to be sure she could keep playing along. She had no doubt in her mind that they were matched intellectually. But emotionally, sexually, she had to at least acknowledge her own vulnerability. But if that's what he wanted from her, then that was her bait. It may even lower his guard a little. At the very least she needed to talk to him and start to get what she needed.

She sprayed on her perfume, and stepped back out into the room.

The door was still closed and the room empty. Caitlin strolled over to take the paper bag off the counter and took it over to the sofa. Accepting food from him felt like treachery, but she was hungry. She needed to keep her strength up. More than that, any defiance would only get his barriers up and she needed them as low as she could get them. She lay the napkin on her lap and took out the croissant, picking off mouth-sized chunks as she glanced at the TV.

An engine revved in the room beyond, making her flinch, but it was an engine being tampered with, not driven. And it wasn't a car, but the guttural roar of a motorbike. She took the croissant with her as she stepped back over to the recess. She leaned against the door again and listened. The engine died down. She heard the clunk of metal. She waited a few minutes to hear anything else, but as silence persisted she wandered around the room.

She strolled into the kitchen, sliding her hand over the table that lay central in the small space. The window was boarded up like the one in the sleeping area. She looked in the fridge. There were beers, bottles of water, some snacks, but not much else. She pulled out the kitchen drawers, most were empty but she lingered over the cutlery one – over the few knives that would have a hard enough time damaging a steak let alone a hardened vampire. She checked through cupboards to find them mostly bare so strolled back over to the sofa.

She took her time eating, picking and playing with her food, each mouthful as laborious as the next, but it gave her something to do, something to try and ease the nerves. Finishing her juice, she found the bin and discarded her rubbish before strolling back into the bathroom to clean her teeth.

She climbed back up onto the bath. Outside, the pitch-blackness had turned to a misty grey. Dawn would be here in an hour or so. And that meant either Kane would be retreating to wherever home was or she'd be locked for several hours in his company.

Wandering back into the kitchen, she helped herself to a bottle of water and, resuming her place on the sofa, curled her feet under her, pulled a cushion into her lap and turned her attention to the TV screen.

The time ticked by and she watched a few more music videos. Then she sauntered around the room again, examining every inch of it for what must have been the fourth time, confirming again that there was no way out other than through the door where Kane had disappeared. She made two more trips to the bathroom and on the second noticed that dawn was already sending its muted warm glow through the reduced cracks in the bathroom windows. She wandered back out, paced a little more, before wandering back over to the sofa again.

She'd just settled in amongst the cushions when the door opened, and Kane stepped inside.

His jeans were not the dark ones he'd headed out there in. These were pale and threadbare, showing up every oil and grease stain. The white vest that had replaced his shirt exacerbated the marks even more. Smidgens of oil and grease lined his arms, neck and his cheek. He stopped at the fridge and pulled out a beer, flicking off the lid on his way back to the counter. He leaned back against it, facing her, her stomach flipping at the flexion in his smudged bicep as he raised the bottle to his mouth.

Knowing she was inadvertently gawping, she lifted the remains of her bottle of water to her lips, and swallowed a little harder than she intended. She could see he was appraising her change of clothing, but, despite the hint of a smile on his lips, he said nothing to compliment her. He said nothing at all before strolling back out of the door, this time leaving it ajar behind him.

Caitlin clenched her bottle as she waited to see if he would reappear. But he didn't.

As the minutes passed, her attention didn't leave the recess. But when clinks echoed towards her, clinks that told her he'd just returned to whatever he had been doing, she finally relented to her curiosity and headed over to the doorway.

The stark room beyond was at least fifty by fifty feet. The sleek black car she knew to be his sat directly ahead, its bonnet jacked open. In front of that and to her left was his motorbike. Kane sat on the floor behind the bike, cleaning and tightening something, tools and dirty cloths spread on the floor around him. A garage door dominated the left wall, a small corrugated-steel door to its right. A workbench sat just off to her left on the back wall, a toolbox spread open on its surface. Ahead there was a corner reserved with some exercise equipment, a punchbag hanging from the A-frame rafters. The room smelt of diesel and oil.

He snatched a glance in her direction as she strolled further into the room, the concrete cold and rough beneath her bare feet. She leaned against the workbench as he turned his attention back to what he was doing. The concentration in his eyes was intense as he screwed another component back on, those sexy fingers working swiftly and deftly with tiny fittings, as adeptly as they did the larger ones.

He seemed neither irritated nor bothered by her presence, the unlocked door indication enough that she could wander. And she needed to show him that she wasn't intimidated.

She reached for the helmet beside the toolbox – black, glossy, the visor blacked out. 'Have you any idea how many times we've tried to impound that bike of yours? As well as your car.'

'Then you guys should learn to drive faster.'

'Anything over fifty miles per hour is prohibited, Kane. Even for the unit.' She glanced at him to see his attention was still on his bike, so she subtly assessed the array of tools in the box beside her. She focused on the crowbar, the chisel and the screwdrivers. A couple were small enough that she might have a chance of concealing them. 'Not that prohibited means anything to you, right? What was your last recorded speed? Eighty?'

'At least I can handle the speed. Which is more than can be said for your lot.'

'We have to watch for civilians, which is clearly the last thing on your mind.' She pulled the helmet on. She lifted the visor up and closed it again before taking it back off.

'You never get told about not touching things that don't belong to you?' he asked with a fleeting glare.

'The rule doesn't seem to apply to you.'

As his navy eyes met hers, her stomach jilted, but instead of confrontation, his attention turned back to what he was doing. 'You've got an answer for everything, Caitlin. That tongue needs taming.'

'And are you planning to be the one who does it?'

He almost smiled. 'I'm planning all sorts for you, shadow reader.'

The instant stirring she felt was inexcusable, her heart skipping a beat. 'For someone who seemed very keen to get their hands on me earlier, you're suddenly very lax with your time.'

'Time we're going to have to make up for, but I'm sure we'll manage.' He reached for another tool, his eyes narrowed in concentration, his jaw tense as he prised something off the machine. He rubbed his hands on a cloth before swiping the back of his hand across his forehead. There, in the garage, she could almost mistake him for human, had his sneer at whatever was causing him difficulty not given a hint of those incisors.

As the stir in her abdomen deepened, she tried to distract herself by focusing on some of the things he had done. The sadistic streak he was renowned for. Behind those intoxicating eyes and enticing smile was a compassionless and twisted heart and mind. He was damaged. She'd never been able to segregate the reports sufficiently to prove it, but what had happened to Arana had made him worse. She was sure of it. Before then he had been bad; since then he had become monstrous. Xavier could say what he liked but she had no doubt that plenty of those cases they wanted to convict him for were the result of his seeking answers. And a part of her, a tiny part that remembered the outrage she'd felt on reading those psychic reports of what had happened to her parents, understood.

But it didn't excuse what he'd done. And she had to keep telling herself that, just as she needed to keep reminding herself there was nothing appealing enough about him to warrant her attraction. Nothing at all.

And then he frowned, frustration emanating from his stunning eyes – eyes that had once emanated love. Because he had loved his sister. No one could dispute that. They had been inseparable – a bond that had been tightly formed after witnessing their parents' slaughter on their homeland by anti-vampiric vigilantes. From a young age he had protected her and cared for her. In many ways it seemed she had been his salvation. Then she had been murdered. And the darkness had been unleashed.

Caitlin snapped from her thoughts.

She needed to get closer to the corrugated door to check it out. She had to make the most of every opportunity.

She folded her arms and strolled over to stand beside him, to look down at what he was doing. She saw his gaze linger on her ankles, her calves before turning his attention back to the machine. It gave her a warm flush to know he was checking her out, until she berated herself, reminding herself it was all just game playing. A game Kane Malloy was more than adept at.

She backed away and wandered over to the corrugated door to examine the padlock. It was as basic as the locks on the door.

'Back where I can see you,' he said.

'I'm not doing anything.' She glanced back over her shoulder at him to see he was glowering at her. She pulled away from the door and circled past the other side of him. 'So where do you really live? Because it sure isn't here, is it?'

She looked down at the trapdoor in the floor and ran her hands over the cool leather of the punchbag on her way back across to the car. She stopped at the exposed engine and assessed it as she waited for him to answer. She sauntered around the periphery of the car, her fingers tracing over the silky paintwork before coming full circle to the driver's door. His refusal to answer didn't surprise her. Resting her hip against it, she folded her arms. 'Did you go out to feed earlier?'

His eyes remained narrowed pensively on the engine.

'Do you need to feed often?' she added.

'You mean is it different for us master vampires?'

'Is it?'

'What else have you been itching to ask me, Caitlin? Where I hang out? When I took my first bite? What kind of women I like? What I do when I'm not committing crimes? Where on the human body I like to feed?' He reached for another tool. 'All those uninventive little questions.'

'You hang out mainly on the east side of Blackthorn but sometimes come west. You prefer the basement bars and clubs. You like your females experienced, a little obvious but sexy without being slutty. You like mechanics, obviously, and playing cards. When you feed you prefer the neck or the inner thigh. I don't know when you took your first bite, but I'm guessing that you were fairly young.' Her attention on him didn't flinch as she tentatively awaited his confirmation.

It felt like a lifetime before he responded. 'What's my middle name?'

'James. Kane James Malloy. If the records are correct.'

He almost smiled, his gaze meeting hers fleetingly before he turned his attention back to what he was doing. 'Genuine little stalker, aren't you?'

'I've studied the archives. You moved into the area just before the regulations came into force. You bought out most of the east side, some of the south and north. We don't know where you came from exactly, but have indications it might have been somewhere north. The Malloy clan dominated areas up there for centuries. Your family line dates back pre-1200s, though where you fit into that timeline we don't know. It's unusual for a vampire to migrate that far from their homeland. Especially a master vampire.' She paused. 'There must have been good reason for you to leave. Maybe the challenge of getting somewhere new under your thumb?'

'I'm not here for control, Caitlin, just to have a good time. One long vacation.'

'Most people swim, read or go trekking on vacation. They don't murder, maim and assault other campers.'

She could have sworn she detected another fleeting smile, but it could just as easily have been a sneer. 'When I see something out of line, I do something about it. It's what master vampires do. We keep order. It's what our bloodline dictates. And we're sure as fuck better at it than the Higher Order sat on their thrones in Midtown bowing and scraping to the likes of your self-elected powers.'

'The Higher Order work actively with the Global Council on many issues to improve the situation of your kind.'

He exhaled curtly. 'You don't believe that any more than I do. Any more than any vampire who doesn't live in the privileged Midtown believes.'

'I know the situation isn't perfect, but agreements were made. Agreements your Higher Order signed.'

'They are not my Higher Order. I have nothing to do with them.'

'So it's true – master vampires are a separate race within the species.'

He wrenched another piece from his bike.

She frowned at his silence. 'Is it true you dual feed? That you use blood and energy? Is it true that's what makes you different?' She knew she had to be wary of how far she pushed. 'The Higher Order are nervous of you, right? Because you're stronger?'

He acknowledged her only with a glance.

'So when you see something out of line, you say you do something about it,' she added. 'You think you have that right?'

'I don't harm anyone who doesn't deserve it.'

'So everyone you've ever hurt was asking for it?'

He reached for his bottle and leaned back on a braced arm, every taut muscle in his biceps, shoulders and chest tensing enticingly. 'The problem with you third-species agents is you spend so long focusing on what I've done, you don't ask why I did it. Like I've said, we have different lores. Why do you think the people you interview don't speak? You think it's purely out of fear? Has it never crossed your mind it's because they understand that's the way it is? That they're loyal? Things go on that your kind have no understanding of.'

She strolled back across to the bench. 'Then tell me. Help me understand.'

'There's nothing to understand other than that there's an order to things. An old order. Some get told what to do; others take charge because they're born with that right or earned it. That's all there is to it.'

'And which are you?'

'I was born with it, and my actions have justified me keeping it. Whatever your reports say, there are two simple reasons you can't corroborate half those accusations – it's either lies or unwarranted. And your so-called witnesses know it.'

'You've had plenty of opportunities to be judged fairly. You prefer to avoid it.'

'Which, as far as the VCU is concerned, is representative of my guilt as opposed to me not giving a fuck about your systems. I'm not accountable to the VCU – or anyone.'

'That's right – you're above any lores except your own.'

He placed his bottle back on the floor and wiped his hands on the nearest cloth. 'I'm above Carter's, for sure. And I sure as hell don't need to justify myself to his supremacy mission. His ways are nothing to do with protecting our species, no matter what he claims. He wants to control us. He wants to keep humans at the top, while he's too arrogant to realise there's no competition.' Picking his beer up again, he stood and strolled towards her. 'If we wanted to be on top, we'd take you down overnight.'

She clutched the edge of the bench as he stopped in front of her, his now undivided attention making every hair on the back of her neck stand on end. His masculine scent lingered tantalizingly on his skin, mixing with the scent of beer and engine oil. 'Confident of that, are you?'

'We have our way of dealing with things. Effective ways.'

'Through threats, torture and murder, you mean?'

He ran the rim of his bottle across her collarbone. 'Look at you taking the moral high ground. There's nothing less moral than peering into a species' most intimate part and stealing their thoughts and memories.'

Caitlin swallowed hard against the resentment in his tone. 'Unless it suits,' she said, refusing to be intimidated by the intimacy of the act.

'Your species used to help us keep order; there was nothing wrong with that. Now you just buckle and bow to control-freaks who think they have the right to tell my kind how to live.'

'As opposed to shadow readers being enslaved to the likes of you,

you mean? Selling information that caused disputes and riots and dis-loyalty. It's the place of the courts to judge. I just act as a mirror, expos-ing truths – nothing more.'

'Truths of a world you know nothing about. Have no experience of.'

'I've seen enough.'

'Really?' He lifted the bottle back to his lips. 'You know that's why Carter wants me, right? You do know he doesn't want to imprison me? Or did he forget to tell you that part?'

Unease swept through her. 'What do you mean?'

'I mean you know he wants me to work for him. He has told you that, right?'

She exhaled curtly. 'Yeah, sure he does. He's desperate for a vampire on the payroll.'

He frowned pensively. 'So he didn't tell you?'

Caitlin tried to read any hint of a lie behind his eyes, but they were as sincere as they'd been when he'd had her pinned to the table. 'Work for him doing what exactly?'

Kane stepped beside her and placed the bottle on the bench. 'Carter wants to rule the third species with a rod of iron,' he said, packing his tools away. 'Why do you think he's one of the most vehement advocates for keeping the third species divided? He keeps us apart because if we ever got together, you lot wouldn't stand a chance. And the prospect of having a master vampire under his control in case it ever does kick off, well, that's just too much power for one man to ignore. He knows the best way to control the third species is with one of their own. And Carter likes control.'

'And what makes you so special?'

He smiled, reached for his bottle again and leaned his hip against the bench as he took a mouthful. 'Asks my stalker.'

'I think you have a serious case of delusions of grandeur, Kane.'

'How many other master vampires have you come across, Caitlin? Or even heard of in the past fifty years? I strolled into Carter's space and he saw opportunity. Just like he would have seen opportunity in me coming after you. The very reason you're here now.'

Her pulse raced. 'This has nothing to do with Xavier.'

'What? You bring me in and Carter doesn't climb down from his ivory tower to get involved?' The knowing glint in his eyes escalated her unease. 'Why no safe house, Caitlin? Why was I able to just walk into your bedroom and take you?'

'You know I needed to see you again.'

'But from what you tell me, they didn't. Surely it would have been insisted upon that you were taken to safety after our intimate little encounter. So what's your instruction from him? What have you been told to do?'

She felt herself falter, but didn't break away. 'I don't have any instructions. I've been suspended.'

He frowned slightly, his eyes still rife with suspicion. 'Is that right?'

'Pending a full investigation for conduct unbecoming. Over how I captured you.'

His lips curled into a hint of a smile. 'The untarnished Caitlin Parish. That's got to hurt.' He raked her swiftly with his gaze. 'So this just between you and me now, is it?'

'Seems that way.' She knew she had to divert him and quickly. 'So why don't you be upfront with me as well, Kane. And tell me what you want with me.'

He pulled away, strode across to his car and slammed down the bonnet. 'Are you getting bored already, Caitlin?'

'Sitting and staring at the TV for nearly three hours? Watching you tend your machines? I'm having a ball.'

'So you'd prefer a little more one-to-one time?'

'I'd prefer you just to get to the point and tell me what you want with my soul.'

He strolled back over to the door, his confident smile unnerving her, frustrating her.

She quickly reached into the toolbox and grabbed one of the smaller screwdrivers. She pulled away from the bench just as he looked across his shoulder at her.

She kept her gaze lowered as she followed behind him. She kept the screwdriver handle hidden in her palm, the body flat against her wrist as she subtly tucked her hand amidst the folds of her dress. She'd slip over to the sofa and hide it under one of the seat cushions. She'd have to be quick and she'd have to be discreet.

He waited at the threshold, his back against the open door, his arms folded.

Her heart pounded, her pulse racing as she stepped forward to slip past him. But as soon as she crossed the threshold, Kane held out his hand.

He clicked his fingers, his palm upturned.

Her stomach leapt. Caitlin swallowed harder than she would have liked. She gripped the screwdriver tighter. But as she looked back up at him, those remorseless eyes told her she either gave it to him willingly or he was taking it. And it was more than obvious who was going to get hurt in the process.

Reluctantly, grudgingly, she dropped the screwdriver into his waiting palm.

He was going to be angry. He was probably going to strap her back down to the bed.

With baited breath, desperate to break from his gaze, she took another step to pass him, but Kane immediately pressed his palm against the wall in front of her, blocking her way.

He threw the screwdriver back into the outer room, closed and locked the door.

She backed flat against the wall as he placed his hand the other side of her head, barricading her in, the air crackling between them, the claustrophobia of the recess uncomfortably intimate.

She looked back into his navy eyes, a sudden flush of arousal heating between her legs. She desperately wanted to feel repulsed, but it just wasn't happening. Again she tried to fill her head with all the terrible things his profile said he'd done, anything to curb the shallowness of her breaths that, at that moment, had nothing to do with fear. She wondered how much of it he was picking up on, and if he'd use it to his advantage right there and then.

She wondered if she'd try to stop him.

'You need to accept that only one of us is going to be in control of this, Caitlin,' he said, that steady gaze unrelenting. 'And you trying to grab the reins like you did last night, like you tried to do just now, only makes me want to control things more. You try anything stupid like this again and I will strap you back down on my bed. Only this time, it'll be wrists and ankles. Do I make myself clear?'

Resentfully, she nodded, the calmness in his tone only adding to the sincerity of the threat. Her throat constricted as she used all her willpower not to break from his gaze.

'Good,' he said. He lowered his arm that was blocking her way. But instead of letting her pass, he took hold of wrist, easing her away from the wall.

He tucked his keys in his coat on the hook as he led her out of the recess.

'I don't need an escort,' she said as he continued past the kitchen, grabbing a beer from the counter along the way. She wanted to tug her wrist away but the strength of his grip already told her it would be futile. 'You've made your point.'

'Yeah, well I need a bath. And as I clearly can't turn my back on you for a second, you're coming with me.' He looked across at her. 'Unless, of course, you'd rather take the bed option now?'

# CHAPTER TEN

Caitlin clutched the sink behind her as Kane turned his back on her to kneel on the steps of the sunken bath.

He leaned forward to turn on the taps, his taut behind and lean thighs outlined against his jeans, the muscles in his forearm and biceps tensing as he braced himself.

She tried to look anywhere but at him. 'You can't blame me for planning my escape.'

'No,' he said, turning to face her again as he sat down on the steps. His strong, nimble fingers worked deftly to unlace his boots. He kicked them off, removed his socks. 'And you can't blame me for not letting you out of my sight.'

He stood and took the last couple of steps down. 'You're too tenacious for your own good.' He pulled off his oil-stained vest, fully exposing his sculpted lithe perfection, every taut and defined muscle in his back, shoulders and arms flexing with the motion. He unfastened his jeans, dropping them and his black shorts to the floor.

Caitlin snatched her gaze to the windows, but took a sneaky peek back at him as she heard him lower himself into the bathwater.

'But continue to prove yourself to be a pain in the arse and I'm going to start to lose my patience,' he added.

He washed the motorbike oil and grease off his arms before reaching for his beer. He sank a little further into the water so she could only see his upper chest, one wet arm resting on the steps, his other hand holding his bottle against the wall. It was as if she wasn't even there. He even had the audacity to close his eyes.

'What – like you did on the bed? When you forced yourself on me?'

'If you call that someone forcing themselves on you, you've led a very sheltered life.' He lifted the bottle to his lips and took a slow, steady mouthful.

'What would you call it?'

'You were the one who goaded me. You shouldn't say what you don't mean.'

'So it's my fault you can't control yourself?'

'I think I controlled myself very well.'

'You bit me.'

'I tasted you.' He looked across at her. 'Despite what your reports say, I've never forced myself on a female in my life.'

'I suppose that's along with all the other crimes you've never actually committed.'

'Like I keep saying – I haven't done a third of what Carter claims I have.'

'So he's set you up? He's lied because he wants you so badly?'

He closed his eyes again. 'Believe what you want, Caitlin. It doesn't make any difference to me.'

She watched him in the silence, his indifference fuelling more than just her irritation. She lingered over his hand coiled loosely around the bottle, before her gaze wandered to the arm nearest her. She took in every curve before dragging her gaze up to his glistening shoulder. She focused on his sculpted chest, the heart within just waiting to be read. She lingered on his eyes, the dark thick lashes that lay lowered, concealing the beauty beyond. She tongued her teeth as she examined those sexy bow lips she could so easily lean over and kiss.

Hell, she needed to focus on the job she was there to do. And quick. 'If you'd let me read you, I'd know the truth for myself.'

His glimmer of a smile warmed him to her far more than she needed right then. 'Nice try, but reading me would kill you.'

She frowned. 'Since when?'

'Since always. Trust me, you don't want to go there.'

'I've probably seen darker than what's inside you, Kane.'

He opened his eyes, looked across into hers and then closed them again. 'I doubt it,' he said, the ease in his low, guttural tone sexy, enticing.

'You have no idea what I've seen over the years.'

'I know you've never seen inside a master vampire. You try and delve into the depths of my shadow and you're never coming out again. The energy drain alone would kill you in minutes. My secrets, let alone the ones of my race, are on total lockdown. Call it a self-defence mechanism.'

'Or call it a convenient warning to prevent anyone trying.'

He smirked, lifting his bottle back to his lips.

'So you're saying I could never read you?' she added.

'Even if you got through the block – and that's one big if – I can guarantee you wouldn't survive.'

'Isla survived.'

'Because it really would have helped me get out of that place if she hadn't. She was too weak to fight beyond first base anyway.'

'I'm not. And I'm willing to take the risk.'

He looked across at her, his eyes narrowed slightly. 'Did you not understand what I said? You put those sensitive fingertips on any of my pulse points, and I will bind you and gag you before you sense even a single beat – do you understand me?'

She stared into the intensity in his navy eyes and knew he meant every word. Reluctantly she conceded rather than sustain the challenge. 'Perfectly.'

But this time he didn't look away, his gaze lingering on hers for an uncomfortable couple of seconds. To her annoyance, she broke first and lowered her gaze again.

'Come and take a seat.'

Her stomach flipped, her grip on the sink tightened. She glanced back at him. 'I'm fine here.'

'That wasn't a request, Caitlin.'

She looked back to meet his unrelenting gaze. The fact it was a directive was enough to urge her to defy him, despite her resolution to be acquiescent. But, begrudgingly, she opted for the sensible option and crossed the bathroom towards him. Her defiant streak tempted her to go and sit in the far corner of the steps, as far away from him as possible, but she knew he'd only summon her closer. Instead she sat halfway up and in the middle, facing the sink, avoiding the intimacy of anything more than sitting side-on to him. Resting her feet on the next step down, she wrapped her arms around her knees. She could feel the heat of the steam on her back, the early morning breeze wafting through the windows. The patter of the emerging rain resounded against the glass and paving outside, echoing around the bathroom.

'Have you always been this shy?'

She frowned, irritated by the flutter in her chest. She glanced across her shoulder at him. 'I'm not shy.'

'Your gaze hit the floor quicker than my towel earlier.'

'Maybe images of you naked aren't ones I want engrained on my mind.' She looked back towards the windows, giving him the back of her head. Even in the dim light she worried he'd see her blush.

'So you want to know everything about me – as long as I stay fully clothed.'

She focused on the patter of the rain. This was not the time to recoil in on herself. She had to turn this into an opportunity. She had to think of all the things she had been longing to learn about him. She needed to try and tease into the conversation why he'd been communicating with Jask Tao, let alone what he knew about her parents' killer.

She looked across her shoulder at him. 'How old are you?'

'A little over 400.'

Her estimations had only been off by a few decades – the approximate timing of the notorious death of his parents the only indicator they'd ever had. 'So you remember what it was like before. Before your species came out in the open, I mean.'

'Life before the Global Council? Before segregation?' He knocked back another mouthful. 'Sure. It's these eighty years since they took over I'd like to forget.'

'Did you not agree with the regulations?'

'What do you think?'

'The Higher Order thought it was for the best – to work openly towards common goals.'

'You're not one of those who believes we'll ever find common ground, are you?'

She frowned at the mocking in his tone. 'Something had to be done.'

'Yes, like dumping us all in places like Blackthorn with all the dregs and criminals of your kind and throwing up borders to make sure we stay contained there.'

'Why did you come here, Kane?'

He silently held her gaze until she had no option but to look away. He was only ever going to disclose what he wanted to disclose, that much was apparent.

'I know the set-up isn't ideal,' she said, looking down at the tiled floor.

'Then why do you support it?'

'Because there's no alternative at the moment.'

'Because you also don't believe there's any common ground, more like. Because you know your kind will never trust us enough to let us mix with your family, your friends, to work alongside you, to contribute to constitutions and regulations, to anything that might knock you off your power pedestal. Because when all is said and done, your instincts tell you we're the enemy. And you lump all the third species in together because if one is let in, we all come in.'

'We know about the prophecies, Kane. We know your kind tried to keep them secret but they've filtered through. Maybe the prospect of vampires taking over one day might be a small factor in the Global Council resisting your pleas for equality. Something that tells us that same equality won't be the vampires' key agenda if that prophecy is right.'

'So we stay imprisoned until some fairy tale is proved right.'

She glanced across her shoulder. 'And that's what you think? That it's a fairy tale?'

He almost smiled as he lifted the bottle to his lips again.

'So that's not why I'm here?'

Irritated by his silence, she looked ahead.

'Who's Rob?' he asked.

Her heart skipped a beat. That was the last name she needed to hear. She almost asked how he knew of him, but then she remembered the cards in her apartment.

'And why did he give you five years of birthday cards at once?'

She glowered across her shoulder at him. 'You went through my things?'

'Post. Paperwork. Drawers. You've got some sexy lingerie considering no one ever sees it. Or is it just in case Rob comes round?'

She snatched her attention back to the sink, away from the coaxing in his eyes. 'You had no right to read those cards.'

'Is he an ex?'

She maintained her silence.

'Was he your first?' he persisted. 'Maybe even your only?'

She pressed her lips together, embarrassment warming her face.

'Who finished it?'

She scowled back over her shoulder at him. 'What's that got to do with anything?'

'I'm interested.'

'So you can use whatever you learn against me?'

'Was he any good?'

She looked back across to the windows, giving him a full view of the back of her head again. 'I'm not having this conversation with you.'

'Is that what ended it? Was he not up to the job? Or was it you?'

She focused on the gentle smatters of rain as she struggled to collect her thoughts.

'A beautiful and sensual girl like you. Maybe he just didn't have the skills to make the most of it.'

Heat flushed her cheeks again. It was a double-edged compliment, she knew that. Mocking. Derisive. She moved to stand, but he caught her upper arm, kept her seated, his hand, warm from the water, feeling almost human.

'I didn't say you could move,' he said, his grasp, albeit gentle, reminder enough that he was still in charge. Equally a reminder to herself not to be over familiar. He was being pleasant only because her acquiescence allowed him to be.

The stirring in her lower abdomen was instant. Her heart pounded. She kept her gaze ahead, refusing to make eye contact, and hoped her lack of struggle would evoke him to let her go.

'Maybe I should ask him as you're clearly so reluctant.'

She glared back at him. 'You leave him alone.'

'Protective over him, too. Sweet. Shame he can't do the same for you.' He released her arm. 'Have you told him about me?'

'I don't discuss work outside of it.'

'But I'm more than work, aren't I, Caitlin? I'm the vampire who can save your life.'

She looked deep into his eyes. Kane confirming it for the second time only made her more resolute. 'So you claim.'

'And did you tell your boyfriend that? Does he know what you really want with me?'

'He's not my boyfriend.'

'All your male friends send you cards like that, do they?' He knocked back a mouthful of beer. 'I'm assuming that, as the cards were never posted, it wasn't a pretty ending.'

'Why are you so interested in him?'

'Why are you so defensive about him?'

'How would you feel if I pried into your love life, Kane?'

'I don't have a love life.'

'Just a sex life, right?'

His lips curled into a hint of a smile. 'You really think you know so much about me, don't you?'

'I've heard the rumours.'

'And I keep telling you that you can't believe everything you hear.'

'How many individuals have you killed, Kane? Across all the species.'

'I don't have enough fingers to count.'

She frowned at his nonchalance.

'Did he break that resilient heart, Caitlin?'

She desperately wanted to stand, to get out of that enclosure that seemed to be contracting more by the minute. But she wasn't going to give him the satisfaction of trying again. 'Rob is nothing to do with you. Nothing to do with any of this. Leave him out of it.'

'Wow, he sure meant something to you once.' His gaze didn't flinch. 'Is he the reason you've been alone ever since? Or had you already seen what you wanted elsewhere? Someone you wanted more?'

She frowned at the taunt in his entrancing eyes. 'And who would that be, Kane?'

He moved his hand to rest just behind the small of her back, her awareness of its presence making her spine ache. 'Why the VCU, Caitlin? I mean, out of all the units you could have worked for, why vampires?'

'I went where the opening was.'

'Still, it's a bit of a dark and risky place for a girl like you.'

She felt like rolling her eyes at the number of times she'd heard that line over the years. It still didn't suppress her need to challenge it. She turned to face him a little. 'A girl like me? And what am I like, Kane?'

'One who has no place chasing vampires like me.'

She narrowed her eyes. 'What was it you said to me – a little girl doing a man's job? And yet here we are, wasting time in one of your dens as you helplessly wait for me to fall in love with you. Does that not strike you as a little tragic?'

There was a hint of amusement in his eyes. 'For a girl who looks at me the way you do, you're very confident in your ability to abstain, Caitlin.'

She exhaled a terse laugh as she turned away from him again, fearful of what he might see otherwise. 'We're not all victims to our libidos, Kane.'

'Is that what you have against us, Caitlin? Do we not meet your moral standards?'

'I don't have anything against vampires. I've met plenty of decent ones. And I'm just as willing to protect those as humans or any other third species, which is why I do the job I do. I focus on the ones that don't take their meds or advice, the ones who don't follow the guidelines.'

'Guidelines created by humans.'

'We're still the morally dominant species, like it or not. Souls will always outweigh shadows.'

'According to your lores. Your religions.'

She looked back at him. 'In any lore, the soul is the base for morality.'

'And I thought it was the decisions someone made.'

'Based on what you know to be right. And that's what your soul dictates to you.'

'So someone without a soul is incapable of making good decisions?' he asked.

'Self-sacrifice is the greatest sign of morality. Unfortunately, it's something third species are incapable of. They can do the right thing, but it's always about self-preservation in the end. Those shadows inside of you where your souls should be prove there is no hope for redemption.'

He smiled. 'You really believe that, don't you?'

'Why did you hold back earlier on the bed? Is it because of conscience? A basic understanding of what is wrong? No, it's because you want something out of this. You thought holding back would make you appear to be in control of your emotions so you could start to gain my trust. You held back because you want me to want you. You need me to want you, to give you my consent so your plan can work.'

'I remember telling you I wouldn't need to seduce your soul out of you.'

Unease squeezed her chest. 'It's the only way you can get to a shadow reader's soul.'

'Is it?'

She stared at him. 'Are you saying it isn't?'

He broke a hint of a smile. 'You almost look disappointed.'

She exhaled curtly and looked ahead again. 'You are so unbelievably arrogant, Kane.'

'I'm not arrogant. I just say it as it is. And you most definitely have a little spark in there for me,' he said, clipping the base of her spine with his thumb in a way she found provocatively and surprisingly playful.

She didn't bother denying it. She wasn't even sure she could sound convincing enough even to attempt it. Instead she clenched her hands around her knees and kept her attention ahead. The rain continued to patter, the tension in her chest tightening as the minutes passed in silence. She rubbed her hands down her shins for reassurance, a sheen of humidity from the bathwater steam lightly coating her skin.

She berated herself for flinching as he reached up and tucked her hair back over her shoulder, slid the back of his fingers over her artery. 'Have you ever been bitten? For pleasure, I mean.'

Her heart lunged at the thought of his incisors sinking into her. She subtly shrugged him off and pulled her hair back over her shoulder. 'I don't agree with feeding. There are systems. Protocols.'

'Is that the real reason? Most people are put off by the pain. But it doesn't have to be painful. No more painful than sex anyway. Not if it's done right. It can't be or people wouldn't give themselves over time and time again.'

'And I've seen what that addiction does to people. Whatever neurotransmitter or enzyme or whatever else it is you use to drug them into thinking they need it.'

'People keep coming back because it feels good. Some even prefer it to sex. It's a whole different high, a different kind of intimacy.' He traced the back of his hand up her upper arm, his cool fingers tantalizingly fresh against the heat of her skin. But she wouldn't move. She wouldn't give him the reaction he was seeking. Not this time. And something, something in the sensuality of those fingers, compelled her to wait to see what he'd do next. 'Bites aren't supposed to be aggressive. The very opposite, in fact. Bites used to be about protection as much as the feed itself. If someone was bitten, other vampires would leave them alone. The vampire would get a regular feeder and the feeder, in turn, would be safeguarded for their loyalty. It was a special bond. The original friends with benefits.'

'And a great way to create your own harem. Sounds more like a protection racket to me.'

'You have such a low opinion of me, Caitlin.'

'I know too much about you.'

'No, you think you know about me.'

'You've done little to prove me wrong.'

'I've done nothing to prove you right other than kidnap you. Other than that, I think I've been more than civilised.'

She looked back over her shoulder at him. 'And if I hadn't stopped you on the bed, just how far would you have gone?'

'As far as you wanted me to go.'

Her stomach clenched at the subtle intimidation in his gaze. She looked back ahead. She couldn't stay there. She couldn't sit there like that. Not with that low rasp challenging the most intimate parts of her. But running would give him all he needed to know that she was faltering.

'Don't tell me you've never wondered what it would be like.'

'You really do flatter yourself, Kane.'

'What I'm flattered by is the way you look at me,' he said, running the back of his hand up her spine. She held her breath at the slow caress to the nape of her neck. And as he traced the back of those fingers across her shoulder blade to the shoulder nearest him, every tiny hair on the back of her neck stood on end. A shiver ricocheted through her as he stroked down her upper arm to her inner elbow, but Caitlin kept perfectly still.

She could feel him watching her every reaction. But she wasn't going to falter like he expected her to. Especially not when his touch was so shockingly compulsive as he worked up under her short, fluted sleeve, his hand enveloping her shoulder.

As he slid his hand across the upward curves of her breasts, she gripped the step either side of her. She shuddered at the intense surge in her abdomen, the intimacy almost unbearable.

She thought she'd break when his fingers adeptly unfastened the first three buttons on her dress, but she found herself unwilling to move. And as the loosened fabric allowed him to lower the sleeve of her dress, he slid down her bra strap so her shoulder was completely bare. She could only focus on steadying her breathing as she relished in the sensuality of his thumb massaging into the knots in her shoulder, her fingertips tingling with the need to touch him, but still she refused to give him the satisfaction of moving.

Kane slid his hand across her collarbone, but instead of retracting again, he reached all the way across to her upper arm. Water splashed around him as he eased onto his knees behind her. Shoulders inches from hers, the temporary heat from his wet chest radiated through the cotton of her dress. 'That much tension is bad for you,' he said.

'So are your fangs being that close to my neck.'

'They're incisors. Fangs are so feral.'

'And you're not?'

'I have my moments. But don't worry, I'm not going to bite you,' he said, his tone betraying his smile. 'Not without your consent.'

'How very chivalrous of you.'

He brushed her hair aside again, but this time to expose the right side of her neck. 'Curb the sarcasm,' he said, his thumb caressing the exposed pulse pumping beneath her skin. 'Or I might be tempted to change my mind.'

His soft, sensuous kiss at the nape of her neck stunned her. She shuddered and gripped the carpeted step. But she still wasn't going to move. This time she'd see just how far he was willing to go. Just what the infamous Kane Malloy would do next.

Still holding her upper arm, simultaneously trapping the other, he kept her against him, the dampness of his arm sinking through her dress. The move had been so carefully orchestrated that she could almost admire him for it. And as he slid his other hand up her throat, his fingers encompassing it with ease, she thought of how easily he could snap her neck. Instead he tilted her head to the side to expose her neck more.

Her heart thudded painfully, the rush of warmth between her legs disconcerting her. She knew she couldn't move now even if she wanted to, even with his possible instability from being knelt in the bath still.

But she didn't want to move. That was the simple fact. She didn't want to go anywhere. The secure grip of his arm wrapped around her and the hardness of his chest against her back was shockingly reassuring, not terrifying as she would have expected.

'Tell me,' he said, leaning enticingly close to her ear. 'What are you most scared of, Caitlin? What I can do to you or how I make you feel?'

Hell, she wished he'd stop using her name. Every time he said it, goosebumps swept over her skin, the word like a melody from his subtle rasp. She swallowed against her arid throat as he released her neck to slide his hand further down her body.

'You don't make me feel anything,' she lied.

She felt his smile as he kissed her ear. 'No?' he asked, slowly bunching up her dress.

She breathed heavily as his cool hand touched the warm, now-exposed flesh of her inner thigh, steadily sliding up to find the intimate heat between her legs.

Caitlin flinched, her hands clenching. She slammed her thighs together, locking his hand in place.

'Felt that, didn't you?' he said, kissing her gently on the neck, his teeth grazing her sensitive flesh through his smile. He tightened his arm around her, clenched his hand into a fist and twisted to encourage her thighs apart.

He slid his fingers gently down to the crotch of her knickers, the teasing pressure and insistence almost unbearable. He kissed behind her ear, distracting her enough to part her legs a little more, allowing him more freedom as he slid his fingers gently back and forth, his thumb working dangerously close to her clitoris. She tensed, stunned at what she was allowing him to do, her own dampness, her sex swelling and throbbing in response to his expert touch. And he clearly sensed it, his fingers adding more pressure. She suppressed her gasp and closed her eyes, relishing in the sensation as tendrils of arousal squeezed her body.

He teased the crotch of her knickers aside, his cool fingers meeting her most intimate flesh. A bolt of shock soared through her as his middle finger slid through the folds a little way into her sex, his thumb expertly finding and applying pressure against her clitoris. She finally gasped and wrenched her left hand free, slamming it down over his, her nails on her trapped hand digging into the step.

But as Kane persisted, Caitlin bit into her bottom lip to prevent herself from crying out. And as his middle finger delved deeper into her wetness, she could do nothing to curb the heaviness of her breaths, her grip tightening on his hand as he pushed deeper.

But as his thumb sent another bolt of electricity through her, it was all too much.

She forced his hand away, stumbled away from his loosened grip and marched out of the bathroom.

# CHAPTER ELEVEN

Caitlin paced the room, her legs shaking, hands to her mouth. She hated the way she trembled, her sex throbbing and aching for him, the bolt of arousal that had knocked her off guard still forefront in her mind.

His touch, though firm, had been gentle and controlled, and not urgent like she'd expected. The thought of his fingers running sensually over her skin and the expert ease with which he found her most sensitive core made her shudder. No fumbling. No misdirection. He knew exactly what he was doing and there was something dangerously appealing in that. Something that was equally as terrifying.

Her resistance wasn't going to last three days. Not trapped in there with him. The whole plan had been crazy. She needed out. Just a few hours and she was already questioning her convictions.

It unnerved her how much she wanted him. And she knew it was wrong because it was nothing about feelings. It was sexual – pure and simple. The way she'd reacted to his touch in the corridor and in the interrogation room had only confirmed it - he had electrified her. And the fact he saw it, and felt it, and wasted no time in responding to it was too much of a turn-on to bear. She wanted him to be brutal, clumsy, crude even, because then she could resist him, but he was none of those. Instead, his self-control and self-assurance were dangerously thrilling.

This wasn't going to work. The realisation hit her hard and fast. She was no competition for him. The tension wracked through her, and she berated herself again for running out on him like some nervous teenager, not a twenty-nine-year-old woman. But one touch of his fingers had told her she wouldn't stand a chance if she gave in to him.

She reminded herself he was just a vampire, albeit a master, but still a vampire. It was her area of expertise. She'd seen inside enough of them, hunted enough of them over the years not to have the excuse of fear or apprehension. The only thing clouding her judgement was her insane attraction to him and she had to get a grip on it quick.

Hearing him step out of the water, she took a few steadying breaths. Just the thought of those insistent fingers made the blood rush back to her most intimate area. She backed away from the door and braced herself.

He stepped into the doorway looking like some honed centurion wrapped only in his dark-grey towel, his erection pressing against it. He leaned against the doorframe, his folded arms emphasising their strength – confirmation again that if he wanted to overpower her, even with her training, it would be effortless.

'You're trembling,' he said, his eyes glinting with amusement.

'I'm fine,' she said, clenching and unclenching her hands before she realised she was doing it. She concealed them behind her back.

'You didn't have to run out on me. You just had to ask me to stop.'

'And you would have?'

He advanced steadily towards her. 'If I thought you meant it.'

She didn't dare break from that gaze as she backed up in sync with each sure-footed casual step he made towards her. 'And you'd know that would you? You'd be willing to take the risk?' Her heel hit the skirting board, making her flinch.

His eyes twinkled with mischief as he drew level, his proximity igniting a spark in her again. 'Is that a challenge?'

Her nails scraped against the wall at the small of her back. 'No.'

He placed one hand beside her head, his other loose and low on his hip. 'You're not used to being hit on, are you?'

'Is that what it was?'

He smiled fleetingly, offering her a flash of incisors. He leaned closer.

'You might be able to play these kinds of games with the wholesome, naive boys you date in coffee shops, Caitlin, but I'm not like that. But then you wouldn't be so turned on if I was, would you?' His lips almost touched her ear. 'I'm already inside your head. And your body's most definitely next.'

Her stomach flipped. He was expecting her to crumble, but her defences kicked in. She wouldn't be seen as the weak adversary. He needed to know that it was him who needed to tread carefully – not her. She was not going to be intimidated by his mind games. She was not going to back down. The defiant streak in her ratcheted her adrenaline up a few notches. His arrogance struck every nerve ending, but more than that, the dark and dangerous promise he had uttered compelled her to challenge him. That aura he held around himself was not beyond breaching.

'You think you've got your fingers on all my buttons, don't you, Kane? But you don't know me. I'm not porcelain – I don't crack easily. It's taken me years to prove that to the VCU, so three days with you will be nothing. You might think you're in control, but you're not. The only control you have over me is hurting me or killing me, neither of which you can risk if you're to get what you need. Because despite what you say, I know you need me to fall for you or you wouldn't be taking your time. You need me, Kane. Maybe even more than I need you.'

His eyes narrowed slightly, but she couldn't tell if it was amusement or annoyance. 'Is that right?'

'For all I know, you might have lied when you said you could kill whatever it is that's coming for me. Maybe that's why you need to get to me before it does. Maybe you're not capable of protecting me, just like you weren't capable of protecting Arana. Where were you when your little sister needed her powerful, master-vampire brother, huh? Where were you when she was being tortured and abused and slaughtered? That's right – fulfilling your baser needs, like you always are.'

The moment she said it, she regretted it.

The playful and mischievous look in his eyes was replaced with sudden anger. His glower unnerved her more than if he'd yelled at her. The fury simmered behind his eyes with an intensity that terrified her. And it terrified her because beyond the fury was pain. Pain that she had inflicted. Pain that had cut somewhere deeper than she'd intended with her stupid remarks.

His eyes darkened, but within them she saw something she thought him incapable of, that every report said he was incapable of: she saw guilt and, amidst it, the tiniest glimmer of vulnerability.

She could see he hated her for evoking it. Worse, she hated herself for mocking him. Kane, who had found Arana's torn and ravished body.

It was unforgivable.

Her hands clenched against the wall. She felt sick with guilt, fear squeezing her chest.

His retaliation felt inevitable, but he didn't lash out. Any other time, any other circumstance, she had no doubt he would have killed her in an instant. But Kane was in it for the long haul, and his reaction proved it.

Clearly he did need her. Really needed her. And because of it, his self-control during those moments was terrifying. More than ever, she now knew he was going to be one hell of an adversary.

'You know nothing about what happened to my sister,' he said too quietly.

He had no way of knowing she'd read the reports. How could he when he didn't even know those who were responsible had given themselves in years before she was even a part of the VCU?

But she'd felt it even as she'd read them – just what he would have gone through. That pain never went away. She knew that only too well – the anger, the injustice, the need for revenge.

And it must have eaten away at him. Kept eating away at whatever heart he had left. His revenge against the vigilantes who'd killed his parents had been merciless. There had been over thirty of them, but he'd got every single one of them and everyone they knew. It had been the start of the tirade that had earned him his reputation. The vigilantes had hoped to evoke a warning by taking down a master family – a caution to all vampires who thought they could share human territory. Instead, they'd learned the lesson of what messing with master vampires, of what messing with Kane, induced. More terrifyingly, he had taken his time over years, filled each with the terror and dread of knowing he was coming for them one at a time. Eventually he'd got his family's land back, their status, their dignity. Before the regulations came into being.

But that same vengeance for his sister had been, unbeknownst to him, thwarted by a wall of silence the Third Species Control Division had no choice but to maintain. They'd had no choice but to cover it up or the consequences would have been dire – for the families of those responsible, for the entire lycan community, for law and order in the locale. The lycans responsible had handed themselves in the night after the incident, had given full and frank confessions and had since been held in the detainment unit, terrified of the wrath of Kane.

And like an epiphany, the pieces started to merge for Caitlin. The gut-wrenching possibility she had already suspected.

He had found out. He'd finally uncovered the truth.

That was why he wanted her. That was the link. Only now she'd worked out how she fitted in. He wanted justice his way. He wanted them out of detainment so he could deal with them. And to get that, he needed a bargaining tool.

Her.

She thought of the quiet resolve it had taken to get each of his parents' murderers. Kane had taken his time for a reason, and history had taught her that this was the time to be really afraid.

This was just the start.

The fear gripping her stomach intensified as he stared deep into her eyes as if he was going to say something. Instead he seemed to think better of it.

As he strode away, her whole body sagged with momentary relief.

He ripped off his towel and opened the wardrobe. He tugged on clean boxers and jeans, pulled on a T-shirt as he strode over to the sofas.

Not only was the moment dead but with it any semblance of hope.

Because if she were right – if this was about redeeming Arana – nothing would steer him off that path.

And if he had been telling the truth in the bathroom when he'd said he didn't need to seduce her to get her soul, she didn't even have the leverage she thought she had. Worse, she'd walked willingly right into his trap.

He picked up his cigarettes and lighter from the coffee table. Placing the cigarette between his lips, he ignited the tip with steady precision before sitting back. He exhaled a curt, swift stream of smoke, his attention locked on the TV.

She needed to know. She needed to know there and then.

And somehow she had to get to the truth without letting him know what she knew or she was about to let slip the biggest secret her division had ever held. She could instigate the vampire-lycan war they all dreaded. And she'd be responsible for the fallout.

She took a few steps towards the sofa, watched him for a moment, the deep but detached concentration in his eyes as they remained fixed on the silent TV screen. 'I'm sorry for what I said. It was unforgiveable.'

He didn't look at her. He didn't even flinch.

'I know she meant a lot to you. I can't imagine what you must have gone through that night when you found her.'

She hovered in the silence before sitting on the edge of the sofa opposite him.

This was what Xavier had sent her in for. This was the information they needed. Inadvertently she had uncovered it and, despite his silence, she needed to persist.

Jask had to have been the one to tell him. The lycan community in Blackthorn was too small for him not to know. If he'd told Kane voluntarily, he was playing a hell of a dangerous game. Either that or Kane already had him well and truly in his grasp.

'I know you tried to find out who was responsible,' she added.

'I know who's responsible,' he said, his gaze snapping to hers, the steadiness as he held it almost unbearable.

'Who?' She hated the quiver in her voice that she knew he'd detected. 'Who did it, Kane?'

'How are they doing? Still being fed and watered? Being good lycans and taking their meds?'

Acid rose at the back of her throat. 'Is this why you and Jask have been communicating? Did he also tell you they gave themselves up the next night? They were scared of you, Kane. They were terrified. I read their confessions. They didn't know who she was. They hadn't taken their meds. It was a full moon. They were out of control.'

'Everyone knew who Arana was.'

'They made a mistake.'

'With my sister.'

She gripped the edge of the seat. 'Is that why you hate the Third Species Control Division so much? Did we take your revenge away from you? Is this the vigilante justice you talk about? Are you planning to use me as a bargaining tool for their release? Do you want me to read them? Is that why you chose a shadow reader? For proof that it was them?'

He looked back at the screen, lifted the cigarette to his lips.

'What are you planning – some kind of execution? Because if that's what this is about, you have to know they'll never be let out. I understand your need for vengeance, Kane—'

'Really?' he asked, his gaze snapping to hers.

'You know I do. Why do you think I risked everything hunting you down – my reputation, my job, my life?'

'Then help organise their release.'

'I couldn't hand them over to you, even if I wanted to.'

'Even if I offered to give you what you want? Even if I agreed to delay my plan and kill for you?'

The perfect solution to both their problems – if she agreed to being responsible for anarchy in Blackthorn, in the locale. Anarchy that was guaranteed to spread to other locales once they heard that the justice her kind so openly proclaimed had been handed over to a vigilante vampire.

The death toll alone was unthinkable.

All for one self-seeking decision.

She didn't operate like that. She didn't operate like Kane or others of his kind and, if she agreed, she was no better than them. Her kind was no better than them.

'You expect me to say yes knowing what you would do to them?'

'That's where you and I differ, see, Caitlin. I don't do rehabilitation. I don't do protecting criminals from justice. I don't waste money, time and resources on those beyond redemption.'

'And how do you know who is beyond redemption?'

'If you read their confessions, you know what they did to her.'

And it had been the most disturbing report she had ever read. At twenty-three, it had dragged her out of her innocence and shaped her view of the world. 'Yes. But you have to see that what you're planning is not going to make this better, Kane.'

'Neither is killing what you're hunting. Yet you think you have a right to avenge your family, whereas I have no right to avenge what has been done to mine?'

'That thing will get away with it if I don't stop it. Those lycans aren't getting away with anything. This is why the unit exists: to stop things like this happening. They are paying for what they did.'

'Safely tucked up in your detainment unit as opposed to being at my mercy? I tell you what stops things like that happening – your kind butting out of issues that do not concern them. Lycans don't need to be medicated any more than my kind needs to be filled with that shit you encourage them to feed on to help curb their cravings. It's about respect and self-control and keeping the balance by a natural order. A natural order that us masters are more than capable of maintaining. They should never have been taken in. They should have been left to me. You're nothing but a hypocrite asking me to help you get your vengeance when you have no intention of helping me get mine.'

She couldn't argue. She didn't blame him. More than ever, she understood. But all that was irrelevant. Kane was no innocent victim merely seeking retribution for his sister. He remained the most dangerous vampire to their district for over fifty years. His potential was still terrifying, let alone the fact the consequences of an inter-species civil war would be horrendous. And if he did persuade the TSCD to let the lycans go, their reputation would be demolished. They would no longer be trusted. The TSCD sanctuary for those third species at risk or those who helped them with their enquiries would mean nothing. There would be fear in the district again. Everything they'd fought for would be in shreds.

She had to get out of there and warn them. If they'd ever had justification to take him in, it was now.

'Even if I did agree with you morally, it's not even possible in the next couple of days,' she said. 'You don't have time for this. You've left it too late. And if what you said about Xavier is right, even attempting this is just giving him reason to take you in. Is that what you want?' She hesitated for a moment. She had to try, as futile as it seemed. 'Let me go and I won't say anything. They don't have to know you took me. I can just say I took some time out because of the suspension. I promise you, I'll say nothing.'

He exhaled curtly and looked back at the screen, his hint of a derisive smirk unsettling her further, his resoluteness seemingly impenetrable. 'Nice try.'

'Max has no power in this if that's why you took me. Xavier is the only one who can arrange for those lycans to be released and there's no way he'll do it. If you want me to read them, if that's the proof you want, let me go. I'll get in there. I'll confirm it for you. It won't work any other way. Just tell me how my soul fits in all this. Why do you need to extract it? How will that aid your vengeance?'

She waited for him to answer, but Kane said nothing, his attention still locked on the screen.

In frustration, fearful of what she might say next, she marched over to the bed. She sat on the edge and clutched the bedpost as she rested her head against it.

Kane wasn't going to help her. She had to face that fact. She was insane for thinking he would. But at least she now knew why he was involved with Jask and what he was planning. That gave her the answers Xavier wanted. Her official job was done.

She had to get out of there. She had to get out of there now.

But it still didn't give her the information she so desperately needed. A name. Just a name. Armed with that, there were people out there she could talk to – shamans and witches she could persuade. As closed a community as they were, she'd get answers somehow. Plenty owed her favours – some who, once they had the name, may even be able to disclose a way for her to kill it herself. Someone other than him had to know something. Other ancients who may talk for a price. Beyond those doors was hope. In here she didn't stand a chance.

Once she had a name, she could turn all her attention to getting out of here.

She needed to bargain with him. She needed to offer him something. Something too tempting for him to turn down.

She hated even considering it. In so many ways it was unforgiveable, but it was a one-off. A small exchange for what she could potentially get in return. It could sate him. It could lower his guard. It could send him to sleep maybe long enough for her to escape. It could mean getting the information she needed and a way out.

It was daylight outside. It was her best chance. Maybe her only chance.

She'd let him calm down first. She'd calm herself down. And then she'd offer him the one thing no vampire, however smart, savvy or powerful, could refuse.

She'd offer him her blood.

# CHAPTER TWELVE

Kane kept his attention on the flickering images on the screen as he turned up the volume. He was relieved she'd stepped away. Relieved she'd had enough sense for that. Even after she'd taken herself away, it took all his self-control to suppress the searing heat burning inside him.

How he'd contained himself when she'd jibed him over Arana's death, he had no idea. But he knew he had found it somewhere between needing his vengeance more and knowing how easily she'd snap if he unleashed his true self on her.

Right then he'd wanted to hurt her so badly. Possibilities had lashed through his mind – thoughts that only confirmed just how depraved he had become. Twisted, sickening thoughts. He'd nearly let it all out. But it was too soon. He needed that soul first. The soul that was locked behind a defiant and dogmatic heart.

And he'd seen in her eyes how afraid she was. She knew what he was capable of but still she'd come after him. Still she'd pressed him for information.

She was desperate for resolution.

But unfortunately so was he.

And righting the wrongs done to his sister was the only thing that mattered. The only thing he had left. And he wouldn't rest until he'd achieved it. He owed Arana that. He owed her what little justice he could get. It wouldn't bring her back – Caitlin had been right. It wouldn't bring back her smiles, the comfort of her touch, her laughter and playful pranks. It wouldn't bring back her companionship on cold, lonely nights or her lively conversations and alluring perspective on the world. It wouldn't bring back her infuriating nonchalance towards risks and danger. Her impulsiveness. Her mischievous streak that had given him far too many sleepless days and far too many confrontations with suitors who'd dared to think they were good enough to get in her bed.

It was the least he could do to go some way to ease the all-consuming guilt that had become as much a part of him because he'd allowed it to happen whilst he'd spent the night in the arms of a female whose name he couldn't even remember, whose face was a distant memory. Another night of meaningless, unsatisfying sex while his sister lay on some cold, concrete floor crying out for him.

His little sister, the one he'd promised to always protect, the one he swore no one would ever hurt.

Arana may not have died in peace, but she'd rest in peace.

And there was only one way for that to happen.

He stubbed out his cigarette and stood from the sofa.

Stepping out of her sight into the depths of the kitchen, he clutched the worktop as he bowed over it. This was the part he wouldn't let Caitlin see, couldn't afford for her to see. The part that had nearly come out as he had her backed against the wall. If any of the venom inside had leaked out, she'd have known there was no hope for her.

She was smart. Smart and sensitive and perceptive. She'd been reading him from the moment she'd woken on his bed – assessing her situation and making plans. She had to believe she could succeed or it wouldn't work. If she knew the truth of how impossible her cause was, she'd close down on him and make her soul even less accessible than it already was.

He had to stop her seeing the dense, impenetrable chasm she was in.

It was cruel but it was necessary.

He gripped the counter.

And because of that he couldn't afford to feel the way he had when he'd wrapped his arm around her in the bath. When he'd felt just how vulnerable she really was. When he'd detected every tiny response to him. It hadn't been just sexual as he'd intended – finding out what might make her tick. A connection had sparked – the last thing he could afford. He'd enjoyed it. He'd enjoyed seeing that side of her. That side so tightly concealed inside her. For a split second, she'd forgotten who he was. Or for a split second, she hadn't cared.

That was what he needed.

He needed more.

He needed to get back out there and allow her to get closer. Allow himself to get closer – closer than he'd dared let himself get to anyone in a long time – if he was going to succeed.

Kane hadn't even looked at her in the hour or so that had passed. His coldness only made what she was about to do harder. Caitlin clenched her hands in her lap as she watched him from the bed. No time yet had felt like the right time to approach him. But she knew no time would.

She thought of the witness statements she'd read about his feeding habits. They were as contradictory as everything else produced about him. Some claimed him to be rough, brutal and insatiable, the sex acts that followed the feed equally fierce and self-sating. Others reported him to be sensual and considerate, but still controlling. None ever wanted to prosecute. All were happy to boast of their encounter. Those that had survived. All said they'd offer themselves to him again.

He stubbed out his second cigarette before standing from the sofa. Crossing the room to the kitchen, he re-emerged a few minutes later with a beer and a bottle of water. He left the latter on the table rather than take it over to her. She wondered if it was her cue to join him.

Her thudding heart resonated in her ears as she forced herself off the edge of the bed. She stepped over to the sofa opposite his, tentatively sitting on the edge.

Kane took a mouthful of beer, the solemnity in his eyes telling her she hadn't been forgiven even if his anger had dissipated.

She knew she couldn't hesitate or she'd lose her nerve. 'If you tell me what killed my parents, I'll let you feed.'

He lifted his eyebrows slightly in faint amusement. 'Excuse me?'

'You heard me.'

'Yeah, I heard you. I just want you to say it again.'

'It's a fair exchange.'

'You're offering to let me feed? On you?'

She nodded.

'What happened to the systems and protocols?'

'I want a name, Kane. I need to know.' She dug her nails deeper into her perspiring palms. 'Before you're going to do whatever it is you're planning to do, I want to know what it is.'

He lifted his bottle steadily to his lips, took a slow mouthful then lowered it again, his gaze not flinching from hers as he subtly licked away the remnants. 'I'd need to control you for every moment of the feed. Are you sure you can take that?'

She couldn't let her gaze falter. 'More than sure.'

Her stomach flipped at his flicker of a smile as he turned his attention back to the TV.

'This is not an open-ended offer, Kane.'

He was a vampire. It should have been the easiest thing in the world to tempt him to bite.

'What's the problem?' she asked, her tone laced with an urgency she hadn't intended.

His eyes snapped to hers again. 'The problem is that I could forget myself, Caitlin. I could decide I want more than just your blood. Like you said, if I do anything you don't like, it could jeopardise my plans. And believe me, during a feed I could do a lot of things you don't like.'

There was a stirring low in her abdomen at the threat, but she forced herself to focus on the significance of what else he'd said. 'So you do need to get to my heart.'

He narrowed his eyes slightly. 'You do know what goes on in a dual feed, don't you? A vampire gets you to the height of arousal until all that built-up energy gets fit to explode and then he bites – hard and fast. And just as you climax, at that exact moment, he drinks, taking every last shred of energy. You don't remember who you are, where you are, you don't even care. Humans can't survive it. Even you shadow readers, with your constantly self-generating energy, can only take so much. And I'm capable of taking more than you can even imagine.'

She refused to look away despite every facet of common sense screaming at her to retreat. 'But you won't forget yourself, will you? Not if your need for vengeance is that strong.'

'That's still one hell of a risk you're willing to take.'

'I have nothing to lose, do I?'

Her chest tightened as he held her gaze for an uncomfortable couple of seconds.

'And you thought me trying to seduce you was tragic,' he said. 'You offering yourself to me in exchange for information you won't be able to do anything with is what's tragic, Caitlin.' He lifted his bottle back to those sexy, bow lips. 'It almost breaks my heart.'

She pressed her lips tight together and breathed steadily through her nose for a moment. 'I just want to know what it is.'

'You really want to trade that flawless skin for information you can do nothing with?'

'Do you really want to turn down a free feed?'

He licked the bottom of his lip as his gaze swept from her throat to her mouth. 'I'd want to bite you full on,' he declared, the intensity behind those navy eyes as they locked on hers telling her he meant every word. 'No numbing. I'd want you to feel me go in. And I will hold you down. I can't risk those magic fingers wandering.'

She nodded despite knowing he was still angry enough to make this difficult for her. But she knew if she pulled away now, she was unlikely to regain the courage to offer herself to him again.

Kane assessed her carefully for a few moments longer before pushing the coffee table aside with his foot, freeing the space between them. He placed his drink on the edge of the table before leaning back, draping his arms over the back of the sofa. 'Come here,' he said, resting his gaze squarely on hers.

She could barely breathe as she forced herself off the sofa to stand in front of him. All she kept telling herself was that she was insane – insane to even be considering giving herself to him.

He wrapped his cool hand around her wrist and guided her down onto his lap to sit astride him, facing him. The rush of heat between her legs as she spread them across those strong, powerful thighs was too overwhelming for her to dare meet those compelling eyes scorching into her.

After a few moments of silent contemplation, he brushed her hair back from her neck. 'Undo your dress.'

Her stomach leapt, her pulse racing. She lifted her fingers to her buttons, fumbling as if she were wearing gloves. She unfastened the first and then the second, glanced at him only to see he wasn't watching her reveal herself, but examining her eyes instead. She unfastened the third and the fourth then hesitated.

He slid his hands up under the hem of her dress to hold her thighs – hands that felt more familiar than they should have. 'A couple more.'

She stopped mid-stomach then looked back at him. Uncertain where to rest her hands, she interlaced them and held them awkwardly at her stomach.

'Have you ever been bitten?'

She shook her head.

'So you're jumping straight in at the deep end,' he remarked, his eyes flashing darkly.

'Sometimes that's the best way.'

He smiled fleetingly, flashing his incisors. 'Spoken like a true bite virgin.'

She stared into his eyes, the shadows of the room intensifying around her, blackening the corners. 'Which I'm sure doesn't bother you.'

He smiled again – a smile that was as sexy and entrancing as the light but firm grip he held on her thighs. But it didn't manage to over-shadow the dark intent in his eyes. 'Not at all. Even if it does make you a little jittery. Unpredictable.' He lifted his hands to her shoulders and slid her sleeves down to mid-arm, exposing the cups of her lace balcon-ette bra, the upward mounds of her breasts. He gently eased down each lacy shoulder strap, leaving her shoulders bare. He ran his tongue down his incisor. 'But I can work with that.'

She pressed her lips together, reminding herself that she could do this. Every survival instinct in her cried for her to tell him she'd changed her mind, but she knew it wasn't just about the information. She knew that for too long she'd wanted to know how it felt to have Kane at his most primal. Despite the danger, despite the blood loss, despite the potential energy drain, she wanted to experience firsthand the binding intimacy.

Kane cupped her behind with both hands and tugged her tight against him. As his contained erection pressed against her sex, a breath caught in her throat. She hoped he hadn't noticed but didn't dare look at him to check. He caught her hands in his, pushed both behind her back to hold them there with one of his. She closed her eyes for a brief moment, her spine tingling as he rubbed his thumb hypnotically from shoulder blade to shoulder blade.

She looked back at him and her heart lunged. His eyes were differ-ent, his pupils dangerously dilated, his incisors more elongated.

And he could never have been more captivating.

This was not just the vampire, but the master vampire emerging. She was learning more in those few minutes than she had learned in years from notes and photographs and witness statements. This was the part of him she most feared and was most fascinated by. She sensed the power but also the need – the deep, sensual, instinctive need that he orchestrated like a finely tuned instrument. Any lesser vampire would have already pinned her to the floor and all but drained her dry.

He didn't need to.

She tried to relax as he rubbed his thumb along her jaw before turning her head to the side to expose her throat. But as he leaned in, licked over her artery, his incisors meeting soft, tender flesh, she tensed.

He pulled back and studied her eyes. He frowned and let go of her wrists. 'You're not ready for this.'

Her stomach flipped. A cool perspiration swept over her. He wasn't going to risk it. He was playing carefully. 'We had a deal.'

'A deal you're not ready for.' He stretched his arms across the back of the sofa again, his sullen gaze locked on hers.

She nearly yanked her sleeves back up over her shoulders and pulled herself up off of him, but there was no way she was having him turn her down. Despite the fact it could be her only opportunity, his self-control was humiliating. As she crumbled inside, her willpower increased. 'You're actually scared of the consequences, aren't you?'

He lifted his eyebrows a fraction. 'You seriously think goading me is a good idea?'

'I want you to bite me, Kane,' she said, knowing that, despite her fear, the words couldn't have been truer. 'I want that name.'

'Last warning. I don't play nice. Sometimes I forget how much more fragile humans are than third-species mates.'

She didn't dare break from his compelling gaze. 'Bite me, Kane,' she said, her eyes narrowed in a taunt to emphasise her double entendre.

He almost smiled as he gently pushed her hands back, his gaze not leaving hers. He raked back her hair, cupped the nape of her neck and leaned in. He slid his lips and then his tongue over her artery, her neck tingling before becoming numb to his kisses. He was anesthetising her, the very fact he chose to ease the pain despite what he'd said making her feel more for him than she knew she should have. But she convinced herself he was just being strategic again, minimising risk of alienating her.

She breathed faster, knowing there would be no stopping him once he'd bit. Not until he fed. And he wouldn't feed gently.

And she was right.

His bite was hard, his incisors piercing her skin in one easy move.

Caitlin buckled as she felt him go in – slow, deep, controlled. But he held her firmly as he began to draw.

She clenched her thighs. The sensation was like one she'd never known, as if he was dragging her whole heart out of her, luring it, tempting it forward against its will. And the more he withdrew, the harder her heart beat, her neck filling with heat. It was painful. Not searing, scream-out painful, but she hated to think what it would be like without the anaesthetic. It was a sickening feeling, but at the same time created a sense of elation, of disassociation as the pain dissipated into a dull ache.

Caitlin didn't struggle as he withdrew from the feed to lift her slightly and lower her onto her back on the sofa, his hard and powerful body immediately containing her with ease.

Slamming her hands either side of her head, he interlaced their fingers as his lips glided to the other side of her neck, capturing her earlobe before licking gently back down to her artery.

'Tell me,' she said.

He met her gaze, studied her eyes for a moment as he licked the traces of her blood from his lips.

'What is it?' she asked.

'It's called a soul ripper. Nasty shape-shifting bastard, or bitch, depending on the form it chooses. It's a fourth species. Ethereal most of the time. It lives on the astral plain and only appears here when it wants to. It's impossible to trace. The psychics were right. It rips the astral body out of its victims so it can keep the soul contained within in, preventing it from going into the afterlife. It imprisons the victims on the astral plain with it, feeding off the energy generated by their souls. It sucks them dry until the soul finally evaporates. It can take decades, centuries, before the soul dies out. No peace. No rest. Like I said, nasty. And unfortunately for you, they're compulsive. Once they start on a family line, they have to finish it. Every two years, every five, every seven – each one differs. But they'll come back, precisely on time.'

The very prospect of her parents being trapped in that agony incensed her, made her heart ache. 'But you've seen one? Here? If they're shape-shifters, how do you recognise them?'

'They can only take on the form of the dead. And they're like aswangs. You look in their eyes and your reflection appears upside down. If you're human and you see that and it's looking right back at you, you know you're fucked.'

'But they can be killed.'

'Yes.'

'What happens to the souls then?'

'The astral body dissipates and their souls get freed into the afterlife.'

'Have you ever killed one?'

'Yes.'

'How?'

'It's impossible for anyone with less strength than a master vampire.'

She frowned. 'But you won't help me.'

'That would mean delaying my plans long enough for it to appear. Why would I do that?'

No reason. No reason whatsoever. Not if he truly believed he was capable of getting what he wanted.

'Feel better now?' he asked. 'Now you know the truth?'

'I'll feel better when it's dead.'

He almost smiled, then without hesitation he bit into the area he had prepared. This time he was slower, more intense.

Caitlin clenched her hands in his as he fed smoothly but hungrily. She closed her eyes, lost in the sensation, in her helplessness, as he consumed her with an ease that was inherent to him.

It was as intense as she'd imagined. More. Those times when she'd dared fantasise about it. When the things said by the females who had experienced him had played on her mind. She'd lingered on their recollections, sometimes putting herself in their position before guilt and shame had overruled.

Frustration consumed her as her physical need for him to stop took over, her light-headedness disorientating her. But she knew he hadn't fed enough, not if she wanted to sate him into sleeping. Because instead of feeding as he should, as he was renowned for, he was being temperate with her, just like he had been in the bathroom. To her annoyance, he was clearly more than capable of containing his appetite both for blood and for sex. At least he was with her. Capable because she was a means to an end.

At that point his self-control didn't reassure her; it angered her. It insulted her because she knew exactly the extent he was capable of when driven by desire and need. That was the Kane she needed to see. That was the mercilessness she wanted to experience to quell her own desire as it burned in her chest, as it built beneath her belly button. She wanted him to desire her that much. She needed him to forget himself.

She needed out of there.

But as he licked her again, she knew he was licking away the final traces. He was done. Nothing but a small taster for him despite how much she had given.

As he released her hands ready to move off her, she caught hold of his arm, felt the curve of hard bicep beneath her palm. She knew then she had no right persisting. That something inside her was about to overstep the mark. 'That's it?'

For a moment he didn't react. But his hesitation told her he hadn't expected that response, and that alone gave her a sense of triumph.

His eyes narrowed with intrigue. 'I've taken enough.'

As he broke from her gaze to move away again, she tightened her grip. She knew it was more than just wanting him to feed himself to a stupor – her entire body reluctantly ached and throbbed for him not to pull away. 'I'm not so sure you have,' she said.

It was one step too far. She knew it was. And in that moment she didn't care.

He rested his forearm beside her head, his eyes glinting with curiosity. 'I meant for you.'

'I'm offering you more,' she said. She let go of his arm and tentatively lay her hands either side of her head. In the ultimate act of acquiescence, she broke from his gaze to turn her head to the side, exposing her neck to him.

If he turned her down now, it would crush her. Not just for the sake of her self-esteem, but the loss of the opportunity the perfect moment had created.

He caught hold of her jaw and forced her to look back at him. 'What are you playing at?' he asked, his eyes staring so deep into hers she wondered if he could see the answer for himself.

Her stomach flipped. Her breathing was dangerously shallow. 'Do you want more or not?'

He licked his incisor, his eyes darkening with suspicion.

He took her hands in his again, pinned them above her head. With only a second's delay, he bit into her neck again.

Caitlin jolted as his fangs entered her full force. She gasped despite not wanting to. This time the feed had an edge of punishment – she could feel it. His grip on her wrists had tightened, his groin pressing hard against hers.

She wondered if the more he took, the harder he took. If even in him, there was a certain instinctive loss of control that came with the feed.

She wondered what it would take for him to forget himself. Totally forget himself. What it would feel like. Whether he would still be capable of being as sensual and controlled as he was in the bathroom. Whether he'd have any sense of boundary.

Her stomach flipped, damp heat gathering between her legs.

She knew she needed him to stop. Despite the tension in her head, her body felt shockingly relaxed. Too relaxed. The thought hit her that the anaesthetic he'd used on her neck had filtered elsewhere into her system. Or that the feed had made her delirious somehow.

But if she asked him to stop, he'd have to. For fear of alienating her, he'd have no choice.

If it still was a choice for him.

Her defences were low, because she didn't even flinch as he reached down to unfasten his jeans.

Sex. Sex with Kane Malloy. Right there, right then.

Why the hell wasn't she scared?

He lowered his head to her chest, licked over the upward mound of her breast to her earlobe. As he pushed aside the crotch of her knickers, the tip of his erection quickly and accurately finding her sex, she caught her breath. He pushed in just an inch, and Caitlin tensed and froze.

It was insane.

She was on the brink of giving herself to him unless she pulled back now – unless she pulled back from the bad, dangerous and compulsively sexy vampire who pushed into her a little more.

It hurt despite her arousal, the entrance to her body stretching to accommodate him. But he was shockingly controlled, shockingly steady. He was showing her things. He was showing her just how in control he was. A further taunt. Proof of power.

She closed her eyes, her body already screaming out for him. The pressure at her sex begged for release, his hard body holding such promise.

But even just his pushing only an inch or so inside her already felt too much. Like a mist lifting, she knew it wasn't just stupid to consent – it was dangerous.

She was giving herself to him. More than just physically.

'Enough,' she gasped, as the room's darkness intensified around her.

She looked back into his navy eyes, could feel her lower lip trembling uncontrollably.

But instead of glowering down at her, the last thing she saw was his eyes glinting in amusement before he bit into her again.

Kane eased off her, yanked up his shorts and jeans and sat on the edge of the coffee table. He wiped his mouth with the back of his hand, before licking any final traces of her off his lips.

She'd been trying to play him, but, hell, she'd been convincing. Lying there, offering herself to him. He knew exactly what she'd been trying to achieve. The fact she thought he'd fall for it was just a little too insulting. He'd had no choice but to knock her out with another feed before he ended up doing her some serious damage and because of it she'd left him aching painfully with frustration.

She lay unconscious amongst the cushions. He could tell by the rhythm of her breathing, her lack of swallowing, that she wasn't faking. He reached forward and pushed her hair back to assess his bite marks. Marks that should, by rights, make her his. But Caitlin wasn't for keeping. Caitlin was just a means to an end.

And he'd almost had her. Instead she'd pulled back at the crucial moment, closing down, just like she had in the bathroom. She was too guarded – her emotional barriers too far up to relax enough to accept him yet, even in the subdued state the feed would have got her into. But it was only a yet. She had wavered. It may have only been for a moment, but the temptation had been there.

He should have felt triumph. He'd got her close enough to the brink to make her question herself. For a girl like her, that would mean something. Caitlin was used to ruling with her head, especially when it came to sex. But so was he. Only this time pulling away had been harder than it had been on the bed. This time it had taken a hell of a lot more self-control on his part. And that unsettled him.

She'd tasted so good and felt so good, her every response dangerously evocative. There was a rawness to those responses. An innocence. An inherent sensuality that was hard to find. He thought of her eyes fixed on his, watchful and wary, her pupils fiercely dilated. Those beautiful soft lips, parted slightly and swollen with arousal. The flush to her delicate, pale skin. The beautiful, soft skin of her shoulders and collarbone still exposed. The tempting upward mounds of her breasts contained behind the lacy cream fabric. Her dress bunched around those lithe, warm thighs.

It would have been so easy to spread those thighs and thrust into her as he fed, built her to her climax, to his, and had the sweet, sweet taste of a dual feed. He could have enthralled her. Exhausted her. Taken everything.

And it had taken every reserve of willpower not to. As he'd heard her snatch back a breath, felt the tension in her body as he pushed just a little way inside her, he'd had to calm himself.

Even at the thought of it his erection twitched.

He headed over to the kitchen to grab himself another drink.

He shouldn't have allowed himself to get that worked up. He was going to have to be the master of restraint. But right then, with every part of him aching to consume and dominate her, he wasn't quite as confident he could do it. He had tasted the potential and he wanted more. Much more. More than his plan accounted for. That had been about more than vengeance, more than the response of the vampire in him – it had been about the male in him. He wanted to break her, overcome that tenacity and that resilience. It was a dangerously compelling pull and one he couldn't afford to feel.

He slammed the fridge door and flicked the lid off his beer. He leaned back against the counter as he took a mouthful.

He needed to get a grip. Forget his primal instincts. He only had two and a half days left and there was clearly still a lot of work to do as far as Caitlin was concerned. Her resistance ran deeper than just being a shadow reader. But even if her mind was in control, her body clearly wasn't. And that was the weakness he needed to focus on. Caitlin wanted him sexually, of that he now had no doubt. And her responses told him she liked his self-assurance, she was aroused by his insistence and she enjoyed him taking the lead. She might not have known it yet or, more likely, wasn't willing to accept it, but she liked him in charge of the one area where she wasn't confident enough to take that control. Her turn-on was his – a perfect match.

Maybe upping the ante was what they both needed. Maybe he was playing too gentle.

He knocked back another mouthful and strolled across to his coat. He took out his keys, unlocked the door and headed over to his car. He took her case folders out of the trunk and the book and packets from the glove compartment. He locked the door behind him, placing the keys back in his coat, and stood at the kitchen counter. He unfolded the cloth. One little book to hold a soul as beautiful and powerful as a shadow reader's. He folded the cloth back up, carried the book and the packets over to the wardrobe and tucked them in behind some sweaters on the top shelf. He picked up the folders from the counter and stepped back over to the sofas.

Caitlin hadn't stirred.

He should have revelled in her defencelessness. But he didn't. He should have at least been pleased with the progress, but as she lay there asleep, he wasn't sure he was. Beneath the defiance and the belligerence, beneath the sanctimony and dogmatism, she was just a girl. A lonely, isolated and frightened girl who was even more vulnerable than she realised. But she was also brave and refused to be intimidated. She wanted redemption for her parents and she wasn't going to be taken down without a fight. Because Caitlin was a fighter and he liked that more than anything else about her.

It was a trait working to his advantage. She'd hold on until the bitter end because she believed he was her only hope. And that was exactly what he needed. He had her right where he wanted her.

Caitlin would be his within the next twenty-four hours. He'd make sure of it. Because sex, to her misfortune, had always been his favourite game.

And she'd just opened the floodgates.

# CHAPTER THIRTEEN

It took her a moment to remember where she was. The sofa was warm and comfortable beneath her chest, the TV a distant hum. She could have easily been at home, having fallen asleep in front of a movie again, but as Caitlin opened her eyes, reality hit her hard and fast.

Kane was sat on the sofa opposite, surrounded in paperwork, a pile of A4 sheets in his hand.

He was wide awake and could very well have been the whole time she'd been out. Even if he had slept, it was too late now. Her heart plummeted at the opportunity missed, a sinking feeling coupled with anxiety again. She lay there watching him for a moment, his eyes narrowed intensely on the content of the papers.

The moment lingered in her mind, the moment he had almost pushed himself into her. The moment she had nearly given in and let him go all the way. Something stirred low in her abdomen again.

She should have been gone. Long gone.

Looking more closely at the array of cardboard folders sprawled over the coffee table, she recognised them as hers: her personal reports on him. Every dark little detail. All her scribbles. Embarrassment and discomfort surged through her. She sat up slowly, trying to counteract the sense of imbalance provoked by her light-headedness. She pulled the sleeves back up over her shoulders and refastened her dress. She grabbed a cushion and pulled it against her chest as she curled her legs under her. 'Have I been out long?'

He glanced up at her before turning his attention back to the report.

'Just a couple of hours.' He frowned and exhaled tersely at what he read. 'Do you guys just make this stuff up as you go along, or what?' His eyes narrowed in concentration as he continued to read. A smile followed a frown. There was a slight widening of his eyes, and then a shake of his head. 'I never did that,' he said, chucking the report aside. He flicked through the next. 'Or that.' He looked across at her. 'All these sordid claims and you still came after me?'

'I had no choice, did I?'

He threw the reports on the table and reached for his beer. Leaning back in the sofa, he stretched his legs out on the table. 'It's a shame there wasn't a report on how it takes more than a few minutes of feeding to knock me out, isn't it? It would have saved you a lot of effort earlier. Still,' he said, lifting the bottle to his lips, 'I'm not complaining.'

She narrowed her eyes at his goading, unease squeezing her chest that he'd worked it out. 'I got a name, so neither am I.'

He almost smiled. 'You coming after me was about far more than just getting that name and unearthing a few hidden vampire secrets. There's a third strain in all of this. A very convenient third strain.' There was a glimmer of an arrogant taunt in his eyes. 'You would have pursued me regardless.'

'And what makes you say that?'

He reached for the report beside him and read, 'Kane has a deadly appeal, undoubtedly from being such an accomplished lover. Despite his disturbing and somewhat sexually sadistic inclinations, he has a fatal charm. The females who have engaged in sexual acts with him proclaim loyalty in spite of his subsequent characteristic disregard for them. His good looks alongside an intelligent and astute mind no doubt add to the fascination.'

She frowned. 'Would you like me to frame it for you?'

'Your words, sweetheart.'

'My objective words, yes.'

'As objective as that pulse rate when I pinned you to the wall? Those curt little breaths? That fluttering heart? Rumour has it you've always had a thing for me.'

He could have at least given her time to wake up properly and come to her senses. 'Is that why you're arrogant enough to think you can get my soul? Because you think I fancy you?'

'I didn't for sure. But I do now.'

Caitlin exhaled curtly. 'You're unbelievable.'

'Say yes next time I've got you on your back and you'll find out just how unbelievable.'

Even knowing him as she did, his blatant audacity took her aback. 'You're shameless.'

'You're curious.'

'Taken from the bite, I can assure you you're not my type.'

'Taken from the way you flinched when I got inside you, you haven't had enough experience to know your type.'

She felt irritation simmer. 'I've had all the experience I need.'

'I'll show you otherwise.'

'Do you really think I'm going to give my soul up to you that easily?'

'When you were teetering on the brink of consenting to me after only one night? Let me think about that.'

'I was toying with you.'

'Be careful what you confess to, Caitlin. Next time it might convince me not to be such a gentleman.'

'You make such sweet threats.'

'They're not threats. Unless you think you're at risk of feeling something more.'

How she managed to hold his gaze as she told such a blatant lie, she had no idea. 'I can assure you, I'm not at risk of feeling anything.'

'So let me fuck you.'

The shock of his directness made her stomach flip. She should have felt appalled at his crudeness, but the rawness of the statement coupled with the intensity in his eyes caused heat to rush between her legs. 'I don't want to sleep with you.'

'I wouldn't hurt you, Caitlin – whatever is intimated in those reports.'

'And what else have they got wrong, Kane? You're just an innocent being set up by Xavier Carter, right? Because he craves your power so much?'

'I'm no innocent. Nor would I claim to be. But I'm not the egotistical, self-seeking, barbaric and sadistic bastard those reports suggest either.'

'And it must be a real effort to convince me of that – to hold back on your true nature. Has the frustration set in yet? Did you think I'd give in to you earlier? I warned you – you help me or you don't stand a chance of getting what you need. In three days, it's going to be here. You don't want to help me kill it, fine. But if you haven't got my soul by then, you won't have any choice, will you?'

His eyes narrowed. 'Is that what you're counting on?'

'You're going to have to kill it one way or another.'

His gaze didn't waver. 'Your defiance is such a turn-on. It's a good thing I don't believe your soul to be as inaccessible as you claim, or I'd be tempted to use you up right now and find myself another shadow reader. Maybe I should give Isla a go.'

Her heart skipped a beat, and his smirk told her he'd sensed it.

'What? You don't think you're expendable? Who's the arrogant one now, Caitlin?'

Arrogant enough to think she'd worked him out. Arrogant enough to think taking her was all about the lycans. He'd never actually confirmed it. Even she had to acknowledge it still made no sense why he'd need to extract her soul.

Maybe he had only picked her because he thought she had a thing for him. Maybe their confrontation in the club had been part of confirming what he'd already suspected. Maybe those responses she'd fought to conceal had saved her life.

Maybe it was nothing to do with the lycans or Arana at all.

She needed air. She needed to get away from him. She couldn't think straight with him looking at her. She pushed the cushion from her lap and marched over to the bathroom. She closed the door firmly behind her and hurried up onto the bath. There was only a small gap in the window but it still let in a small amount of late-afternoon light and an all-important breeze. She clutched the windowsill and let the air fill her lungs, despite knowing the toxicity renowned in Blackthorn. It still helped clear her head.

He was just upping the ante – making her doubt herself. Her resistance during the bite had worried him. He was cornering her. He was bound to be feeling the pressure of time. But if he were telling the truth about not needing her specifically, there was no telling how much more of that depleting time he would allow her.

She looked down at her hands to see they were trembling again. One lingering look from those intense navy eyes, one sentence of sexual intent, and she was a pathetic wreck again.

Damn it, she couldn't let this happen. She needed to be stronger. She needed to work out what the hell was going on if she stood any chance of winning this. Another night would soon be passing. Another night wasted when she could be out there with the name he had given her.

She needed to sleep with him.

Her own train of thought startled her.

It was out of the question.

But it could break the spell, like letting the venom out of the bite. Sleeping with Kane could release everything she had pent up for too long. It could also buy her time while quashing everything she was feeling for him and give her a fighting chance.

She could see what he was like firsthand, if she dared put herself in that situation. Like Rob had said – he wouldn't be gentle, he wouldn't be kind, he wouldn't be patient. And maybe that was what she needed – maybe that wasn't a bad thing.

On the flip side, she could risk feeling more for him. Already he had proved himself to be far more capable of gentleness than she had imagined. Intuitive. Perceptive. Attentive. She thought of how easily she nearly let him continue, so lost in the moment. She could end up giving him exactly what he'd brought her there for. Because, as much as she despised admitting it, it could never be just sex. It could never be just sex with a vampire who made her shiver meeting his gaze, who sent waves of arousal through her with one touch, who was already suppressing a lifetime of inhibitions and convictions of celibacy.

She used the toilet, washed her hands and sank onto the bath steps.

She rested her head in her hands. Max and Rob had been right. She was stupid to think she could take Kane on. Her training, her expertise, even her bucket-loads of knowledge on him meant nothing when she stared into his eyes. Only Xavier had believed she could do it. If he had at all. Feelings of doubt crept over her at recollections of the sincerity of Kane's claims out in the garage.

Kane had been right to suspect Xavier had sent her in. He'd been right to suspect he'd come down from his ivory tower. Xavier, who was clearly intent on catching Kane in the act, who had sent her in undercover knowing anything could happen to her. Anything to give him the hard evidence he needed to bring Kane in.

Because Kane had never been caught in the act. Witnesses had never come forward. And so much of what Kane had said about his own kind made sense. It was easy to assume it was fear that kept witnesses away. But there was still so much about the inner workings of third species they didn't know. And there was even less they knew and understood about the masters of the species.

A master of the species who was waiting beyond the door for her. A vampire who knew how to get what he wanted. A vampire with a sensual, sensitive touch that sparked parts of her she thought inactive and even defunct. A vampire who promised to be a sexy, exciting and fulfilling lover.

She clenched her hands between her tense thighs and stared at the door. A vampire who was using her for one thing only.

That's what she would keep at the forefront of her mind. That was what would keep her heart safe, however her disloyal body responded to him.

She couldn't fall for someone who used her, who manipulated her. Someone who was so arrogant they didn't even at least pretend to like her. If he was conceited enough to believe she'd fall for him despite that, maybe she'd play that game. There was too much for her to lose not to. That untouchable aura of his was created just as much by her head as his reputation. She felt intimidated by him, inferior to him, but she had no reason to. Maybe she was fighting too hard. Maybe she was fighting herself too hard. Maybe she needed to call his bluff. Maybe it was time she upped the ante.

And somewhere deep inside, somewhere she was beginning to willingly acknowledge she wanted to press a few of his buttons. She wanted to dare to toy with him. She wanted to push her professional role aside for a while.

She forced herself up off the steps and opened the bathroom door. Kane was still on the sofa, reading through the paperwork. Her heart pounded and she instantly felt herself flounder again. She needed a few more moments. Just a few more. She veered into the kitchen, opened the fridge and took out a bottle of water. She wrapped her trembling hand around the top but struggled to twist it open. Tightening her grip, she exhaled tersely when it still didn't budge.

She was so focused on the task that she flinched when she realised he was behind her. She let him take the bottle, turned to face him and watched him twist the cap off with ease.

For all her resolution in the bathroom, her nerves gave way.

'Thanks,' she said, as she moved to brush past him.

But Kane braced one arm on the fridge, blocking her as he placed the other on the counter beside her. 'What's it going to take to get inside you?'

Her heart lunged. 'That's been your burning question all along, hasn't it, Kane?'

He almost smiled at her flashback to the interrogation room. 'Look me in the eye and tell me I'm wasting my time.'

Her pulse pounded in her ears as she refused to falter under the intensity of his gaze. 'I'm a little old for playground bully tactics.'

'Yet here we are – just you and me, all alone behind the bike sheds. So what are you going to do now?'

Heat flushed through her body. When she'd played through these fantasies in her mind it had been safe – she'd controlled the outcome. But this was real. She was about to play a dangerous game she knew there was no turning back from. And she'd never felt such a surge of arousal, her whole body aching and tingling. Arousal that gave her the courage she needed as his navy eyes penetrated painfully deep into hers.

She needed him to say the right things, to do the right things. She had no doubt he was more than capable. 'No, Kane – what are you going to do now? You like to be in control, so you make the next move. Then I'll let you know.'

He took the bottle of water off her and braced his arms either side of the counter, his mouth dangerously close to hers. 'Admit you want me.'

She swallowed harder than she would have liked. 'I think you've convinced yourself enough for both of us.'

He moved closer, his hips touching hers as he slipped his hand up under her dress.

As he thumbed the band of her knickers at her hip, her stomach tensed. She gripped the counter, silently pleading that she wouldn't make a fool of herself again.

'Why does sex with me scare you, Caitlin?'

'I'm not scared. I just don't like you.'

'Is that right?' She was sure she saw a glimmer of a smile as he brushed her hair back over her shoulder before leaning in to lick then kiss the rapid pulse in her neck. 'We can play these games all day, all night, and they can get darker and more dangerous with every passing hour. But I will have you,' he whispered against her ear. He nipped her lightly on her earlobe and Caitlin's legs nearly buckled.

'You can do what you like to me, Kane. I know that. But you need to get it into your head that doing what you want to me and getting what you want from me are two very different things.'

He placed his left hand over hers, trapping it against the counter. 'And what is the worst thing I can do to you, Caitlin?' he asked, easing his other hand between her legs. She flinched as he tucked her knickers aside, slid his fingers over her moistness. A warm flush swamped her, her legs weakened. 'Just how bad a vampire do you imagine me to be?'

As he eased his finger inside her, Caitlin shuddered, her nails digging into the counter. 'I'm warning you, Kane,' she said, catching her breath. 'You do something I don't like, and you've lost. I'm losing my soul either way. How confident are you that you know me? Or are you so arrogant that you think you can do anything to me and I'll still want you? Or so good that you can do anything and I'll still want you?'

She felt his smile as he nipped her earlobe again. 'That's very dangerous talk, Caitlin. I've played this kind of game before,' he said, easing his finger out of her to replace it with two. The pressure and discomfort caused her to snap back a breath again. She slammed her free hand against his hip to forge what little distance she could. 'You only play it when you know someone inside out,' he added, sliding his fingers back out again to caress her clitoris. She shuddered and bit into her lip. 'It's a game that will make or break you.'

'You're expecting me to say no again, aren't you?' she said, more breathily than she intended.

'Am I?'

As he slid his finger in her again, she felt that stirring deep in her abdomen that she had neither the desire nor the will to walk away from. If these were her last few days, and one way or another she knew they were, she was going to have at least one time with Kane Malloy. She owed it to herself. Whatever his intentions, it made no difference. He was never going to declare undying love. That wasn't what it was about. She wasn't that naïve. And she wanted him in all his rawness. She wanted to get as close to him as she could. And right there and then she had never wanted him more.

She knew as much as he did that this had been a long time coming. Hell, she'd fantasised about it long enough. She just had to keep her eyes open and remind herself he was just using her. And she could use him too. She was a consenting adult and so was he. She needed to get him out of her system. She needed to sate the surge that his touch sent through her body. He could disappoint her. Hurt her. Fail to arouse her. All her preconceptions could fizzle into nothing.

Because she knew, as undoubtedly as he did, that bringing shadow readers to orgasm was notoriously difficult. Even Rob, an experienced and tender lover, had never succeeded. And something deeply sexual inside her itched to know if Kane was capable. If she could be sated. Truly sated.

She buckled as he pushed his finger all the way in, a cold perspiration sweeping over her. And as he placed his hand on her hip to keep her against the counter, she trembled, his strength and his confidence an evocative combination. His kiss was intoxicating as he traced down her neck to her shoulder – exploring, caressing, cool and wet and provocative.

She knew it before and she knew it even more then: he had been right about the third strand. The third strand that had always been there. And it refused to be suppressed, refused it even more with his hard body against hers, a body that could become part of hers if she'd just reciprocate.

He withdrew his finger, his thumb finding her clitoris. 'Did Rob ever make you come?'

She frowned, angry that Kane had broken the magic, angry that she could almost believe he'd done it on purpose. Tension ricocheted through her body. 'More times than you'd think possible.'

'Liar,' he said, easing her knickers down to mid-thigh before they slid to the floor. 'Do you want to know how it feels?'

She glowered at him, her body aching. 'You're a conceited bastard, aren't you?'

'Decades of practice.' He lifted her up onto the counter, spreading her legs around his hips in one easy move. He tugged her towards him so his erection pressed against her damp heat through the softness of his jeans.

Caitlin wanted to be scared, would feel better for being scared, could despise him if he scared her. But he didn't. She wanted the controlled façade to slip. She wanted to overcome the feelings she was developing. 'You are so going to fail, Kane.'

'You are so going to learn,' he said, his navy eyes sparkling with mischief as he lifted her off the counter and onto to the table behind him. He kicked the chairs away and lay her down so she was flat on her back on the surface.

She watched him strip off his T-shirt, the flex of those muscles, the feel of his body against hers quashing the surge of panic she felt. He unfastened his jeans, and she felt his bare thighs between hers. And as she felt his hardness press against her sex, she braced herself.

She tried to suppress everything she'd heard about him. His twisted sexual endeavours, the beautiful females he'd been with. The consensus was that he was a proficient and demanding lover. Probably too proficient and demanding for her. But she needed that – she needed someone whose sexual confidence brought out hers. She needed his persistence and tenacity and she needed the way he was looking at her right then as if he could devour her.

He pinned her hands above her head and gazed down into her eyes, his delay arousing her
further.

The pressure building at her sex was uncomfortable, her stomach tightening to the point of pain. She knew her breaths were erratic, she knew her body was flushing with heat and she knew he was picking up on every little response.

He pushed in just a little like he had before, the sensation making her gasp, the enticing playfulness in his eyes outweighing the darkness of his intent. She closed her eyes to avoid looking at him, to avoid that intimacy.

She clenched her hands. It felt shockingly good, shockingly intense as he started to push his way inside her, slow, deliberate, giving her time to adjust, giving himself time to enjoy the sensation. She was unsure how far he was entering her, but knew from the discomfort it was further than last time. As she started to accept him, he pushed harder, the arm around her waist keeping her in position as he partly withdrew to ease inside her again.

And as her body finally adjusted, her arousal easing the penetration, he pushed all the way inside her.

Caitlin buckled and shuddered. She bit into her bottom lip to silence herself, but was unable to curtail the heaviness of her breaths.

She'd never felt so complete. Never felt so alive. But she wouldn't give him an indication. She wouldn't give him the satisfaction.

His moves were shockingly calm, surprisingly controlled. They spoke of someone experienced, someone who knew how to pleasure a woman, who enjoyed the sexual act. This was as much about sating her as sating himself. It wasn't a selfish act, a selfish penetration.

She shuddered as he withdrew only to push all the way inside her, this time one slow, complete penetration, setting her nerves alight. She clenched her fists, a whimper escaping. But the hurt gradually became less painful, the discomfort became pleasurable.

He combed back her hair over her shoulder, braced himself up on one arm as he pushed back inside her in another single, slick movement. But this time the thrust was intentionally forceful.

The warm rush flooding her body stunned Caitlin and made her tremble as he penetrated her hard and deep. He twisted the hair at the nape of her neck, coiling it in his hand, his tongue gliding up from her cleavage to her throat as he increased his pace. The carnality sent her reeling, his playful but threatening nips on her neck adding to her arousal.

And as he continued to thrust, he released her hair and pinned her hands above her head, his other hand moving to find her most sensitive core, caressing her already engorged nub. And as his thumb found pace with his thrusts, she no longer had any control over her body, of her escalating arousal, until an alien climax built in her fingertips, her toes, heat washing through her body.

On the cusp of demanding he stop, he moved his hand from between her legs. He interlaced his fingers with hers again, lowered himself back onto her, his arm back around her waist as he held her with total control. He penetrated her with a force that should have hurt her, her body already aching from his onslaught, but her body was getting used to him now, finding it easier to take him.

She caught her breath in shock as she felt her arousal starting to peak. Arousal that rose from her aching toes, at first icy cold then hot, the pins and needles almost unbearable. Her body throbbed to the point it was almost painful, her fingertips numb. Thoughts slipped from her mind other than Kane inside her, as she felt the tension in his body at his own impending climax.

But she couldn't come. Her whole body cried out for it. She teetered in agony on the brink of what she had no doubt was an orgasm.

But nothing happened.

Tears trickled down her cheeks as Kane tensed inside her before ejaculating hard and powerful, a cruel reminder of her own inadequacies.

Kane remained inside her for a few moments. He stayed inside her until her breaths calmed and he stopped pulsating. Then he gently withdrew.

He pulled up his shorts and buttoned up his jeans as Caitlin eased off the table to the nearest, upright chair. She kept her gaze lowered, smoothed down her hair in what appeared more to be an act of self-assurance than concern about her appearance. She was still blocking him out. She might have let him in physically, but emotionally those barriers were now even further up. She was still in control. Irritatingly in control.

Which was more than could be said for him.

He should have felt nothing, but instead he felt aggravated. He knew she'd feel good but he hadn't expected her to feel that good. Her tight body had closed around him for the perfect fit – slick, hot, silky. But it was more than that. He'd come hard and he'd come fast and it had been because of more than just the feel of her body. Instead of lurid and salacious thoughts as he was thrusting into her, thoughts of violating her and degrading her, he'd found himself turned on just by the intimacy. All he could think of was how she was giving herself to him, found himself turned on knowing how much she must have desired him to have consented. A simple penetrative act shouldn't have been that intense. Sex was supposed to have created distance for him, not made him desire her more. Instead she had intoxicated him with that fragile body and those intense eyes, that nervousness, those enticing breaths. And the fact she had emotionally fought so hard against him had further fuelled his arousal.

He'd been inside too many females who writhed and moaned and accepted him easily, been willing to do anything to please him. Sexually he'd done everything that was physically and emotionally possible over the decades. He'd experimented and played and found satisfaction through all sorts of means, but it had been a long time since he'd come that powerfully. He'd never come across a female he'd wanted to consume as much as he did her in those moments. Moments when he'd nearly forgot himself. She had put him in dangerous territory, which could so easily ruin everything.

And as he looked at her, he felt something stir. Something he had no place feeling. Something he needed to get control of. If it had been anyone else looking that vulnerable, he would have already got their coat and told them to go home.

He should show her some affection or compassion. Give her reassurance or even just a compliment. Because making her feel safe was the next way in. Safe was a way she hadn't felt in a long time. Something that would seal the deal further.

But she wasn't safe. And he wasn't willing to play that game.

And when he detected what looked like shame and embarrassment in her eyes, he almost felt a glimmer of guilt.

She'd wanted to climax. She was ashamed she hadn't. In her naivety, she'd thought it could happen that easily. She didn't see that what they'd done was just the start.

He stepped away from her, tried to get a grip on himself. He opened the fridge and grabbed himself another beer and her a bottle of water. He flicked the lid off his bottle, picked up a chair and placed it adjacent to hers. He put the bottle of water in front of her on the table.

She didn't flinch.

He took a mouthful of beer, the silence uncomfortable even for him. 'Conception's impossible unless there's an eclipse,' he said. 'Just in case it crossed your mind.'

'It didn't.' She shoved her chair back and stood a little too quickly. She pressed her hand to the table for support, before regaining her balance and striding past the table and through to the bathroom.

He could have reached out and caught her, but he let her go.

The honesty of her words cut him deeper than they should have. She had no reason to worry because in her mind it was pointless. She might have been hell-bent on killing the soul ripper, but she didn't expect to survive it. She was fighting with everything she had even though, deep down, she believed her own survival was a lost cause. He had been her last resort. It had taken everything, had gone against every instinct, to ask for his help. She'd done it because redemption for her parents was more important than her own pride. Getting one over on the soul ripper that had killed them was more important than her own safety. Caitlin wanted this badly, needed it. And he understood those feelings only too well. But he wouldn't let it cloud his judgement.

And he couldn't give her time to close in on herself again. Her mind was fending him off only because her heart was sending out signals that it was feeling vulnerable.

That was exactly what he wanted. Instead, he felt like a complete and utter bastard for what he needed to do next.

He'd give her a little while. Maybe finish his beer. She could try and avoid him if she wanted to, but there was no way he was going to give her that luxury.

Not now.

# CHAPTER FOURTEEN

No. No. No. No. No. That was not supposed to have happened. Caitlin clutched her head as she paced the bathroom. What the hell had she been thinking? She dragged her hands down to her mouth as she faced the windows. And how the hell had it happened so quickly? Sleep with him, yes, but not less than fifteen minutes after resolving to.

She sat down on the steps and rested her forehead on her clenched knuckles.

She'd lost it. She'd totally lost it. She cursed in frustration, still aching and throbbing and tingling, every inch of her skin alive from his touch. Her stomach flipped at the recollection of how easily he had got her on the table, just like he had back in the interrogation room. She hadn't even thought about how easy it would have been for him to bite her too. It could have taken her hours to recover from that. Hours she couldn't afford to lose.

Damn it.

She wondered if her walking away had made it worse. If she should have just stayed there and shrugged it off as if it was nothing.

But it wasn't nothing. She'd just had sex with a vampire. Worse than that, a vampire she had craved since she'd first laid eyes on him. She'd had sex with Kane Malloy. And he'd just proved himself to be everything she'd imagined him to be and more.

But even that hadn't been enough.

She impatiently wiped away an irritating tear of embarrassment. He'd proved it – she was useless. He was flawless and still she couldn't be sated. She truly was defunct. She'd given herself to him – and for what? To have him laugh at her ineptness? Or to smear his masculinity? Because if he didn't already hate her before, he'd hate her even more now.

She'd proven to him just how unbreakable she was – even more unbreakable than even she knew. If he didn't need her, he may as well just kill her.

Her plan had backfired in more ways than one. A plan she'd deluded herself into thinking could actually work. Just like she'd deluded herself into believing she could abstain from him long enough to get what she wanted.

She couldn't go back out there. The way she was feeling, she didn't want to go back out there ever again.

She'd had the most gorgeous male she'd ever come across, and she'd just lain there, too tense and frigid even for the basics.

She snapped her attention to the door as the handle turned.

Kane pushed the door all the way open and leaned against the doorway with a nonchalance that made what they'd just done all the more painful. He took a mouthful of beer before lowering his arm to his side. 'Are you okay?'

She looked back ahead. 'Fine.'

'You don't look fine.'

'Really,' she said, meeting his gaze, unable to conceal her glower. 'I'm fine.'

'Then why are you looking at me like you could kill me?' He lifted his bottle back to his lips, concealing the hint of a smile that had crept there.

'I wouldn't have to look at you at all if you gave me some privacy.'

He lowered his bottle again and pulled away from the doorframe. He placed his bottle on the corner of the sink and sauntered over to her. He sat on the floor directly in front of her and leaned back on braced arms, his legs splayed.

She curled her toes into the carpeted step as she refused to look away. She would not let her gaze wander. She would not let herself be distracted by the honed perfection displayed in front of her.

But rather than being aggravated by her defiance, the glint in Kane's eyes told her he was amused by it. She averted her gaze and focused on the patter of the rain at the window rather than the excruciating silence between them.

At first she thought him touching her toes was an accident. But as she looked back at him, she saw from his hint of a smile that his caress was very much intentional.

'You need to think less and play more,' he said.

She knew she should have withdrawn her foot up onto the next step out of his reach, but she didn't. 'Whereas you play games all the time, don't you, Kane?'

'I nearly lost control out there. You do know that, don't you?'

She warily met his gaze.

He slid his big toe into the gap next to hers, the rest of his toes covering hers. 'What happened on that table, that spark, it doesn't happen often.'

Her heart skipped a beat. 'I didn't feel a spark.'

'No? I don't remember the last time I came that quick or that power-fully.'

Her pulse raced. She was looking for the mocking in his eyes, but they were devoid of it. She'd assumed he'd got impatient. Had sensed he was getting nowhere so had sated himself to get it over with quickly. Even now heat scorched her face at the humiliation. He'd probably felt nothing the entire time, nothing but triumph for finally getting her to concede. And now he was trying to make up for it.

She withdrew her foot from his, lifting both feet onto the next step up as she tucked her dress beneath her thighs.

'You put yourself under too much pressure,' he added.

'Maybe I just didn't enjoy it.'

'Did I not misbehave enough for you? Because you like me playing the bad vampire, don't you? It makes you feel safe.'

She stared at him aghast, his words striking too deep a chord. Apprehension squeezed as a damp heat renewed between her legs.

'Ironic,' he added. 'But true. It terrifies you how much I excite you, how easily you gave yourself to me out there, how that heart of yours isn't quite as impenetrable as you think.'

'This has nothing to do with my heart.'

'For a girl like you, when it comes to sex, it's always about your heart.'

'So you hoped you'd get me swooning? You thought it would be that easy? You were good, Kane, but obviously you weren't that good.'

His smile resonated in his stunning navy eyes, but also revealed a hint of those lethal incisors. 'Ouch. Stake me through the heart, why don't you.'

'Trust me, if the opportunity arose…'

He laughed. It was the first time she'd ever heard him laugh. It was the first time she'd ever seen him laugh. It was fleeting, but intoxicating.

'Maybe I should try again,' he said, 'Maybe I shouldn't take it so easy this time.'

Her heart lunged. 'Once was enough.'

'No. Clearly you think I failed.'

'I never said that. You just weren't as good as I'd thought you'd be.'

'You're just full of compliments, aren't you, Caitlin?'

'I'm sure you'll get over it.'

A smile escaped then dissipated. 'I warned you these games could get darker.'

'And I keep telling you I'm not fragile.'

'You're more fragile than you can possibly conceive, little girl.'

She stared as deep into his eyes as she dared. This was him – the real Kane seeping out again. The Kane that would remind her how stupid she'd been. The Kane she couldn't possibly feel anything for. 'I'm guessing you've worked out you're out of your depth thinking you can break a shadow reader. It'll take more than a handsome face and a few well-rehearsed moves.'

'You can stop that soul ripper getting what it wants, Caitlin. You just need to make a choice. You can keep blocking me, keep that self-control and keep fighting me for the next two days until it comes and takes exactly what it wants all over again, or you can give in to me. Let me get there first. And then you can look that soul ripper in the eyes and tell it to go fuck itself. You might not have your soul, but at least you'll be alive. You win and I win. All you have to do is learn to let go.'

The insult of how easy he made it sound was too much to bear. 'Is this what you meant back in the interrogation room about me giving you my soul willingly? You making me an offer I can't refuse? Or am I to take it as an ultimatum? Well, you can go to hell, Kane.' Her heart pounded, but she wasn't going to be the first to look away. Not this time. 'I'll take my chances with the soul ripper before I give you what you want.'

As soon as she'd said it, she knew she'd made a horrible mistake.

His gaze was as immoveable as hers as the rain smashed against the window, his eyes flashing darkly with unnerving sobriety. She caught her breath and braced herself as he stood up. But he didn't look at her as he lifted his bottle back off the sink and strolled back out of the bathroom.

She couldn't move. Her heart pounded in her ears. Every instinct, everything she knew about him, told her this silence meant trouble.

Big trouble.

# CHAPTER FIFTEEN

Caitlin stood from the steps, but remained rooted to the spot as she stared warily at the open bathroom door. She wrapped her arm around her waist and chewed on her thumbnail.

She heard music, music that became louder. Louder because Kane was turning it up until she could hear every word of the pounding rock song. The room beyond became dark as he switched off the wall light, only the flashing glow of the television igniting the space. Curiosity urged her to step up to the threshold, but nerves made her legs leaden.

She sat back down, clutched the step either side of her, not daring take her attention off the gaping doorway.

But he didn't come back.

Minutes seemed to pass, but she was sure it must have been less. She tucked her hair behind her ears and then clenched her hands in her lap. Whatever he was up to, he was taking his time.

The smatters of rain intensified and poured like a mini-waterfall from clogged guttering above. The breeze was picking up, whistling through the small gaps in the windows. She should have felt cold, and she did to the touch. But panic made her perspire, a thin coating already lining her palms.

If there had been a lock on the door she would have run over and slammed it shut, secured herself inside until she'd at least got a grip.

It was all part of his games – leaving her there suffering and pondering, imagining the worse.

*Just how bad a vampire do you imagine me to be?*

She scowled at the door. He couldn't do this to her – manipulate her like this. Because that's what he was doing by walking out of there and saying nothing. By leaving her alone in the silence. He was treating her like a petulant child, so petulant was subsequently what she felt. He was punishing her. Or he just didn't care.

He couldn't have given up. Kane didn't give up on anything. Her chest clenched. He could have tried harder. He could have tried again. He could have persisted a little. If only he'd known how painfully close she had been. How he had made her feel.

Her throat constricted. She was upset. She had to acknowledge it. She was upset because Kane had walked out on her. She should have heaved a sigh of relief, been grateful for some time alone. But all she wanted to do was go out there and find him. Even arguing with him would be better than being sat there in isolation wondering if it was all over – if that was it.

Because it might have been.

Her heart thudded. He might have taken her at her word. Her failure on the table might have convinced him it was a waste of his time and energy pursuing her any further. He might have already been making plans to find another shadow reader. Maybe she wasn't as integral to his plans after all. He might even have already left to go and find one.

Another shadow reader to spend time with. Another shadow reader to taunt, tease and seduce.

The pang in her heart wasn't panic. It was something even more terrifying.

She stood up despite the tremor in her thighs. She couldn't just sit here as he made decisions about her fate. She couldn't let him discard her like she was nothing.

She tentatively crossed to the door.

There were no obvious signs of him. But the door to the outer room was halfway open. Her heart skipped a beat. He was still around. He hadn't left her. He'd probably gone back to do some work on his car –

to take his frustrations out on that. And if he'd resolved to kill her, he clearly wasn't intending to act on it yet.

She needed to talk to him, not that she knew what she'd say. More than that, she needed to see him. She needed to look him in the eyes to see if he'd given up on her.

The music resounded in her ears, the increased darkness softening the room around her as she headed over to the door.

She stopped at the gap. She couldn't see anything in the shadows beyond, not from the angle she was stood at, so she opened the door a little further and stepped up to the threshold.

She froze. Her mouth dropped.

He was pounding into the punchbag, every move swift, precise and controlled. He was in nothing but a pair of low-riding sweatpants that showed off his sculpted, lithe perfection in all its physical glory as he punched and kicked. Even partially masked by the shadows, he looked phenomenal in action.

Her heart skipped a beat, her mouth dry, a rush of heat flooding her lower abdomen.

Frustrated, angry, bored, routine – whatever his reasons for punishing the bag, she knew it was an image she would never recover from, even if her life did only extend to a few more hours.

How she managed to cross the room towards him, she had no idea. But she did manage it, even if she didn't remember the journey. She leaned back against his car, facing him, her hands at the small of her back.

He didn't stop straight away, but when he did he faced her fully. His usually undetectable breathing was more frequent and heavier. A sheen coated his skin, a few traces of which he wiped off his forehead with the back of his hand. He unravelled the white tape from around his left hand, something he clearly used to protect his knuckles. His eyes were terrifyingly dark as they met hers.

Right then, right there, she could have thrown herself at him whatever the consequences. The sense of liberation was intoxicating.

She should have been frightened, but those eyes – dark and intense and unyielding as they were – also glinted with a self-possession that had a lure all of its own.

As he walked across the few feet towards her, she couldn't speak, her toes digging into the cold, rough concrete.

His appraisal of her was swift, almost cold.

She bit back a breath.

It took no effort on his part to spin her around and pin her up against the car.

She was instantly back in the shadows of the corridor, his hard body taking her by surprise, giving her heart the biggest jolt to life she had ever known. The spark, even back then, telling her she was playing a far more dangerous game than she'd been willing to accept.

This time he didn't say anything as he kicked her legs apart, slammed her hands onto the bonnet of the car.

She could hardly breath, uncertain whether it was from fear or arousal. But this could be it – the moment he ended it. One fatal bite, one twist of her neck, and it would be all over. But all she could feel was that capable body; all she could see was those strong, masculine hands holding hers; all she could smell was that musky, woody scent. And close to her ear, she heard those subtle, infrequent breaths that reminded her he was far from human.

'What took you so long?' he asked softly against her ear.

Words failed her as he forced her wrists together, encircling them with just one hand, keeping them on the roof of the car.

'Remind me, how long have you been hunting me, Caitlin?'

All she could think of was his lips – those beautiful, cool, masculine lips against her ear. She tersely licked her own, but her mouth was still too dry. 'Tracking. Not hunting.'

'Semantics.' He raked her hair back from her neck, lowered his mouth to her ear again. 'That's all it's been for years, isn't it? Me and the soul ripper consuming your every thought, every motivation, every waking moment. You've hunted me for so long that you think you know me. But you don't know me. You don't know me at all. But I know you. I've been watching you for a long time. Wanting you. Wanting to break you. And now I know how. I've worked out that to make you lose control, I've got to take that control. Completely.'

Her stomach flipped, her heart lunged. He'd asked her how bad a vampire she imagined him to be. Right then, she didn't care. She knew his idea of bad and her idea of bad were probably two completely different things, but something told her she was about to find out how different.

He moved his hips just an inch to drag the back of her dress up to bunch at the small of her back.

Caitlin flinched and instinctively tried to free her hands, but his slap on the exposed side of her behind made her still.

'Don't move,' he warned. He nipped her lightly on the ear, his cool thumb gliding firmly over the curve of exposed flesh. 'Careful now, I can hear that heart pumping. There's only so much temptation a vampire can take.'

She bit into her bottom lip as he pressed her hard against the car again, the metal cold against the heat of her thighs and sex through the thin cotton of her dress. 'What are you going to do?' she asked, the tension in tone unnerving her, but not as much as the undertones of arousal seeping through with it.

He tugged down his sweatpants, pressed his erection flat against the cleft between her buttocks as he closed the gap again, his chest hard and tight against the back. 'What do you think I'm going to do?'

She raked her nails against the roof and braced herself. 'Don't you hurt me,' she warned breathily, surprised it wasn't more of a plea. But some sixth sense told her he had no intention of hurting her, that it was nothing about causing her pain. Not entirely.

But sometimes he forgot. Sometimes he forgot just how fragile humans are compared to third-species mates.

'But Caitlin,' he whispered against her ear, his rasp igniting every nerve ending. He lowered himself slightly to direct his erection up between her legs. Pressing the tip against her sex, his lips hovered over her ear again. 'I thought you said you weren't fragile.'

And he pushed.

It wasn't the gentle nudge it had been before, a gradual breaking inside her, building her arousal with his own. This time he gave her no time to adjust. This time he made the most of her wetness. This time he was feeding his own hunger as well as hers as he entered her in one slow, steady but unrelenting move, filling her to the hilt.

Caitlin cried out and arched her back, but he pressed her hard back against the car. She flexed her fingers. Closed her eyes. Her body shuddered. Her own dampness masked her thighs as he withdrew only to thrust again. This time it was harder and intentionally so. She dropped her head back against his shoulder and cried out again, her nails digging deep into the palms of her hands.

'I wanted you from the first moment I saw you,' he said against her ear. 'And when I had you up against the wall in that corridor, I could have taken you so easily.'

Tension gripped the pit of her stomach, the stirring in her lower abdomen distracting her from the ache as he penetrated her slow but deep.

'Do you know what it took not to?' he asked.

He kicked her legs further apart, his thrusts picking up pace.

'And I know you wanted me too,' he said, hints of a growl in his gravelly tone. 'You've always wanted me. And only me.'

If he hadn't pinned her so firmly against the car, she knew her legs would have given way, her whole body already trembling, her breathing shallow, her throat tight.

'Just like I've wanted you. But I never expected you to feel this good,' he declared, the strain of arousal leaking into his tone. 'Or I might have taken you sooner.'

His words struck straight to the core and imploded as his pace increased, her discomfort at his onslaught tempered only by the arousal already taking a tight hold deep inside her.

She was sure she'd wake any moment, fantasy and reality merging indistinguishably. One of those raw, sexual moments she had let herself indulge in, in the privacy of her own thoughts now having life and movement and sensation. Once-powerful fantasies now appearing weak compared to reality.

Because she had only been able to imagine what Kane was like. And she realised just how limited her imagination had been as he consumed every inch of her, thrusting into her with such controlled force that every part of her ached.

Bright lights ignited behind her eyes, the floor feeling off kilter. Stars exploded, the room surging in heat around her. Caitlin clenched her hands as her climax kicked through her system at an increasing rate, building, surging. She jolted as she lost touch with reality. She cried out, buckled with the force of her climax almost too powerful to bear. Tears trickled down her cheeks, her whole body absorbed in the aftershocks.

Every part of her ached and tingled. Every part of her felt alive with both pleasure and pain. The sensations made her feel sick, sated, an alien sensation of ease flowing through her body.

He had managed it. Kane Malloy has managed the impossible.

And it had been perfect.

# CHAPTER SIXTEEN

Caitlin's dress dropped back into place as Kane pulled away.

She turned around, her hands against the car to help her keep her balance. But her legs felt too weak, her quivering thighs barely able to hold her more than a few seconds. She slid down to the cold, hard floor, her legs coiling under her.

She still struggled to catch her breath, wiped the tears from her cheeks. He'd done more damage in that climax than she would have thought possible. Kane Malloy had just proved himself a far more lethal opponent than she could have even conceived.

She warily looked up at him as he unwrapped the tape from his right hand. For a moment she wondered if she'd just inserted the entire scene in her own mind, somewhere between him removing the first lot of tape and the second. But she knew what had happened was real – terrifyingly real. Her aching body told her so.

And so did the ache in her heart.

She couldn't fall for him. She wouldn't let herself.

But she had the terrifying feeling if he didn't say something nice to her, her too-fast-beating heart would splinter.

He crouched down on his haunches, agilely remaining poised on his bare toes. He reached out and gently brushed a few stray strands of hair from her eyes. 'Are you all right?'

Her heart jolted. She managed a nod.

He clipped her under her chin, the gentle act, coupled with his hint of a smile, one she could almost mistake as affection.

'Let's get you off that floor,' he said, standing upright, catching her by the hand.

He guided her to her feet, Caitlin pressing her hand back against the car to ensure she didn't fall over with the motion.

'Can you walk?'

She nodded.

'Sure?'

'I'm fine,' she said, though she wasn't sure she was.

Kane led the way back across the room, his hand on the small of her back as he guided her back inside the living area, closing and locking the door behind them.

'Go and lie on the bed before you fall over,' he said.

She looked across at it. Never had it looked more inviting. But she couldn't allow herself that comfort. She certainly couldn't afford to sleep. Now more than ever she had to remain on her guard.

He knew. He had to. He must have sensed it – the change in her. If she looked at him he'd surely see it in her eyes.

She lowered her gaze from the intensity of his as he stepped alongside her.

'Did you hear what I said?'

'I don't need to lie down. I'm fine.'

'Did I not tire you enough?'

Apprehension squeezed her chest. Suddenly their intimacy left a bitter taste in her mouth. She looked back at him. Tire her enough to let down her guard and let him probe at her heart a little more – test the water? 'Is that what you were hoping?'

He scooped her up in his arms in one easy move and carried her across to the bed.

'Kane, put me down!' she demanded, but he got her to the bed within seconds.

He knelt astride her hips as he pushed her wrist back towards the cuff, locking it in place. She stared at him aghast as he grabbed her other wrist, reached over to the beside table and pulled out another set of cuffs from the drawer.

'No,' she said, panic consuming her. He couldn't act that quickly. He may have chipped a great chunk of defence away but even she knew it was nowhere near enough yet for access to her soul. 'What are you doing?'

He glanced down at her, his eyes sparkling darkly as he looped the cuff single-handedly and with expert ease around the headboard before locking it around her other wrist.

'Kane, let me go!'

She wasn't ready. If he even tried to remove her soul, it could kill her. It could kill them both.

He didn't answer her as he moved off her hips, prised her legs apart and lowered to his haunches between them. She tried to buckle and wriggle, but he pressed his thumbs into her hips to hold her down against the bed.

'What good is that going to do, Caitlin?'

She pulled her knee to her chest ready to kick at him, but he caught her behind the knee, tugging it back down, took hold of her ankles, containing her legs either side of his hips. She tired quickly, no fight left, her energy levels teetering on totally inadequate.

She heaved a sigh of frustration and stared up into his eyes. Even in the darkness she could see they were calm and dangerously resolute.

'Are you done?' he asked.

'What are you going to do? If you think you can take it, you–'

'Take what?'

'You know what.'

He almost smiled. 'This isn't about your soul, Caitlin. Not right now. I haven't finished with you yet.'

Her heart pounded painfully.

She clenched her hands as he broke from her gaze to lower his head, lift her ankle a little to his lips. He kissed her slowly up the inside of her calf to the back of her knee. Caitlin parted her lips in shock, flinched at the cool caress of his lips. A kiss that became a lick as he traced his tongue slowly up the inside of her thigh. Her heart fluttered as he reached the mid-way point and she braced herself for his inevitable bite as his incisors pressed against her tender flesh.

Sex and then the feed. She should have seen it coming.

But it wasn't inevitable.

Neither was him stopping as he reached the top of her thigh. And as he released her ankle to use both hands to push up the hem of her dress, Caitlin froze.

She shook her head, more out of instinct than will. 'Kane,' she warned, her throat dry, embarrassed by the heat rushing between her legs.

But Kane was taking no warning as he moved further down the bed into position.

She held her breath.

And as he lowered his lips back to her thigh, as those kisses traced slowly and tauntingly inwards and upwards, Caitlin closed her eyes and pressed her head back against the pillow. He was going to drive her to insanity with his taunting, the pressure once again building at her still-sensitive sex. But as his cool lips met the heat deep between her legs, her heart nearly stopped. She gasped, unable to contain her exhale of pleasure, of fear.

She knew what he was about to do was far more intimate than penetration. Far more invasive. Far more risky to her state of mind when it came to him.

Kane held her hips in place as he licked perilously slowly from the core of her sex to her clitoris.

In her head, Caitlin cursed – something she couldn't recall ever having done during the sexual act. And as the intensity between her legs surged, as he kissed and licked and sucked unashamedly, she couldn't contain it anymore. As Kane pushed his tongue through her folds and deep inside her, she cried out, clenching the metal bar that held her cuffs.

Hissing at her own reaction, she bit deep into her bottom lip.

She felt him smile as he withdrew his tongue, licking back up to her throbbing nub. He took it in his mouth, encircling it with his tongue, adding just enough pressure to her folds again to make her squeeze her eyes shut and arch her back towards him.

It was all the cue he needed to tighten his grip on her hips, keep her in position as his tongue, his lips, his whole mouth became hungrier – tasting her, consuming her. The ache between her legs became painful with her need to climax again, every tiny hair on her body standing on end, her spine tingling. She could no longer think of anything but the cold perspiration that swept from her toes to her head, Kane working her to the point where she knew there was no turning back. That if he stopped, she would have begged him to continue. She hated him in that moment and she adored him. If she'd had any regrets, they'd gone. And as he performed the act she'd never experienced, she couldn't imagine ever letting anyone else that close.

As her orgasm erupted again, she cried out. Despite not thinking it possible, it was harder and more painful than the first. She didn't care if he saw the effect he'd had on her. She didn't care about anything but the quenching heat that sated her so totally again.

Kane braced himself above her, pulled down his sweat pants and shorts. She couldn't imagine taking him again when she still ached and throbbed, every part of her tingling. But clearly he'd decided she could.

She flinched and tensed involuntarily as the coolness of his erection met her heat, his rigidness meeting her softness, breaking through her folds again with ease.

Warily, tentatively, she gazed back at him, his eyes so dark in the shadows that they looked like opals. He'd never looked more stunning, more powerful, more in control. She tried to fill her head with negative thoughts about him: his callousness, his arrogance, his salaciousness, his cruelty, his depravity. But instead her head was filled with his attentiveness, his sensuality, his authority, his strength, his sincerity.

He looped his arm around the small of her back, tilting her up towards him slightly, still bracing himself on one arm as he pushed.

She closed her eyes, cried out, her body shuddering at the shock. He tilted her up slightly further, thrust into her again. She yanked her wrists against the cuffs, crying out again as he filled her to the hilt, stretching her until she felt nothing but him.

She'd barely even noticed he'd released her cuffs, her wrists falling free as he withdrew himself gently to pull her up onto his lap. He tucked her thighs either side of his, encircling her waist as he lowered her back down on him.

Caitlin winced at the new position, but Kane held her waist firmly, tucking her hands behind her back, containing them.

And did the last thing she expected.

He cupped her neck with his strong, steady hand, his fingers cool against the heat of her flesh. He gently pushed her chin up with his thumb as he slowly, excruciatingly slowly, leaned in.

Her heart leapt as his lips met hers, as he tenderly prised them apart with a kiss that was unashamedly deep and sensual. An exploratory kiss that made her knees buckle, an intensity that made her stomach flip. His detachment and coldness was suddenly so much more preferable to a tenderness that was far too unsettling for her already battling heart.

Not even Rob had ever kissed her like that and, for a while at least, he had loved her. Yet this vampire, the hardened Kane Malloy, expressed more emotion, more passion in that one kiss than she'd ever known.

But she couldn't think like that.

If she thought for one moment that Kane felt something, anything, for her, the game was over. She had to believe he hated her. She had to keep her barrier up and beguile him as much as he beguiled her. She had to play the game even if she was staring into the eyes of temptation incarnate. Because if it was part of the act, it was shockingly manipulative to the point of being evil.

She leaned back to catch his gaze, desperately trying to read whatever was going on behind those shielded eyes.

But his next kiss was deep and primal as he thrust into her again, making her accommodate him, making her succumb to him. She gasped between his kisses, opened her neck to him as he kissed down her throat to her cleavage, ravenous kisses between licking and sucking, nipping and grazing her flesh.

And this time when she met his gaze again, she wouldn't look away.

This time she stared deep into his eyes.

He'd broken her body. That was well and truly his. And now he was so deep in her head she knew she would never be free of him. But let him into her heart?

He was perfection. Perfection for her. She'd always known it. But perfection like that hurt. Something that ran that deep hurt like hell when it was torn out. She knew that. She knew it too much. And she couldn't take any more pain. She couldn't take that hollow feeling again.

And she couldn't lose everything she had worked for. Not for one sordid session with the last vampire she had any right desiring.

She'd given him enough. He'd taken enough. She'd already surrendered more than she would have ever believed herself capable.

'Stop,' she said, trying to free her wrists.

He pulled back from her neck to look into her eyes. But he didn't withdraw and he didn't loosen his grip.

Caitlin held his gaze, shocked by the panic she felt bubbling inside, a burning in her throat that usually preceded tears. She couldn't cry, that would be crazy. She had no reason to cry. And she'd never been more grateful for the dark.

'What's wrong?' he asked.

She pressed her lips together and glanced down at those hard, curved shoulders, arms that held her so firmly. She looked back into his eyes. She really was at his mercy.

'I've had enough.'

But as his lips hovered a couple of inches from hers, she wasn't sure she was stopping him for any of the right reasons.

He adjusted his position to lower her onto her back, but he still didn't withdraw. He released her hands from the small of her back only to pin them either side of her head. 'And what am I supposed to do with that? Me being the immoral, self-sating bastard you've made me out to be.'

She was eased only by the playful coaxing in his eyes. The words fell out before she had time to deliberate them. 'But you're not. Help me, Kane.'

She could feel his gaze burning into her in the darkness.

'Whatever you want me for, it can't be so urgent that you can't delay by a couple of days,' she added, 'or you would have taken me long before now.'

Kane released her wrist, eased up on to his elbow to rest his head on his palm. He studied her in the darkness, the rock music still reverberating in the background.

'Why do you want to hurt me, Kane? What have I ever done to you?'

'We're not going to do this right now.'

'Help me and I will give you my soul.'

He lifted himself off her, released her wrist to turn her over, smoothly, fluidly before she had time to protest. She clutched the sheets as he nudged her thighs apart, lowered himself back onto her.

'You're already giving it to me, Caitlin. Would I be able to get this close to you if you weren't?'

She moved in protest as much as she could in only the inch she had available, before he nudged a little way inside her again.

She stilled, catching her breath as he pushed back inside her. Already aching and throbbing, her whole body shuddered.

And as he thrust, she dug her nails into the sheets. The new angle almost tipped her over the edge, her climax impending terrifyingly quickly.

She took that moment and held it. Held it as she felt him come, his jolt and pulsation inside her erupting another orgasm.

Another orgasm that had her crying out against the sheets.

How the hell was she going to walk away from him? How the hell was she going to let it all go?

And as he kissed her tenderly on the shoulder, Caitlin squeezed her eyes shut. His absence as he withdrew and moved away was almost more than she could bear.

# CHAPTER SEVENTEEN

Caitlin woke up not knowing if it was day or night, but as she opened her eyes she could see Kane lying next to her in bed. Ironically she couldn't remember the last time she had slept so well or woken feeling so safe.

He lay acquiescently on his back, torso exposed, his head turned slightly in her direction. The sheet was low on his flat stomach, barely covering his hips and groin. He was still naked. His left arm lay between them, his right under his head as if basking on a summer's day. He appeared to be sleeping soundly and peacefully.

This was Kane Malloy with his defences down. Something, she was sure, only a rare few ever saw. Females he'd brought into his bed and trusted enough to stay the night. Maybe one or two close friends, if he had any.

In the minutes she stared at him she only saw his chest move once. Aside from that, he could almost look human. The curve of those thick lashes concealing those preternaturally compelling eyes, the lethal incisors hidden behind those closed bow lips. She gazed down his honed, taut chest, examining every defined muscle, his tattoos, up over the curve of his broad, strong shoulder, the biceps that had held her down with such ease. Her master vampire. Her dark prince who lay asleep next to her, oblivious to her thoughts as she looked at that hard, cold chest. She could so easily make contact, wait for the pulse, that all important beat that would give her a true glimmer inside of him, that would finally allow her to get inside him.

But it was also a touch that would inevitably wake him.

He could have been that way for minutes or hours, but it had happened. It had finally happened. She should have felt elated. Instead she felt an ache in her chest at what she knew she had to do.

As she gazed at him, she knew more than ever that she needed to get out of there. She was already feeling an intensity she'd never thought possible. As strong as her feelings had been for Rob, she'd never felt like this. Even on the day he'd left her, she hadn't felt that gut-wrenching pang like she did right then.

There was something about Kane. Something inexplicable. Something that had burrowed deep from the first time she'd seen him. Even as he'd pinned her up against the wall in that corridor, she'd felt she'd known him. But now, in his bed, as up close and personal as she could get, even after what they'd done, she knew she was feeling something more.

Something he was never going to feel back. He was never going to feel anything for the neurotic, detached, awkward, sexually inept VCU agent who had once got the better of him. To him it was all a game. A game he was a master at – getting people to fall for him, beguiling them into getting his own way. And he had been right. She was no match for him and the longer she stayed, the less of a match she would be.

And he knew it or he would never have slept without cuffing her. Lying next to her as if she were a compliant lover. He had chosen to lie with her. More than likely because he wanted her where he could feel her. But it was no doubt equally to encourage the sense of familiarity and safety he sensed she needed for him to progress.

And now more than ever she had to remember who he was. Who she was. Why she was there. She had to get a grip. This was about survival. This was about getting back to the VCU, to Xavier, and hauling him in. That was what she worked for. That was why she was there.

She had the evidence for Xavier. She had a name for herself. And, armed with the latter, she would go it alone. Something she was more than used to.

She looked at where the cuff hung loose above him. It would secure him long enough in case he woke, and give her a head start. But she knew her reflexes weren't quick enough. If he woke, he'd have her in a second. If she even intimated what she was doing, she'd be strapped to that bed again.

Still Kane slept soundly, the absence of breathing broken only every few minutes disconcerting her, not allowing her to be sure just how deep asleep he was. Caitlin held her breath as she eased away from him, sliding slowly, dispersing the weight carefully so the mattress didn't sag, waiting to see if he woke, if he stirred.

If he did, she could claim she was going to the bathroom. But then he'd be awake and she would have lost.

She counted through the seconds before sliding closer to the edge of the bed. Her foot touched floorboard, then the other alongside it as she slid to the floor onto her knees.

She stood up carefully, padding slowly and silently around the foot of the bed, praying nothing creaked. She made her way quickly into the bathroom, rummaged around in her bag for some knickers and slipped them on. She stepped back into the living area.

He was still asleep.

She kept her full attention on him as she backed up silently and slowly towards the door.

Reaching the threshold to the recess, she tucked her hand into the soft leather of his jacket. She dipped her hand into the inside pockets, searching for the one where he had placed his keys. As her fingertips touched metal, she grasped hold of them, using her fingers to keep the metal segregated so as not to cause a clink as she gently withdrew her hand.

She backed up into the dark recess of the doorway and slipped the key in the lock, glancing over her shoulder in dread.

He still slept soundly.

She held her breath as she turned the key. The first didn't move. She tucked it in her palm as she thumbed through to find the next. On second failure, she glanced over her shoulder again, her heart pounding to the point she was sure it was going to wake him up. She thumbed for the third, placed it in the lock. This time she felt it turn, heard the subtle click.

She flinched and looked over her shoulder.

Just one more lock. One more and she was out of there.

She tried the fourth key first but it wouldn't fit, so went back to the first she had tried on the other. Hands trembling, a sheen of perspiration consuming her palms, she finally heaved a sign of relief as the key turned.

She reached for the handle and slowly pulled open the door, grateful it didn't creak or the game would have been over.

She glanced over her shoulder once more to check Kane was still sleeping soundly on the bed.

She felt a pang. Of what, she wasn't sure. But it made her uncomfortable and teary and panicked.

Reaching back for his jacket, she lowered it off the hook and crept outside. Closing the door carefully behind her, she locked it again and slid the bolts across.

She rested her head against the wood for a moment, sagging with relief. But she knew she had no time to waste. Turning around she looked at his car. It was a much safer option for getting through Blackthorn territory, but there were no car keys on the fob.

She ran across the stone floor, cold and rough beneath her bare feet, and reached the car. She tugged the car handle in the vain hope it might be unlocked. It didn't give. With the right tools she knew she could break in and hotwire it but she had no doubt Kane had his own security on the car. There was no saying what that might incur.

She stepped back over to the toolbox and quietly opened it up. She took out one of the screwdrivers and hurried over to the corrugated door. Searching through the bunch of keys, she found the most likely and slotted it in the padlock. She unlocked and pulled open the door and stepped out into the winter breeze.

It took her eyes a moment to adjust to the moonlight. More so, to adjust to her freedom. Feeling an unnerving sense of sickness, she leaned back against the garage door. And as she breathed in fresh night air, despite knowing she should have felt liberated, she felt lost. And never more alone.

What was she running to? A life back in the VCU? Max? Rob who she already knew she no longer felt the same about? But the only other option was to turn back. To go back to Kane and his plans. Kane who had no intention of helping her, and even less now he was assuming he was close to getting what he wanted.

No, she had to sort this by herself. And she had no time to waste. In just over a day it was coming for her and now she knew there was a way to kill it, she had to find out how. She had to run because it was the only way she was going to save herself and prevent him from getting what he wanted. She had a responsibility to run. If he got what he wanted, if he somehow persuaded Xavier and killed those lycans, the uprising would be beyond their control. And she was the only one who could do anything about it.

She looked left and right along the desolate, unlit street. Wherever she was, it was industrial as opposed to residential. The expansive four- and five-storey buildings loomed down on her ominously, their faded signs and broken windows emphasising their neglect. The silence was eerie, exacerbating the whistle of the bitter wind that rang in her ears like tinnitus.

She turned around and backed away from the garage door to examine her prison. Aside from the garage door being painted grey, there was little to distinguish the building. Holding her hair back from her face, she turned to look at the building opposite. Above the doors, a faded blue sign with the name Sable on it was still distinguishable. It would be clue enough.

Pulling on Kane's coat, she looked up at the night sky. The clouds dispersed across the pending full moon, igniting the street enough for her to see a safe distance in front and behind.

Nothing looked familiar and she knew every nook and cranny of vampire territory. But she also knew she was disoriented. At some point she'd recognise something to tell her which direction to take. She zipped up Kane's coat that swamped her to mid thigh, the sleeves consuming her hands – a grateful cover for the screwdriver she clenched in one, and the keys, tucked through the gaps in her fingers as a makeshift knuckleduster, in the other.

She turned left and marched ahead, the winter breeze whipping around her legs. She needed to find a payphone, preferably one on the street. Failing that, she needed to find one in a store, a bar or a restaurant. But that would be a last resort. She needed to stay as far out of sight and away from attention as she could. There were plenty in Blackthorn who would recognise her. She could ask for help, but there was no telling whom she was talking to. There were plenty of the third species who willingly supported the agents' work but there were plenty of others who held Kane's view. She had to keep watch for someone who was human enough not to pick up on the vampire scent and who would willingly respond to her call for help without fear of retribution.

She quickened her pace, her feet numbing against the chilly, dank pavement as she nimbly tried to avoid the ice-cold puddles. She glanced warily over her shoulder as Kane's building became consumed by the darkness, but no shadows or footsteps indicated she was being followed.

After several minutes, she took her first turning, taking a left onto what looked like a residential street. The streetlights paved the way ahead, going someway to ignite street corners left and right.

The sign said Borough Street. Not even that sounded familiar. She tightened her grip on her makeshift weapons and hurried on ahead. She took another left and crossed the street to take a right. Soon she heard the distant sound of voices, the hum of a community. A couple of stragglers appeared from around the corner ahead, but didn't seem to notice her as they staggered across to the other side of the street before disappearing around the corner opposite.

She felt helpless without her gun. Blackthorn never worried her when she was kitted-up and psyched-up, but she felt drained, fuelled only by adrenaline and the need to get away. They were never good defence mechanisms when you needed to be on full alert, and right then she needed everything firing.

If she got to a phone, Xavier would find her. He'd have the whole place on lockdown within the hour if he had to.

She took a right and hesitated at the corner. There were a few stragglers, mainly twos and threes. And there was a large group congregating around what looked like a bar, its bright red sign illuminating the littered pavement around them. But between her and them, on the opposite side of the street, was a phone booth gleaming under the streetlight.

Her instinct told her to turn away and look for a phone booth somewhere else, but sense told her it was potentially her only opportunity to get to one. She knew she was cornering herself by entering the booth. She knew from her training, from common sense, to avoid such situations, but there was no saying where the next one would be. For all she knew, Kane had already realised she had escaped and was hunting her down. Even in that vast district, it wouldn't take him long to find her.

She glanced anxiously over her shoulder into the darkness behind, then back down the street ahead. Everyone was engrossed. No one was going to take any notice of her. No one had any reason to take any notice of her. The sign to the right of her said Orkney Street. Again, she'd never heard of it but it would give them something to go on. Clenching her weapons, keeping her head low, she padded down towards the booth.

She tucked the keys in her pocket and yanked open the heavy door, stepping inside. She glanced up at the lit ceiling mottled with the shadows of dead flies and moths as she tried to tentatively avoid the sticky, unpleasant patches on the floor. Sending a wary glance over each shoulder, she noticed she had already caught the attention of a group across the street. Keeping the screwdriver tight in her hand, she lifted the phone off the cradle. The absence of tone made her curse in frustration. She dropped the phone back in place and took a moment to calm her nerves before turning back around to see two males were already only a few feet away.

She reminded herself not to panic. To take a steadying breath. Her pulse raced, her adrenaline kicking in as it always did when she was faced with combat. But she controlled it adeptly, keeping her body lax, her eyes downturned as she yanked the door open.

Instead of moving aside, they locked shoulders.

Caitlin took a wary step back and first assessed the one who'd pressed forward to lean against the doorway. His grey almond eyes raked her rapaciously as an irritating smirk spread across on his stubbly, chiselled face. The other one held the door open as he leaned back against it. His eyes were blue and colder despite his gentler, boyish face. They weren't vampires. They were human. And if they were residents in Blackthorn that meant even the penal prison system in Lowtown was too good for them. Grey-eyes was around six-foot, lean but not sturdy looking. Blue-eyes was a few inches shorter and didn't have the body of someone adept at running or combat. She could take both of them if she had to.

'Hello, sweetness,' grey-eyes said. 'You look a long way from home.'

She met his gaze, but suppressed her aggression. 'Why, where am I?'

Grey-eyes looked at blue-eyes, who smirked back at him.

Grey-eyes grinned. 'You are lost.' He folded his arms. 'Would you like some assistance?'

'Seriously, where am I? North, east, south?'

'North. As far north as it gets.'

Her heart skipped a beat. 'Lycan territory?'

Clever Kane: stashing her on the outskirts of the tiny lycan territory of Blackthorn, let alone stashing himself in the last place anyone would come looking. It was no wonder she didn't recognise the area. The LCU handled this part. She may have been there once or twice at most. Only now it was as a lone female with vampire scent all over her. If they were telling the truth, and there was no reason why they wouldn't be, she had nowhere to hide. She'd be sensed by every lycan in a quarter-mile radius.

'No more than it is ours, honey,' grey-eyes remarked. She wondered what he'd done to deserve being confined to the area. What both of them had done. 'So how can we be of assistance?'

'Is there another phone booth near by? One that actually works?'

'About a mile away. Can't say whether it works though.' He looked down at her bare feet. 'So what you running from, sweetie?'

'Do you have a phone?'

Grey-eyes slipped his phone out of his back pocket and held it up for her to see.

'Would you mind if I used it?' she asked.

He grinned. 'Not at all. Do you have a means of payment? Something in that coat? Or under it preferably?'

She offered him a closed-lip smile as her heart began to pound to the point she could hear it reverberating in her ears. She was tempted to take them both down there and then, one clean in the face, the other clean in the groin. She would have been out of there before they'd had time to recover, but with him still holding the much-needed phone, she knew it could be worth a few more minutes of her time.

She glanced over to the bar front where the larger crowd had already disappeared. A few others were still gathered and chatting, but the fact not one of them came over to assist didn't bode well.

'I thought you wanted to be of assistance,' she said, looking back at grey-eyes.

'I do. I'm just saying maybe you can assist me back.'

She blew out her lips and lowered her gaze for a moment before looking back into his eyes. 'You know you are such a cliché. Why can't you be helpful?'

'Cliché?' he asked, frowning.

She wasn't sure if it was a rhetorical statement, but something told her he wasn't sure what she meant. 'If you're not going to help me, let me pass.'

Grey-eyes looked back across at blue-eyes. 'Did she just refuse to pay me for my services, Boyd?'

'Looks that way, Karl,' Boyd replied.

'Let's not do this,' she said, glaring at each of them in turn.

'She's not very friendly, Boyd.'

'Certainly isn't, Karl,' Boyd responded as coaxingly as his friend.

'Do you think we can make her friendly?'

'I think we could persuade her.' Boyd glanced over his shoulder before looking back at her with a smirk. 'With a bit of privacy.'

'I'd advise you don't touch me,' Caitlin warned, glowering up at him.

Karl laughed. 'A fighter. This could be fun.'

'A fighter and VCU Agent,' she said. 'I have an obligation to warn you that if we enter into an altercation, I have a license to use whatever force is required.'

Karl frowned, the uncertainty in his eyes telling her he was deliberating over her statement. 'Where's your ID?'

'I'm undercover. There's been a problem. I need to contact my unit.'

'She's bluffing,' Boyd declared. 'She's too little for an agent.'

Caitlin's gaze rested squarely on his again. 'That's why I work so well undercover.' She looked back at Karl. 'I need to use your phone. I suggest you co-operate.'

Karl frowned, studied her gaze for a moment then handed her his phone.

She accepted it warily, backing into the booth. 'And some privacy?'

Karl held up his hands and backed away, slapping Boyd on the arm to let the door go. She watched them as they turned their backs on her. Karl's shaved head lowered to Boyd as he whispered something to him. Whatever it was, she had the feeling it wasn't good.

She looked down at the phone. Xavier's number was still held in her head where she'd practised it so many times. She started to input it, but stopped as she got to the fourth digit. The things Kane had said crept into her mind. Max was the better option. She needed to talk to Max. She needed to ask him about the things Kane had said before contacting Xavier. She inputted Max's number and held it to her ear as it rang. As it kept ringing, she bit into her bottom lip, looked out of the booth to see Karl and Boyd had turned to face her, hands shoved in their pockets as they glanced warily and guiltily over both shoulders intermittently. They weren't going to let this go. They weren't going to let her go.

Max's voice-mail resounded in her ear and her heart plummeted. 'Max, it's Caitlin. I'm okay. I'm far north in Blackthorn. Lycan territory. I'm in a phone booth near the corner of Orkney Street. Kane's got a place on the industrial estate a twenty-minute walk down Bishop Street. He's about ten minutes down Hove Avenue. You need to look for a grey corrugated garage door. There's a blue sign on the building opposite that says Sable. Behind the grey door is a garage. There's a door to the far left as you go in. It goes into a living area. He's after the lycans that killed Arana, so we've got cause to take him in.' She hesitated for a moment. 'Max, leave Xavier out of it for now though, will you? I need to talk to you first. I'm going to hang around Orkney Street and lay low, but I'll keep a look out for you.' She paused. 'Just make it quick.' She disconnected and took a steadying breath before pushing the door open.

Karl strolled towards her and held out his hand for his phone. Boyd tucked in tight beside him, re-forming the barrier.

Karl dialled a number and held his phone to his ear.

Caitlin frowned, but resisted asking him what he was doing as she tucked her hand back in Kane's coat. She subtly threaded the keys back into place between her fingers, removing her screwdriver hand from her pocket and tucking it behind her back.

He smiled as he disconnected. 'That didn't sound like a unit on standby. Who's Max, honey? Boyfriend?'

He was smarter than he looked.

And it was pointless trying to explain herself.

She rammed the screwdriver into Karl's thigh, leaving it in for good measure as he instantly dropped to his knees. She slammed her keyed knuckles into Boyd's side and withdrew. It was quick and sharp enough to throw them both off balance and disorientate them enough for her to slip between them and run.

She pounded through the puddles, rainwater splashing her legs. She avoided heading down the main street, opting to take cover somewhere less exposed. She tried to memorise the names of each street she passed so she could find her way back.

Feet and calves numb, her face cold against the breeze, she weaved left and right down quieter side streets, sending a wary glance over her shoulder to see she had been successful in leaving them behind.

She stopped to catch her breath and faced the way she had run. She rested her hands on her hips as she looked around her, panting, composing herself, renewing her strength. She'd have to go back there. For the sake of Max finding her, she at least needed to be close to where she'd told him.

She took a few paces forward and flinched as a car revved around the corner, the thrum of the heavy-beat music inside pounding through the tarmac, the neon under-light glowing blue against the ground.

To her relief, it raced past her, but then it slammed to a halt, the white of the reverse lights suddenly ignited.

She didn't need to know that whatever was in that car, it meant trouble.

Caitlin ran, taking a left and then a right. As she heard the car reverse, she picked up pace, adrenaline burning in her chest, unable to feel her feet beneath her as though she was running on air as she ploughed past street after street, the car pursuing her.

She knew she had to get into the lanes despite it going against her better judgement. If they were humans, it was her best chance to hide out. If they were lycans they would have already been out of the car and pursuing her on foot, her scent impossible not to follow.

She took a sharp right down a lane between two houses, tunnelling into the darkness, taking a left past a chain-link fence before circling around to another alley. She pounded forward until she felt excruciating pain as something hard and sharp sliced into her foot, embedding itself. She stumbled and tried to stop herself crying out.

She leaned back against the wall behind a dumpster and regained her breath again, lifting her foot as she rested her head back against the wall in agony. As the car revved past her, she lowered to her haunches, the car's headlights igniting the alley for a moment before speeding away.

It hadn't seen her.

Silence swamping the alley, Caitlin stood slowly and warily. Every muscle burned with exhaustion making it harder for her to balance and keep the weight off her foot. Thighs trembling, she wiped a tear from her eye at the pain aching through her whole lower right leg. She lifted her foot and touched the underside. She knew immediately from the sharpness that she'd stood on glass, a good fraction of which was still lodged in her sole. And her foot wasn't just wet from water – it was too thick and warm to be water. Smelling of vampire and now of fresh human blood too, lycan territory suddenly became even more threatening.

She cursed under her breath and rested her head back against the wall. She wasn't going to be running anywhere now. She'd be lucky to even walk. And from guessing what the state of her foot was, she'd be leaving a convenient trail wherever she went if she did.

But she had to get back somewhere near the booth. She rolled her head to the right towards the alley entrance and her heart leapt at the figure there.

She could only make out an outline, but whoever it was, they were more than likely male from the height and stature. Her first instinct was Kane, but the figure was too stocky. Besides, Kane would have already been storming towards her. This one lingered, exhaling cigarette smoke into the night air. He could have just stopped for a smoke or maybe to use the alley as a toilet. He might have been waiting for someone. Maybe waiting to be picked up. But he remained motionless other than his smoking hand.

She tried to quiet her breathing, grateful she had at least had a few minutes to rest. She just had to remain as quiet and still as she could until he moved away, then she could make her way back out onto the street.

At least the car was long gone, and Boyd and Karl were more than likely either getting bored with trying to find her or seeking some form of medical treatment.

But the figure didn't move.

Feeling light-headed and exhausted, Caitlin didn't dare take her attention off the shadow. After a couple of painful minutes, he threw down his cigarette, filling Caitlin with a sense of relief – until she saw him turn in her direction and stride forward.

Caitlin hurriedly reached inside Kane's jacket pocket for the keys, threading them through her fingers again. She'd never outrun them, human or lycan, and she had no balance to fight nor the strength.

As soon as he stopped in front of her, she knew he was a lycan. He had to be at least six foot four, broad, his long dark hair tied back in a ponytail, his features hard in the dim light, his eyes sparkling preternaturally. And from the subtle flaring in his nostrils, the curiosity behind his eyes, he was picking up the vampire scent.

She clenched the keys.

His gaze darted to her hand, he grabbed her wrist in an instant, slamming her hand once then twice against the wall, grazing her knuckles, forcing her to release the keys into his hand. He shoved them in his pocket then bent forward to lift her up over his shoulder.

'Get off me!' she demanded, digging her nails under his jacket and into his back but he barely flinched as he carried her further into the depths of the alley.

Caitlin buckled and flexed futilely as it took little for him to control her, his bulk as well as his supernatural strength keeping her bolted down against his shoulder. Caitlin eventually stopped fighting him, reserving her energy for whatever he had planned.

It was over. Down the depths of some dark and unpleasant alley in lycan territory. She was stupid to have run from Kane when she had no idea what she was running into. And in that moment, she wished she were back with him. She wished he were there now. The lycan wouldn't have stood a chance against him. But there was no Kane, only more putrid darkness.

The lycan carried her past the large metal bins, the strewn-aside cardboard boxes and crates. If he was going to interrogate her or attack her, he'd had opportunity enough. The street was already a distance away. No one could see them in the shadows. No one would hear them.

Instead he dropped Caitlin back to her feet, pushing her through the chain-link fence before forcing himself through it behind her. Despite her continued protest, he lifted her back up over his shoulder with ease and carried her across an open expanse of concrete, towards what looked like the back entrance to a warehouse.

'What you got there, Hank?' the lycan guarding the door asked. 'She reeks of vampire.'

'Yeah and lurking in an alley bleeding all over the place.' Hank passed through the metal door held open for him and stomped along the bare corridor.

They passed a few lycans sending intrigued glances in her direction, but she lowered her gaze from the humiliation, desperate for Hank to put her on her feet despite the pain.

Hank shoved open another door and stepped into a large, vacuous room. He dropped her to her feet, Caitlin nearly yelping with the agony.

She stumbled forward to have him catch her by her upper arms, forcing her down onto her knees, concrete scraping the skin.

Ahead was a table, at least six lycans sat around it, cards held in their hands.

She heard the scraping of a chair and her attention snapped to the only one who rose from the table and strolled towards her.

Kane couldn't smell her. There was a faint scent, but nothing strong enough to tell him she was close by. He sat bolt upright and scanned the room. The place was silent, void even of her breathing.

His first thought was that she had done something stupid. He shoved back the sheets, kicked open the bathroom door and scanned its emptiness. He stepped over to the kitchen then stared across at the door.

Hell, the girl was insane.

His jacket had gone and with it his keys. He marched across to the TV and reached behind it to take the spare set of keys off the hook.

He turned both keys in the lock and tugged. As he'd suspected, the door didn't budge. She wouldn't leave without bolting it from the other side. He slammed his hand in fury against it before storming back across to the bed.

There was no way to say how long she'd gone. An hour maybe. But an hour was a long time in lycan territory. Her only saving grace would be that she smelled of him. Unless she came across rogue lycans stoned or drunk enough to be willing to take the risk with a pretty human girl. Or came face-to-face with her own kind – the worst of her own kind.

He yanked on his shorts and jeans. He pulled on a T-shirt and hurriedly laced up his boots.

The thought of anyone other than him with their hands on her, the thought of anyone hurting her, wrenched at his chest. But he knew that should be the last concern he had. The bigger concern was that she might, just might, get out of there. And it was going to be a hell of a bigger challenge getting her back than just slipping into her apartment.

He clamped his hand around the bedpost and pulled the whole bed aside. He ripped the rug up from underneath, exposing the trapdoor. He released the catch, lifted the door and took the wooden ladder down into the darkness.

He should have cuffed her. He should have known better. He should have known it would be what she'd be planning. But no one had ever slipped from him without disturbing him in his sleep before. No one. But she was stealthy and nimble and far too light on her feet. And he had slept deep. For some reason his sleep had been the most restful he'd had in a long time.

He crossed the cellar and marched up the wooden ladder on the other side, yanking back the bolts on the trapdoor.

Every single nerve ending sparked in anger but he also had a stirring in his gut that he didn't like. Something he hadn't felt for a long time. Something he didn't want to acknowledge. But he recognised it and he hated it.

Worry was an alien concept. Something he hadn't felt since he'd lost Arana.

He slammed back the door and stepped up into the garage, kicking the door shut behind him again.

He marched over to the bench, took his car keys out of a metal tin in the drawer and stormed across to his car as the garage door began to open.

She could be anywhere. With anyone.

But she was a smart girl. She'd stay away from the crowds. She'd stay away from anyone who might recognise her. And once she realised she was in lycan territory she'd lay low because of the scent.

She'd also put out a call for help if she got to a phone.

He needed to find her quick.

He wasn't going to let it happen again. The thoughts of what he might find brought the painful, sickening memories back too hard and too fast.

She was his to use. His and no one else's.

Pulling out onto the street, he dropped his phone onto the passenger seat. There was enough of a breeze that he'd pick up a scent. That others would pick up on the scent.

He'd find her. Wherever she was.

Because if anything happened to her, he'd never forgive himself. Ever.

# CHAPTER EIGHTEEN

Caitlin watched the lycan leader approach, each of his heavy foot-steps mindfully, tauntingly purposeful.

'Well, well, well,' Jask said, stopping in front of her. 'Caitlin Parish. You're a long way from home.'

Pulling her shoulder from Hank's grip, Caitlin glared up into Jask's sharp azure eyes. Eyes intensified by the darker shade of his lashes and stubble, compared to his blond hair.

He cocked his head to the side as he crouched in front of her, his loose, shoulder-length hair falling forward slightly with the motion. 'Shouldn't you be out somewhere chasing vampires?'

'Tell him to get his hands off me,' she said, yanking against Hank again.

'With your reputation. I don't think so. The girl who brought down Kane Malloy. Your name is all over this district. Even more than it usu-ally is. Only I heard Kane had got his own back.' He indicated for Hank to pull her back to her feet.

For fear of her arms being wrenched out of her sockets, she con-ceded, hobbling slightly, trying to keep her weight on just one foot. She glanced at the other lycans sat around the table, then back at Jask.

She'd seen pictures of him but they hadn't done him justice. His chiselled features were more striking up close.

He looked down at her bare feet and smiled an unnervingly wide smile. 'Oh. I see.'

She tried not to let her mind go there but she immediately pictured the images of Arana's brutalised body. Vampires were notorious for bad press but she wasn't naive to the capabilities of lycans. They may have been the more insular and easily contained of the third species, but only because of the effectiveness of the meds that had been perfected to manage their condition. What had happened to Arana was proof of their instincts when they weren't effectively controlled.

She glanced once more across at the table of them then warily back up at Jask.

He was smart enough to keep himself to himself as far as the control units were concerned but she didn't underestimate his potential. It took something to keep all those lycans in line. And it wasn't all based on fair leadership and positive praise.

'You let me go, Jask. Keeping an agent against their will is a serious offence—'

'Save it, Caitlin. No one knows where you are because no one's come looking. So forget the speech, you're going nowhere.' He indicated for Hank to let her go. He did so with such force she stumbled forward slightly before regaining her footing, hopping slightly to avoid the pressure on her foot. 'You're up to your neck in it, little lady, so don't come shouting the odds in my territory. You haven't got your army behind you now.'

Caitlin brushed the hair from her eyes, glanced back over at the other lycans. Panic clenched her stomach. 'You clearly need yours to back you up though, don't you?'

Jask breathed in slow and deeply through his nose, his gaze to the ceiling before he looked back at her with a smile. 'Is that fear I smell?

'What's your problem with me, Jask? I'm nothing to do with you.'

He laughed lightly. 'Nothing to do with me?' He looked around the room at his henchmen. 'Did you hear that?'

She followed his gaze, watched him warily.

'You've got two of my boys in that big old containment unit of yours. I think that makes an agent of the regulations my business.'

'We've got a lot of your boys in our containment unit. None of them are anything to do with me.'

'But you know which boys I'm talking about, you being Kane's biggest fan and all. You know exactly which two.'

'They went in voluntarily. Full confession. Like I said, they're nothing to do with me.'

'You've read the reports then. You know what they did.'

'I know exactly what they did. And that they deserved to be locked up for it. And that they came running with their tails between their legs proves what cowards they were.'

As Jask lifted the back of his hand to strike, Caitlin caught her breath and braced herself.

'Jask!' one of his henchmen warned, shook his head.

There was a silent exchange between them. Caitlin frowned. She stared back at Jask as he lowered his hand and stepped closer.

Why the hell was he looking at her like it was her fault?

'They have families,' Jask said. 'One of them had daughters of his own.'

'They also both have a history of being negligent of their meds, defiant of laws, unruly behaviour. Their DNA was found all over her. We have a confession. They admitted they were intoxicated. They admitted they were three days out on their medication. It was near the full moon and they were in a heightened state. Arana might have been in the wrong place at the wrong time but they took advantage and have to pay for that. Families or not.'

'That's right – Arana on the edge of lycan territory during full moon. Has that never struck anyone as strange?'

'Everyone knows Arana liked to live as close to the edge as her brother. But that doesn't excuse them.' She frowned. 'The LCU know you've been talking to him, Jask. They're watching you. What are you up to?'

'It's all about closure, little lady.'

'The TSCD kept those lycans' identity secret for all your sakes. But I know he knows who they are. I know you told him.'

Jask smiled.

'What's in it for you, Jask? Why are you betraying your own? Is Kane paying you off with something, or has he got you scared too?'

'Me and Kane have an understanding.'

'You're lucky he hasn't killed every single one of you. Do you think this means you're off the hook? He's not letting this go until he gets vengeance. And we both know it. If you're linking with him, you're a fool.'

'As much a fool as you?' He leaned in to her. Breathed deeply. 'Screwing the vampires you're hunting part of VCU protocol now, is it, Caitlin? Smells like he's had you right where he wanted you. Until you escaped.' He circled around her. 'So how are you liking being up close and personal with the vampire of your dreams? Word on the street is you've had a crush on him for quite some time. Less than two days in his arms and look at you.'

Caitlin frowned as he drew level again. 'Are you really that desperate for his approval that you would put those lycans' families at risk?'

He smiled. A smile that was more of a sneer as he walked away again.

'What they did was despicable, Jask. I believe as much as the next person that they deserve whatever they get, but this is about justice and justice is being served. You cannot let him get them. It's murder.'

'We have our ways. You have yours. When are you agents ever going to understand that?' He raked his gaze over her with disdain. 'Standing in your place of authority and making us live by your rules. Drugging us. Controlling us. Telling us how to live. You know nothing. You create this division but we are talking about respect. Respect for each others' territories. We live by our own order. It has been the way for centuries and when ours step out of line, we punish them. Our way.'

'You know, you even sound like him. He really is working your strings, isn't he?'

Jask glowered at her. 'He needed to know who was responsible.'

'And you told him. Do you know what it will do to them if they find out Kane knows who they are, if they know he's going after their families? Because he will. And he won't just kill them. And you know it. What you are contemplating is beyond inhumane.'

He laughed. 'You're not getting this at all. When I said me and Kane have an understanding, I meant it.' He looked across to one of the henchmen. 'Call Kane. Ask him if he's lost anything.'

'No!' Caitlin reached for him, his sleeve snatched from her grip by his quicker reflex. 'Kane wants to use me as a bargaining tool to get those lycans out. And if they get released in exchange for me, Kane will slaughter them. The TSCD will know it's Kane who's done it—' She stopped herself abruptly, an uncomfortable feeling spreading through her. 'Is that why you're doing it? Are you trying to get Kane inside?' She frowned. 'Have you been speaking to Xavier?'

Jask raised his eyebrows. 'Xavier Carter?'

'Jask, if you are double-crossing Kane then you are insane. And you can't trust Xavier. If he's setting you up for something—'

'Oh, don't insult me. You think he could fool someone like me. Like he fooled you into coming here. Like he fooled your father?'

Caitlin stared at him. 'What did you say?'

Jask raked her swiftly, before indicating for the other lycans to leave.

'What the hell are you talking about, Jask?' she demanded. 'What do you mean he fooled my father?'

Jask's eyes narrowed. 'You really don't know, do you?'

'Know what?'

'Kane hasn't told you yet?'

'Told me what?' Her heart pounded.

As the lycans left them alone, Jask stepped up to her. 'If there wasn't a no-touch policy on you, I'd tear you apart myself.'

'What no-touch policy? Jask, what's going on?'

Jask pressed his lips together as he glowered at her. 'You really think those lycans were there by accident that night? Just happened to be on the wasteland out of sight where Arana happened to be wandering?'

'Rumour was she arranged it.'

'She despised lycans. She would never go near them let alone arrange to meet them for some sexual experiment. But it was a very convenient motive.'

'Convenient for who?'

'Who do you think?'

Caitlin frowned. 'Are you saying they were set up?'

'Selected because of their plausibility and their dubious background. Starved of their meds. Told they either went along with it or their families would pay the price. Families that would be protected if they gave themselves up after it. Lycans who were given sanctuary in the detainment unit if they spoke nothing of the truth. If they kept quiet until Kane was caught.'

Caitlin's heart pounded.

'They didn't run into the containment unit with their tails between their legs, Caitlin. They had no choice.'

'Why? Why would anyone set that up?' Her gaze rested uneasily on Jask. Then dread flooded every nerve.

'Xavier wanted Kane and he wanted Kane bad. What better way to send the most controlled vampire off on a self-destruct vengeance mission than to have his sister slaughtered and debased by a pair of out-of-control lycans?'

'Xavier? Are you telling me Xavier Carter set up Arana's murder? Are you insane?' Caitlin held his gaze. She wanted to deny it, but the things Kane had said started seeping in. 'He would have been creating warfare.'

'Think about it, Caitlin. Was there anybody who didn't know who Arana was? Any third species who didn't know of Kane and his reputation? Do you not think she would have mentioned it in her last desperate pleas? No one would dare touch her. Let alone what they did. You think she didn't scream it from the rooftops as they finished her off?'

'They would have been too far gone to care.'

He stepped up close. 'They came to me for help and swore me to secrecy. They were terrified after what they did. I had to go along with it and advise them to hand themselves in. Not even I could protect them. I know Xavier expected word to leak out and for Kane to go on the rampage. And Kane would have if I hadn't got to him first. I told him it had been a set-up. Kane's got a temper but it never outweighs his need for justice. When he wants that, he's meticulous and calculated and logical.'

'So why doesn't he just go after Xavier? What the hell does it have to do with me?'

'You know Xavier never does his own dirty work. Do you think he was the one who starved those lycans? Do you think he was the one who stood guard when it was happening? Made sure there were no witnesses? No interruptions? How do you think Arana got to lycan territory in the first place?'

Caitlin's stomach clenched. Sickness rose at the back of her throat.

'It took three of them, Caitlin. One of the VCU's finest to collect Arana. One of the LCU's finest to deal with the lycans. And one rookie who worshipped them both to be their lapdog. You want to know what this has to do with you? You ask Max. You ask Robert. It's just a shame your father's no longer around to face the storm Kane's got coming.'

Caitlin dropped to her knees, partly in pain and partly in shock.

His words rebounded in her mind, bouncing against numb walls.

Jask crouched in front of her. 'You really didn't know, did you?'

She glowered up at him, the fury catching at the back of her throat. 'You're lying.'

'No, your father was the liar. Max. Robert. And Kane is going to make them pay. He's going to make all of you pay. Slowly and painfully. He's waited a long time for this, Caitlin. He's waited a long time for you.'

The door opened behind.

She heard boots against stone. Footsteps whose rhythm she had come to know. A rhythm that had excited her and had made her heart skip a beat in anticipation. Now it filled her with nothing but fear and fury.

Kane stopped in front of her, his lace-up black boots cuffed by his jeans.

She couldn't bear to look up at him for fear of what he would see in her eyes. She didn't know what she would say to him or how she would react, her emotions too difficult to place.

'I told her,' Jask declared.

Kane said nothing, but she could feel his eyes burning into her.

'And you were right,' Jask added. 'She didn't have any idea.'

She didn't know how the hell she didn't cry. Probably the shock. The prospect of the three men she cared most about, had trusted most, allowing that to happen. To help set it up. To be so weak as to follow Xavier's orders. It made her feel sick. But it had to be a lie. She knew them and they were not capable of that. Not of those atrocities. She'd seen the pictures of Arana's mutilated body. No one she knew, no one she cared about, could ever stand by and let that happen. Even her heart had been torn out. Only a monster was capable of standing by and listening to those screams and doing nothing to stop it. Jask was setting them up. But that didn't matter to Kane. He had his scapegoats. If she ever needed proof she meant nothing to Kane, this was it.

She felt numb as Kane slipped his hand into the crook of her arm, hoisting her to her feet. She swayed, struggled to stand, blood pooling on the floor from her torn foot. She kept her gaze lowered from his, said nothing.

He pushed her chin up with his thumb, gazed into her eyes, but she couldn't stand it and broke away. She had too much to think about, too much to say and she was just about holding it all in. Meeting those navy-blue eyes for too long was just going to make her erupt one way or another. And neither were going to happen then and there.

He instantly scooped her up. She didn't argue. She didn't fight him. Instead, she let him carry her across the room, down the corridor and out into the cool night air.

# CHAPTER NINETEEN

His relief should have been because she hadn't managed to ruin his plans, not because she was still breathing. When he'd received the call, when he'd heard she was okay, his heart had jolted from its temporary paralysis. And when he'd seen her on the floor, when he realised as soon as he walked in the room that Jask had let it slip, it wasn't triumph he felt because she finally knew, it wasn't disappointment that he hadn't been able to revel in telling her, it was angst. Angst that she sat alone on the floor, crumbled to her knees, the look in her eyes one he never imagined would pierce him so deep.

Caitlin remained silent next to him for the short car journey back, her head against the glass as she stared out, her hands clenched in her lap. Tears from shock, no doubt also from pain, occasionally leaked from her eyes and more than once he'd seen her hurriedly wipe them away. For the first time, the composed and collected Caitlin looked close to breaking.

She was still trembling and shivering despite the heater being on, her lips a light shade of blue, her complexion pallid. Never had she looked so fragile, so emotionally worn and tired, and he took no pleasure in that. He took no pleasure in seeing the sadness and confusion in her eyes. Her discovering the truth might have been the worse scenario at that stage, but he had to find a way to turn it around again. He certainly couldn't afford to be governed by sympathy with the perfect outcome so close.

He opened the electronic garage door remotely and drove inside, letting it close behind him as he shut off the headlights and engine.

He looked across at her and her reddened eyes met his. 'Jask is lying, Kane. He's lying to protect his own back. I know what happened to your sister. There is no way my father, Max or Rob had any part of that.'

He studied her eyes carefully, the accumulation of resentment and panic simmering behind them. Resentment and panic either at realising her family's closely guarded secret had been uncovered, or, if she hadn't known the truth, panic and resentment as she struggled to accept what she was faced with.

'Jask isn't lying, Caitlin.'

'He's playing you for a fool, Kane. Don't you see he's doing what he can to prevent a third-species civil war? Preventing you from taking revenge on his kin? That is what this is about. Those lycans messed up and Jask knows it and he is using the people I care about as scapegoats.'

'Because the whole unit are squeaky clean, right? Just like your intentions coming after me were purely professional.'

'So where's your proof? Your evidence? Nothing was found at the scene. The only reason those two lycans were detained was because they confessed. Confessed, Kane. I read those confessions. It should never have happened, but it did. And it was nothing to do with my family.'

But this was not the time to argue. Not with the state she was in. He stepped out of the car, closed the driver's side and opened the passenger side for her.

He reached in to help her out but she pushed him away, not even looking at him.

He stepped back, hating watching her struggle as she lost her balance against the bonnet before limping across to the door, determined to keep her pride intact. It irritated him, but at the same time only made him admire her more.

Kane got there first, unlocking and opening the door before stepping inside. He made his way over to the bed that still sat yanked from the wall. He pulled the rug back across the trapdoor and tugged the bed back into position. It didn't matter that she'd seen it, there was no way she'd shift the bed on her own – not that she was getting out of his sight again. She was in shock and she was angry and that made her more unpredictable than ever – and that meant he'd guard her closer than ever.

She leaned against the counter, clearly unable to take the weight on her foot, her elbow resting on the surface to help support herself. She still trembled but that seemed to be more to do with the shock than being cold now, the colour returning to her cheeks and lips.

He stepped into the bathroom and started to run a bath before making his way back out into the lounge.

'We need to get that foot sorted before you develop an infection in it.'

'As if that will make a difference,' she said, irritation swamping her eyes.

He reached for her arm, but she pulled back. 'Don't touch me.'

He instantly scooped her up again. She protested despite her weakness, wriggling in his arms. 'Put me down!'

'And have you bleed all over the place?' There was no way he was leaving her in that much pain for the next 24 hours. The pain she was trying to ignore because she was so caught up in her own fury.

He carried her to the bathroom, ignoring her futile protests, and placed her fully clothed down in the half-filled bath. She flinched but avoided eye contact, clearly knowing she had no choice but to concede. Instead, she drew her knees to her chest, holding up the foot that pained her, her eyes emanating defeat.

He sat on the step and reached across the bath for the soap, handing it to her. 'Here.'

Reluctantly she took it, lathering it up slowly in her hands before cleansing her wounded foot.

'You're lucky that's the only damage you're suffering. You could have got yourself seriously hurt out there, Caitlin. What the fuck were you thinking running out on me?'

'More hurt than being stuck in here with you? Disappointed you weren't the one to tell me your insane theory?' she asked, glowering at him. But she lowered her gaze as quickly as she had met his, returning her attention to her feet and calves. 'You're making a terrible mistake, Kane.'

'No. Your father, Max and Robert made a terrible mistake the day they agreed to tie my sister to a post and set those lycans on her.'

'It was not a set-up, Kane. That's just what Jask wants you to believe. I know my family. They would never have done that. They would never be capable of that.'

'You were a child at the time. What would you have known about anything?'

'I wasn't a child when I was with Rob. Far from it. He wouldn't have been able to keep that from me. We—'

'Shared a bed. I know. And I don't need reminding.'

Caitlin stared at him, her eyes emanating disgust, shame. 'Is that part of the reason you slept with me? Was that part of your revenge? Is that what all those questions about my relationship with Rob were about? This is about more than you taking my soul. I'm intricate to your little revenge plot, aren't I? You're using me. Making me pay just as much for what you think they did to Arana. That's why you chose me.' Her eyes widened into panic. 'Am I to suffer the same fate? Is that what you're planning?'

'They spread the rumour that she had gone there to meet with the lycans for her latest kick. They stood by when they tortured and defiled her and let it happen. Your family and boyfriend ripped away the only thing I had left to care about and all because Xavier wasn't getting his own way. They purposely left her there for me to find. They killed her to get to me. How the fuck do you think that makes me feel?'

She seemed momentarily startled by the venom in his voice, the venom he could no longer suppress as she defended her loved ones so fervently.

'It was an accident, Kane. Arana was in the wrong place at the wrong time with lycans who should have known better. It was not a conspiracy.

It was not a set-up. Do you seriously believe Xavier would go to that extent, murdering Arana just to get you on side? It doesn't make any sense.'

'No, because having me seek retribution on the lycans wouldn't give him all the evidence he needs that I'm out of control. Having me as a risk to the peace of the district wouldn't give him all the power he needs to take me in and keep me in whilst he bartered with me for my freedom. Carter wouldn't think to use the only thing I had left to care about in a last-ditch attempt to show me who's in charge. Just as he wouldn't send you in here as a spy despite knowing all of that.'

She shook her head, but her eyes leaked contemplation. 'You're paranoid.'

'Are you going to add that to the rest of your infallible psych evaluation?' He held out his hand. 'Let's have a look at your foot.'

She lifted it out of the water as if accepting she needed it sorted out, just to reduce the pain if nothing else.

He studied her sole now it was clean enough for him to see. 'You've got a couple of nasty shards in there. We're going to have to get them out.'

'You need to get me to a hospital.'

'It's nothing I can't sort,' he said. 'Get yourself warmed up and dried off and I'll take them out for you.'

'I don't think so.'

'The sooner they come out the better.'

She stared at him. 'You leave them alone, Kane. I'm warning you. Don't you touch the people I care about or you are getting nothing from me.'

She believed every word she was saying. Those eyes staring back at him were not those of someone trying to cover their tracks. Caitlin hadn't had a clue, and that made it neither the time nor the place to tell her the rest. It wasn't the time to see the last of her hopes shattered when she learned she stood no chance of getting out of it alive. Because the minute she knew that, he knew she'd close down on him completely. And he had too little time to risk that.

He could take her anger and anything else she had to throw at him – it would make no difference.

'You have no control over that heart of yours,' he said, 'any more than you have control over any of this. And the sooner you accept that, the easier this will be.' He stood up, pulled a towel off the rail and held it out to her. 'Do you want help getting out?'

She shook her head.

'I'll get some stuff together,' he said, and strode back out of the bathroom.

Caitlin watched him pull the door half-shut behind him as he left. She rubbed her hands down over her bare legs. Her feet no longer stung, the warm water instead soothing now she'd acclimatised to it.

She had to stay calm. It would only be a matter of time before Max tracked her down and then it would all be over. She could ask Max for the truth in front of Kane. Because she would ask him. She wanted to look him in the eyes as he stared back in horror and bewilderment at the very prospect of what Kane was claiming. Because there was no truth in it. There couldn't be.

But there had been something about the look in Jask's eyes when he'd said it – something that chilled her. There was real anger in those eyes as if he believed it. And Kane was no fool. He was astute and perceptive enough to pick up on a liar and this meant too much to him to make a mistake. But she also knew how deeply he had loved his sister. Those kind of situations left someone demanding answers, actively looking for resolution and sometimes in the wrong place.

Of course Jask would protect his own. No one wanted Kane baying for their blood. But Jask had picked the wrong people for scapegoats. And her job was clearly more than just taking Kane in now – it was also now redeeming the name of those she loved. And if she could redeem their names, she might even be able to persuade him to help her. Help her before they took him in.

But she was kidding herself. This wasn't about her surviving the soul ripper anymore. This was about surviving Kane.

She shuddered, the shock of it all still working its way through her body.

And everything she knew told her nobody survived Kane.

He was going to kill her. He was going to tear out her soul and kill her. The ones she loved would never have been capable of inflicting what happened to Arana, but Kane was. He was capable of duplicating that. And more. So much more.

Horror of her looming fate left her disassociated even from the bathwater she was sat in. Thoughts of the pain, humiliation and degradation Arana had suffered. Reading that report was the first time she'd ever thought death could be a blessing. No one was capable of surviving that and wanting to live. She hadn't needed images – the lycans' confessions had been enough. Seeing it with her own eyes would have tipped her over the edge. Just like she was sure it had tipped Kane over the edge.

He hated her. He hated the ones who loved her more. And there was no better vengeance than putting her through what his sister had gone through. Poetic justice. Kane style. It didn't matter that he was wrong. What mattered was that he'd feel right about it.

But he wouldn't feel right about it. He couldn't feel right about it. Not when they'd been so intimate. Not after she'd felt the tenderness of his touch and the affection of his kiss. They hadn't just had sex – even she knew that. There had been some kind of connection, on some level, at least on her part.

But the thought of him inside her, of her giving herself to him, when all the time he was imagining brutalising, torturing and degrading her made acid rise at the back of her throat, her stomach twist in pain.

She stared across at the door.

And he was out there, waiting for her.

She had to stop him. She had to persuade him he was wrong. She had to. She was not going down without a fight. It was not over yet. Max was coming. She just had to keep herself alive.

She eased out of the bath, struggled down the steps and wrapped the towel around herself. She slipped out of her soaking-wet dress and dried herself off before taking clean clothes out of her bag.

She hobbled back out to where he sat on the coffee table, a first-aid kit beside him. He indicated for her to sit on the sofa facing him and she did so.

He handed her a bottle of water before lifting her foot to take a look at it again. 'I'm going to have to anaesthetise this or it'll hurt like hell taking those shards out.'

As he took a needle and small glass jar out of the box, Caitlin recoiled, yanking her foot from his hand. 'No way are you sticking that in me.'

'You won't cope without,' he said, drawing the clear fluid back into the syringe.

'I don't care. I hate needles.'

'Would you like me to pin you down and rip out the shards?'

'No.'

'Then give me your foot. Because they're coming out whether you like it or not, Caitlin. You're in agony and it's not going to improve unless you let me do this.'

'Nursing another of your many skills, is it?'

'I've cleaned up a lot of wounds in my time – bigger and worse than these – so I know what I'm doing.'

She held her gaze warily on his. For all she knew there was enough anaesthetic in that syringe to knock her out completely. But if that was what he wanted, he'd just do it. The pain was excruciating and getting worse by the minute, and she knew that if she didn't get it sorted out she was going to pass out anyway. Besides, the more focused Kane was on her, the less aware he'd be of what was going on outside. And she was certainly no use not being able to walk let alone fight or defend herself.

Reluctantly she lifted her foot across to him. She clutched the cushions as she watched him tentatively.

'Look away,' he said.

She looked across her shoulder and closed her eyes. She felt the needle go in and sucked in air, tears welling up in the corner of her eyes, her knee recoiling as she flinched at the pain, but he held her ankle tight. Her foot numbed quickly. She thought she wouldn't be able to feel him pull out the glass but she could; it made her wince but what she was experiencing was no more than an uncomfortable ache. He dropped the shards into the lid of the box one by one before cleansing her sole again. His hands were gentle, his strong fingers working deftly as he applied antiseptic and finally a bandage to her foot.

She examined the attentiveness in his eyes, his glance at her making her heart skip a beat. She lowered her gaze again as he finished and tucked her foot up on her lap, rubbing it to encourage the circulation back in. 'What are you planning to do?'

He pushed the first-aid box aside and took a mouthful of water, his gaze steady on hers as if deliberating whether to tell her. 'In order to save your life, Max and Robert are going to go public with a confession of their role in the murder of Arana. They are going to clear my sister's name and at the same time sully Xavier's and everything your precious organisation stands for. And whilst that is happening, Xavier will be with us.'

'With us? What for?'

'So I can kill him.'

Her heart pounded. 'Why do you want my soul?'

'Because the soul ripper does. When I say they're compulsive, I mean it. It'll need to finish the line it started. If I get my hands on your soul before it does, I can get it to do my bidding.'

'What bidding?'

'Simple death is too good for Carter.'

She stared at him aghast. 'You're going to set the soul ripper on Xavier? Is that why you've waited this long? Because you knew it would come back?'

'Seven years is a small price to pay.'

'But how did you know about it? How did you know it was coming for me?'

'There were a lot of questions being asked by agents around the district after your mother was killed. Max and Rob had a few private questioning sessions of their own. During their interrogations, it leaked out that they suspected your father had been killed by the same thing.'

'They said they didn't believe me.'

'Seems they have a habit of lying to you, doesn't it? Anyway, it didn't take me long to work out what it was from the descriptions – astral body gone, soul not at rest. There's only one creature that can do that.'

'So, all this time you've just been waiting? If I hadn't tracked you down, you would have just come and snatched me right out of my room anyway, wouldn't you? You've timed all this to perfection.' She frowned. 'What a shame you've got the wrong people.'

'Seven years, Caitlin. I wouldn't waste seven years on a hunch.'

'No, but clearly you have on a lie.'

'Those lycans weren't lying to Jask. And Jask hasn't lied to me. If he believed in their guilt he would have handed them over to me, not encouraged them in to detainment. Resolution and justice is the primary objective of every leader. Like I said to you, we resolve things effectively our own way. He'd gain nothing by setting agents up.'

'They didn't do it,' she snapped, shocking herself with her own vehemence. 'To stand by and let that happen would make them monsters. And the people I love are not monsters.'

Kane held her gaze fleetingly then picked up the first-aid kit as he stood.

'And how do you suppose you're going to persuade Max and Rob to confess?' she asked.

'Like I said, it's the only way they'll save your life. I'm going to tell them if they confess, I'll save you from the soul ripper.'

'They'll never believe you.'

'That'll be their choice. But I think they'll take a punt.' He stepped across to the kitchen.

Caitlin forced herself up onto her feet and limped across to him, clutching the counter as the light-headedness took over. She watched him put the first-aid kit in one of the cupboards. Her hands trembled. Her head ached. 'And then you'll kill me anyway? Is that how it'll work?' She stared at him in the silence. 'Or you'll let the soul ripper kill me. You can't help me because you can't kill the soul ripper because you need it to kill Xavier. And you can't kill it afterwards because that will release Xavier's soul – which defeats the whole object of you using a soul ripper in the first place rather than killing him by your own hand. There's no way I'm getting out of this is there?'

He met her gaze fleetingly, not needing to confirm it as he stepped past her back into the room.

Caitlin's heart ached, an empty void filling her stomach. He'd looked her in the eye with the arrogance indicative of him that he could still succeed despite telling her the truth, despite giving her every reason to close her heart to him again. But he had been right – it was something she had little control over. Her heart had been responding without her consent. Even then, when she'd never wanted to hate him more, she didn't.

But that didn't mean she couldn't.

She had to open her eyes. He was tending her wounds and disclosing his plight in order to further reinforce her growing feelings for him. He didn't even have to lie and deceive his way to her heart, and that was his greatest triumph of all.

He was winning. Kane, who, if he got the confessions and brought down Xavier, would also single-handedly bring down the reputation and success of the VCU and subsequently the entire TSCD. There would be mistrust and anarchy. The uprising they all dreaded. The devastating consequences.

She had to stop him. She had to somehow block him getting her soul long enough for Max to come. They had enough to prosecute him. It could be over within the hour. Kane had no compassion for her – that was clear. She owed him nothing. He would use her right up to the last minute. She had to remember who she was. Who he was. He wasn't going to stop and if she didn't stop him, the only people she had left to care about were going to suffer.

She had to toughen her heart. She'd had enough experience of shutting off the feelings and emotions. She would hate him. She would make him do something. She'd anger him. She'd make him lash out. She'd make him hurt her. She'd make him forget himself and reveal who he really was. Maybe worse than she had ever thought he was.

But she had to have one last stab at convincing him he was wrong. Something deep in her wanted to give him that chance. He'd been right to call her a hypocrite when she'd gone after him seeking equal retribution for her own loved ones. She had to reason with him.

'If Xavier set all this up, if he's as manipulative and powerful as you make him out to be, then maybe those I care about were just as much the victims in this as those lycans. Have you thought of that? Maybe they had no more choice than those lycans.'

He strolled back over to the sofas. 'We'll know when we get their confessions, won't we?'

'Surely you know this isn't going to work, Kane. Xavier is not going to fall for it. If what you're saying about him is true, he knows it'll be a set-up. Arana's gone, Kane.' She limped over to him. 'A long time ago. You need to accept that and move on.'

'Like you've moved on from the death of your parents?'

'I haven't got that luxury, have I?'

He reached for his drink. 'No,' he said, knocking back a mouthful, 'but at least you've got the option to be reunited with them.'

The coldness of the remark chilled her, adding to her escalating fury. Her hands trembled as she stepped between him and the television. She wasn't going to get through to him, so she had no choice.

She knew how to get the reaction she needed. Kane had only one weakness – she'd seen it already. Her stomach clenched at the cruelty of what she was about to say.

'Your sister was no saint, Kane. Maybe you should accept that. I know what happened to her wasn't pleasant, but how do you know she didn't go there on purpose? Everyone knows what she was like.' Kane's gaze rested unnervingly on hers as she twisted the knife a little further. 'And maybe it didn't help her always thinking she had her hero older brother to help her – his reputation to save her. Maybe she wouldn't have got herself in the situation if it wasn't for you always looking out for her. So why don't you try and take some responsibility for what happened instead of blaming everyone else? Maybe if you'd given in to Xavier none of it would have happened. It's a shame you weren't thinking of Arana then instead of yourself and your pathetic pride.'

She waited for the onslaught, but he said nothing. He did nothing. His eyes narrowed slightly in a way that terrified her. She swallowed hard and braced herself.

'Arana suffered because you're too arrogant to accept your place,' she continued. 'Just like you and Arana suffered as kids because your parents couldn't. Your father was too conceited to accept defeat and so are you. It's your inflated sense of self-importance that killed Arana in the end, just like your father's killed your mother and nearly killed you. You're nothing Kane. Master vampire means nothing anymore.'

His gaze didn't flinch as he stood up and sauntered over to her. Caitlin backed against the wall, her heels hitting the skirting board as he braced his hand beside her head. She held her breath, not daring to move.

'Are you trying to incite me, Caitlin? Do you want me to do something to hurt you so you can hate me? Do you really think I'm that gullible?'

'I'm stating facts, Kane: those little things that seem to be eluding you in all this.'

'Your precious Max and Robert held those two lycans captive for three days before a full moon and starved them of their meds,' he said, his tone unnervingly calm. 'They delivered them in a cage to where your father had tied my sister to a post. They hid in a van and watched it all on screen as they deactivated those cage locks. They didn't even give her a chance to run or defend herself. Those are the facts.'

'According to Jask. According to the lycans who killed her.'

'Your father was a cruel and merciless coward. Max, the man you look up to in place of him, the man who shared your mother's bed after your father died, is a liar and a self-seeking hypocrite. Rob, the man you loved, the only man you've ever loved, abandoned you and ran away because he was scared of what was coming after you. You keep defending them all you want, but I know the truth. And you can push me all you want, but I'm not going to hurt you. I wouldn't give you or them the satisfaction.'

She exhaled curtly as he pulled away. 'No, you're just using me to get to Xavier, just like Xavier used Arana. You're no different. You're both the same you and him. If anything of what you've said is true then he's won. You're as much a monster as he is and you're going to prove it to everyone, just like you're already proving it to me. You can't even see that you've already lost. I couldn't hate you more right now if I tried.'

He turned to face her again.

Her hands clenched, but she refused to move as he stepped up to her again.

She flinched as he cupped her jaw, as he ran his thumb across her lips. But then he kissed her, a full, slow, lingering kiss that knocked her off guard until she tore her lips from his.

'Hate, right?' he said, the mocking clear in his eyes.

She lifted her hand ready to swipe the infuriating smirk off his face, but he caught her wrist in an instant, pressed her hip back against the wall with his other hand, her glower clearly meaning nothing to him.

'Do you really want to do this?' he asked.

She pulled on every reserve and every resolve. 'My family have done nothing wrong. Legally or morally. Your sister had it coming, Kane. Just as you have.'

Caitlin shivered in the passing moments as Kane's attention remained painfully unwavering, his eyes disturbingly unreadable. She braced herself, fear consuming her to a point she was sure she stopped breathing.

'Finished?' he asked.

The simplicity of his response made every hair stiffen on the back of her neck.

He leaned closer as he pressed her wrist back against the wall beside her head. 'Do you know what I'm seeing when I look into your eyes right now? One very desperate and very scared little girl who's clutching at whatever she can. That's the same look that your father, Max and Rob would have seen in my sister's eyes when she realised what they had set up. So do I treat you the same way? Do I tie you to a post now? Do I torture you and rape you and beat you? Do I humiliate and degrade you? Do I leave you here for Max and Rob to find you? Will that make me feel better? Will that allow me to exact my revenge? No. Because the very thought of it sickens me to my stomach. Because I'm not the same even if you do want to convince yourself otherwise. I would never enact it nor would I stand by and allow it to happen. To anyone. That's the difference between me and those you know and love, hard as it is for you to take. So you keep looking for an excuse to hate me and rebuild that wall around your heart, but I'm giving you no reason because you have none.'

'No, you're just planning to rip out my soul to use it to your own ends before shoving it back in so the soul ripper can get me. Where's your morality in that, Kane? Tell me how I deserve that any more than Arana deserved what happened to her? You might have held back on what you could have done to me but that's only because you've had to. You are still a brutal killer. Hide behind whatever mask or guise you want, I know what you are and I am going to give you one hell of a battle for my soul. Try and take it now. Go on – I dare you.'

He assessed her eyes then smiled before releasing her and stepping away.

'You know, don't you?' she said. 'You know you're not in there enough. You've tried every trick and you've failed. Less than a day to go and you haven't won the heart of the one woman you need. And you're not going to. Any self-respecting vampire would already be opting for plan B.'

He stopped at the footboard, clutching it, his back still to her as she took a few steps closer.

'Come on, Kane, you're no hero so you might as well play the villain to the full. All that pent-up frustration must be fit to bursting point. You know what you want to do to me. It's the only way you're going to get any kind of payback for Arana and we both know it.' She paused, her throat constricted in fear, in desperation. 'If you loved her, you wouldn't even be hesitating.'

'Desperate, Caitlin. So desperate,' he said quietly. He looked over his shoulder at her. 'Because you'd have to be to even be contemplating what you're suggesting.' He turned to face her. 'Taking one for the team who have got no respect for you anyway. For the people who care about you so deeply that they let you come after me knowing what I could do to you. Is that all you're worth?' He reached out and pulled her towards him, pressed her up against the bedpost. 'Do you really want to call my bluff? Shall I call yours? One more little shove, Caitlin, and who knows what I'll do.'

But as she held his calm, intense gaze, she dropped her own in irritation.

He gently caught hold of her jaw, forcing her to look back at him again. 'Do you want to know how I know it was your father who was responsible? The soul ripper is passed on by a curse, Caitlin, not by chance. And it can only be incanted by the spilling of archaic blood. In this case, Arana's. Now blame her if you choose, but ask yourself what you would have done in her situation? Gone out quietly or left a trail for your brother to follow? Xavier is to blame for this. And your father, Max and Robert were a willing part of it. Everyone's using you, Caitlin. It just depends if you're going to stand by those principles of yours, your claims of the selflessness of humanity, and let the right one win.'

Caitlin felt the tears welling up behind her eyes. 'My father was a good man.'

'Your father was a dogmatic power seeker.'

'You didn't know him.'

'I know he had a taste for female vampires.'

'You're a liar,' she said as she lashed out to punch him in the arm, but he caught her hand. 'Everything you say is a lie,' she added, swiping with the other.

He caught both. 'Why? Because telling you these lies would help my cause? I'm telling you them because I think you deserve the truth.'

'I don't believe anything that comes out of your mouth,' she snapped, trying to struggle free, but his grip was firm and unrelenting. She blinked away a tear of frustration. 'Get off me!'

'They allowed you to come after me because they think I don't know about their dark little secret. They think they've got away with it. And as far as Xavier is concerned, everyone's expendable on his quest for me. This is never going to stop unless I end it. You want to hate me? Try – but you already know that it makes sense. You understand why I'm doing this. Deep down you know I need to do this. Deep down you know I'm right.'

She pulled away from him, rubbing the tears from her eyes with the heel of her palm as she limped across to the bathroom. Slamming the door behind her, she fell back against it.

# CHAPTER TWENTY

Jask was lying. Kane was lying. The alternative didn't bear thinking about.

Caitlin's body ran cold. If it were true, Max knew and had said nothing. He'd let her track Kane without any word of the history. Xavier, Max and Rob had all let her come there and not one of them had told her the truth. Not even Rob that night he had come around. But it explained why both had tried so vehemently to persuade her otherwise. And other things niggled such as Rob's sudden departure from her life and his and Max's fervent denial of any link between her parents' deaths. Then there was Max's insistence she shouldn't take Kane's case all those years ago.

And those questions during the disciplinary interview. All Xavier and Max had wanted to know was what Kane had said: if he had mentioned why he wanted her. The same questions that Rob had asked when he came to her apartment the following night. They were worried. But why wouldn't they be? Kane Malloy had her in his sights – of course they'd be worried. She clutched her head. He was toying with her mind – making her believe what he wanted her to believe. He was shifting the blame to her family so she'd feel no loyalty to them, so that she'd feel empathy with him. He was playing her and she was letting him.

She needed Max there now. She needed to know that he and her father were not capable of such an atrocity. That Max would have cared enough about her to warn her rather than hide his dark and nasty secret. More so, that Rob would have done more to stop her.

She grabbed a bunch of toilet paper. She stepped up to the sink and ran the paper under the cold tap before dabbing the red patches and blemishes around her eyes, cooling her cheeks and calming her tears.

But if Kane and Jask were telling her the truth, Xavier was responsible for the worst atrocities. And her father, Max and Rob had gone along with it. Xavier who could, at that moment, be on the way to collect Kane. And he wouldn't let him go this time. Xavier could do anything to him – anything to the monster he was responsible for creating. Xavier who had encouraged her there even though he knew her life was at risk.

If Kane was telling her the truth, every principle told her she had to tell him the VCU were on their way.

But if he was lying…

She used the toilet and washed her hands before slumping onto the bath steps. The cool night air was refreshing against her skin as the breeze tunnelled through the small gaps.

There was only one way she'd know for sure and that was to look directly into Rob's or Max's eyes when she asked them. The only problem was, by then it would be too late.

She looked across at the door as the handle turned.

Kane leaned against the doorframe, gazing down at her with those beautiful navy eyes that captivated her so easily. As he sat down next to her, she turned to face him.

'Let me out of here to confront Max and Rob. If you're telling the truth, I'll get the confessions out of them and I'll go to the governing board. We'll bring Xavier down that way. It'll do him a hell of a lot more damage than setting the soul ripper on him. This plan you've got will point every finger in your direction. You will have every unit agent after you. It'll be over for you. Xavier will still win. Vindicate yourself and vindicate Arana that way.'

'And get it all cleared up by tomorrow night?'

'It can be done if you let me go now. Because if you're telling me the truth, I owe Xavier just as much for this as you do. I will see this through.'

'You're not going anywhere, Caitlin.'

'I've done nothing wrong, Kane. You don't need to make me suffer when there are alternatives.'

'This has never been about making you suffer. But I am going to do this my way.'

'And to hell with what happens to me?' She exhaled curtly and moved to pull away from him, but he caught hold of her lower arm to keep her beside him.

'What would you prefer, Caitlin? False promises like everyone else you know?'

'And what then, Kane? When you get what you want: when you bring down Xavier and the VCU, the entire TSCD.'

'This is about vengeance, Caitlin, not power.'

'And you'll just walk away?'

'I will have done what I had to do.'

'You're not going to change your mind, are you?'

His gaze was steady. 'No.'

The ache in her heart was all-consuming as she stared deep into his eyes. She wanted to tell him he'd regret it. She wanted to tell him that maybe in a matter of hours she'd be the only advocate he had. But it wasn't the time for personal outbursts. And she couldn't bear to look at him anymore. Because even then, even knowing the risk he posed to her and her family, she couldn't help the pain in her chest. She had no option but to let them take him. Once she told them he knew about the soul ripper, they'd let her read him to find out how to kill it. It was the best she could hope for.

'I was right the first time,' she said. 'You and Xavier are the same, using whoever you can to get what you want. Whatever justice you think you can assign to your actions, they're embedded in the same justifications as his.'

'Fine,' he said, standing and stepping over to the door. 'Believe what you want. It'll make no difference.'

'Don't turn your back on me, Kane!' she warned, following him out.

'Turning my back on the great vampire hunter, hell no, we can't have that.' He turned to face her. 'Despite the fact it's been me protecting your arse the past seven years.'

'What's that supposed to mean?'

'What do you think it means? You think you would have survived this long without some protection? Especially when you took it on yourself to become a VCU agent.'

Caitlin exhaled curtly. 'I've achieved what I have on my own merits.'

'You're good, Caitlin, but you're not that good. Come on, do you really think you would have survived in the field this long without some help? Like I've said before, it's no place for a girl like you.'

'Is that what Jask meant by a no-touch policy on me?'

'You've got bubbles bursting all over the place tonight, haven't you?'

She couldn't move for disbelief. 'You bastard.'

'Great – now I'm a bastard for keeping you safe.'

'I am a damn good agent!'

He stepped up to her. 'And you're also impetuous and obstinate and yes, at times, fucking suicidal. You ran in after me, remember? You think under any other circumstances I couldn't have snapped your neck within seconds? You're a survivor because I needed you to survive. You go on about my arrogance, but I've got nothing on you if you think you could have done this without me.'

She stepped up to him. 'I could have killed you if I'd wanted to. If I hadn't needed you. Remember the hemlock in the handle? That could have been a lethal dose if I'd chosen it to be.'

He exhaled tersely, his hands loose on his hips. 'Darling, you're forgetting you only got that close because I let you.'

'Honey, the only reason you're still alive is because we had orders that you had to remain that way.'

'Exactly,' Kane said. 'From Xavier. Ask yourself why.'

'Because you're a master vampire.'

'Because he wants me. For power. How much do you want the truth to bite you on the arse, Caitlin, before you accept it? Your boss has used you, your stepfather has deceived you, your boyfriend abandoned you and your father caused the death of your mother. Those are the truths here.'

She stood there, unable to contain her trembling, unable to contain her tears any longer. And when he turned his back on her again, it was the final wound. She turned away from him and hurriedly wiped her tears away. She hadn't even let her mother see her cry. Nor Max. Rob had been the last. And she'd sworn then he'd be the only. Once had been enough – an awkward and uncomfortable moment when Rob hadn't quite been sure what to do with himself. So she sure as hell wasn't going to let a vampire who clearly hated her see that part of her. She needed to get a grip. She couldn't afford for him to see even an ounce of vulnerability. She pushed her hair back from her face before clutching on to the footboard for balance, her efforts to suppress her already silent tears constricting her throat.

And she flinched as his body touched hers, as his hand slid between her and the footboard to catch her hip, turning her towards him.

She shoved his hand away, but he turned her fully to meet him, easing her against him. She twisted away but his insistence was unrelenting as he pulled her against his chest. Caitlin struggled for a moment until it got too much – the pain and the confusion and the exhaustion tightening its grip until she couldn't breathe. And as his insistent grip loosened, her anger morphed into despair. She didn't want to sink against him, but her reluctant lack of fight gave her no choice. His arms were, ironically, a comfort, his silence calming, his head resting against hers the final act of tenderness that pushed her over the edge. And she sobbed. And as Kane stroked her hair, as she felt the strength and reassurance of his shoulder against her cheek, the hardness of his chest pressed against her, the gentleness of his hand on her neck as he held her against him, she let her tears dampen his shirt.

And despite knowing why Kane was doing it, she absorbed herself in his closeness because, for those few minutes, she needed more than anything to feel him there. Sobbing against him didn't feel strange, even though it should have. It had been years since she had been held and comforted. But she knew why it felt so easy. And if she felt that comfortable being that close to him, that exposed to him, even after what he had said, she was in more danger than even she had been willing to acknowledge.

But luckily for her, years of practice had made distance easy, had made anger and frustration easier emotions, safer emotions. She pulled away, wiped away the dampness on her cheeks. 'Oh, you're good,' she said. 'Very smooth.' And as she backed away, the void she'd created caused her pain to a point that terrified her.

It was perfect. That one act of her pulling away told him everything he needed to know. It was even more telling than how she'd curled into him to accept his comfort. She'd pulled away in panic, and there was only one thing that was going to evoke that response: her soul was ready for the taking.

It should have given him a kick of triumph but, to his annoyance, it didn't.

And as she glowered at him, her eyes wary with trepidation, he wanted to pull her back to him and tell her how insulting her last statement had been. That all he had thought of when he'd heard her almost silent tears was of comforting her. And maybe if he'd told her that, it could have secured his goal.

But confessing the truth then would have been cruel. He clearly already had her. Anything more was unnecessary.

She was right to pull away. And he needed to forge that distance again – for her and for him.

It irritated him that holding her that close had made him wonder what could happen if he did play hero. It shouldn't have even have crossed his mind because playing her hero meant letting those who had hurt his sister get away with it. That could not happen. Not for her. Not for anyone.

And for what, even if he did? He couldn't be what she needed. Sexually, maybe. Intellectually even. But emotionally, no. She needed a deep connection, something he wasn't willing to grant anyone. Not since Arana. Not since his heart had been torn out. He would see this through and then five, ten, fifty years from now, Caitlin would become a distant memory – just like the female he'd been with the night of Arana's death. He owed his sister far more than some VCU agent. That had to stay forefront in his mind.

But still it simmered: how he could let Max and Rob go with a confession; leave the lycans in the detainment unit to rot; get them to drop Xavier in it first. But none of those things were sufficient justice for what they had done to Arana.

Not just because of the way he was feeling about Caitlin right then.

She had no life anyway, just a lonely and solitary existence based around work. And now even that had been torn apart; she wouldn't trust anyone again. Her life was over anyway.

But she had fallen for him. The beautiful, brave, closed-off shadow reader had opened up to him. And he could never have softened to her more as she gazed deep into his eyes, her own resonating a deep and painful hurt. It was more than a physical attraction. More than just the thrill. She had seen something in him that she had liked.

And he couldn't deny how he'd felt when she'd escaped – that excruciating emptiness of not having her there. But he couldn't live like that. He couldn't have her in his life when she'd started to mean something to him. He couldn't have the pressure of worrying about her every day, of needing to protect her, of keeping her happy, of being what she needed him to be. For her to walk away one day when she realised just how damaged he was. Because he was damaged. He was too used to being on his own, of not feeling responsible for anyone, of doing whatever he wanted. Of keeping his finger off the self-destruct button only so he could make the people who had hurt Arana pay. And once that was dealt with, he didn't know what was out there for him.

He had no place falling for Caitlin. Not for the girl whose self-preservation, even then, was astounding. Many would have given up faced with the things she was, but she was going to fight him to the bitter end. And because of it, one way or another, he was going to end up hurting her.

He needed to get out of there before he acted against his better judgement. He needed fresh air. He needed space from her. He needed to remind himself that she meant nothing. She was just a means to an end.

Her beautiful eyes narrowed in their distress. 'What was going through your head as you saw me falling for you?'

'Trust me, you don't want to know.'

'Why? Because if I finally see you for what you are, all your progress will be shattered?'

'Because what is going on in my head is none of your business. I made it clear what I wanted you for. I fucked you, you were willing. That's all there is to it.'

Caitlin drew back her hand and slapped him hard across the face.

He knew he could have stopped her. But he also knew it was justified. And the pain in her eyes at that moment was excruciating, twisting his insides and sickening him. He took a moment to compose himself then looked back at her. He couldn't be angry with her or feel indignation towards her when she looked as startled and uncomfortable as she did. It had been an instinctive emotional response and one he could clearly see she hated herself for.

'I guess I deserved that,' he said.

Her eyes glossed, her lower lip trembling almost undetectably had he not become used to studying her so closely. 'Do you really feel so little, Kane?'

He broke from the intensity of her probing gaze, from the need in her eyes. And he hated himself for bringing her to that. Out of all the questions she could have asked him, it was the one that pierced the deepest. And as he looked back into her heartbreaking eyes, honesty slipped from his lips before he could contain it. 'Sometimes when I touch you it's almost painful. Standing this close to you now just makes me want to consume you. It makes me want to forget my principles and intentions and just let myself go with you. And right now I'm feeling so close to the edge, it's taking everything I have to stop myself throwing you down on the floor and forgetting every part of my plan just to have one moment as I really am with you. Only, sure enough, you'd hate me for it. You'd hate me for what I really am. So that's why I can't back down, Caitlin. For both our sakes.'

Caitlin snapped back a breath, her eyes flared. He'd thrown her off kilter. He could almost see her playing his words over in her mind. She didn't know how to respond. She didn't know what to do with herself.

He glanced at her clenched hands then back at the lips he wanted to graze with his own. And because of this, never more did he need to remind himself of who and what she was, and the damage her family and the people she cared about had done. He had to remind himself of how much she irritated and aggravated him with her dogmatism and defiance. She was a VCU agent. She was the one arrogant enough to think she could hunt him down. He couldn't feel anything for her. She couldn't feel anything more for him than infatuation. And that would pass. She could never love him. Not enough. She'd come to hate him. They'd tear each other apart.

But those eyes didn't glimmer with hatred or anger now, they softened with shock and confusion.

But there was something else. Something he couldn't work out.

Her lips were parted ready to speak. But she was hesitating. Deliberating. She looked worried. Panicked even.

Betrayal struck him hard and fast, wounding him more than he knew it should have as he realised what had happened.

He caught hold of her wrist and pulled her close. 'You got to a phone, didn't you?'

She didn't even need to answer him – the flare in her eyes said it all.

He let her go and marched up to the wardrobe. He gathered the book and packets from the top shelf.

'Kane, you have to let me go,' she said, tears welling behind her eyes.

He didn't even look at her as he passed her on his way across to the door. He yanked it open and marched across to the car. He opened the passenger door and shoved the book and packets into the glove compartment before pressing the remote for the automatic garage door.

He strode back towards her as the late-night breeze seeped into the enclosure.

'Kane, please,' she said, taking a backward step to the threshold.

He caught a scent. Human. Male.

Felt the shot in his back.

Three further shots sent him to his knees.

He heard footsteps. Two sets.

He didn't need to look over his shoulder.

He knew exactly who it was.

# CHAPTER TWENTY-ONE

Caitlin stared at Max and Rob approaching from the open garage door with their guns still poised, then back at Kane laying face down on the floor.

Max hurried over. 'Are you okay, Caitlin?'

She nodded as if on autopilot. She should have been elated, over-whelmed with relief. Instead, unease stirred in the pit of her stomach. All she could think about was what Kane had said. Those words hadn't been about getting her soul, they had been about bearing his own – a soul that didn't exist but was represented nonetheless by depth and pain and turmoil.

She looked from Kane's unconscious body back to Max. His face seemed different, unfamiliar, as if she'd been away for weeks. But she knew it wasn't that. He felt unfamiliar to her because of the secrets that had leaked out. A secret she needed him to deny, even more than she needed Rob to deny it. She needed to know that her father, and Max – the man who had then stepped into his breach – were not capable of what now seemed all too real in her head.

And she felt sick. Had felt physically sick as Kane had looked deep into her eyes during those last moments and told her how he'd felt. Because she'd believed what he'd said. And right there, right then, she needed to know she hadn't made the worst mistake of her life calling them for help.

Max stepped past Kane and hurried over to her as he tucked his gun back in his shoulder holster. He swiftly assessed the grazes on her knees and knuckles, the bandage around her foot. 'What's he done to you?'

'What really happened to Arana, Max?'

She didn't intend for it to come out that quickly. That directly. She wasn't even sure she was ready to ask.

The silence was palpable. The panic and disconcertion in his eyes was all the confirmation she needed. But he wasn't panicking because she had found out – Max was panicking because he realised Kane had found out.

Her heart pounded, almost deafening her. Her attention snapped to Rob, his gun still poised on Kane. The look in his eyes only verified the truth in Max's.

Max took another step towards her. 'Caitlin…' he began, adopting the negotiator tone she was all too familiar with.

She took a step back, uncertain how she would react, flinching and wincing at the pain in her foot despite the generous bandaging. 'Tell me you didn't help set her up. That you didn't give her to those lycans.'

'Caitlin, this is not the time or the place. I don't know what Kane—'

'Tell me!' she demanded, trembling fiercely.

Max reached for her arm. 'Okay, Caitlin. We need to get you out of here. We'll talk back at mine.'

She clenched her fists and took another step back, sickness gathering at the back of her throat. 'Kane told me Xavier wants him alive. Is that right? That he wants him to work for him. That you killed Arana to get him to do just that. That Xavier set him up because he wasn't getting his own way.'

Max sighed, his eyes sullen but patient. 'Caitlin, not even you know how dangerous Kane is. Why do you think he moved to this area? He wants to own this place. Just like he's owned every other place he's been allowed to slither his way into. He would take over. Our unit, everything we stand for, would mean nothing compared to the influence he would exude. We couldn't allow him that power.'

'So you set him up.'

'We had to do something to incite him. We had to have him go after the lycans. We had to get enough to convict him outright.'

She swallowed the anger responsible for the lump in her throat. She had never felt the need to defend someone so strongly. Someone who now lay on the floor at her feet because of what she had done. 'I read those reports, Max. I read what happened to her.'

'We did what we had to. We did it for the good of this district.'

'The reports said the lycans tied her to a post, but they didn't, did they? You did. You all did. Then what? You stood back and watched?'

'Caitlin, we had tried everything else. He was no innocent. You know the crimes he's committed. You know how impossible it has been to pin anything on him. Xavier had tried for years. It was a last resort.'

'So he went after the one and only thing Kane cared about.'

'He'd already weaved his way into the community. The fact we couldn't get anyone to speak against him was proof of that. With Kane in control, this district wouldn't stand a chance. Everything we have to keep order would have been out-ruled. This is what we're about – to stop them getting too powerful, to protect the masses. You advocate that.'

'I would never advocate what happened to Arana, what she was subjected to. If Xavier was that desperate, he could have killed Kane. He's not untouchable. He could have sent in a task force to execute him. But he wanted him alive, right? Xavier wanted Kane Malloy under his thumb to extend his own authority. This is about his power trip, not Kane's. And you went along with it.'

'It's my job. It's our job.'

'Our job is to keep the peace and to keep the third species in line, but only to protect them from their own as much as to protect humans.'

'Be real, Caitlin. You knew there was more going on behind the scenes than just that interrogation room. Do you really think shadow readers are our only ways to get convictions? There are two sides to this business. You knew that the VCU was the darker side of law enforcement. You were warned when you joined that things happen that probably shouldn't. But we are combating things that have no regards for principles, or morals or laws of any kind.'

'And some of us fight that with fairness and justice and by upholding what is right.'

'Kane was a risk to us all. To everything we advocate. He could wipe out our influence within months and then there would be anarchy, and it would be our kind that would suffer. People get caught in the crossfire of a war. It's a fact. This time it was Arana.'

She stared at Max. The only man she had trusted those last few years now felt like a stranger. 'How long did it take them to kill her?'

'It was over in an hour.'

'An hour.' Her stomach clenched. 'You stood by for an hour. You let her be brutalised and murdered and you did nothing. You slaughtered an innocent vampire just to control her brother.'

'She was no innocent,' Rob cut in. 'You don't know the half of it. She was as dangerous and unruly as him. It was the only option we had to protect our own kind and to protect vulnerable third-species members.'

'To protect them?' She exhaled curtly. 'If Kane hadn't discovered the truth, you could have started a civil war with your stupidity! Which is exactly what Xavier wanted, wasn't it? Discord in the ranks and Kane the instigator. Or every lycan baying for his blood until he did exactly what Xavier asked and turned to him for protection. Xavier must have been very disappointed when everything fell quiet. And you must have thought you'd got away with it.'

'We covered our backs and the backs of those lycans. It was part of the deal. The lycans gave themselves up and we offered them anonymity in order to protect their families.'

'You put them in an impossible situation, you mean. Damned if they did, damned if they didn't. And they chose a lifetime in detainment rather than face Kane's wrath. And you took them in because you didn't want to risk them spilling the truth. And Xavier let them live in case they ever became useful in his quest for Kane.' She glanced to the floor and shook her head before looking back up at them. 'Just tell me

Xavier made you do it. Just tell me he threatened you like he threatened those lycans. He threatened my mother. Or me. Tell me you had no choice.'

'We did what was good for the district.'

Their resoluteness infuriated her. 'Illegally and immorally. Did my mother know about this?' she asked, dreading that Max might say yes.

Max shook his head and the sincerity in his eyes told her it was the truth. 'No.'

'We have to go,' Rob said. 'Now. Those sedatives will only last so long.'

'Frightened of facing him, Rob?' she snapped. 'Because I would be if I were you. I'd be terrified.'

'I'm sure he hasn't told you the whole story.'

'Between him and Jask, I know enough.'

Max's eyes flared in panic. 'Jask?'

'Yes, Max – Jask. They both know. They both told me. Those two lycans went to Jask before they came to you.'

Max glanced across at Rob then looked back at Caitlin. 'The car's outside. We'll get Kane in it and then we'll talk.'

'All these years,' Caitlin said. 'All these years and you said nothing. You let me chase him down, you let me come on this mission and you said nothing.'

'I tried to talk you out of it,' Max reminded her.

'You should have told me the facts the minute I walked out of that interrogation room!'

'I tried to stop you. But how could I without letting you know everything else that had happened?'

'Without telling me the truth, you mean.'

She turned her attention to Rob. 'You could have told me the night you came around. If you cared anything for me, you would have.'

He should have looked remorseful, but he didn't. She thought of the times they had shared, the person she thought he was. Now to think of what he was capable of sickened her. Any confidence she'd had in her ability to read people had been torn out by those closest to her. Those she should have been able to trust more than any others.

'We didn't think Kane could have possibly found out,' Rob said. 'We thought he was after you for your shadow-reading. He was coming after you regardless. If you'd known the truth you could have let it slip, and then you would have been at worse risk.' He looked back at Max. 'We really have to go.'

'You're not taking him to HQ,' Caitlin warned, her gaze snapping from one to the other. 'Not now.'

'We're not taking him back to HQ,' Max said.

Caitlin frowned, her chest clenching. 'Then what are you going to do with him?'

Max looked at Rob. Rob met his gaze. The exchange sent a chill up her back. She was about to demand they tell her, when Max spoke. 'We need answers from him.'

'Answers?' But a split second later, she didn't need any clarity. Pain lanced her chest at the betrayal. 'You've known all along. Kane was telling the truth about that too. You know it's coming for me.'

Max held out his hand again. 'Caitlin–'

Caitlin recoiled. 'You let me think I was insane for believing there was a link. For thinking it was coming for me. You kept telling me that I was imagining things, looking for patterns in things that weren't there. Do you know that's what the counsellor told me? She said I needed resolution. I was punishing myself as sometimes people do when they lose a loved one. And thinking of something coming for me was a comfort. A comfort? She actually used those words.'

'I wasn't going to let you live like that, Caitlin,' Max declared. 'Letting the years tick away in fear.'

'You looked me in the eye,' she said to Max, 'and you told me there was no link.' She glowered at Rob. 'And worse than that, so did you. Is that why you left me, Rob? Were you too ashamed to face me? Or were you too scared of what was coming for me?'

'We tried to find out what it was,' Rob insisted. 'We worked flat out trying to get a name for it so at least we could ask the right questions. But no one would talk to us. No one knew anything.'

'Do you blame them, if they suspected what you'd done? Do you really think any third-species member who had heard what had happened to Arana really believed it was the lycans? They knew, Rob. The whole community knew it was a set-up. No wonder they never talked. No wonder no one would ever answer my questions. The community closed in on itself because of what you all did. And do you know what? You just made them respect Kane more. You just made them admire and trust him more because he showed intelligence and control and dignity. He didn't tear the community apart like Xavier was hoping. He wanted to turn Kane's own people against him. And he failed. And he'll keep failing because Kane is untouchable.'

'Clearly not,' Rob said. 'Not anymore. We got him in the end, didn't we?'

Caitlin's stomach clenched as the whole truth unravelled before her. 'You didn't just come back for me, did you? You were already coming back. You knew the clock was ticking.' She stared at Max aghast. 'You could have locked me away somewhere if you'd wanted, but you used me for bait, just like Xavier did. You wanted Kane just as much.'

'We had no choice if we were to help you,' Max said. 'We needed to find a way to stop that thing.'

'The soul ripper.'

Max frowned. 'What?'

'That's the nickname for it. Why do you think I took the task, Max?'

Rob looked across at Max. 'I told you there was more to it.'

Max's eyes widened in disbelief. 'Kane told you what it is?'

Caitlin nodded.

'Did he tell you how to kill it too?'

Caitlin shook her head. 'But he will.' There was no way they were taking him now. No way. She'd sort this. She'd sort this with Kane her way. 'And for that you both need to walk right back out of that door. Now.'

Rob exhaled curtly and stepped up to her. 'Not going to happen. Come on, let's get you in the car.'

She pulled back, snatching her arm away. 'Don't you touch me,' she warned, her tone dangerously low.

Rob pulled back, impatience emanating in his eyes.

He and Max exchanged glances in a way that made Caitlin's skin crawl with unease. She saw Max reach into his jacket pocket, and knew what he was planning.

Caitlin tried to back away, but Rob caught hold of her, clamped his hand over her mouth to silence her protests.

She tried to kick out again as Max slid the needle into the crook of her arm.

'I know you're angry right now,' Rob said. 'But you'll understand. We started this and we're going to finish it. Tomorrow night we will kill that soul ripper and this will all be over. I promise.'

# CHAPTER TWENTY-TWO

Kane woke with an adrenaline-infused start. He quickly scanned the basement.

Rob stood directly ahead, a few feet away, arms folded as he leaned against a bench, his blue eyes stony.

Placing a wooden chair equidistant between them, Max eased back in it. 'Hello, Kane.'

Kane assessed the manacles that held his arms outstretched and gently twisted his arms to test their resilience. The hinges were tight, melded. He had no numbness or ache so he hadn't been there long. The manacles that held his feet secure to the floor gave him no room for flexion. He wasn't going anywhere fast.

He surveyed the implements hanging from the walls – the iron and silver tools. The bench running along to his right looking like some-thing out of an operating theatre with its sharp implements, syringes and jars of liquid and paste. Soundproofed. Airtight. He wondered how many other vampires had been brought to the torture chamber when legal methods weren't yielding results. And he'd heard Max always liked to get results.

There was no sign of Caitlin. Equally there was no sign of Carter. If he had been involved it would have been him waking him – he wouldn't have been able to resist. This had been done on the quiet – which meant one thing: this was purely personal. And it took no guesses to work out what they wanted. Max had woken him quickly and that meant he needed information quickly. This was about saving Caitlin.

'I'm going to keep this simple, Kane,' Max said. 'I want to know how to kill the soul ripper.'

Kane glowered at Max and flexed his wrists in the restraints. 'Is this you asking nicely?'

'This is me telling you nicely.'

'Because that's going to work.'

Max leaned forward, his elbows resting on his knees. 'Let's not play games, Kane. Caitlin's given us a name. Now we want to know the rest.'

'Where is the lovely Caitlin?'

'Somewhere you'll never get to her again,' Rob said, his glare unflinching.

'I've seen the state of her, Kane,' Max declared. 'That doesn't make me happy.'

'Trust me,' Kane said, sending a glance Rob's way. 'I didn't do anything she didn't want. She certainly wasn't objecting,' he added with a smirk. 'Not in the end, anyway.'

Rob stood upright from the bench and marched towards him, but Max held out an arm, blocking his way. Their glares locked for a moment, then Rob reluctantly took a step back.

'That's quite a temper you've got there, Robert,' Kane declared, meeting his glare square on. 'It must be all that pent-up sexual frustration. Caitlin was telling me about some of your difficulties. While I was helping her work through some of hers.'

Max stood up, drew back his fist and slammed it into Kane's chest.

Kane winced, the tautness of his binds giving him little room for flexion to soften the impact. It was a powerful punch. An emotive one. Max meant business, he had no doubt about that. He glared back up at Max as he took a couple of steps back. 'You're making a bad mistake.'

'No, you made a bad mistake going after Caitlin. You made a mistake getting her involved.'

'I didn't get her involved, Max,' Kane reminded him. 'You did.'

'That was a long time ago, Kane,' Max declared. 'You really should have got over it by now.'

Kane glared up into his steely grey eyes. 'Then untie me and let's resolve this.'

Max lifted the chair and placed it closer, sitting on it so he was less than a foot away. He leaned forward. 'Your bitch of a sister killed my best friend and my wife. That thing she set on them is not going to get Caitlin. I have less than 24 hours, Kane. You will talk. Do it now and preserve your dignity.'

'Which part of "Fuck you" are you not getting?'

'What are you up to, Kane? Why now?'

'You allowed my sister to be brutalised and murdered. I want to feel better about that.'

'By going after Caitlin? She has done nothing to you other than be the unfortunate link in all of this.'

'Like my sister was?'

'Caitlin does not deserve that thing coming after her.'

'I can't help what you caused. What Xavier caused.'

'If you knew all this time, why now? Why have you left it so late?'

Kane held his gaze steadily on Max, and smirked.

Max looked across at Rob. 'I think this is going to have to get nasty quickly.'

'The sooner the better,' Rob said.

Max strolled over to the table and lifted a silver knife. 'I've been doing this for thirty years, Kane – getting information out of species like you. I used to have to use this room a lot. For the unofficial interrogations, of course.' He strolled back over towards him. 'The work to get the leads in the first place. You won't believe some of the things I had to do down here. Lots of it was about you. But nobody would speak about you, of course. Scared. Revered. I never could break one over you. I had one vampire under a UV lamp for fourteen hours. There was nothing left of him, but still he'd say nothing. See, that's the loyalty Xavier wants. That's the power he's jealous of. And he's never going to rest until he's got you. I know that much.' He strolled around the back of him, put the point at his shoulder and dragged downwards, the searing heat making Kane wince. 'The difference is Xavier wants you intact.' He leaned into his ear. 'I just want answers.'

The anger seethed through him, but he knew he had to contain it. If he wound them up too much he didn't doubt they would take their chances and kill him.

'So come on now, Kane,' Max said. 'Don't make this hard on yourself.'

'Maybe he wants to,' Rob said. 'Maybe it's all that latent guilt about wasting time with a whore while his sister was being murdered. You always knew how to prioritise, didn't you, Kane?'

Kane glowered up at him. 'And where were your priorities when I had Caitlin pinned up against the wall in that corridor? When I took her from her own bed where you should have been?'

'Tell us how to kill it, Kane,' Max repeated.

Kane exhaled curtly, his glare on Max unflinching.

Rob wandered over to the table. He picked up a selection of iron nails and reached for a hammer.

'I don't have time for this,' Max warned. 'You will tell me how to stop the soul ripper. Even if it has to be when the last shred of skin is hanging off your body and the last drop of blood is clinging inside your veins, you will tell me.'

When Kane didn't flinch, Max stepped back over to the bench. He picked up a syringe, pierced the foil lid of the bottle with the needle and drew up the contents. Kane could smell the garlic, as potent and concentrated as it could get.

Rob stopped in front of Kane, flipping a nail up in his hand and catching it again before placing it beneath Kane's collar bone. He hammered the nail into his flesh.

Kane flinched and gritted his teeth as he silently cried out. He lowered his head for a moment then glared back at him, his hands straining in the manacles.

Max stopped in front of him. 'Why now, Kane? It's something to do with that soul ripper, isn't it?'

Kane lowered his gaze as he licked the blood from his split lip.

Looking back up, he saw the flare in Max's eyes, a momentary loss of composure. He heard the tightening of his breathing, the tension suddenly exuding from him. Max grabbed Kane's jaw, forcing his head back. 'I'll rip those fangs out of your gums, if have to. Feed you cold, diluted blood via IV for the rest of your pitiful life.'

'Let me see Caitlin.'

'You have nothing to say to her.'

'You know as well as she does that I'm her only hope. You kill me and she dies too. I know you know that or you would have already found what you're looking for. You're on a deadline, Max. This is just wasting time. How much does Caitlin mean to you? More than your pride? More than your fear for your own life?'

'If I thought for one minute this might actually help her, then maybe we'd have something to negotiate with. But you have no intention of helping her, do you? And whatever you're plotting, I'm not going to let it happen.' He forcibly let go of his jaw. 'I'm growing impatient, Kane,' he said, holding up the syringe to let a bead of garlic essence leak out. 'You might think you're different, you might think you're special, but when it comes down to it you're all exactly the same. And I'm going to prove it.'

Caitlin flinched and opened her eyes. She lifted her head from amongst the cushions and scanned the familiar lounge. Being brought to safety, being in Max's house, should have felt comforting. The relief should have been overwhelming, but instead panic clenched her chest. Despite the warmth of the room, the blanket they'd thrown over her, she felt cold.

Temples throbbing, her neck aching, she dropped her head back to the floor and examined the cuff that bound her wrist to the radiator. It was a VCU issue cuff and impossible to break from. They knew her too well.

She kicked the blanket off and scrambled from amongst the cushions to lean back against the wall, despite the further agony sitting up inflicted on her head.

She skimmed over the photographs on the dresser to her left. The photographs of Max and her father together. Photographs of her father and mother. Photographs of Max and her mother. Photographs of her.

The familiarity of the place she'd all but grown up in brought with it the stark light of reality, her time with Kane seemingly like a distant dream. But the throbbing in her newly applied bandage was a reminder it was all too real. And Max and Rob had him. Somewhere. Could be doing anything to him.

And she was responsible. Her chest ached.

But she had no choice. What was the alternative? Kane got what he wanted? Killed Xavier, Max, Rob, her? Destroyed the district? The locale? She might have liked to believe she could change Kane's mind, but the cold light of day reminded her no one could throw Kane off course. Especially not now she knew he had been right all along. What alternative could she offer him? Letting those who had destroyed his life off with a lighter consequence? Would she let the soul ripper off?

She needed vengeance as much as him. If she wouldn't waver from her mission, how could she expect him to? And the only way she'd get that vengeance was by forcing the truth out of him about how to kill that thing. That thing his own sister had evoked.

In choosing him, she'd let the soul ripper win.

In him choosing her, all his enemies would win.

But she'd seen it. She'd seen that look in his eyes – the look that had reignited a glimmer of hope. She had got to him. She had broken through the armour. How, when, why, she had no idea. But those words that he had uttered without restraint had let her see a part of him that told her it wasn't over. It had given her something to work with – something that had been snatched away with Max and Rob's untimely arrival.

She needed to see him again. She had to see him again. They needed to find a way through this. There had to be a way through it. If it had become possible that Kane Malloy's armour had cracked, if it had become possible that her impenetrable heart had been touched, if it had become possible that they had connected on a level deeper than the all-consuming need for vengeance, there was hope in the impossible.

She craned her neck to look at the clock on the dresser. It was already late morning. She needed Max or Rob back there. And quick.

Kane bit into his bottom lip as he tried to control the pain searing through his body. Max was proficient, he'd give him that. Painfully proficient.

He shuddered in the manacles. The iron nails were thickening his blood to the point it was clogging his veins. Every nerve ending ached from the invasive silver nitrate. His pores burned from the garlic essence, his perspiration saturated with it. The open cuts and lacerations Max and Rob had inflicted all over his body scorched from the hemlock they had been coated with.

As he felt himself slide to the edge of unconsciousness again, Max rammed another syringe of adrenaline into his heart.

Kane cried out, but then gritted his teeth against the surge in agony as his brain acknowledged just how much trauma his body was suffering. He closed his eyes and lowered his head.

'You're certainly resilient, Kane,' Max said.

Kane glanced up to see he was already preparing another syringe at the table. 'I want to see Caitlin.'

He needed to see Caitlin. He was not done. That wasn't going to be the last he saw of her. Resent it though he may, he needed to look at her again. He needed to look in her eyes and know she knew, believed, the truth.

Besides, he needed to think. He needed the pain to stop just long enough for him to be able to think.

He could persuade her to let him go. To at least release him from the restraints. He could bargain with her. Or he'd opt for the only other choice he had. Because he wouldn't fail. Even if they killed him that night, he would get his vengeance through her, because she wasn't like them. And if she believed what they had done, she would have no choice but to seek justice for Arana. She was too good a person not to. The truth would eat away at her and she was too strong a person to let that happen. She'd confront it. She'd deal with it. He had to believe she'd make the right choice. And if she gave him her word that she would see justice through, he'd tell her. He'd tell her how to kill the soul ripper.

If he could look in her eyes and believe she would do the right thing, he'd do that for her.

If not, he'd see her destroyed and the lives of those she loved with her.

He had no option. He couldn't let them win.

Max lowered in front of him and held his gaze. 'Why couldn't you have just done as you were told, Kane? Xavier made you a good offer. You could have saved all of this.'

The door opened.

Rob crossed the room towards them. He stood beside Max and folded his arms. 'Still nothing?'

'Give it time.'

'Then why don't you get yourself a drink? Take a break. Let me take over.'

Kane lowered his head again. Him and Max had just got into a stride. He'd got used to his pace, his technique. Rob, on the other hand, was erratic – too driven by his emotions. Rob was the one most likely to cause a fatal injury.

He looked up to see some sort of private exchange pass between the two of them before Max stepped away and left the room.

Rob pulled the chair over and sat down in front of him. He leaned back and surveyed the wounds Max had inflicted on him. 'Tell me how to kill it.'

Kane stared him square in the eyes.

Rob leaned forward, his arms resting loosely across his thighs. 'Come on, Kane, let's play along. At least for Max's sake. He still believes he can get something out of you. You know you're not going to talk. I know you're not going to talk and, to be honest, I'm fine with it. In less than twelve hours, you'll have no further purpose. In less than twelve hours, you'll be mine.' He leaned closer. 'Your sister thought she was unbreakable too. And look what happened to her. It was a shame in some ways, but she had it coming. I'm still not completely sure she didn't enjoy it. In fact, I'm sure I heard her yelling for more at one point.' He smiled. 'You know what a slut she was. Of course you did. I know how close you two were. Maybe closer. Maybe a bit more than just brother-sisterly love?'

Kane glowered up at him, anger and hatred burning the pit of his stomach.

'I mean, even I could see it,' Rob added. 'She was hot. If you like them rough.' He laughed lightly. 'I could hear her screaming. She spent her last few minutes begging for her life. Or maybe it was just for them to keep going. "Harder," I'm sure I heard her yell,' he said in a mocking voice. '"Harder, boys. I still have some dignity left." I was nearly tempted to join in myself at one point.'

Kane buckled and wrenched in his manacles, unable to contain his fury.

Rob pulled back. 'That's more like it. Truth hurts, doesn't it, Kane?'

'You were a coward then and you're a coward now.' He twisted his wrists in the restraints. 'Or you wouldn't opt for these.'

'I'm going to opt for a lot more than that before I'm done with you.'

Kane glared at him. 'Don't worry – I know what you're capable of. I know all about what you've done in your quest to save your precious Caitlin. How honest have you been with her about how far you were willing to go? Only you boys know how to cover it up, don't you? Just how much of that did you blame on me, huh? And you can keep asking all you want, but the only one with answers is me. That's why she came after me. Frustrating, isn't it? Not being able to help her. Me being the only one capable of doing what you can't. Performing where you can't. Every which way she needs. As deep as she needs.'

Rob slammed an angry punch into his stomach and then his side, once then twice then punched him hard in the mouth. 'She told us where you were, Kane. So you're not quite in as deep as you thought.'

Kane spat blood from his mouth. 'I was in deeper than you can imagine. Than you could ever manage.'

Rob sneered and slammed his fist into him again. He shook his hand from the impact.

Kane winced. 'You've never been enough for her, Rob. And you never will be. You failed her.'

'Really?' He cocked his head to the side slightly. 'You think she needs you?'

'You know it. I know it. She knows it.'

'Until I tell her Xavier has a safe room. Well, more an apartment. It's not much but it'll do. What matters is that it's blessed, protected and charmed to the hilt. Nothing is going to cross there. And that's where Caitlin is going to be in a few hours, whether she likes it or not. Because I will keep her safe, Kane. I will save her from this. And from you.'

Kane frowned. If that's what they were counting on, they were making a horrific mistake. He should have been panicking that his own leverage may have been gone, but instead all he could think about was Caitlin. 'Is that what Carter promised you? Protection for her? When he doesn't even know what the fuck it is? It's fourth species, Rob. It's like nothing you've ever come across before. And I promise you, nothing is going to keep it out.'

Rob lifted his hands to his nape as he marched away, trying to calm himself. He stepped over to the bench and picked up the nails. 'That's a chance we'll have to take.' He strode back over. 'The same as we'll have to take the chance Xavier never finds out we took you out of the equation once and for all.'

Kane looked him square in the eyes. 'Think carefully, Robert. You kill me and Caitlin's dead too. And you know it.'

# CHAPTER TWENTY-THREE

Caitlin heard the garage door open and footsteps crossing the kitchen. Footsteps she knew the rhythm of only too well.

Cupboard doors opened and closed, echoing through the open door in the far corner to her left. She heard the hiss of a percolator. A subtle aroma of coffee snagged the air.

'Rob!' she called out, yanking her wrist against the radiator for good measure. 'Get yourself in here!'

Rob appeared through the doorway a second later. From the instant defensiveness in his eyes, her glare clearly spoke the volumes she'd intended. 'You're finally awake then.'

'Where is he?'

'I'll go get us a coffee,' he said, turning on his heels again.

Caitlin growled with impatience. 'We don't have time for this! You need to tell me where you've taken him!' She waited a moment for a response. She heard the clink of ceramic. 'Did you hear what I said?'

Rob strolled back in a minute or so later with two steaming mugs. 'I heard you. You need to calm yourself down. How long have you been awake?'

'Calm myself down?' She yanked her arm within its cuff. 'Get me out of this.'

'When you stop glaring at me like that, I will.' He placed the two mugs on the coffee table before stepping over to join her. 'Stop worrying, it's all under control.'

'What have you done to him?'

'We're talking to him, Caitlin,' he said, lowering himself to the floor in front of her.

Unease clenched her stomach. 'And what exactly does that "talking" entail?'

'It entails finding out how to kill the soul ripper.'

'He's not going to tell you.'

'He will.'

'That information is the only leverage he's got.'

'And we're using the only leverage we've got. He's not going anywhere until we know.'

'So where is he? Is that where Max is?'

She hadn't heard a car pull into the garage, which meant Rob had been there the whole time she'd been awake and that was over an hour. He'd come from the garage. The garage led down to the wine cellar. The pieces slotted together quicker than Rob had time to respond. 'You brought him here, didn't you?'

'Like we said, this is between us. Nothing to do with HQ. Don't worry, he's perfectly secure.'

'In the cellar? Are you insane?'

'It's all in hand.'

'How did you even get him across the border?'

'In the trunk of a VCU car being driven by the head of the unit.'

'You have to let me see him.'

'No, what you have to do is rest. I re-wrapped your foot. How did it happen?'

For some reason a sense of resentment clawed at her that he'd undone Kane's handiwork. 'I sliced it in an alley when I escaped.'

'How did he get you back?'

'I bumped into one of Jask's buddies.'

'You're lucky to still be alive.'

'I know. No thanks to you.'

'Get it off your chest,' he said, standing again. He took the coffees from the table and brought them back with him.

'You said you'd get me out of this,' she said, yanking her wrist in the cuff again.

'You haven't stopped scowling yet.' He sat back on the floor and placed her mug down beside her. He took a sip of his own before sliding over to sit against the wall alongside her.

'And what are you going to do a few hours from now when he's still said nothing?' she asked.

'We kill him. He disappears – no questions and no answers.'

Her stomach flipped. Dread at the thought of losing him, of it happening right beneath her, consumed her. 'You can't do that.'

'I think you'll find we can.'

'Xavier wants him alive.'

'Xavier will never know.'

She turned more towards him, curling her legs under her. 'Rob, Kane is the only thing between me and the soul ripper. We need him alive.'

'So he keeps telling us. Very convenient, isn't it?'

'Rob, please listen to me. You're making a mistake. Whatever you're doing to him, you have to stop.'

Rob took a sip off his coffee. 'What are you most worried about, Caitlin? Us messing up your plans or is it him you're concerned about?'

Caitlin frowned at the accusation in his eyes. 'Don't you dare judge me after what you did. After you've lied to me for all those years.'

'I did it to protect you.'

'I didn't need protection. I needed the truth.'

'And I'm telling you the truth now. Me and Max will sort this out.'

'The only one he'll talk to is me. If he'll even do that now.'

'You were the one who called us, remember?'

'Yes, to take him in so I could find out the truth for myself. Before I knew what you had done, before I knew about Xavier and his power craving. Or believe me, I wouldn't have bothered.'

She snapped her gaze away, aware her frustration was clouding her judgement. Time was of the essence, and giving him a reason to keep her secured to the radiator was not going to help.

'I didn't just abandon you, Caitlin. I want you to know that. I meant it when I said I've been trying to find out what was responsible and how to stop it. We knew Arana was the cause of what happened to Rick, but we never expected it to come for Kathleen too. We tried to get answers, but couldn't. That's why I went further afield and moved to another locale. I never gave up on you; I just had no way of explaining why I was leaving or when I'd be back.'

'So you left me with the excuse that we weren't right for each other.'

'Better that than looking you in the eye and keep lying to you. When you kept probing me about your suspicions that something was coming for you, I didn't know what to say.'

'Max managed to stick around. He even married my mother.'

'And he knew I'd left to find out what I could.'

'So I was right – you had planned to come back all along.'

'I've been back two months tracking him. I'd narrowed it down to three places he was most likely to be. Me and Max had planned to do it all undercover and then you got in sooner. But then Kane waiting for you in the corridor, Xavier getting involved, Kane taking you the night before I'd planned to take him were all complications that got in the way. If we'd pulled you out, if we'd told you the truth, Xavier would have known. We've needed to keep him on side. But that doesn't matter now. What matters is you knowing I did not turn my back on you.'

'Then don't turn your back on me now and listen to me, please. You need me to talk to him. I can negotiate with him. I can offer his release to get him on side.'

Rob shook his head and took another sip of coffee. 'No. You're not going near him again.'

She wrenched her wrist in the cuff. 'If you kill him, I will not make it through the night. Please let that sink in.'

'What happened between you two, huh?' he asked, his cool gaze settling on hers again.

She felt as though she'd been physically winded. She wasn't even sure she knew the answer. She frowned. 'Why, what did he say?'

'Did you sleep with him?'

'What business is that of yours?'

Rob exhaled tersely, his tongue meeting his upper teeth. He lifted the mug back to his lips.

'That has nothing to do with any of this,' she added.

'What, you jumping into bed with the vampire you were employed to hunt? The vampire whose sister was responsible for the death of your parents? The vampire who wants to kill you, Max and me?' His eyes narrowed coldly and accusatorily on hers. 'That's nothing to do with any of this?'

'And what you did to Arana was perfectly justifiable was it? A means to an end? I never would have thought it, Rob. I never would have thought you were capable of those things. How could you stand by and let it happen?'

'We did what we did for the good of this district.'

'What you did was follow Xavier's orders with no thought for morality or the lore.'

'Kane doesn't operate inside the lore.'

'So if you can't beat them, join them.'

Rob held her gaze steadily, not a glimpse of guilt behind his blue eyes. 'You would know.'

In that moment she wasn't just angry, she realised she wasn't even sure if she liked him anymore. 'I was handling it.'

'Just like he was handling you,' Rob sneered, the resentment clear in his eyes.

'I'm the only one who can get through to him.'

He laughed derisively. 'Oh, he's got you right where he wants you, hasn't he? He's using you. He's playing you. And I can't believe you of all people are letting him. He wants you dead, Caitlin. He wants us all dead. And then he'll bring down the TSCD. His rise to power will be overnight. He will rule this territory. Everything we have worked for, everything your father worked for, will be gone. What if this is it? Has that crossed your mind? What if he's the key to these prophecies we keep hearing about? This vampire rise to supremacy. What if it starts with him?'

'We don't even know if they're true.'

'Can we take the risk? Caitlin, he wants only one thing, and that's vengeance. You need to remember who and what you were before all this started and you need to get a grip.'

'Don't you dare patronize me. What makes you so sure you're right? All your opinions are drip-fed by Xavier, just like mine were. But what do any of us really know about Kane and his intentions? What proof have any of us had? This whole mess was started by us, not him.'

'So your parents deserved to die – is that what you're saying?'

'Did Arana?'

Rob stared at her, lost for words, but anger gleamed behind his eyes. 'Look at you – going there determined to bring him down and coming out his advocate.'

'I went after him to find out how to kill the soul ripper. I went after him because I had no other option left because I thought the only people I had left to care about didn't believe me. If you'd told me the truth before all this, we could have worked together. Instead I went in there and all but begged him for his help. Do you know what that took? Tonight, Rob. It's coming tonight. And if you and Max don't let me deal with this, it's taking me with it.'

'It's not taking you, Caitlin. We have a backup plan. Xavier has a safe haven for you where you'll be protected from the soul ripper.'

It took a moment for what he'd said to sink in. 'What?'

'Xavier has kept it over our heads to stop us retaliating against Kane. If we got nowhere with Kane, we knew we had it as a backup.'

'A haven?'

'A small apartment. Fully charmed and protected.'

'And beyond that apartment?' The look in his eyes said enough. 'There would be no beyond the apartment, right?'

'At least you'd be alive.'

'I either die at the hands of the soul ripper or spend the rest of my life in a make-shift jail?'

'Until we find the answers we need.'

She stared back across the room. 'I can't believe how clueless I've been to all this.'

'I've already been scouring all our resources these past few hours after you gave us the name,' he added. 'There's still nothing.'

'Because you haven't found anyone archaic enough – no one with as archaic a bloodline as Kane.'

'We will find a way to kill it. I promise.'

And for as long as they believed that, they wouldn't need Kane. They wouldn't need her to have any communication with him. She wouldn't get a chance to explain herself. She wouldn't even get a chance to see him again. Her heart wrenched. He'd be slaughtered right beneath her. The world suddenly seemed like a painfully empty, dark place.

'Let me read him,' she said. 'Take me to him. It was the one opportunity I didn't have back in his den but I can do it now. I'll find the truth. I'll find out how to kill it.'

Rob shook his head. 'I can't let you do that. I'm not having whatever darkness is inside of him inside of you.'

'It's not your place to make that choice for me.'

'I told you I would keep you safe and that's what I'm doing.'

Fury and panic simmered – resentment that he dared continue to take her decisions away from her. 'I need to see him.'

'And I am not having you blemished by him.'

'Blemished?' She exhaled curtly. 'It's a bit late for that.'

She saw his eyes narrow, his attention distracted only by more footsteps crossing the kitchen.

Her attention snapped to the door.

Max appeared in the doorway. He looked composed, calm, but he was tired. She could see it in his expression, in his sallow face. He gave her something of a placating smile before stepping over to join them. 'How are you doing?'

She held up her wrist, it clinking against the radiator. 'What do you think?'

'Any progress?' Rob asked.

Max shook his head.

'You've got to let me in there,' Caitlin said. 'I told Rob. You have to let me read him. It's the only way.'

Max nodded. 'I know. We might not have any choice.'

She heard Rob's subtle intake of breath, felt his tension escalate despite him being a foot away. He pulled himself to his feet. 'We said we'd talk about that.'

'The clock's ticking, Rob. It's an option we need to consider.'

Caitlin's heart pounded. 'It's a good option,' she cut in. 'It's our only option.'

But the men's attention was firmly locked on each other.

'We said that was a last resort,' Rob said, his voice low.

'It is. He isn't going to break. There's nothing more we can issue other than to kill him.'

Her stomach wrenched. 'What do you mean, "issue"? What have you done?'

'You don't know the risks,' Rob said, his attention from Max not wavering.

'She's the best shadow reader I know. We have to try.'

'Isla failed.'

'I can do this.' She stared from Max to Rob and back to Max again. 'You owe me this chance.'

Max broke away from the glare in Rob's eyes. He took the release device from his pocket and stepped towards Caitlin.

'Think about this,' Rob said firmly, catching his arm.

'I'm only doing it because I have to.' He pulled his arm free and lowered to his haunches. He slid the device across the cuffs, the anti-magnetism releasing Caitlin from the binds.

She rubbed her wrist. 'You're doing right, Max,' she said, looking deep into his eyes.

'She's exhausted,' Rob cut in. 'She needs to rest.'

'We don't have time to rest,' Max reminded him. He stood up and helped Caitlin up with him.

Caitlin passed Rob, purposefully avoiding his glower, and limped behind Max across the lounge to the kitchen. Coffee still lingered in the air and the house was silent. Even the weak sunlight pouring into the kitchen did nothing to soften the atmosphere.

This was it now. This was what was left of her life. The last 24 hours. The last 24 hours with the truth she wished she'd never learned.

Max led the way through the garage door. Caitlin cautiously took the single step down behind him while gripping the doorframe to balance herself.

He took the next door on the left.

Clutching the handrail, she tentatively followed him down the wooden slatted steps, bracing herself for seeing Kane again, for what she might find. But the wine cellar was empty.

Straight ahead, the floor-to-ceiling wine rack was slid aside to reveal an iron door she never knew existed. Unease clenched her stomach. Her heart thudded painfully, reverberating in her eardrums, exacerbated by the deathly silence.

As Max opened the door and led the way inside, she limped towards the bright clinical light. The room looked unnervingly like an operating theatre, but this room wasn't designed to help anyone. It was kitted-out with every possible torture device for vampires. Hung, strung and mounted on the walls were contraptions of iron and silver. More devices lay on the surrounding benches. The air was thick with the aroma of garlic and hemlock.

Max closed the door behind her. The thrum resounded in her ears as they adjusted to the pressure of the airtight silence. The cellar walls seemed to throb as she instinctively turned towards the right-hand corner, and followed the glare of spotlight to the focal point.

Kane was on his knees on the tiled floor, the only thing holding him up being the manacles and chains that bound his outstretched arms to the floor-to-ceiling posts. His head was lowered, concealing his face. He was shirtless, the bright light bouncing off every defined muscular sinew of his back, shoulders and arms. A position that emphasised the power behind the body that now hung lax, damaged and bleeding.

Her heart wrenched. Her stomach vaulted. 'What have you done?' she demanded quietly.

'What we had to,' Max said.

She stepped warily closer to Kane, her pulse racing. She assessed the iron nails meticulously rammed into his shoulder blades, his chest and thighs. Stepping around the back of him, she stared in horror at the wounds amidst his tattoos. They had treated him savagely, the cuts etched into his skin as though torture was a major part of the pleasure of the wounding. 'What the hell is wrong with you?' she said, fighting back rage as she glared across at them both.

'Sometimes extra measures are needed, Caitlin,' Max declared.

She scanned the room again, taking in the torture devices. 'I don't know you at all, do I?' she said, looking back from one to the other. 'I'm not even sure who the real monsters are around here.'

'The only monster around here is the one who kidnapped you and subjected you to hell these past couple of days,' Rob said. A smirk almost graced his lips. 'He had it coming.'

It was a smirk that sickened her. She snapped. Lunged at him. He stumbled backwards, his eyes wide and startled. It was the only time she had ever seen him shocked. If Max hadn't been quick, caught her and yanked her back, she would have smacked the smirk right off his face. 'Like Arana did?' she demanded, fighting against Max's vice hold. But her anger limited her adeptness. 'You think this is okay? You think this is justified? Is this what Xavier has reduced you to?'

'This is what Kane has reduced us to,' Max said.

She yanked free and pulled away from them. 'Torturing him? Did you seriously think you could break him? Have you learned nothing about him?' She raked her hands through her hair. 'All you've done is set yourself up to fail.' He'd wanted them to pay before, but now he was going to want even more. Anything she could have done to convince him otherwise had potentially gone. The gap had been forged even more and she had no idea what she was going to do about it. 'You were never intending to let him survive this, were you?'

'This has to end tonight, Caitlin,' Max said. 'It's time to finish it.'

'Finish what you started.'

'We can argue about the morality all night, but that's not going to help anyone. I'm going to stop this one way or another. Xavier has been obsessed with this for too long. And one day either Xavier is going to make an offer Kane can't refuse or vice versa. I was hoping it wouldn't come to this. I'm not particularly keen at the prospect of you probing inside him, but it's all we have left.'

She needed to be alone with Kane and she needed Max and Rob as far away from her as possible. She needed both of them out of her sight before her temper bubbled over. She couldn't even look at Rob – the man she had once shared a bed with. The man she had once loved.

She needed to tend to Kane's wounds. She needed to do something. She needed them both out of her sight before she exploded and blew any small chance she had. 'You need to leave me alone with him.'

'No way,' Rob said firmly.

'I'm not asking your permission,' she snapped. 'If I'm going to read him, I need to not have any distractions. I cannot do this with you here. Even in this state he's still going to be strong.'

Max stepped over to one of the benches and removed a small black case from the bottom shelf. He flicked the clasps open and took out a syringe. He handed it across to her, the emerald liquid glinting in the dim light. 'In case he tries to block you. It'll weaken him even more.'

She snatched the syringe off him. 'More illegal substances?'

'We're not in the interrogation room now, Caitlin. Get inside him and find out how to kill that soul ripper, and vengeance will be complete for your parents. Do this and it can all be over.'

'But we're not leaving you,' Rob said firmly.

'I don't even want to look at you. You get the fuck out of my sight,' Caitlin said, the vehemence in her tone unnerving even her.

Rob stepped up to her. 'I don't trust him and I sure as hell don't trust you in this state.'

'Why – what am I going to do, Rob? Release him so he can kill us all? I may hate what you've done, but I'm not stupid. I'm still a VCU agent. I can handle this and I will sort it. But I cannot concentrate with you here.' She looked back at Max. 'Give me an hour.'

Max wavered for a moment. 'An hour,' he said. 'That's all.' He looked back at Rob and cocked his head towards the door. 'Let her get on with her job.'

# CHAPTER TWENTY-FOUR

Caitlin stood trembling as she looked down at Kane, finally left alone in the silence with him. Stepping up to him, she lowered to her haunches and tilted her head to the side to check his face. His eyes were closed, dark circles beneath them. Blood that had seeped from the cut on his eyebrow tainted his eyelashes. His lips, the lower of which was split, were slightly parted. The bruises on his jaw looked intrinsically painful.

She crossed to the sink and placed the syringe down. She picked up a metallic bowl and filled it with water before reaching for some cloth, dressing and tape. Stepping around the back of him, she dampened the cloth and used it to cleanse his wounds. She washed the garlic and hemlock paste from within the gashes as well as the remains of silver nitrate. She gently cleansed his back and his shoulders, working her way down his arms. She examined the iron nails and knew she'd have to pull them out before he was conscious.

She placed the bowl on the chair and headed over to the bench for the pliers. She hovered in front of him. The nails were buried deep and would take some wrenching, but she had to do it.

She secured the pliers around the tip of the nail beneath his collarbone and, taking a deep steady breath, she pulled.

She hadn't expected him to flinch. Or gasp.

She dropped the pliers and the nail in shock and took a step back. Her stomach clenched, the tension in the room excruciating as his navy eyes fixed pointedly on her, his pupils tiny within his navy irises.

'How long have you been conscious?'

'Long enough.' He sounded exhausted, the agony clear in his voice, his eyes.

She lowered to her knees in front of him. 'I was trying to tend your wounds. If I get the nails out it should ease some of the pain.'

Kane sighed heavily and twisted his neck from side to side in a slow painful motion that made her wince. 'Yeah, I'll give it to your loved ones, Caitlin, they sure know how to torture.'

'I never would have thought them capable of doing this.'

'Really?' he said, his eyes resting accusatorially on hers. 'Is that why you called them?'

'Before I knew the whole story. They confirmed it, Kane – all the sordid little details.'

'And what have you told them?'

'I haven't told them you want my soul. Or why.'

'Why not?'

'Because we can sort this between us, right?'

He broke a hint of a smile, but winced with the pain. 'Sure, Caitlin. The minute they let me walk out of here.'

'I didn't mean for this to happen. I thought they'd take you to HQ.'

'So where am I?'

'Believe it or not you're in Max's basement.' She swallowed hard, his clear agony causing her pain. 'I really, honestly had no idea about any of this. This place. I'm sorry, Kane.' She reached for the pliers. 'Let's get the rest of these nails out of you.' She pulled the chair closer, so she could reach the bowl and dressings. She dampened some more of the cloth, cleaned the wound where she'd pulled out the nail and taped the dressing down over it. 'It won't take you long to heal once these are out, will it?'

He shook his head. 'No.'

She broke from his gaze, the intensity too much, the intimacy as she knelt in front of him too much for her to bear. 'Did you hear they want me to read you?'

'Yes.'

She pulled another nail from his side, hating seeing him flinch. His teeth clenched as she gently washed out the wound and dressed it. She looked down at the one on his inner thigh, glanced warily back up at him.

'Be my guest,' he said.

She pinched the nail in the pliers and pulled it sharply. She quickly applied the dressing through the tear in his jeans, adding pressure to stop the blood flow for a few moments. She glanced up to meet his gaze, the proximity dangerously inviting. 'They've given me something to suppress you and help make access easier.'

'You know you can't agree to this, Caitlin.'

Caitlin wiped the wound on his thigh clean and applied the some clean dressing. She sat back on her haunches. 'And how do I know you're telling the truth, Kane? What if it's just a ploy to stop me from seeing the truth, from finding out how to kill the soul ripper myself?'

'You try and read me,' he said, his gaze steadily on hers, 'and it will kill you. I've never lied to you about that.'

'But I only have your word.' She dampened the cloth again and wiped the cut above his belly button. 'Tell me how to kill the soul ripper and I'll get you out of this.'

He exhaled curtly then flinched as she cleaned another wound.

'It's your only option, Kane. I am offering to help you if you help me. We both need to trust each other. I cannot get you out of here without that information.'

'And you won't just run with the information? How about you get me out of here and then I tell you?'

She sat back on her haunches again. 'So this is stalemate, is it? And the only lives hanging in the balance are ours. The only one who's going to win is Xavier. You'll be gone and what will that mean for this place? Do you want the whole territory to think he beat you? The minute he knows you've gone missing he'll declare he caught you. Do you want him to win, Kane?'

Kane narrowed his eyes. 'Where have you been all this time, Caitlin?'

She could see the suspicion in his eyes, the accusation. 'Tied to a radiator.'

'What is it about you that makes people want to cuff you, huh?'

The glimmer of playful mischief in his eyes was almost too much.

'I need you to compromise with me, Kane.'

'Then let me go. If those principles of yours are so strong, release me. What was it that you said to me: that it's selflessness that makes your species great? That it's selflessness above personal survival that separates humans from the third species?'

'This isn't just about my survival though, is it? If I release you, you'll kill them, right?'

'We all look after our own, don't we? And you're no different. You know they don't regret one moment of it, don't you? They're still justifying it to themselves. How does that make them differ from the worst of my kind – the ones you work every day to bring to justice? Rob looked me in the eye and mocked Arana's death, Caitlin. There is not even one iota of remorse there.'

She held his silent gaze. She looked at the dignity in his eyes, the posture despite the pain. He wasn't going to give up. He wasn't going to go down without a fight. She knew the traits only too well from herself. But she had faltered – faltered because she felt something. And if he felt anything for her, he might do the same. 'Xavier is the one we both want. If we don't do this together, he will win.'

'And if I tell you what you want to know, they'll kill me – and they win too.'

'In a few hours' time this won't even be open for negotiation.'

'No – and you'll be safe and sound in your prison. At least that's what Xavier's been telling them. It's amazing that he knows how to protect you against something he doesn't even have a name for.'

'Are you saying it won't work?'

'The only way to kill a soul ripper is with something whose power is just as archaic, just as strong.'

'You, you mean.'

'You need to get me out of here.'

'But I keep you here and at least Rob and Max will be safe.'

'You think so? You think Xavier won't work out what happened? You do this and the only winners in any of this are Xavier and the soul ripper – the two that deserve to pay the most.'

'But you've already told me you won't kill it. So what choice do I have? Releasing you means giving myself over to you and the soul ripper. Why would I do that?'

'They are going to kill me Caitlin. What this comes down to is whether you can stand by and let that happen. You know they're wrong. You keep proclaiming the goodness of your species, so prove it to me.'

'You make it sound like it's a simple moral choice, but it's not. I know what you're capable of.'

'Get me out of here and I promise to let Max and Rob live in return. That's the best I can offer.'

'And how do I know I can trust you on that?'

'I have never lied to you. I will never lie to you. It's down to you, Caitlin, if you believe me or not.'

'How do I know betraying them is worth it? If you won't kill the soul ripper for me, if you won't even tell me how to do it myself, what's the point?'

His gaze didn't falter. 'This is the only way we both win.' Something in his eyes softened. Something in the way he looked at her. 'You've seen for yourself, Caitlin. You've seen what goes on here. You know everything I have told you is true. And now that you know that, you know you have no choice. You can't let them get away with this. Let me go.'

She eased onto her knees in front of him, still searching those beautiful navy eyes that brimmed with sincerity. She felt sick at the thought of what they had done and even sicker at the thought of what they were planning. And she knew she couldn't walk away. She needed to trust him. She wanted to trust him.

But he was still a vampire and he still wanted vengeance – revenge that he had openly admitted to. And she was moments away from helping him succeed. Once and for all, she needed to know what was inside him, what was in his heart. She needed the truth – the whole truth, before she made her decision. And she knew there was only one way to find it.

She had been betrayed too many times – thought she knew and understood the truth only to have it thrown back in her face. She couldn't risk it again. Too much was at stake. Too much for her to cross that final line without being sure.

She saw in his eyes that he knew what she was thinking. And he frowned, followed by a flare of panic in his eyes – something she had never witnessed before. As she reached out and placed her palm flat on his chest over his heart, he tried to recoil.

'What the fuck are you doing, Caitlin?'

'I'm sorry,' she said, swallowing hard against her constricted throat, her pulse racing. 'I need to do this.'

He tried to pull back in the restraints, but he was bound too tightly. He looked down at her hand, trembling on his chest, then back into her eyes. 'Caitlin, get your hand off me.'

She shook her head. 'No.'

His stunning navy eyes narrowed into a scowl, his incisors elongating a little more behind those beautiful masculine lips. 'You can't do this.'

'We're about to find out, aren't we?'

'They've weakened me too much to block you completely.'

'Even better. Try and fight me and I'll use the syringe.'

'For fuck's sake,' he snapped, every muscle in his shoulders and arms, his chest, tensing against the restraints.

Her hand hovered tensely against his cool skin as she tried to relax herself, preparing for what was to come. She'd need to hone her concentration, keep the strength in her to hold his gaze, lock his gaze on hers. 'How long is it between heartbeats, Kane? Two minutes? Maybe two minutes thirty? We might have that amount of time or it could be seconds away, right?'

He glared at her. 'It'll kill you.'

She stared deep into his eyes and she could already see that she was having an effect. She tried to relax more, slip into the zone that came so easily to her. And she could see from the look in his eyes that he was preparing himself for a battle – a battle he knew he was too weak to fight.

'Scared of what I'll see? That I'll know the truth, Kane? About how you've played me?'

Redness rimmed his eyes as he was already getting drawn in with her, their energies beginning to mingle. 'Caitlin, don't do this.'

'How do I kill the soul ripper?'

He heaved a sigh in a way that was almost human. 'Take your hand off me.'

'No.'

'Do it!'

'Why? Is the pulse close? Can you feel it coming? It's not nice when you feel the clock ticking, is it, Kane?' Her gaze on his didn't relinquish. 'You know what you have to do.'

'I have told you.' His eyes started to water, whether from fighting her, she wasn't sure. Maybe from frustration or anger. 'Caitlin, you've got to believe me.'

'And I will when I see the truth.'

'Stop this.'

'Stop fighting me,' she said.

'I will not.'

'You can't beat me in this state. Master vampire or not.'

His jaw clenched, his teeth gritted, his eyes narrowed as he turned his head to the side, trying to break away from her.

The energy started to increase – she could feel the drag of the current beneath her hand. The tide was coming and it was building. She felt the trance start to come over her as she always did those moments before. A trance that would allow her to travel deep, to feel every impulse, to tune into the darkness that was within them, like slipping into a dream, everything beginning to merge, disassociated images starting to flicker in front of her eyes.

And it was an intense energy building beneath her palm, an energy like she'd never known. An energy that was dark, powerful and unfathomable. This wasn't going to be a gentle wave. It was like the silence before the storm, a distant rumble then an unnerving hush. She felt a cold perspiration sweep over her. That was no regular wave coming – it was a tsunami that would hit her head on.

'Caitlin, please.'

His voice was becoming more distant, like someone calling on a wind-swept beach.

'Caitlin!'

She heard it but she knew she couldn't tune into it. Tinnitus rang powerfully in her ears. She was close, so close to finding out everything, everything about him – not only about his kind, but him, the most intimate parts of him, how he felt. About her.

But there was something fighting against her. Like an opaque pane of glass she knew there were things beyond, but she couldn't get to them. And the harder she tried, the more dense the glass became. He was fighting her, he was using every reserve of strength to fight her, but the moment that pulse came, that glass would shatter.

And she felt panic beyond the darkness. She felt trepidation. She felt sadness.

'Caitlin, for fuck's sake!'

It was coming closer. The surge was building. Her body ached as she willed herself to stay focused.

She knew it was seconds away. Maybe even moments.

'Okay! If I need to kill it, I'll kill it!'

Something snapped. She didn't know what, but something did. Like a power surge that cut the lights.

His eyes suddenly became clear. Not just doorways but shape and form and intensity and light. She flinched and dropped her hand from his chest and fell back onto her haunches.

Her will or his, she couldn't be sure.

But the connection was broken.

She trembled, catching her breath, coldness consuming her. And as she looked at him, he dropped his gaze as if recovering, his chest heaving in a way she had never seen. That beautifully honed chest damp with exhaustion.

He'd had to fight. He'd really had to fight. For his own survival or for hers, she wasn't sure.

Or maybe both.

After a few minutes, he looked back at her, his eyes tired, angry, irritated.

'You will?'

He nodded, his jaw tense. 'If that's what you want, if that's the only thing that will get me out of this.'

She had broken him. She had broken Kane Malloy. And instead of feeling relief, it pained her.

It pained her because he was helping her not of his own free will, but because she'd forced him.

She eased back away from him a few inches, too weak to pull herself onto the chair.

'That's some strength you've got in there, girl,' he said. 'But if I hadn't been through all this these last few hours, I would have kicked your arse for that.' He raked her swiftly with his gaze before lowering it again, concealing what she could almost interpret as affection behind his eyes.

'Give me your word that you won't hurt Max and Rob.' She looked at the hesitation in his eyes. 'I need your word, Kane.'

'Then you have it,' he said. 'So, can we quit with the party tricks and get the fuck out of here?'

She pulled herself to her feet and warily looked down at him. She knew exactly what she had to do.

# CHAPTER TWENTY-FIVE

Caitlin placed the empty syringe on the kitchen table and pulled out a chair to sit down. 'You're going to have to let him go,' she said, looking from Max, sat adjacent to her, to Rob, sat opposite.

Rob laughed tersely. 'Funny, Caitlin.'

'You kill him and I have no chance of surviving this.'

Max frowned. 'Is that what you saw?'

'Only a master vampire can kill a soul ripper. Or something equivalent to his power – which I doubt very much we're going to get our hands on in the next seven hours.'

'How convenient,' Rob sniped.

'But a soul ripper can be killed?'

'Yes,' Caitlin said.

'According to Kane,' Rob said.

'According to what I saw,' she reminded him.

'And how do we know you saw anything? How do we know he didn't just persuade you to accept what he was saying?'

'Because I'm just one big walk-over – right, Rob?'

'You are when it comes to him.'

'Enough to jeopardise my life? He's the key – Arana started the curse and he can finish it. This is what he intended all along. The only flexibility we've gained is whether or not I survive this.'

Max glanced across at him before focusing his attention on Caitlin. 'Letting Kane go is out of the question.'

'He has given me his word that he won't hurt you. It was part of our deal.'

'And we all implicitly trust Kane's word, of course,' Rob sniped.

'If word gets through to Xavier that we had him, we might as well be dead,' Max remarked. 'I'm sorry but we're too far gone. We can't turn back now.'

Caitlin leaned forward. 'That's it? Sorry, but no? You wanted to know how to kill the soul ripper and now we have our answer. And I'm telling you the only way to save me is to release him.'

'And you seriously think he's going to kill it for you?' Max asked.

'Yes,' she said. Because he would – she had no doubt about that. If her plan worked, he would have no choice. 'And it's the only option we have. I don't trust Xavier. Have you ever seen this safe place he claims he's got? Do you have any proof it works? Because according to Kane, nothing stops a soul ripper. They don't adhere to any lores we know. We have enough trouble trying to understand how half of the third species work, let alone something of that thing's calibre. For all we know, that apartment he claims to have could just be another ploy to get Kane. Xavier was the one who sent me in there, remember? He actively encouraged me to do this. Do you think he had my best interests at heart? He wanted to use me to draw Kane out. And this is going to end in disaster again if I don't do something.'

'Then we keep Kane here,' Max said. 'We keep him down there with you. When the soul ripper comes, if he kills it, we'll let him go. If anything happens to you, we'll have him right where we want him.'

'And how does he know you won't kill him anyway once you've got what you want? He is not going to bargain with you. You have to let him go. And you have to let me go with him.'

Max leaned forward to meet her. 'You're asking us to release a vampire who's baying for our blood.'

'I'm asking you to trust my judgement.'

'He has timed this to perfection, hasn't he?' Rob said. 'Putting us all under pressure. He's been planning this for years and he's executing it with precision.'

Max shook his head. 'I can't accept that he won't come after us. It's too simple.'

'There are terms.' How the hell she was going to sell it, she had no idea. 'We know the soul ripper is due between the hours of eleven and one tonight. He's going to stall it from killing me. He wants you to do a live broadcast at half-past one – confess to your involvement in the killing of Arana. Once your confessions are done, he'll kill it.'

'As in a news broadcast?' Rob asked. He exhaled curtly. 'You are kidding?'

'He wants justice for Arana. Do that and he'll let me live.'

'And he brings down the VCU,' Max said. 'Potentially the whole TSCD. Oh, he really has got this all worked out.'

'If you don't do this, it's over for me,' Caitlin said.

'And what's to stop him letting the broadcast air, killing you and then coming for us?' Rob asked, his tone laced with impatience.

She leaned forward, arms on the table as she looked deep into Max's eyes. 'You owe me,' she said. 'You, Rob, my father. And you owe my mother. I am asking for your help and I am asking you to trust me on this. I can do this.'

Max held his fingers in a steeple against his lips and sighed heavily.

'Max?' Rob asked. 'You're not seriously considering this?' He stared from one to the other in the silence before pushing back his chair and standing abruptly. 'This is not happening.'

'Sit down,' Max said.

'I'm not agreeing to this,' Rob said.

Caitlin looked up at him. 'And where does that leave me?'

Max looked across at Caitlin. 'What have you got planned?'

'You know me, Max – always the backup.'

'I cannot believe this conversation is happening,' Rob said, clutching the back of the chair, his knuckles white.

'I am trying to get the best out of an impossible situation that you created.' She looked back at her stepfather. 'Please, Max. I need this one shot.'

Max got up and strolled over to the window. He braced his hands on the edge of the sink as he stared out of the window.

'Max, this is not an option,' Rob said firmly. 'You are giving Kane exactly what he wants.'

'No, you're giving me what I want,' Caitlin said. 'What I need.'

'You're being played for a fool, Max, and you should know better. Think about this.'

Max turned to face him. 'And what if Kane is her only hope? What if this is her only shot?'

'He won't get to you. I will make sure you're long gone before we leave that room,' Caitlin insisted.

'Max,' Rob said more firmly. 'This is suicide for all of us. You can't listen to her. She's brainwashed by him. Yes, Caitlin – brainwashed. Why else would you think it's okay to screw vampires? Two days with him and he's already turned you into a whore just like his sister.'

Caitlin stepped up to him, drew back her hand and slapped him hard across the face.

He caught his jaw and glowered at her. Then he pulled back his hand and slapped her back.

Caitlin stumbled, but caught the chair for balance before glaring at him in shock, at the lack of remorse in his eyes. A hand that had once held her so gently had struck with a vicious jealousy that sickened her. If she didn't despise him before, he had just ticked the final box.

Max lunged between them. 'What the hell do you think you're doing, Rob? What's happened to you?'

Rob stepped away with a curt exhale. Grabbing the keys, he marched out of the kitchen towards the basement.

Her heart lunged in her chest. 'Wait!'

'Rob!' Max called out, reaching for him, but just falling short.

Caitlin hobbled behind both of them, pursuing them through the garage and down into the wine cellar. Her pulse raced as she struggled to keep up, Max finally pulling Rob back just before he reached the iron door.

'Don't be stupid!' Max warned.

'I'm not having him control us like this.'

Caitlin stepped equidistant between Rob and the door, braced for his onslaught as he pulled free of Max.

'Move out of the way, Caitlin,' Rob warned, marching up to her.

Caitlin pushed him back. 'You stay away from him!'

'Look at you defending him!' he said, frustration and despair emanating from his eyes.

'I need him.'

Max dragged him aside. 'Rob, you kill him now and you might kill the only chance we've got of helping her.'

Rob yanked free, squaring up to Caitlin again. 'How can you choose him over me?'

Caitlin held his gaze but didn't flinch.

Rob grabbed her by her upper arm and yanked her towards him, causing her to nearly lose her footing. 'I asked you a question.'

'Get off me,' she warned, glaring back at him.

'Let her go!' Max demanded, prising them apart, shoving Rob back.

Rob strode to the other side of the room. Head lowered, he thrust his hands on his hips, his back to them.

'This has to stop,' Max said. 'This whole thing. It has to end. And I can't see any other way that's going to happen.' He looked across at Rob. 'We're going to give her a chance.'

Rob spun to face him. 'No.'

'Why? Because you're scared of the consequences? Because your ego can't take it? Or is this just a personal vengeance against Kane now?

Because that's the way it just looked to me.' He paused. 'This was never supposed to be personal. Any of it. We've lost control. One of us has to get it back. And it seems to me Caitlin's the only one who can do it.'

'Then don't expect me to be a part of it.'

'You don't have a choice. If I confess to this, I'm confessing to all of it.'

'You'd implicate me?'

'How much do you care about her, Rob? Really care about her?'

'I'm not doing time for Kane Malloy. I was doing my job, that's all.'

'A job we should have said no to.'

'A job we were doing for the right reasons.'

'In the wrong way. I know it and so do you. We've always known it. And if Caitlin has even the slightest chance of surviving this, she deserves for us to give it to her.' Max looked back at Caitlin. 'This plan had better be good.'

'I'll make it good.'

Despite the anxiety in his eyes, for the first time in years she saw an element of relief. 'And what's Kane got planned for Xavier? I assume he's the one he really wants.'

Caitlin nodded. 'Just do your part and I'll take care of the rest.'

Rob stepped back over to them. 'You against the world – right, Caitlin?'

'I have no choice,' she reminded him.

'We'll take Rob's car,' Max said. 'So you use mine. You should get across the border easily in it. If there are any questions, tell them to call me. The key code for Kane's restraints is your parents' birth dates combined.'

'I know,' she said. 'I worked that one out.'

Rob's eyes flared. 'He's already out, isn't he?'

Max stared at her aghast. 'You released him already?'

'I couldn't let you kill him.'

Max shook his head. 'Always that one step ahead.'

She shrugged. 'You know me.'

He looked down at the floor, contemplating for a moment, then looked back up at her. 'Half-past one?'

She nodded. 'And if Xavier gets even an inkling of this, it's over.'

'I have no intentions of telling him anything,' Max said.

As silence rebounded off the walls, Caitlin stepped up to Max, taking him by the hand and squeezing. 'Thank you,' she said. 'For believing I can do this.'

He held her gaze and squeezed back. 'You just get through this, okay?'

She gave him a fleeting, closed-lip smile and nodded again.

He wavered for a moment and she was sure she saw tears accumulating in his eyes, but he turned away and walked back over to the stairs.

Rob remained fixed to the spot. 'You're making a mistake, Caitlin. He's going to let you down. Just when you need him. I want you to know that.'

'Maybe he will,' she said. 'We'll see. But it seems I need to start getting used to that.'

He looked away, wiped his tongue over the top of his teeth before looking back at her. 'I shouldn't have hit you. I'm sorry.'

'No, you shouldn't have. But there's a lot of worse things you shouldn't have done and you need to face that. This will rot you on the inside, Rob. However much you try to convince yourself to the contrary, you know what happened was wrong. Xavier has destroyed enough already. Don't let him destroy you too. This is your way out too, even if you don't see it yet.'

He held her gaze for a few moments longer. He needed time to think, she knew that. He always needed time to think. But he'd do the right thing. She had to pin her hopes on that.

He joined Max at the steps and led the way up. He didn't look over his shoulder once before leaving her alone in the silence.

# CHAPTER TWENTY-SIX

Caitlin stepped back into the airtight room, her ears taking a moment to adjust to the pressure again.

Kane was sitting behind the door, head and back resting against the wall, legs bent, arms braced either side of him on the floor. He looked exhausted, the journey across the room from where he'd been manacled seemingly all he could manage. She remembered how he'd fallen to the floor when she'd unlocked the binds, her heart wrenching to see him falter. He'd demanded she leave him there and then, his pride clearly as wounded as his body.

But now some of his more superficial wounds had already started to heal, even if the great majority remained in a bad way. Still, she had no doubt he would have put up a fight if the plan had gone wrong – if Rob and Max had gone back in there for him – but she wouldn't have rated his chances.

His hooded eyes locked on hers as she sat on the floor next to him, facing him.

'They're going,' she said. 'Max has agreed to the broadcast.'

He kept his head against the wall. 'And Rob?'

'Rob won't have any choice if Max is going to implicate him anyway.'

'And will he?'

'Max wants this over. He knows he has to do it if I'm to pull through.'

'What did you tell them I wanted from you?'

'Just that you were using me to get them to confess. I said you'd planned to kill me if they didn't. I said I'd bargained with you to kill the soul ripper for your release.'

'And they believed you?'

'They had no choice.'

Kane nodded towards the blemish that must have appeared on her jaw line. 'What happened?'

'A minor altercation.'

'Rob?'

She shrugged. 'I hit him first.'

His eyes narrowed. 'That justifies it, does it?'

She broke from his gaze momentarily, touched that he had noticed and, more so, by the displeasure in his eyes. 'We probably need to get out of here,' she said. 'Max has left his car. We can use that. So what happens from here?'

'I suggest we remove your soul before we run into any more complications. We'll need to go back to where we were for me to get a few things, but then we'll go somewhere where we won't have any more interruptions.'

She knew the question was worthless, but she felt the need to ask it anyway. 'You're not going to double-cross me, are you, Kane? You are going to kill it?'

'We have a deal, Caitlin.'

'One you could easily back out of.'

'I'm not going to.'

'So what about Xavier?'

'I guess I'll being making other plans for him.'

'And you need my soul out before you kill it?'

'It's the only way I'll control it. Then it'll be enough to distract it when I put it back in.'

Unease stirred inside her. 'That's a hell of a leap of faith you're asking from me, Kane.'

'And you could have let me die tonight. You could have taken Xavier's option. So some of that faith must already be there.'

Caitlin studied those sullen, exhausted eyes. 'You don't look in any fit state to adhere to any deal at the moment. How long will it take for you to heal?'

'A couple of hours. Maybe more.'

'Do we have a couple of hours?'

'It depends if your loved ones have a change of heart and rally reinforcements. Or if the soul ripper decides to turn up early.'

The risk of the former was all too real with Rob. She hadn't even considered the latter. It was going to be dark in a couple of hours and there was only one way Kane was going to be fit and strong enough by then. 'Will a feed help you?'

He raked her swiftly with his gaze. 'When doesn't it?'

'Then do it. We need to get this over and done with.'

He frowned a little. 'I feed and it won't be pleasant,' he warned. 'It's going to hurt.'

'I coped last time. It wasn't so bad.'

'I didn't need to feed last time: I chose to.'

The solemnity in his eyes made her chest tighten. 'Well, I'm not going to be able to carry you out of here in that state. And we can't sit around for the next few hours while you recover on your own, so I don't have a choice, do I?'

'I'll likely dual feed.'

Her stomach vaulted. 'Why?'

'Because this has weakened me. Because my instincts will take over. Because with me in this state, you're going to taste too good for me to fight it this time.'

'You could kill me.'

'I won't.'

She glanced over at the bench. 'There are sedatives over there. I could get a syringe full just in case you lose control.'

'I lose control and a syringe isn't going to do you any good. Nothing will.'

Visions of him biting into her viciously, thrusting into her savagely, flooded her mind. But she had to suppress them. She had made a decision and she had to stick with it. Her life was guaranteed to be over if she didn't.

'Are you sure you can do this?' he asked. 'You need to give me your consent now because it'll mean nothing once I start.'

She eased up onto her haunches and nodded.

He winced as he straightened his legs out flat to the floor. 'Sit astride me.'

She took a steady and resolute breath then closed the gap between them as she tentatively eased across his thighs.

He brushed the hair back from her neck, assessing her swiftly before holding her gaze again. 'You need to go with it. Don't fight me, it'll only incite me further.'

'That's reassuring.'

He flashed a hint of a smile, going someway to appease her tension. But she could see even that caused him pain. Pain that she had inadvertently caused. The urge to lean forward and kiss him tenderly on the lips was overwhelming, but it was unthinkable. This was a business deal – that was all. He was only going to help her because she'd finally forced him into it. And she couldn't have done that had she not got him into an impossible situation with Max and Rob's help. She couldn't feel guilt for fighting for her own survival, and that was exactly what she had done – she had fought back. And she needed to keep fighting. He may have been on the cusp of getting access to her soul, but she needed to keep her head clear even if her heart was less controllable.

She coiled her hair up from her neck and tilted her head to the side to expose it to him. With his one hand at the small of her back, the other firm around her nape, she braced herself and closed her eyes.

As he bit, she gasped, the absence of his anaesthetic this time meaning she felt every millimetre of the puncturing. She slammed her hand to his upper arm, the other gripped the waistband of his jeans.

The taste of her blood or the carnality of the act, maybe both, seemed to instantly incite him, making his feed both feral and fast. She wasn't sure if the strength and tension in his arms, as well as in his feed, was escalating or whether it was a reflection of her own weakening, light-headedness overcoming her quickly in the passing minutes.

His grip on her neck tightened, his other hand clawing at the fabric at the small of her back, clenching it as he tugged her tight onto his groin. Feeling his erection, she tensed. This feed was raw and unrestrained. And she knew if he wanted sex next, it would be the same.

She wanted to be afraid. Every ounce of decency and common sense told her she should be, but the clench deep in her abdomen was nothing to do with fear.

Her pulse raced, not just with her heart fighting the pressure of the withdrawal of its essence, but from the pressure of his hard body pressed against her. A body that, even within just a few minutes, was already fast recovering. A body that, from his unfamiliar low growls, still wanted more. Much more.

Kane swapped to the other side of her neck and bit again. Caitlin jolted, her nails digging into his hard upper arms. But he caught her wrists, forcing them behind her back, holding them there with just one hand as he used his other to keep her neck exactly where he wanted it.

The power returning to his body increased as he relaxed fully into the feed, his grip more assured and his movements more fluid. It was no longer just about necessity. The feed was gradually being replaced with enjoyment. He lapped away the blood at the wound he had created, kissed up her jaw where Rob had struck her, before his lips met hers, the metallic taste of her blood mingling in her mouth as he kissed her deeply.

His lip had already healed along with the cut on his brow. The spark was returning to his eyes, their sharpness replacing exhaustion and pain.

She braced herself as he nuzzled down her cleavage and tensed at the prospect of him biting down into her breast.

'Kane,' she said breathily. 'Kane you've had enough.'

But he was paying her no attention. Through the thin fabric of her knickers, his erection was already throbbing against his jeans. If she had had any doubt of what was to come, now she was sure.

He ripped the first few buttons on her dress as he tugged the fabric aside. Pulled down the cup of her bra so he could take her in his mouth.

She froze, fearful he would bite, but he didn't. Caitlin shuddered and whimpered, the tenderness within the brutality creating a heady mix for her own arousal.

Sensing it, he released her hands momentarily to push her down onto her back, the tiled floor cold and hard against her shoulders, her behind. He tore away her knickers, yanked down his jeans and shorts before parting her thighs around him. It felt unnervingly natural as she lay beneath him, her body acquiescent to what he needed. Not that her acquiescence made a difference. This wasn't just about Kane taking what he needed – it had the lethal undertones of him taking what he wanted.

But still she didn't feel afraid, despite anxiety overwhelming her. Memories came back hard and fast of walking into that room and seeing him. The sickness she had felt at the pain they had put him through. That feeling deep in her gut that had paralysed her when she knew they had every intention of killing him. The prospect that they could have taken him so easily still terrified her. If they had, she may as well have stepped into the grip of the soul ripper because having Kane die would have torn her soul out anyway.

As he pushed his way inside her without further warning, she bucked and gasped. The sensation was completely different, as if it were the first time all over again. Forcing her thighs further apart to allow himself deeper penetration, he withdrew slightly to thrust again, this time filling her to the hilt in one go. A tear escaped her eye from the building pressure inside her body, the heat overwhelming her despite the coolness of his body, of the floor.

She almost didn't notice him raking back her hair until he bit again. This time it was passionate and impulsive. She cried out, but it only made him feed on her harder and push himself mercilessly deeper, his renewed body uncompromising as he drank.

She arched from the floor, instinctively pressing herself into him as his bloodied lips covered hers again, his kiss voracious. The throb between her legs was overwhelming, all-encompassing. She closed her eyes, lost in the sensation, aching for her climax. She clenched her hands, held her breath. Forgot where she was.

His pace increased, his growls alarming her, momentarily distracting her from the intense heat rushing through her body.

And as he bit into her again, his thrusts unrelenting, she opened her eyes in shock only to slam them shut again. Dust particles sparkled and glinted in the darkness. Particles that darted around chaotically. Particles that became sparks. Sparks that ignited into flashes of light. She flushed from icy cold to hot, the flashes colourful, vibrant.

The room felt off kilter, the thrum resounding in her ears disorientating. Her body ached and her eyes filled with tears. She felt nothing around her but his arms, nothing but him inside her. And as her body shuddered into climax, she cried out. She tried to open her eyes again, but something more powerful was making the decision for her. Something that was determined to win. Something that held her still despite her struggles. Something that absorbed every last bit of energy she had left.

And she knew she couldn't fight it as unconsciousness consumed her, as she sank into darkness as comforting and enveloping as a warm ocean.

Kane withdrew from her and sat back on his haunches, catching his breath, surprised at how much his body trembled and ached. He'd never had one that powerful. Even with the shadow readers who had made it into an art form, they'd never brought him to climax like that.

He wiped away the blood on his lips and sucked it off his hand, a taste that intoxicated him as much as her touch. Caitlin lay beneath him, her body languid, pale and sated. He tenderly checked her pulse. It was slow but steady. She was lucky to be alive. And he was lucky he'd come when he had. She was strong but he'd pushed her hard and fast and her body wasn't used to it. What he'd done was dangerous.

Her body had gone into shock, but the glow around her told him she was quickly recuperating. He ran his hand over the softness of her face and lingered where Rob had hit her. The thought of it incited him in ways it never should have.

He sat back on braced arms as he continued to watch over her. The same feeling stirred in his chest as when she'd run out on him: that uncomfortable and unfamiliar feeling that he didn't want. All the while he had been trying to seduce her, to win her heart, she had been silently burrowing into his. And he already knew she had burrowed deep, too deep for comfort. And as he gazed down at her, he wondered how the hell he was going to let that soul ripper anywhere near her.

She opened her eyes and glanced up at him, obviously sensing his presence but slipping straight back into unconsciousness. His heart splintered somewhere deep. He leaned over her and did what he knew was the last thing he should have done. The very last thing he should have considered. He kissed her gently and tenderly on the lips, so tender that he had to pull away as soon as he'd done it.

He had to stay on course. He had to see it through to the end. He couldn't let this compromise his position.

He had to do this.

# CHAPTER TWENTY-SEVEN

Caitlin opened her eyes to find she was inside Kane's car. She looked out of the window at the run-down towering building that seemingly had once been a hotel. So many of the buildings like that had become residential – if they could be called that. No one visited Blackthorn for pleasure anymore, not wholesome pleasure, even though decades before it had been a thriving tourist city.

She pulled herself more upright.

That meant they'd successfully crossed the border.

'We're back in Blackthorn,' she said, as if to confirm it to herself. 'How?'

'I left the car at the border. Took the tunnel.'

She stared across at him. 'The tunnel is real?'

He almost smiled. 'But let that be our little secret.'

He drove them into the multi-storey car park and descended the first ramp.

She looked down at the sweater he had pulled over her torn dress to cover her modesty. It was clearly his from the size of it. Heat rushed between her legs as she remembered the rawness of the act. She wondered how much of it he had been aware of. She wondered how much of it had been out of his control, how much had been about punishing her for putting him in that situation, and how much of it had been just him unrestrained. She pushed back the sleeves. 'Where are we?'

'You were right to suspect I didn't live at the other place,' he said, driving deeper and deeper towards the subbasement. He stopped at the steel barrier at the end of the next ramp and pointed a remote at the wind-screen. The barrier grated as it recoiled and folded back against the wall.

She looked across at him, his features now barely discernable in the darkness. 'This is where you live?'

He glanced across at her and offered her a hint of a smile before driving into the darkness again, the barrier closing behind them.

He parked in the far left-hand corner of what was clearly the lowest level of the building. He reached for the glove compartment, his arm brushing her knees, every hair on the back of her forearms standing on end.

He met her gaze but it was fleeting, before he pulled away again.

Caitlin got out as he did, the chill in the basement compared to the warmth in the car evoking goosebumps. The echo as they both slammed their doors ricocheted around the expansive, empty darkness surrounding them. As the inner car light dissipated, he took her by the hand and led her over to what she could just about make out to look like a maintenance door, from the hazardous symbols and motifs it displayed.

As the car light finally switched off and threw them into pitch darkness, Caitlin clutched Kane's hand tighter. Her heart skipped a beat as he interlaced his fingers with hers while he did something barely audible to the door.

It opened automatically, triggering a light to come on at the top of the tiny stone stairwell, igniting the dusty flecks in the air.

Her stomach clenched. 'Down there?'

He squeezed her hand. 'Not scared of the dark are you, Caitlin?'

She offered him a feigned smile of rebuke, and followed his lead down the steps. The door shut behind them, intensifying the already dense silence. She pressed her hand to the wall for balance, the steep stone steps cold against her soles.

Kane stopped at the metal door at the bottom and unlocked it in two places before indicating for Caitlin to step in first.

She stepped over the threshold as Kane flicked a switch, causing a domino effect of erupting low-wattage lights igniting the darkness.

It was nothing she had expected from the dim and grimy entrance, but everything she expected of him.

This was his place. This was where Kane lived.

It was a cavernous maze of halls and doors and rooms partially hidden behind heavy jacquard or velvet curtains. It was opulent and luxurious, lavished with forest greens, navy blues and deep-crimson rich-textured fabrics to match the walnut and mahogany frames, doors and furniture. And silent. It was so silent. A warm labyrinth scented with cloves and mandarin, with cinnamon: scents that made her think of Christmas and all its promise.

She followed him down the hallways, passing floor-to-ceiling gilded mirrors that reflected the rooms opposite – mirrors she could mistakenly walk into. It was confusing and bewildering, but enchanting. Intricate tapestries draped the walls amongst metal sconces, elaborate carvings and renaissance images. Catacombs and recesses exposed ornate curiosities. Further objects of fascination covered shelves and bookcases: filigree wooden boxes, enamels and metalwork goblets and rings. Swords with stunning hilts as detailed as the one she had seen scrawled onto his back, were resting high on the walls or in glass display cabinets.

This was Kane – intense, dark and private, with a world of fascination in every recess. This wasn't just a home, it was a retreat. This was his nest.

He unlaced his hand from hers and veered off right into the lounge. Caitlin hovered for a moment as he pushed open a set of double doors directly ahead, turning right again.

She looked to her left, drawn towards the gap between the emerald velvet curtains, before glancing right once more to see if Kane had reappeared. He hadn't.

She pushed the weighty curtain aside to step into the enclosure. It was a lounge just like the one Kane had walked through, but this one was smaller and swamped in clutter. She passed a nearly finished cross-stitch of a Labrador and an easel with a half-finished oil painting of a woodland landscape. Resting against the wall behind them were numerous canvasses. She crouched down and flicked through. They were of scenery, still life, wildlife and portraits. And almost all of the latter were of Kane. Her heart skipped a beat at the assortment of wry and amused smiles and stoic glances he was offering the artist, or that the artist had been keen to capture. And because those images had clearly been created by someone who adored her subject, she instantly knew who that artist was: someone who got close enough to see who Kane really was; someone who loved him; someone whom he looked back at with equal love and affection.

This was Arana's room.

Arana, whose self-portrait smirked down at Caitlin from across the room. She was as stunning as Kane. Her thick black hair was long, wavy, untamed; her eyes an equally dark blue though large and doe-like. Like his, they were full of mischief and sharpness.

She thought of backing out of the room, but she didn't feel unwelcome there. There was no hostility in the environment. She stepped forward and pushed back another emerald curtain and stepped into Arana's bedroom. The bedroom of a girl who could just as easily never have left her teenage years. It was packed with fans and trinkets, metal and wooden trinket boxes. Elaborate and extravagant costume jewellery held stones that sparkled in the artificial light. Scarves and clothing were draped over mirrors and a domineering changing screen adorned with images of proud peacocks. This was the boudoir of a girl who loved life and all it had to offer. This was a girl who loved spontaneity. This was a girl who would buy something just because she liked it. Someone who accepted gifts readily and happily. A girl who loved textures and scents and patterns.

Arana had been exuberant and wilful and a lover of the beautiful. She had been impetuous, maybe self-indulgent, but she had been real and had lived every moment of her life until it had been cruelly snatched away from her.

Arana was all Kane had had, all that meant anything to him. And Caitlin's family, her boss, everyone she was linked to, had cruelly torn it away from him.

She was finally seeing inside Kane, the real Kane. Kane who'd had no choice but to leave his parents at the hands of vigilantes for the sake of escaping with his sister. His sister who had clearly been the exuberance in his life before hers was extinguished so unjustly. Never had his pain been more apparent. Never had she understood him more.

She stepped up to the dressing table and ran her finger through the dust that had lain there for fourteen years – gathering and waiting. He'd let it fall. He'd let it fall because that's what he did. He let the dust fall until he was ready to do something about it.

She felt a pang in her heart. She felt a pang for his pain and the agony of the past fourteen years, but also a pang of admiration for his restraint. A pang that confirmed that her heart hadn't just opened a little to him, but fully.

Caitlin didn't hear Kane step in behind her, but she felt him. She turned tentatively to face him, but instead of being angry at her intrusion, he stood watching her pensively.

'I'm sorry,' Caitlin said as she gazed deeper into his eyes than she'd ever dared. 'For what they did to her. For what they did to you.'

He didn't say anything. After a few prolonged moments, he turned and sauntered back out of the room, Caitlin knowing it was an indication for her to follow.

He led her through the lounge and the double doors, and out into the hallway beyond. He pushed open the second lot of heavy doors on the right and indicated for her to enter first.

The ornate walnut bed dominated the cosy windowless room, gold and red jacquard bedcovers draping and bunching onto the wooden floor. Floor cushions lay in front of the fire to her left, a chest directly ahead at the foot of the bed. A domineering wardrobe sat behind the door like something she'd read of in the Narnia Chronicles. The whole room was luxuriously regal. If she'd ever doubted his past status, she saw it now. The prince trapped in the cavernous underground. This was a fairy tale. Just without a happily ever after.

This was the very essence of Kane. This was the heart of Kane. This was where he came when he wanted to be alone and when he wanted to get away from it all. When he wanted peace.

She'd wanted this for as long as she'd known – to get right inside him, to see him in his true surroundings. And she knew what else she wanted. For just a few hours, she needed to forget everything she was supposed to be, everything she was supposed to know and experience. For just a few hours, she wanted to be herself with him. If she even knew who she was anymore.

She hovered awkwardly, watching him as he stood in front of the fire, his hands on his hips as he gazed pensively into the flames. Their glow warmed his skin, casting an amber sheen on his dark hair. And she felt the loneliness in the place, the isolation too indicative of her own life. But there and then was the first time she hadn't felt lonely in as long as she could remember – just standing there watching him, sharing some silent understanding with him. They were both doing what they could to survive. And, whatever happened, in just a few hours she was losing him. Whether her plan met with success or failure, this was the last time she'd stand alone with Kane Malloy.

When he glanced across at her, her stomach leapt the way it always did. There were still a few hours left until it was all over and this was probably her last chance, her only chance, to experience one shared intimate moment with him where she wasn't worrying about the consequences or trying to protect her heart.

She stepped over to join him, stared into the flames as their heat caressed her legs. She was drawn to the crystal flute glass on the grate, the amber flicker dancing in its transparent liquid content. 'What will you do when this is all over?'

'What I always do.'

The simplicity of his response cut her deeper than she knew it should have. 'Life goes on, right?'

'Something like that.'

'Xavier has got a lot of connections, Kane. Even if Max's and Rob's confessions are enough to take him down, he won't let this lie.'

'He'll have no choice.'

She pushed up the sleeves of the sweater again, the refined heat quickly burrowing into her skin. 'Rob's convinced you're going to betray me.'

He glanced across at her, the flames igniting in his navy eyes. 'And what do you think?'

'I think you're out to win and I think it would be dangerously naïve of me to think anything to the contrary.'

'But you're still going along with it.'

'I have no choice. I can't face this alone. Besides, I think you appreciate what I did for you tonight. And despite who I am, I'd like to think you'll stand by your word.'

He studied her eyes for a moment, Caitlin breaking away to stare back into the flames, unsettled by the intensity of his assessment.

'How can you still look at me like that?' he asked. 'After everything you now know.'

'It's because I now know.'

Kane turned to face her. Her heart leapt as he brushed her hair back from her shoulder, ran the back of his hand down her exposed neck, over the blemishes from his passion. He reached for her hips to turn her to face him. 'And what will you do after this is over, Caitlin? What do you want?'

'I haven't thought that far ahead.'

'You're really not expecting to make it, are you?'

'If I do, I'll think about it then.'

'Just do your part. Do as I say when I say, and you'll be fine.'

'Trust you with my life.'

'You could have walked out on me and left me in that cellar, Caitlin.

You could have listened to Max and Rob, taken what Carter had to offer. What you did took courage. Real courage. You did the right thing.'

'We'll see,' she said, turning away from him again, worried he'd probe too deep. 'So how is this going to be done?'

He stepped up to the mantelpiece and reached for the small, worn-looking book along with the three small plastic bags that held what looked like herbs. 'We dissolve these in warm water,' he said, indicating towards the flute glass on the grate. 'Once you've drunk the contents, there's a spell I perform.' He held the book across to her. 'Your soul gets transferred into here.'

She accepted it off him. Despite its size, the book was surprisingly weighty in her hands. 'Will my soul be safe?'

'We won't be able to open the book until the moment we plan to return your soul to you, or we risk tarnishing it. A hint of damage and it won't bind in you again.'

'And at what point will you return it?'

'As soon as the soul ripper has done what I want it to.'

'Which is?'

He took the book back off her and placed it along with the herbs on top of the mantelpiece. 'It's best if you don't know.'

She assessed him warily. 'But as soon as my soul's back in, you'll kill the soul ripper?'

'It being distracted by you will give me the best opportunity. It's the only shot we've got.'

'Can it kill you? Even though you don't have a soul, I mean?'

'The soul ripper can kill anything.'

'And what if it kills you for removing my soul in the first place? What if it doesn't want to bargain with you?'

'It will. It has to.'

She looked back down at the drink. 'And what effect will drinking that have?'

'It'll disorientate you. Maybe make you hallucinate. It gives you a sense of detachment and disassociation so it's easier to separate your soul from your astral body. When you're far enough gone, I'll conduct the spell. The book will draw your soul towards it and suck it in.'

'And how long will it take to get my soul out?'

'Minutes maybe.'

'Will I know what's happening?'

'It'll be just like having blood drawn.'

'And when it comes to returning it?'

'I reopen the book and you just need to consent.'

She looked away again, for fear of what he might see. But he'd confirmed it again – those words he'd said as he'd lowered her into the bath. The words both their survival hung on. 'And that's all?'

Kane nodded again. 'That's all. Putting it back in will be nothing more than a slight impact in the chest.'

She heaved a heavy breath and lowered herself to the floor. She pulled her knees to her chest and crossed her ankles, hypnotised by the flickering flames exacerbating the dark shadows around the room.

He sat down beside her, stretched his legs out towards the fire and braced himself back on his arms.

'What would you have done, Kane, if I hadn't fallen for you?'

'What would you have done if I hadn't waited in the corridor for you that night?'

'I would have walked right into one of your haunts and demanded to see you.'

He smiled. 'Oh yeah, that's right – and threatened to expose my links to Jask Tao, right?'

'No, I would have hemlocked you and read your shadow against your will.'

'That easy, huh?'

'Obviously I didn't know then what I do now. What about you – what was your backup plan?'

'I knew I wouldn't need one.'

Caitlin shook her head as she looked back into the flames, fighting to suppress her smile. 'Not even you're that confident.'

She lingered on the crackle of the fire, surprised how relaxed she felt in his presence, how safe.

'There was a time when I nearly asked you out, Caitlin.'

She looked back across her shoulder at him, lifted her eyebrows slightly. 'Asked me out?'

'You must have been about twenty-three. It was after Rob disappeared, but before you joined the VCU. You wouldn't have known who I was back then of course, but I knew you. It wasn't long after I worked everything out. I walked past the café and there you were – all alone. I was going to walk in there, invite you back to mine and do the most horrendous things to you. I wanted to tear you to pieces and deliver you back to Max.'

Caitlin frowned. 'So why didn't you?'

'It wasn't a moral choice. It would have meant nothing to Xavier except embarrassment. He would have covered it up just like he did your parents.'

'So you spared me until you could make us all suffer just that little bit more.'

'Be glad of it. My viscous streak then has turned out to be your salvation now.'

'But that's what you would have resorted to – if your plan hadn't worked?'

He looked into her eyes and held her gaze. 'That was my intention. My intention was also not to feel anything for you. Didn't quite turn out that way, did it?'

Her stomach flipped. Her heart lunged. She gazed deep into his eyes. 'Didn't it?'

'Do you really think the only reason I stopped you reading me was to save myself?'

'You wouldn't have agreed to help me if I hadn't threatened to read you.'

'You'll never know, will you?'

She searched his eyes for sincerity until the intensity got too much and she looked back into the flames.

'I'm not completely heartless, Caitlin.'

Her gaze snapped back to his. 'I know,' she said, surprising herself with her own conviction. 'And I don't think Xavier has won completely. I know the Kane Malloy I saw in your sister's paintings is still in there, behind the vengeance and anger and the hatred.' She lowered her eyes from his gaze for a moment. She pulled off the sweater to prevent the heat becoming uncomfortable. The cups of her bra were back in position but the first five buttons of her dress had been torn away. She closed the fabric for all it was worth and wrapped her arms back around her legs. 'Were any of those reports true, Kane? Had you done any of that stuff?'

'I've done a lot of bad things for a lot of bad reasons, most of the time to bad people but not all. Some things I regret, some things I don't. But I can't change any of it.'

'What happened to Arana was a catalyst for a lot of it though, wasn't it?'

He studied her for a moment. 'The only other time I felt helpless was watching those human bastards murder my parents.'

Her chest clenched. 'You saw it happen?'

He looked back into the fire. 'I was under the floorboards. We were supposed to already be running – me and Arana. There was a way out underground. Our parents sent me down there with her as soon as they saw the vigilantes coming. I got down there but I couldn't move. I watched through the cracks. Arana was only small. I kept her eyes covered, her mouth. I needed to see their faces. I needed to know who I was going to hunt down.'

'How old were you?'

'Old enough to know who I was and that I'd make them pay.' He stared pensively at the flames, silent for a moment. 'When they started to rip the place apart looking for us, I ran, leaving the place to burn behind us.'

She frowned at the darkness in his eyes, the amber glow within them, and also the sadness – the deep, unfathomable sadness muted only by the anger that still simmered.

'I promised I'd look after her. Arana. Instead I was in some grotty, dank basement giving it to some female whose face I can't even remember.'

'How did you find out what had happened?'

'Someone found her body the night after. I'd been out looking for her when she hadn't come home. She was always home by dawn.'

She stared back into the flames alongside him.

'Arana was the only goodness left in me,' he said. 'So maybe you're right, maybe that was the catalyst. Maybe it exposed who I really was when I didn't need to love or think of anyone else. To be honest, I don't even know anymore. Nor do I care.'

She studied him in the firelight. Those beautiful masculine features. Those tender, passionate lips. Those deep, emotional, untamed eyes. 'There's still good in you.'

He exhaled curtly and looked back at her.

'There is,' she insisted. 'I've felt it. I've seen it. I know most of it has been about making me fall for you – I'm not stupid. But there were still parts of you, real parts of you that slipped out.' She looked back into the fire. 'I wouldn't have been able to fall for you otherwise.' Composing herself in the silence, she looked back at him. She wished she didn't need to ask it. 'Do you hate me?'

He shook his head. 'No.'

She believed him, but it was still irrelevant with what was to come. She looked down at her bare toes curling into the carpet.

'You need to have more confidence in yourself, Caitlin.'

She frowned. 'I do have confidence.'

'Do you?'

'I have enough.'

'You have no idea how strong you are.'

She looked back across her shoulder at him. 'Are you scared of anything, Kane?'

He frowned. 'Why?'

'I want to know.'

He looked back into the flames. 'Honestly? Not much.' He was pensive for a moment. 'Serryns I guess. But that goes for every vampire. I suppose I'd say I'm more unnerved by them though, rather than scared.'

'They're the ones with the poisonous blood, right?'

'Poisonous to us. And infused with all the charm and prowess to get us to bite. They're a walking advert for vampire celibacy if ever there was one.' He broke a smile before looking back into the flames.

'Have you ever come across one?'

'I wouldn't be sitting here now if I had. Not with my lack of self-control over the years.' He glanced back at her. 'Unfortunately for you, they've kept away from me.'

'Only scared of one thing. That's impressive.'

'Why, what are you scared of, Caitlin?'

'It would be quicker to list what I'm not scared of.' She hesitated and took a steadying breath. 'Like you, I guess it's not being in control. Being helpless. A failure. Being alone. I'm scared of you taking my soul. I'm afraid about how it will feel not to have it anymore.' She interlaced her fingers and clenched. 'I'm frightened of feeling that emptiness again. I'm frightened of the pain that comes with it.' She felt him tense, knew he hadn't taken his eyes off her. But she didn't dare, couldn't bear, to meet his gaze. She looked down at her hands. 'I sometimes wonder if I'd even have come down this path if I hadn't lost them both. If Rob hadn't walked away. I wonder if I could have made myself normal.'

'What's normal?'

She looked into his eyes, eyes that studied her intently. Too intently for her to sustain it. She looked back into the flames and shrugged.

'Strong isn't about not being afraid, Caitlin. It's about facing what you're scared of.'

'Like you,' she said, holding his gaze. 'And what you can do to me.'

'I don't want to scare you.'

'No?'

He shook his head. He brushed her hair back from her shoulder, but didn't withdraw his hand. Instead he gently smoothed down the hair on the back of her head before tenderly cupping her neck.

She warily met his gaze, a gaze that lingered as if in contemplation. But he didn't need to say anything more. His touch had said it all. His eyes had brimmed with compassion enough to break her.

She didn't think about it and she was glad she didn't, or she'd never have had the courage to do it.

She leaned into him, the energy crackling between them as their legs touched.

She knew it was a tentative kiss, but he didn't seem to mind. He accepted her willingly, lips parting to hers, tongue meeting hers as they kissed slowly, lingeringly. He cupped her neck with both hands, his thumbs tracing across her jaw as he moved onto his knees, straddled her, guiding her gently onto her back.

His kiss was deep, intense, as he took his time, teasing her mouth open, creating enough pressure to make every hair on the back of her neck stand on end.

She traced her palm down his chest, taking in every hard curve, his skin warm from the heat of the fire. She absorbed the static as she ran her fingers over the top of his jeans, the ridge of his toned stomach.

He unfastened his jeans and led her hand down to his erection. He guided her hand around his girth, held her there until she relaxed it enough for him to slide it up and down his length before wrapping her fingers around the ridge, guiding her thumb over the tip so she could feel his wetness.

Arousal shot through her, his grip tightening over hers as he sighed against her lips. He was enjoying it. He was enjoying her touch. And he kissed her slowly, tenderly, on the mouth, down her neck, her cleavage, rubbing his thumb across her breast through her bra before sliding his hand to her neck again, her whole body ignited.

Hell, he was going to break her heart, tear her to pieces, but still she couldn't stop reacting to him. She had fallen and fallen deep. And as she kissed him again, she could feel her heart wrenching.

She'd never make him love her. It was a battle she'd never win. But she'd hold on to the way he looked at her right then, the way he touched her as he gently pushed her hair back, running his fingers through it.

'Let's just do this,' she said against his lips. 'Before I change my mind.'

He nodded, his head pressed against hers. He stood and took the herbs and books from the mantelpiece. He emptied the contents of the plastic bags into the crystal flute glass, the dried samples melting into the warm water surprisingly quickly.

Kane handed the flute across to her as she sat up. 'You have to drink it in one go.'

She accepted it off him, the glass warm between her fingers. She looked down into the liquid then knocked it back. It was sweet to taste but the bitterness quickly snapped in, a dry wall forming in her throat. She felt nothing else for a few seconds, but then felt consumed as if dropped in a warm pool. Feeling her body sway, she clutched the floor.

She frowned, her head feeling heavy. If it hadn't been for the aware-ness of Kane's arms guiding her back down she would have sworn she was falling slowly. The rug felt soothing, warm and comfortable as she relaxed into its softness. The darkness of the room added to the inescap-able calm seeping into her body and mind, the flicker of the flames on the ceiling compellingly hypnotic.

Kane's kiss was deep again, sensuous as he pulled off his T-shirt and lowered himself onto her, melding against her. She slid her hands up the tautness of his biceps to his shoulders and down his hard, cool back, before gliding back up to the nape of his neck as his kisses trailed back across her jaw.

It was all she could concentrate on as she felt herself drifting into languidness. Her eyes were an effort to keep open, the coolness flushing over her skin adding to her sleepiness. The shadows on the ceiling took on shape and form, mingling and merging, swirling in each other's midst. What she knew to be 2D became 3D, reaching out for her, looming down on her like stalactites. She reached her hand up to touch them but felt nothing but warm air, each time the tips of the stalactites receding just out of reach. The rug felt like liquid, dissipating between her fingers.

She turned her head to the right as Kane kissed down her neck, the room following a split second behind, adding to her queasiness. The flames curved and bowed towards her, stretching and morphing into shapes, into faces, elongated then squashed.

She closed her eyes, needing to rest her weighty lids.

'Still with me?' Kane whispered in her ear.

She nodded.

She let him spread her legs and push himself into her.

She caught her breath and clenched the back of his neck and forearm as he eased all the way inside her.

Her body felt shockingly relaxed, surprisingly at ease. His cool fingers interlaced with hers and squeezed, but he still felt distant, her hand feeling as though it was someone else's. And as he began to penetrate her, the darkness seemed more intense, its depth almost breathing as it contracted and expanded.

She knew she could have died then and would never have felt more complete. She knew she could want nothing more than having him inside her, feeling him that close to her, a part of her. She pulled him closer and kept him against her as he kissed down her throat, down her cleavage. He withdrew to slide down further, pushing up her dress to kiss her inner thighs. She arched her back, knowing where he was leading to and longing for him to get there. His cold tongue instantly met her heat, licking at her folds and encircling her clitoris until she grabbed the back of his head. He pushed his tongue inside, the sensation almost knocking her to the brink of climax. But he sensed it, his mouth again meeting hers, as he pushed himself back inside her.

'I could never hate you,' he said softly in her ear. 'You make me feel too much.'

Her gaze met his. He was blurred, but she could tell from the way he was looking at her and the sincerity of his tone that he was speaking the truth. A truth that made her heart ache.

His thrusts became slicker, his grip firmer as he started to bring her to climax. The relaxation of her body made every tiny pulse almost too intense to bear, her arousal consuming her, overwhelming her. She didn't care that she couldn't contain it. She didn't care that she whimpered in elation. She didn't care that she called out his name or cried as she broke into another climax. A climax Kane lingered in until he kissed her tenderly on the ear and withdrew.

Words. She heard words. Distant muffled words as if she were under covers or in another room. But she knew Kane's voice. She picked up the rhythm of an incantation. He'd started the process.

She could hear the crackle of the fire, the flames seeming to vibrate on the ceiling as they leapt unnervingly fast as if they were panicking, trying to get away.

A wave hit her, the whole floor seeming to undulate beneath her. Then again. The next one came harder and faster as if a tidal wave was not crashing against her, but flowing out from within her. It took all her concentration to keep herself steady, her toes and fingers curled into the rug.

A thrum resounded in the room, in her ears, like a distant drumbeat only softer, like a large bird preparing itself for flight, beating its wings in slow motion. She could almost see them: those heavy brown wings outstretched, picking up air with every beat. And they got faster, louder, lighter, flapping now instead like tiny bird wings. The stronger the pull inside, the more the wings flapped frenetically. And she realised it was paper – pages turning rapidly – turning because the incantation was working. Her soul was being drawn out, its content transferring to words on the paper.

The flapping became so frantic it hummed in her ears. Her body ached, her chest tight. She felt empty, lost, just as she had the day her mother had told her about her father, just as she'd felt the day Max had sat her down to reveal the same news about her mother. And tears trickled down her cheeks. Disassociation overwhelmed her, the pain too great to acknowledge, the emptiness all too real and all too encapsulating. The void grew with every passing second, until she heard a thunk as the book slammed closed.

The water rushed away, Caitlin feeling as if she was laying in an empty bath, not moving as the darkness pulsated and throbbed behind her eyes.

She clenched her hands and they felt like hers again, the rug felt warm and soft beneath her. She opened her eyes and looked up at the ceiling, the flames flickering on the ceiling a surprising comfort.

Kane gazed down at her as he rested on his forearm. 'It's done,' he said softly.

She sighed and turned her head to look across at the book that lay closed beside her. She scanned the room. Everything looked the same. Everything felt the same. Everything smelt the same. Apart from that nagging feeling of emptiness inside, she didn't feel any different. She looked back at him through heavy, sleepy eyes. 'Now we wait?'

He nodded. 'I'll get us some pillows. We can bed down here.'

Kane pulled a couple of pillows from the bed.

Caitlin had moved onto her side, her back to him. He stood captivated by her feminine silhouette in the firelight – the inward curve of her slender waist, down over her rounded hip, her slender, shapely legs, those delicate feet, her toes curling and uncurling in the rug. Her sandy-brown hair cascaded over her beautiful shoulders, her head resting on her forearm, that tantalizing neck exposed. A neck he had fed on and ravished. A body he'd come to know nearly every part of. A body that sent a pulse of excitement through him from just a touch. A body he had been so close to doing so many atrocities to – thoughts that now sickened him.

Because, tough though she may be, fiercely resolute, irritatingly stubborn, her vulnerability overrode it all. A vulnerability that had never been more apparent. A vulnerability that he could no longer deny had entranced him since the moment he'd pinned her up against the wall in the corridor and stared into those milky-coffee eyes. Eyes that even then warned him she was going to break him and that she was going to change things – that she was going to make everything different.

And he'd suppressed it and fought it because his plan necessitated it. His plan could not have him falling for his target. His plan could not have him softening for one moment. And he would defile her and toy with her and destroy her to prove that point.

And he was going to succeed. He was going to succeed even after she'd saved his life in that cellar. Even after she'd put her trust in him enough to unfasten those shackles. Even as she'd given herself to him willingly for the dual feed.

Up until then it had all gone so smoothly. Even her escape had allowed him to get deeper inside her. Even in her distress, he'd seen the way she'd been looking at him as he'd tended her foot. She wasn't used to being cared for. She wasn't used to someone else picking up the pieces for her. And when she'd cuddled into him for the first time, he knew she wasn't used to being comforted.

And he'd managed it – the guilt, the deceit. He'd managed his feelings. He'd accepted them.

Until that crucial moment. That moment she'd looked in his eyes and saw him. The real him. Looked at him with warmth and understanding and love. That moment she'd opened her heart and broke his. Until she kissed him without barrier and without refrain. Until, for the first time in fourteen years, he'd made a connection and felt a glimmer of contentment. Contentment at knowing her. The real Caitlin. Contentment he still felt watching her lying in front of his fire as if she'd always been a part of his life and always would be.

And he realised he'd lied when he said only one thing scared him. Nothing compared to this: the thought of being without her.

He'd felt it as soon as her hand had closed on his chest to force-read him. The sheer panic he had felt, not that his plan would fail, but that within seconds she would have been gone.

Gone by his hand.

It had only been three days of being with her. Three days of being close to her and she'd crumbled walls to parts of him he thought lost forever.

And as she'd looked him in the eyes and asked if he hated her, she may as well have asked him to love her.

But loving her wasn't the hard part. It was sacrificing his love for Arana to be able to love her that was the problem.

The problem that chained him to the darkness that had become a part of him. A darkness that was too interwoven for him not to be ripped to shreds from its release.

He placed the pillows beneath their heads and he lay down behind her. In her semi-conscious state, she settled back against him, her head on the pillow beside his. As he interwove his fingers through hers, she languidly toyed with his fingers, running her thumb over each short nail in turn before massaging each of his knuckles.

He could kill the soul ripper as soon as it appeared. Drive the dagger deep into its spine and give Caitlin her soul back. Keep her there. They'd never find her. They could live out the next few days, even weeks, locked in his haven while he plotted another way to get those responsible.

And then she'd despise him when he succeeded. She'd be torn apart even more.

He had no choice.

He leaned forward and kissed her, eased her lips apart gently, his tongue meeting hers. She relaxed into his kiss quickly and easily, her soft, wet mouth accepting him willingly. He ached for her again, hardening in readiness again, but as she closed her eyes, her hand becoming lax in his, he spooned against her, holding her close.

She was asleep within moments, her breaths deep, heavy, sated.

He could feel the depleted strength in her, her deflated resilience because of her absent soul. She probably didn't feel any different, other than being exhausted. But he could sense it. Like a lover sensed sadness or worry or anxiety, he sensed the difference.

He kept his fingers interlaced with hers, rested his head against hers as he stared into the fire.

She was going to hate him anyway, but at least it would be over quickly and painlessly. Hatred was essential if it was going to work.

# CHAPTER TWENTY-EIGHT

'Caitlin, wake up.'

Caitlin opened her eyes. The fact Kane had whispered it close to her ear unnerved her more than anything else. Unnerved her more than the fact the fire now lay dead and the room had turned icy cold. More than the fact the silence was more intense than it had been in the sound-proofed cellar. She sat bolt upright beside him and stared at the figure stood at their feet.

If she hadn't felt so angry she would have cried. For one split second, for that tiny amount of time, she thought her mother had come back. Thick, wavy hair cascaded around the vision's shoulders, the floor-length nightdress reminding Caitlin when and where her mother had been the night she had been taken.

But it wasn't her mother. Her eyes alone revealed it wasn't her mother, because the eyes that glowered back at her were dark and cruel and lifeless.

The eyes of the soul ripper.

Caitlin gripped Kane's hand, partly for reassurance and partly to curb her anger at the creature that focused on her.

'Take it easy,' Kane said softly to Caitlin as he handed her the book. 'Don't move.'

The soul ripper glanced at Kane. Its eyes were unreadable, but it clearly wasn't bothered by his presence. Instead it snatched its attention back to Caitlin and advanced the few steps towards her, its jerky movements like jumps in a movie roll. It crouched in front of her, its face less than two inches away as it stared deep into her eyes.

Caitlin dug her nails into the rug, her trembling hand clutching the book to her chest as she forced herself to look back at it.

And, just as Kane had described, she saw herself upside down in the murky, fathomless pool of its black eyes, eyes that flicked to the book before staring back at her.

It retreated, more quickly than it had advanced, clearly disgruntled with what it saw. Its eyes snapped to Kane as quickly as its body did.

But Kane didn't flinch, his sullen eyes unwavering on the creature.

'Go and get on the bed,' he instructed Caitlin.

Caitlin eased away from him, clambering back, not taking her eyes off the soul ripper as it watched her every move. But as it stepped forward to pursue her, Kane stood and blocked its way. It cocked its head to the side in what could have been mistaken for a nervous twitch, but it was clearly an unspoken enquiry that Kane understood.

'You want her, you do my bidding first,' he said, without so much as a quiver in his tone.

Caitlin's stomach clenched, her heart pounding as she watched him fearlessly square up to the creature.

If it could sneer, she was sure she saw an attempt to. 'You dare to command me, vampire?' it said, drawing out vampire with disdain, its voice huskier than the feminine frame it embodied would have allowed.

'I dare and I do,' Kane said. 'Do my bidding, sphariga, and I will give you what you seek.'

Caitlin couldn't see enough of Kane's face, but from the indignation in the soul ripper's eyes, he was glaring right at it.

The soul ripper didn't move, its stare melting into Kane in rage.

The thought that those eyes were the last things her parents had seen filled her with renewed anger. She had no doubt what form it had taken to appear to her mother and how cruel that would have been.

It drew its lip back slightly in a snarl, losing the feminine features it had stolen. 'You took it?'

'Yes,' Kane said. 'Do as I say or I will kill your prize.'

It leaned back in an unnatural bend, the wrath and, at the same time, horror emanating from its eyes. Whatever it was thinking, it believed Kane and it didn't want to lose what it had come for. Namely her.

The soul ripper was quick. It drew a clear line towards Caitlin, charging at her with an unnatural balance, defying gravity as it leapt onto the thin ridge of the footboard in one easy move before pouncing in front of her.

She flinched and it snarled.

Then it withdrew.

Its head snapped towards Kane.

And it nodded.

# CHAPTER TWENTY-NINE

The soul ripper sat in the back of the car in the middle of the seat, its hands in its lap, its attention fixed ahead.

Caitlin looked across at Kane for reassurance and he glimpsed across at her, sending her a wink. She turned her attention back out of the passenger-seat window, trying to ignore the tension in her chest from having that thing behind her. The thing that had filled her nightmares for seven years. The thing that had murdered both her parents and was itching to kill her. The thing void of emotion because it felt none. It had one purpose and that one purpose alone had driven it to bargain with Kane.

Kane drove down the slope and along the length of the chain-link fence, before driving through the gateway into the wasteland. It was unnervingly still outside, unnervingly silent. Caitlin surveyed the warehouse in the distance, the dark, stormy clouds its backdrop.

He pulled inside the derelict building, his headlights igniting a stone pillar as they passed. He couldn't have picked a more perfect location to enact his revenge.

He turned the car around and reversed so he was facing the doors, then shut off the engine and looked across at her. 'Are you okay?'

She nodded. 'This is where they did it, isn't it?'

'Yes.'

'Is this where you found her?'

He nodded.

Caitlin looked back out of the window and scanned the dark and murky expanse before looking back at him. 'You've planned every last detail.'

'I've had a long time to do it.' He took his phone out of his jeans and checked the time. 'Carter should be here any minute.'

'What am I to do?'

'You stay quiet.' He held her gaze. 'I mean it, Caitlin. As far as Carter's concerned, you're here against your will.'

She nodded and followed him out of the car.

Their doors echoed as they slammed each in turn. She strolled around to the bonnet and leaned back against it, Kane coming to sit beside her.

'He won't come unarmed, Kane. He's not stupid.'

'It'll make no difference.'

'What if he just takes you down?'

'He won't. He's waited for this moment longer than I have.'

'What did you say to him?'

Kane looked across at her. 'What I needed to get him here.'

'Do you really think he believes you're going to give yourself up?'

'All he'll see is a compromise, but that's good enough for him.'

'What if he does take you down, Kane? What do I do then?'

'You'll live. Just soulless until they let me go.'

She frowned. 'And what about the soul ripper?'

'Everything is accounted for.'

'Plans fail, Kane.'

He looked back ahead. 'Not mine.'

Caitlin followed his gaze to the doors – to the distant sound of engines and tyres over shale.

Within minutes, a sleek black car pulled up, two vans lining up either side of it. Another larger van drove past them all and stopped to the right of Kane's car.

The vans either side of the car opened. Four black-clad soldiers dismounted from each, forming a circle around Kane and Caitlin. They lifted their tranquiliser guns in perfect unison, aiming directly at Kane.

'You sure better know what you're doing,' Caitlin whispered to him.

He looked across at her and smiled. 'Have you learned nothing?' He stood up from the bonnet, his attention focused on the car as its doors opened.

Three more black-clad soldiers stepped out, equally raising their guns. And, following behind them, was Xavier Carter. He strode forward a few steps then stopped about fifteen feet away, hands tucked deep in his long coat. 'Hello, Kane,' he said, a glimmer of satisfaction overriding the uncertainty behind his grey eyes.

Kane took a few casual steps towards him, the guns following his every step. 'I see you've brought your friends.'

'I'm no fool, Kane. You know that.'

'I could take offense.'

'I'd prefer you take it as a compliment.'

'Have you brought what I wanted?'

Xavier nodded to one of the soldiers who in turn advanced towards the third van. He banged his fist on the door three times.

The lycans were led out in turn and, from their lack of fight, they were clearly heavily drugged. They were gagged, blindfolded, their hands bound behind their backs, their ankles linked by chains.

Caitlin glowered across at Xavier. Xavier who had handed them over so easily to the fate they should never have been facing. And, as he met her gaze, she felt sick with fury, more so at the glint of approval in his eyes as if she had done a job well.

'And I see you've brought Caitlin back safe and well.'

'As per our agreement,' Kane said.

The soldiers shoved the lycans over to the concrete post, kicked them onto their knees and secured them to it.

'I'm glad you finally took me up on my offer,' Xavier said. 'I hope this is the first step in the right direction.'

'So much for your claimed protection of everyone in your care,' Kane remarked.

'I have no sympathy with what they have done. I understand your need for vengeance for your sister. Who am I to stand in your way?' He took another step towards him. 'I'm willing to do what it takes, Kane. To convince you that you can trust me. Of what a formidable force we can become. This territory will be yours. You'll never want for anything again.' He held out his hand towards the lycans. 'See this as the first offering of my loyalty. You only had to ask for them. This is how it will be. You ask and I'll give.'

'Humans and vampires will never be able to form an alliance – not a true alliance. We are both too inherently in need of control.'

'But that's not to say a vampire and a human who will mutually benefit cannot work together. Keep your territory under control – that's all I ask. And enforce what I need you to enforce. And in return, I will let you do whatever you want to do with no fear of retribution. You have nothing to lose and everything to gain, Kane.'

'Loyal to me, but not to your own, is that right?' Kane asked.

Xavier took a step closer to him and lowered his voice. 'I will do whatever it takes to have this happen.' Xavier clicked his fingers and held out his open palm towards one of the soldiers.

The soldier marched over to the car and came back with a small wooden box. He placed it in Xavier's hand and stepped back.

Xavier took a few more steps closer to Kane, the soldiers closing in on them a little more.

As Xavier opened the box, Caitlin pulled herself off the bonnet to take a few steps closer.

The tension in Kane seared through her.

'They told me where they'd stored it. I told you I'd kept it safe,' Xavier said.

'I knew you would have,' Kane said, Caitlin knowing him well enough now to know it was the tension of restraint. 'You're not going to squander a trophy like that, are you?'

Caitlin's heart pounded audibly in her ears.

'Not a trophy for me, Kane. I wasn't the one who tore it out of her body.' He glanced across at the lycans. 'I'm not the beast that guts its victims like they were animals.' He looked back at Kane. 'It's my gift to you. The final sealing of our loyalty. Arana's heart and the blood of the lycans who murdered her,' he held his hand towards Caitlin, 'and the soul of a shadow reader to complete the resurrection.'

Panic encompassed her. Sickness burned the back of her throat as she drew level enough to stare down at the withered heart in the sickening epiphany moment.

She stared back at Xavier in horror.

He smiled.

Resurrection. Arana back. The only thing Kane would ever bargain for. What Kane had been planning all along now hit her like a concrete wall.

And she'd fallen for it.

But it wasn't him she lunged at – it was Xavier.

'You're nearly as ruthless as me,' Kane said to Xavier, wrapping his arms around Caitlin and tugging her against his chest to restrain her effortlessly as he clamped his hand over her mouth. 'Sacrifice all to get what you want. That's dedication. Maybe you and I are alike after all.'

'I'm glad you're beginning to see it.'

His words paralysed her. If Kane hadn't held her so tight, she would have dropped to the floor, the distance in his eyes as he focused on Xavier chilling her.

'You see, Kane – I can bring light out of the darkness. Those beasts stole your sister from you, but I'm giving her back to you. This is how it can be. We can do immeasurable things.'

He didn't know. Xavier was still clueless. Caitlin's heart pounded. He still hadn't worked out that Kane knew he was responsible. Somewhere in-between, they had made this deal and it clearly had seemed like a perfectly reasonable exchange to Xavier if it had got him there.

She glanced anxiously around at the soldiers. Kane was going to kill them all. Somehow he was going to end it all.

She needed to yell at Xavier and warn him. She needed to give her unit a chance. She shouldn't have hesitated. Kane had clearly betrayed her. He had tricked her, just like he'd tricked the others.

But as her heart splintered enough for her to cry out, Kane, as if sensing it, weaved his free fingers into hers, squeezed lightly, the private exchange of his thumb sliding over her hand enough to make her hesitate.

'You understand me,' Kane said, words that could have been directed at her as much as they were at Xavier.

'That's right,' Xavier said. 'I understand you perfectly.'

'Then nothing I do will surprise you,' Kane said, gently easing Caitlin away from him.

She reluctantly took a few steps back and looked over her shoulder as the rear passenger door of Kane's car opened.

But it was no longer the image of her mother that stepped out. She saw the head first, the long dark hair. There was no mistaking the porcelain skin or the large dark eyes.

The soul ripper stood perfectly still, its head tilted slightly to the side, those eyes staring intently across at Xavier.

He glanced around the room nervously as if checking it wasn't an apparition of his own mind, searching to see if anyone else could see what he could. They could, but they kept their guns on Kane.

'Impossible,' Xavier said, staring at the likeness of Arana as it approached. 'It's impossible. What is this?'

Caitlin took a wary couple of steps back.

'Impossible as you arranged her death so perfectly,' Kane said, his arms folded.

Xavier stared back at him in shock. 'You know?'

Kane held his gaze. 'Just as I know what my sister cursed the Parish line with.'

Xavier's attention snapped back to the soul ripper, his frown deep as he tried to work out what was happening.

'I know things you could never know, Carter. I know third-species secrets that will never fall under your knowledge – and all this is an example of why. Your kind has an agenda – always has had and always will have. Under your guidance and control, all hell would break loose in this district. So, as I keep telling you – no, I will never work with you.'

'You're a fool, Kane,' Xavier said, trying to look calm. But even from where she was stood, Caitlin could see the perspiration trailing down his temple. 'It doesn't have to come to this.'

'Come to what, Carter? Me getting you to accept my refusal once and for all?'

Xavier glanced nervously at the soul ripper again as it stood beside Kane. He looked back at Kane. 'But your sister. You must have the shadow reader's soul for it to work.'

'A lie to get you here. I can't bring her back. My sister has gone, Carter,' Kane said. 'You saw to that. But she left me this legacy,' he said, pointing at the soul ripper. 'Just so I'd know how to track you all down.'

Xavier backed up further as the soul ripper stalked towards him, its eyes fixed on his. He lifted his hand to command the soldiers to shoot, but the soul ripper was quicker.

The guns were simultaneously ripped from their hands first, smashing into the walls behind them. In perfect timing, the men were lifted swiftly and horizontally into the air before being slammed down onto the floor on their backs.

Panic flared in Xavier's eyes as he scanned the room before looking back at the soul ripper. He took a few wary steps back. 'What's it doing?'

'What I've told it to do.'

The soldiers writhed as if in agony then slowly their ethereal bodies rose from within them, the phosphorous glow of their souls still intact, hovering a couple of feet above their unconscious forms like translucent shadows.

'I could have killed you before now, Carter,' Kane continued. 'So many times. But I resolved this was worth the wait.' He strolled back over to the car, placed the wooden box containing Arana's heart safe on the driver's seat before coming back out with a dagger. He spun it in his hand as he sauntered over to the two lycans. 'You have to be stopped, Carter,' he said as he carved an A for Arana into their foreheads.

As he turned to face Xavier again, Xavier took a step back.

'You can't do this, Kane. Everyone will know. You'll be finished. I protect you. My no-touch policy on you is the only thing that keeps you alive.'

'We'll find out soon enough, won't we?'

Xavier stumbled backward as the soul ripper closed the gap. 'Get away from me!' he demanded, falling against the bonnet of his car. 'You hear me? Stay away from me! Keep it away from me, Kane!'

'You have no idea how hard it's been waiting this long,' Kane announced, following behind it. 'But I knew when it was coming back, you see. All I had to do was find a way to command it. I just had to take the one thing it craved – Caitlin's soul. And then I could make it do whatever I wanted it to.'

'Stop it,' Xavier said, his tone laced with panic. 'Stop it and I will do whatever you want.'

'I don't need anything from you. Max and Rob are about to go live with confessions of exactly what they and you did. You're finished, Carter. But prison is too good for you. Death at my hand, however agonizing I could make it, is too good for you. It's going to tear out your astral body and soul and take you into an eternity of slavery. Just like what happened to Rick and Kathleen Parish.'

The soul ripper arched its back, ethereal white tendrils streaming from its body, lunging towards Xavier's chest.

He screamed as he fell back against the bonnet. 'Whatever you want!'

As Kane stepped back, as he glanced across at the soul ripper, as its tendrils lunged into Xavier's chest, Caitlin flinched and momentarily turned away.

That was what happened to them. That was the cruelty that stole her parents from her. Her life. Her dreams. Her peace of mind. And it was coming after her. Within minutes, it would turn on her, ready for Kane to meet his side of the bargain.

'I know about the prophecy!' Xavier cried out, his tone wretched. 'The secret.'

Caitlin snapped back to look at him.

'I know what you need!' Xavier added. 'I know what you need to make it happen! I can get it!'

'Wait!' Kane commanded the soul ripper, his hand raised.

It ceased and looked back over its shoulder at him. Its tendrils disappeared back inside its body.

Xavier sank to the floor as Kane stepped over and crouched in front of him.

'And how do you know what's needed?' Kane asked.

Xavier stared at him warily.

Caitlin took a couple of steps closer.

If Xavier bargained with him, if Kane had reason to keep him alive, Kane could kill the soul ripper. Her pulse raced. She wouldn't have to resort to what she'd planned. It could work out. But at what cost? She stared back at Xavier. Selfish to the end. He couldn't seriously be talking about helping the vampires fulfil the prophecy. It was everything he stood against. Everything she worked for to stand against.

Enraged by Xavier's silence, Kane grabbed him by the throat. 'How do you know?' he asked, his tone dangerously low.

'Call it off,' Xavier said. 'Give me your word you'll call it off and I'll tell you.'

'You'll tell me now,' he said as he squeezed.

'You won't kill me. You said it yourself that I deserve worse. Give me your word. Give me your word and I'll tell you.'

The seconds ticked by.

'You have my word,' Kane said.

Caitlin sighed with momentary relief, albeit muted. But it couldn't be true. Kane wouldn't give up that easily. He was just getting what he wanted.

Xavier hesitated for a moment longer before saying, 'Feinith. Feinith told me.'

Feinith? The only Feinith Caitlin knew of was one of the Higher Order vampires. She was one of the diplomats with the Global Council and occasionally communicated with the TSCD on particular matters, but only those related to strategic vampire management issues.

Kane's silence told her he knew exactly whom Xavier was talking about. His continued silence told her he wasn't happy. But he released his grip just enough to let Xavier take a few panicked deep breaths.

Xavier glanced warily back at the soul ripper. 'Get it away from me.'

'Why did Feinith tell you?' Kane asked.

'Because she wants me to help get it.'

Kane released him and stood. He took a step back.

Xavier rubbed his throat, his gaze warily locked on Kane. 'Join us. Make this happen. Rule our army.'

Caitlin took a few steps closer, shock coiling through her. 'What are you saying? Are you insane?'

But Xavier didn't break his gaze from Kane to acknowledge her. 'Did you hear me, Kane? Feinith has plans. Big plans. And she wants you to be a part of them. That's why I needed to get you.'

As Caitlin pulled level, Kane caught hold of her forearm, preventing her moving any closer. He didn't look at her either, but he didn't need to.

'Own up to what you did to Arana,' Kane said to him. 'Publicly. Hand yourself in.'

'What? I'm offering you a deal.'

'I thought I made myself perfectly clear.'

'Do you understand what we're offering you?'

'You have until dawn. If you don't confess, I'll send it back after you. Wherever you are and whatever you're doing, it will find you. Only I won't be around to stop it.'

'You gave me your word.'

'And I've called it off. But I never said I wouldn't set it on you again.' He released Caitlin. Holding out his arm, he used the dagger to slice down his forearm until droplets of his blood hit the cold, stone floor.

Words slipped from his lips that Caitlin could barely hear nor understand. Something archaic, something lethal. 'Confess by dawn or you will meet your fate my way.'

'You need me on the outside.'

Kane crouched down again and caught his jaw. 'I don't need anyone, Carter. Not anymore.'

The words cut deeper than Caitlin was prepared for. The sealing of her pending fate. Kane hadn't made a deal with Xavier – he'd just persuaded him to do exactly what he wanted him to do all along.

Kane slammed Xavier's head back against the bonnet with such force that it knocked him out cold.

As Kane stood and turned to face her, she caught her breath.

He was on the brink of the best of both worlds: he'd make Xavier confess to the crimes, bring down the TSCD with it and then send the soul ripper after him anyway.

And he could only do that by keeping the soul ripper happy, by keeping the soul ripper alive.

By betraying her.

Kane checked his phone as he strolled back across to his car. He opened the passenger door, took out the book and placed it on the car bonnet.

She knew what he was waiting for. Why he was looking at his phone. It was half past one. He was waiting for a broadcast.

And then he smiled, albeit fleetingly.

She could hear the voices as he stepped across to her and held out the phone for her to see.

'Looks like your loved ones have come good,' he said.

Max and Rob were on the screen, both seated behind a table, microphones in front of them.

'This is corruption of the highest order,' one of the journalists said. 'Confessing to this will bring the whole of the unit into disrepute. Why would you come forward like this and why now?'

'This community deserves the truth,' Max's voice resounded through the phone. 'It was only a matter of time. That time is now.'

There was a barrage of questions and muffled voices before Kane turned his phone off. He returned it to his back pocket. 'Are you ready?'

Caitlin swallowed hard against her arid throat, her heart thudding. She looked across at the soul ripper, anger interweaving with her fear. Whatever the consequences after, she was going to get at least part of what she came for: the soul ripper was going to die that night. She was going to succeed in that if nothing else.

'Do you think I'm stupid?' she asked, her attention snapping back to Kane.

Uncertainty glinted in his eyes. 'Caitlin?'

'You seriously think I'm going to give you my permission?'

Kane's eyes flared then narrowed. 'What game are you playing?'

'I'm not playing a game. But we both know what happens if I don't let you put my soul back in.'

Kane glowered at her. 'Very clever, Caitlin,' he said, admiration in his eyes despite his irritation.

'Our agreement,' the soul ripper said to Kane, stopping a couple of feet behind him.

Caitlin circled around to the car to keep distance between her and the soul ripper, her eyes snatching warily between it and Kane.

He held his hand up to the soul ripper before lowering it again. Stepping up to Caitlin, he caught hold of her arm, pulling her close. 'You know what will happen.'

'Not if you kill it,' Caitlin whispered into his ear. 'You want to live, you don't have a choice. You've got what you wanted, or close enough. Now I want what I want. I want it gone. I want my parents free. And you are going to help me, Kane.'

He exhaled curtly, his grip tightening on her arm. 'Always the back-up plan, Agent Parish.'

'Did you really expect anything less? This is about my family, not my job.'

'The agreement,' the soul ripper said behind him.

'It needs to be distracted,' he whispered against her ear. 'And right now, its full attention is on you. If you want it dead, you need me to put your soul back in.'

Caitlin exhaled curtly. 'Oh, just perfect, Kane. My soul goes back in and you won't need to save me, will you?'

'And what if I want to save you?' he asked. 'Has that possibility ever crossed your mind?'

Caitlin pulled back slightly to stare at the sincerity in his eyes. But she wouldn't let herself falter; she wouldn't allow herself to be vulnerable. She needed to be in control of this. She needed to be in charge. Love him? Yes. Unequivocally. She knew that from the pain surging in her chest at the prospect of what might happen to him if this went wrong, if he called her bluff. But trust him? No. 'And why would you want to do that, Kane, when everything is so close at hand? Your word to me doesn't have to mean anything once I'm gone.'

'I want her soul,' the soul ripper said, Caitlin's blood turning cold as fury jarred its motions.

'Caitlin,' Kane said, catching her jaw, 'we had a deal.'

'Then fulfil it.'

He frowned. 'You've been planning this all along, haven't you?' She saw the genuine despondency in his eyes. 'Hemlock in gun handles is one thing, Caitlin, but this is insane.'

'You said you can kill it. And nothing will drive you more to that than saving your own life, will it? Do what you will to me after, but you are going to do this.'

The soul ripper stepped alongside them. 'Soul back in!' it commanded, its form shifting and changing, appearing to grow in height, in width, a cold darkness flaring in its eyes as they turned black.

Caitlin glared at the soul ripper. 'You're not getting me,' she snapped, pushing past Kane. 'You hear me? Sorry, but go and feed your compulsion elsewhere.'

Kane yanked her back to him, grabbing her upper arms, forcing her to look at him. 'This cannot happen unless it is focused on you,' he said. 'You have to trust me.'

'I don't, Kane. I'm sorry.' Her heart ached as she gazed into his eyes. 'Especially not after what Xavier said. Kill it,' she whispered. 'Now.'

'Vampire,' the soul ripper warned.

'If you don't want to believe me, Caitlin, don't, but at least believe in yourself and what your gut is telling you.'

In the corner of her eye, she saw the soul ripper grow bigger in its impatient rage.

'Last chance,' Kane said.

'No, Kane. It's yours.'

Kane hissed with frustration. 'Trust me.'

She wouldn't look away. She refused to break from his glower. 'Give me a reason to.'

'I love you,' he said.

Caitlin's heart skipped a beat. The room closed in. It didn't matter that the soul ripper was less than three feet away, the dreamlike state his three simple words had yanked her into muted the fact that they were minutes away from it all being over. And though her intellect told her to deny it, her heart cried out to her to believe him as she gazed deep into his eyes: eyes that were intense with earnestness.

'Please,' he said. 'I know everyone has let you down, but I won't. Trust me and I will prove it.'

He made it sound so simple: putting her life in his hands. Believing that he was capable of loving anyone. Believing that he was capable of loving her. Love her enough to let ultimate revenge slip through his fingers.

She shook her head slightly in confusion and took a step back to forge some sanctuary from the intensity in his hypnotic navy eyes. She opened her mouth but nothing would come out.

He couldn't love her. Kane couldn't love anyone anymore. But why did every instinct in her scream for her to believe to the contrary?

'Caitlin,' he said, the plea in his tone breaking her almost as much as the hope in his eyes. He closed the gap between them, reached to tenderly cup her face, the coolness of his hand reminding her too much of their intimacy – how she'd felt alive from the touch of his fingertips, how, from the moment they'd met, he'd given her hope.

She broke away only to anxiously glance across at the soul ripper rising for attack. It was maybe seconds before it lost its temper. It would kill him. Rip him away from her just like it had everyone else she had loved. She glared at it before looking back at Kane.

She couldn't lose him. She couldn't lose the only thing that had kept her living and breathing and fighting those past seven years.

He didn't deserve to die that night. She wouldn't let him die. And if there were any truth, any truth at all, in the words he had uttered, she'd do whatever it took to hear him say it again.

It was one hell of a test, but as she gazed back into the vampire's eyes, she knew it was a chance she was going to have to take.

With no time to dwell, she backed away from him to rest against the car. Fighting back the tears of frustration, of fear, she offered him a single nod.

He placed the book on the bonnet beside her, opened the cover and gazed back into her eyes.

As he recited the words, the rush was intense enough to throw her off balance. She clutched the bonnet of the car as the pages flickered. She closed her eyes from the pressure of the power surging back inside her, until she felt she'd been hit in the chest with a baseball bat.

She gasped and bent forward, clutching her abdomen. She coughed and trembled, perspiration lining her palms. Her heart felt as though it was going to break from her chest. The floor felt off kilter.

She snatched her gaze back up only to see Kane backing off and the soul ripper take the one easy stride towards her.

Straightening up, she looked up into its eyes, into the darkness within. Darkness that throbbed like molten tar, thick and fathomless, putrid and angry – the eyes that had stared into her parents' before it had stolen their life force.

Glowing white tendrils were unleashed from the soul ripper's abdomen within a split second, spiralling and thickening before piercing inside her.

Caitlin fell back against the bonnet with the force as the tendrils speared her astral body, hooking inside her. Every nerve ending sparked and ignited in fiery pain. Thinner tendrils lanced her alongside them, weaving between them, entangling around her soul, squeezing as they secured themselves around the orb of light that was her soul.

She snatched a glance across at Kane as he backed further away. If he was going to act, now was the time. The pressure inside her was building, scorching her from the inside as she felt the soul ripper's power build.

But Kane stayed away, a blur in the distance behind her glossy eyes.

She needed him to act. She needed him to lunge at the soul ripper. But instead he kept a safe distance – motionless, watching, the dagger lax by his side.

'Kane!' she called. And she reached out to his blurred image that didn't even flinch.

She closed her eyes and felt the tears build as all her fears were confirmed.

She'd made a mistake. A mistake that had cost her everything. An unforgivable mistake considering she knew better. Should have known better.

And nothing hurt more than the pain of his betrayal, nor her stupidity at allowing it. Kane felt nothing – wanted nothing but to see every last one linked to his sister's death punished.

And that included her.

As the tears trickled down her cheek, so her rage built. Her anger coiled and twisted inside, overwhelming the fear. She slammed her hand through the tendrils that bound her as she glared defiantly up into the soul ripper's eyes. She wasn't going out willingly. She wasn't going without a fight. She tore at them, trying to yank each from her body. But as she tore them away, others slipped into their place, weaving tighter, hooks plunging deeper.

Caitlin kept fighting, her body like a furnace, the irritation of the soul ripper escalating with hers. She jolted as a thick and powerful tendril pierced the centre of her soul. She cried out, feeling the rip as it started to tear her astral body from within her, her whole body shivering and aching.

She wasn't going to let it take her. She wasn't going to let it win. She wasn't going to let it end like this. She slammed her hand up to the soul ripper's throat and glared into its eyes

She felt it freeze.

Her first thought was that Kane had finally come to rescue her.

But something else had happened.

The soul ripper's eyes flared. It jolted, its jagged toothed mouth gaping down on her.

It yelled piercingly, the screams nearly bursting Caitlin's eardrums. She let it go to clamp her hands over her ears as the soul ripper retracted, its hands flaying, its whole body shuddering as if on fast-forward.

And it ignited into a blinding white glow.

She felt the flurry of wind as the astral bodies were sucked back into the bodies on the floor, the room surging with energy.

Then there was silence.

And it was gone.

Only a blackened singe remained on the concrete to show where it had been stood.

# CHAPTER THIRTY

Caitlin slid off the bonnet and stared down at the blackened concrete, not daring to take her attention off it as she staggered away.

She clutched her chest and looked up to see Kane approaching, the dagger still in his hand.

'What happened?' She stumbled backwards, still trembling from shock as she glanced around rapidly. 'Why am I still here? Why am I still alive?'

He glanced down at the scorch mark. 'It looks to me like you just killed your first soul ripper, Caitlin Parish.'

She stared back down at the concrete then back at Kane. 'Killed it? It's gone?'

'I'd say that's a definite,' he said, giving her a hint of a smile.

As he stepped up to her she took a wary step back. 'I don't get it.'

'You don't get that the shadow reader's soul is impossible to remove without getting to the heart first? I thought we'd just spent the last three days establishing that.'

She stood perfectly still. Her whole body felt numb. 'I killed it?'

'That's what you wanted, wasn't it? That's what you really wanted. You asked me to kill it for you, but I knew you wouldn't get the same satisfaction as being responsible for making the little fucker explode yourself.'

She stared at him in disbelief.

'You had me worried for a moment though,' he said. 'All that not letting me put your soul back in. You nearly screwed me over, you know that?'

'I killed it,' she said again, still trying to let the truth sink in. 'But that means I could have killed it all along.'

'Of course. Those lores surrounding that precious soul of yours apply to any species, Caitlin. Thing is, your soul was already out when it arrived so it wasn't going to know what you were.' He smiled. 'But when it pierced your soul it sure did. By then it was too late. It was trying to get back out of you, Caitlin. You gave it one hell of a struggle. Your anger wasn't letting it go.'

She frowned. 'You knew all this. You knew before now.'

His silence said it all.

She stared at him in horror. 'You never intended to do anything, did you?'

'I'd have stepped in if I had to, but you seemed to be doing just fine on your own.'

Caitlin swung her fist back before punching him across the jaw. 'You bastard!'

He rubbed where she hit, but looked far from disconcerted. 'I guess I deserved that one too.'

She stabbed her finger towards him. 'I could have done this on my own all along! I didn't need you – you needed me!'

'You got this far because I let you get this far. Don't forget that. You got what you wanted. You killed the soul ripper.'

She looked down at the dagger then anxiously back at him.

He exhaled curtly. 'What? You think I intend to use this?'

He closed the gap between them, pressed the flat of the blade against the underside of her chin. 'Open your eyes, Caitlin.' He studied her for what felt like a lifetime before he lowered the blade and flipped the dagger in his hand as he stepped past her.

She turned to face him as he collected the book off the car bonnet. 'So you're letting me go?'

As he opened the driver's door and eased inside, her stomach flipped.

'I am.' He looked around the room to where the bodies on the floor were already starting to flinch and stir into consciousness. 'You're going to have a few questions to face though.'

'What about Xavier? What about your vengeance on him now the soul ripper is gone?'

'I've got plenty of time to catch up with him. And a few others by the sounds of it.'

'Feinith?'

'Oh yeah. Feinith is one for sure.'

He leaned across the passenger seat to tuck the dagger inside the glove compartment along with the book.

'What was Xavier talking about? What did he mean about what you needed for the prophecy?'

Kane met her gaze fleetingly. It was a glance that told her that one was going to remain undisclosed. He switched the engine on.

A sudden sense of loss clutched her stomach. He was leaving. Just like that, he was driving away. 'You're going? Now? I just nearly had my soul ripped out of me. I've just spent three days fighting for my life, and that's it?'

He looked back across at her. 'What do you want, sweetheart – fireworks?'

She knew exactly what she wanted. She wanted him to utter those words again. She wanted him to pull her close and confirm every single word. She wanted, needed, to believe it could be true.

She clenched her hands by her sides. She realised she was panicking, but it wasn't like any kind of panic she'd ever known. She should have been itching to let him go. She should have been itching to get away from him. But instead she remained rooted to the spot, her throat arid, her legs weak.

She also knew what she didn't want – she didn't want him to go. She didn't want him to leave just like that. She didn't want him to act like it was all nothing.

But neither did she want him to laugh in her face or dismiss her if she told him. She didn't want to embarrass herself any more than she clearly already had. Kane didn't want her. Kane had never wanted her. Not beyond his own purpose. He had told her he loved her merely to get her to concede to give himself a chance at survival. He let her kill the soul ripper because she had saved him in the basement. He was making the score even, that was all. Making it even so he didn't owe her anything. His pride, at least, would insist on that.

There would be no fireworks – just a cold, dark night outside. An empty, lonely night.

And with her vengeance gone, she didn't even have a purpose.

It hit her like a wall. It was over. It was all over. And now there was nothing.

She pointed across at the lycans still bound and gagged. 'What about them?'

'They were leverage. Just like you were. Besides, their testimonies will come in useful.'

'So you were never going to kill them?'

'It was a condition Jask set before telling me the truth that night he came to find me.'

'So you're letting us all live?'

'We had a deal, didn't we?'

A deal. A business arrangement. She gazed into his navy-blue eyes. As if she could think he was capable of anything else. She lowered her gaze, her swallow dry and painful.

'Caitlin.'

Her gaze snapped back to his, her heart skipping a beat.

'You're going to be okay,' he said as he leaned his arm on the open window. 'You know that, right?'

Her heart pounded. She glanced back around the room as a couple of the soldiers started to ease themselves up onto their elbows, looking as dazed as if they'd been out for days. She looked back at Kane. 'I can look after myself.'

He held her gaze for a moment longer then lifted his hands on the steering wheel.

'Wait!' she said, taking a step forward, her throat so tight it was almost a struggle to breathe. 'I'll make sure the truth comes out.'

Going against everything her heart was telling her to do, she took a step back again, creating the distance he clearly wanted.

She had to stay resolute. It was less painful this way. Letting him go had to be less painful. And she had to do it while she still had the conviction. She was used to facing things alone and this was no different. She didn't need him. She needed anything but him if she was going to get her life back on track. The last thing she needed was a broken heart. If any more threads that held it together were cut, she wasn't sure it would ever repair again. And she knew Kane was more than capable of being the one to ruin her.

She had to turn away. She had to walk away. It was the only way she'd know for sure if he cared enough to come after her. It was a risk, a bigger risk than anything else she had ever done because if Kane did leave, she knew the disappointment would be excruciating. But it was better that she did it then and saved herself the prolonged and inevitable pain of his eventual rejection.

She wrapped her arms protectively around herself and took those few steps away from him. She closed her eyes for a brief moment and clenched her hands into fists as she pleaded for the car door to open, to hear his footsteps towards her.

He'd take her in his arms. He'd pull her close. He'd reassure her that nothing else mattered. That they'd find a way to be together.

Instead she heard the rev of the accelerator, she heard tyres scrape on concrete. And as Kane pulled away, driving through the bodies awake enough to roll out of his way, her heart broke.

Caitlin stood alone with only the scent of night air, the chill encompassing her and melding the tears against her cheek as she watched him disappear into the darkness.

# CHAPTER THIRTY-ONE

Caitlin sat at the café table, staring into her mug of coffee. The rain tapped against the window beside her, glistening against the darkness of Blackthorn, the coffee machines hissing in the distance.

She should have gone straight home after the verdicts, but the thought of going back to the apartment filled her with an even greater sense of loneliness than being sat in this room full of strangers. That and the prospect of the barrage of journalists guaranteed to be camping outside her apartment. For just a couple of hours, she'd opt for feeling like a coward instead of a traitor – and no one would look for her across the border.

Cold air swept into the room as the door opened. Three young women burst through the door, scanning the café for seats. Spotting the empty booth next to hers, they rustled towards her, chatting and giggling.

Caitlin stared back into her mug. Their sudden hush told her they'd noticed and recognised her. The case had been plastered across every news channel all day, let alone the three days leading up to it. It was the biggest scandal the VCU had ever faced, and the whole of the Third Species Control Division were out to prove their worth in the face of adversity. Xavier had been disowned along with Max and Rob as rogues amidst an otherwise morally flawless organisation. The fact that Caitlin had given the key testimonial was the biggest shock of all to the establishment. If she'd been held in contempt by her colleagues before, now she was well and truly hated, and not least because of her reinstatement.

After what she was sure were a few mouthed words and overdramatic eye-jerking in her direction, the women's chatter resumed, albeit more hushed.

Caitlin glanced back out onto the rain-soaked street. Rob couldn't even look at her when he'd been led away. But it was the resolution in Max's eyes that hurt her the most. And when he'd looked at her across the courtroom after the decision of guilty was made, there hadn't been anger in his eyes, but pride. Whether as his agent or his stepdaughter, maybe both, he'd told her in that single lingering gaze that she'd done the right thing. It caught in her throat even then and she fought back the tears, stared back into her mug in the hope no one would notice.

Kane hadn't turned up at the courthouse. Too big a part of her had hoped he would. She'd checked out the gallery but there had been no sign of him. She'd hoped to linger outside for a little while afterwards, but the journalists who'd been forced to wait outside had posed too great a threat. The only one she'd come across was Jask. The fact he'd been sat in the lobby when he'd had no reason to hang about after his testimony confirmed he'd been waiting for her.

'We're not done yet,' he'd said as she'd stepped past him.

She'd stopped and stared down at the mosaic floor despite knowing she should have kept walking. She'd turned to face him, his azure gaze penetrating deep into hers.

It had been his testimony that had sealed the verdict, along with the testimonies of the two lycans who'd committed the act.

'You heard the verdict, Jask.'

'You think ten years is enough? Twenty for Xavier? Do you think they're even going to serve that time?'

'That's out of my hands,' she'd said, turning away.

'But you're not out of mine.'

She'd stopped again. Turned to face his rigid gaze.

He'd stood steadily from his ornate mahogany chair, his broad six-foot frame domineering the short distance between them.

'I don't know why Kane let you live,' Jask had said. 'But I wouldn't rest easy if I were you. If he doesn't finish this properly, I will. Those boys in there are owed. Fourteen years of their life at least. Their families are owed. I'm responsible for seeing that happens.'

'I put everything on the line to see that the truth came out. I can't do anything more.'

'Do you think your laws make any difference to us? We have our own lores. There are going to be a lot of angry lycans out there. In this locale and others. I've got to be seen to be doing something if Kane isn't. I only let you off because I had his assurance that he would deal with this.' He'd stepped around the back of her. 'I'm giving him a few days and then I want to see some damaged goods, or I'll see to it myself.'

Caitlin's breath had caught in her throat. She hadn't dared turn to face him, hadn't dared given him the opportunity to look back into her eyes because she would have said something she'd have regretted. She would have laid down a challenge she wasn't sure she could meet.

Because as she'd stood alone in that lobby, as the only people she had left had been led down to containment, as she'd left that courthouse and walked the dark streets of Lowtown and into the top end of Blackthorn, she knew that's exactly what she was now – totally alone.

And she knew the real reason why she had resolved to cross the border – and it wasn't all about being a coward.

She pushed her coffee aside, unable to face the tepid liquid.

'So is he as good as they say?'

Caitlin's attention snapped to the three young women as she searched for the one who had spoken.

The woman who sat the furthest away widened her heavily made-up brown eyes expectantly. 'Worth grassing on your own family for, I mean.'

They were all human. She could see that now.

The one sat next to her sniggered. 'Honey, I'd be tempted to give up my own kids for a night with him.'

Caitlin met each of their expectant stares in turn – stares that were a mixture of accusation, curiosity and jealousy.

She had to keep her mouth shut, that's what she'd been told. She spoke to no one or the thread her job was already hanging by would be cut. They were waiting for an excuse. They only kept her on to reinforce the image they had created that they were representing justice. She was their mascot of proof of that. At least for the time being.

She grabbed her jacket and scarf and slipped out of the booth.

'Word is he's done with you now,' one of the other women called out behind her. 'So does that mean he's open to offers?'

Caitlin yanked open the door and stepped back out into the darkness. At least the rain had ceased. The chill to her face was instant, small puffs of warm exhalation mingling with the night air. But she was sure the way her skin prickled was about more than the temperature. She'd never so brazenly hung around Blackthorn at night, so lost for what to do. It created a feeling of paranoia and she found herself scanning the street warily as she felt she was being watched. A few more passers-by sent her fleeting stares but said nothing. It was a bad idea. She knew she was asking for trouble, but something in her just didn't care. She'd find another café – somewhere to wile away a couple more hours until deciding to go and face the awaiting mob.

Maybe she wouldn't. Maybe she'd find a room somewhere and keep her head down for a couple of days. Maybe she could wake up when it was all over.

A few people nudged past her, chatting and laughing, a couple engrossed in a discussion she only caught part of, all exacerbating her sense of isolation more.

She glanced up at the dense cloud weighing heavily with threat of further rain.

She looked across the street, almost by instinct.

Her heart pounded, every tiny hair on the back of her neck standing on end as he looked back across at her. She didn't need the clear light of the moon to know it was him, she felt it – a dangerous sense of elation albeit one overwhelmed by the feeling it was about to be extinguished.

From the shadows across the street, Kane had watched her in the café.

She'd sat alone in a booth, staring into the mug she'd barely drunk from the entire time she'd been there. She'd been absorbed in her own world in a way he'd come to know only too well watching her all those years. Only now he'd touched her, tasted her, seen parts of her that no one else had seen. And she'd seen too much of him. Far too much.

He'd had her followed from Lowtown and across the border, had received the call as to the café she had entered.

He also knew the results of the verdict. He knew of what she had been put through on the stand when they had questioned her loyalty to him compared with her loyalty to her unit. She'd done an amazing job apparently, even though they'd torn her apart in the stand, with the testimonies of other agents, including Brovin and Morgan, letting leak what they termed her fixation with Kane. But he knew it wasn't just about him. It wasn't just about Arana. For Caitlin it had been about justice and doing the right thing. It was about her standing up for the ideals that she believed in – that the unit could do good work. And she wanted to prove that they weren't all corrupted. She was doing her bit to retain the peace that could implode in the district. It was damage limitation in her eyes – not that her opposition saw it that way. That she believed there were those who needed to be defended. That some kind of order needed to be maintained.

Unfortunately, she'd always believe that that order had to be from humans.

He'd watched her as she'd stepped out onto the pavement – hesitant, lost, wary – pulling on her coat and wrapping her scarf around her. And he'd followed her as she'd kept her eyes downturned. This was not agent Parish walking through Blackthorn; it was Caitlin with all her official status stripped away. It was irresponsible of her, naïve and careless. Stupid even. She was the easiest picking on the street. Lucky for her that word was already out that nobody touched her. That he hadn't finished.

He was far from finished.

He didn't know what had made her look up but as if by instinct, she'd snatched her gaze across to his. He'd felt a jolt through him, her beautiful eyes widening in mixed emotions.

They could have been completely alone on the street for all anyone else mattered at that moment – the moment they'd connected again.

But Caitlin didn't stop. She didn't back away. She didn't run the way she'd come. She looked back ahead and kept walking down the parallel side of the street.

At first he wondered if it was some kind of trap, and she most definitely the honey. But he'd been watching long enough to know she was very much alone. And if she had been on the job of snaring him, she would have been more alert, more purposeful. He knew her too well not to be able to recognise the signs of that rare occasion when her defences were down. But then again, she was the only one who could surprise him. The only one who could ever throw him off guard.

Regardless, she was well and truly in his territory – alone, accessible and deliciously vulnerable. And it was the alone that she clearly wanted – alone with him. She knew he'd follow. He liked to think she wouldn't have dared stroll deeper and deeper into Blackthorn if she suspected otherwise. Because he could so easily leave her to weave herself into her own demise, sauntering along those dark, rundown, isolated streets. The high square heels of the smart black dolly shoes she'd worn to court echoed lightly over the concrete as she turned down a side street, the flare of her demure grey dress blowing lightly against her knees.

He took a cigarette from the inside pocket of his jacket and stopped only for a moment to ignite the tip before continuing behind her, keeping just the right distance for her to know he was there, and so she couldn't slip out of his sight. Not that he wouldn't find her again. It was just whether someone else found her first.

They passed the wrought-iron bars that enclosed what was once one of the grand houses when it had been the heart of a city. Now it was as dilapidated as the rest of the buildings that couldn't be spared the expense of maintenance. She avoided the cobbles and kept to the paving before crossing over and down another dark stretch.

She clearly wanted to make sure they weren't going to be seen. And if they were being followed – by the press, other agents or anyone else who thought they might try their chances – she'd given Kane plenty of time to detect them and eradicate them.

This was purely between them. Every instinct told him that. Caitlin was looking to wrap this up as much as he was.

Halfway down the bleak cobbled street, she turned slowly to face him.

He stopped, exhaled a steady stream of smoke that dissipated into the cool air. She wanted to rein that little bit of control she had. She wanted to take the lead.

She really should have learned by now.

As rain started to bounce on the cobbles, glistening against the backdrop of the only two un-smashed streetlamps, she took a right into the open porch of one of the abandoned houses.

He blinked droplets from his lashes before following her to the splintered stone archway.

Inside, she leaned back against the paint-flaked wall of the left side of the porch, her slightly damp hair already tousling, her beautiful milky-coffee eyes dark in the ungenerous light. But he could still read them, the same as he could read the rest of her. She was prepared for confrontation. When she'd seen him across the street, she was not going to run and hide. She was not going to back down. And those wary eyes were guarded and prepared. She was frightened, but she wasn't frightened to face those fears.

He leaned against the side of the archway furthest away from her, his back to the darkness. 'You should already be heading to some distant locale by now.'

'Is that what you were hoping?'

He exhaled curtly, a simultaneous stream of smoke escaping his nose and mouth. He looked to the cracked black-and-white-tiled floor as he ran his tongue swiftly down his incisor before looking back at her. 'You're playing a dangerous game, Caitlin.'

'Why? Is this where it ends? Have you followed me to finish it, Kane?'

'You're asking me that after leading me into a dark recess?'

'As opposed to sitting and waiting for you to come for me? You know I don't work like that.'

'Do you remember the first thing I said to you?'

'A little girl doing a man's job. How can I forget?'

'Bound to end in tears,' he added, before throwing his cigarette to the floor. He exhaled a final steady stream of smoke as he crushed and extinguished the cigarette beneath his boot before stepping into the porch.

He sensed her tense though she was trying hard to contain it.

He faced her square on. 'Take your jacket and scarf off.'

She frowned contemplatively for a moment but complied. She knew he wanted to be sure she had nothing hidden. No surprises. No hemlock in gun handles. She unravelled her scarf and slipped her jacket over her slender shoulders before laying them down on the worn wooden bench beside her.

He purposely and tauntingly raked her slowly with his gaze up from her delicate feet to her tentative eyes. She was breathing a little faster, shallower, her pulse already racing. He lingered on her exposed collarbone, her smooth, now flawless throat, her lips already plumping with arousal. She still wanted him. Despite her every instinct probably telling her how deeply wrong it was, her heart was well and truly his.

'I hear you did good in that courtroom, Caitlin.'

'What they did was wrong, but that doesn't make me proud of what I've done. I just hope that once all this dies down, people see what I did as proof that not all agents are corrupt. The majority of us are trying to do good for this community. I still believe in the TSCD and I'll continue to stand by that.'

'Dogmatic as ever,' he said, glancing at her lips again, parted and ready for him to graze.

'They're still going to want to talk to you, Kane.'

'And they can still go and fuck themselves.'

'You should have stood up and told them what Xavier tried to do all those years.'

'That hearing was about Arana, not me. They had their key witnesses.'

'One of whom is now no use to you. One who still fervently advocates the establishment you despise.'

He knew she was referring to her. Her tone was challenging but resolute. 'Seemingly so,' he said.

He stepped up to her. Heard her catch her breath. She shuddered a little – partly apprehension, partly the gentle breeze leaking in from outside. Grasping the midway point on the skirt of her dress, he slowly bunched up the thick woven cotton until her thighs were exposed to the cool night air. He slipped his hands underneath, finding the bare flesh above the lace tops of her hold-ups. It was the only place she had left to hide anything. His ready erection throbbed, uncomfortably confined in his jeans. He slid his hand up over her warm and tender silken curves before reaching the lace band of her knickers.

Caitlin didn't flinch this time, but he detected the subtle tremor in her lower lip. Something he now knew, from studying her so closely the past few days, was a sign of competing emotions. She didn't not want this, but she also had all the reasons why she shouldn't contending inside her.

He slowly and purposefully slid her delicate, white lace knickers down until they fell to the floor.

She subtly stepped out of them, not daring to take her eyes off his as he pressed a hand to the wall beside her head. He leaned inches away from her lips as he gazed deep into her eyes, detected her held breath. 'So, Caitlin, are you still out to convict me?'

He could feel her heart pounding. 'You admitted yourself that you've done a lot of bad things, Kane.'

He smiled. 'And I'll continue to do a lot of bad things. I'm a very bad vampire, Caitlin.'

'Then I have no choice, do I?'

'So detain me,' he said as he leaned in to kiss her neck, her skin warm and sweet against his tongue as he licked along her artery. She wore the same perfume – the perfume that had become indicative of her. Her shallow breaths were as enticing as they had been when he'd first slammed her against the wall back in that corridor. Only now they were breaths that were all too familiar – breaths he knew for a fact were the heady mix of fear and arousal. He brushed his lips over her ear and whispered, 'I dare you.'

Hands flat against the wall, she didn't move other than to shudder again. 'Then do something,' she said, a detectable lack of self-assurance in her voice.

He looked back into her eyes. He gave her a hint of a smile. 'Are you trying to set me up, Caitlin?'

'Are you planning to kill me?'

'And why would I do that?'

'Loose ends. Why wouldn't you?' He heard the uncertainty of her swallow. 'No one's expecting me home. No one even cares. What's to stop you?'

The sadness in her tone pierced him deep.

'Would you rather I kill you?' he asked, reading deep into her eyes – the loneliness, the loss, the confusion.

'What kind of question is that?'

'Things are about to get nasty, Caitlin. The TSCD aren't happy with you. The lycans aren't happy. Jask's not impressed you're still breathing and he's going to want to do something about that. The pride of his clan is at stake. So is his pride.'

'He told me part of your deal with him was you finishing me.'

'It was. The only reason I could negotiate him being witness in that courtroom was to start the downfall of your human empire.'

'Is this the start of the prophecies? What Xavier was talking about?'

'No. They're very different.'

'But they're coming?'

'Yes, Caitlin, they're coming. Maybe sooner than we think. And you're going to be right in the firing line doing what you do. Like I said, things are going to get very nasty, very soon. So I'll ask you again, would you rather I kill you?'

'You said "was".'

He frowned. 'What?'

'You said finishing me was part of the deal. Not is.'

'You changed the goalposts when you saved my life in the cellar. I repaid it by letting you kill the soul ripper.'

'So now we're even. But the truth is, nothing will ever even the score with you, will it, Kane? Only I'm fed up of waiting for the inevitable. I've had it for seven years. Waiting for something to come for me. I'm not doing it anymore.'

'So you thought you'd lead me down some dark, isolated place to finish this. Give yourself that sense of control, right? Defy me in my own territory. Prove you're not afraid of me.'

'I don't hide. From anyone. From anything. You should know that by now.'

'And you've got a stronger sense of survival than anyone else I know. So what the fuck are you really up to, Caitlin?'

The confrontation was still emanating from her eyes but it was masked by a hesitation she couldn't disguise. She lowered her gaze only for a moment before looking back at him. 'I want to know if you meant it. What you said. I want to know if you feel enough. For me.'

Her honesty startled him. He expected a little more banter or at least a few more taunts. Caitlin laying her soul bare that soon was not something he had prepared for. The vulnerability in her eyes was crushing. 'Enough for what?'

'To not do this. When you have every opportunity to. I've made it easy for you. As easy as it gets.'

He brushed his lips across her ear, trying to calm the surge inside him at the challenge she was so boldly laying in front of him. 'I like to hunt, remember? Maybe I don't want it this way. Maybe I'll just walk away.'

'Maybe you will. And maybe you'll never find me again if you do.'

The very prospect of it wrenched deep inside. He pulled back to look in her eyes again. For the first time, he couldn't read them. He didn't like it. He didn't like the uncertainty. He didn't like her cornering him – controlling the situation. She was subtle about it but she was good. He shouldn't have expected anything less. She was out for the truth from him and she was going to get it – whatever it took.

He couldn't afford to feel like this. Have a girl who had got so far under his skin he hadn't already let her drained, ravished body slip to the dark, dank porch floor. But he took his time because he liked his time with her. Hell, he loved his time with her. Every minute and every second of studying those intense coffee eyes, of reading those beautiful, tempting lips. Of wondering what she'd say next, what she'd do next. Of experiencing the wealth of emotions she lived with every day, emotions that spilled out so many times, unwillingly, in front of him. Of the way she made him feel – alive, real, validating his existence.

And as the rain beat down outside the porch, exacerbating their isolation and the opportunity for him to do whatever he wanted to her – everything his vampire instincts, his advanced survival mechanisms and his reasoning told him to do – he knew this was going to be harder than he'd ever imagined.

But he knew that if he didn't end it, everything changed there and then. She'd become his responsibility. He either killed her or he protected her. And that meant from then on. But, unlike the past seven years when it had been purely about preserving her for his plans, when he could be detached and calculated, this was personal. This would create conflict for him. Complications for him. His reputation would be questioned along with his loyalties, both within his species and others, not least with the lycans.

And he'd have someone to worry about again. Someone to care about. Someone others would want to use to get to him.

It was Arana all over again – the last time he had dared to love.

By loving Caitlin he was putting her at risk. He was putting them both at risk. Risk with consequences he wasn't sure he could handle again. So love her though he may – deeply, painfully, irrevocably – he needed to walk away. He needed to let her disappear. But she wouldn't. Tenacious, stubborn, dogmatic Caitlin would only get herself into trouble elsewhere, if she resolved to leave at all. He'd put nothing past her. That unpredictability would never change. And that's why he had no choice.

'Is that what you want?' he asked. 'Do you want me to love you?'

Her eyes flared slightly, the intimacy of the question, the probing for her to expose her inner feelings to him, only fuelling her obvious insecurity.

He cupped her face, the warmth of her soft, flawless skin radiating through his fingers, her supple trembling lips pliable beneath his thumb as he graced them with gentle, sweeping pressure.

'I don't want to be lonely anymore, Kane. Neither do you. We can do something about that.'

'And that's why you want me? To fill a gap?'

'It's more than that.'

'And you deserve more than damaged goods.'

'We're both damaged goods.'

He turned his hand around to run the back of it down her cheek and throat. 'You've only seen a fraction of me, Caitlin.'

'I'm not scared of you anymore.'

He exhaled a curt breath. 'Maybe I should do something about that. Maybe I should do the decent thing and let you know what you're contemplating.'

'If every word you uttered was a lie, I don't care anymore. Do whatever you want.'

She meant it. Those eyes he could barely look into in those passing moments meant every single word.

By instinct, he unbuttoned his jeans. From the way her eyes flared a little, even she hadn't expected him to act that quick. She'd clearly expected more conversation, but he was done with conversation. He was done with her burrowing into his mind, making him face things he didn't want to face.

He grabbed the backs of her thighs, lifted her in one easy move, spread her thighs around him and slammed her against the paint-flaked wall.

She snatched back a breath and locked gazes with him as he caught her hands, pinned them to the wall above her head with one of his, before gripping her hip with the other, keeping her contained.

'Say no to me now,' he said. 'And walk away. Walk away from all of this. Or once I'm back inside you, I will own you.'

'Are you threatening me, Kane Malloy?' she asked with a detectable breathlessness, her gaze not flinching from his.

His erection strained through his open jeans. He tugged down his shorts. 'I prefer to call it foreplay, Caitlin Parish. But whatever suits.'

'Hurt me if it makes you feel better,' she said, almost inaudibly. 'If it helps you feel safe.'

He frowned, the challenge in her eyes, her perceptiveness, stunning him to both stillness and silence.

'But I'll have my answer,' she added.

'What's that supposed to mean?'

'You're scared of loving me. Just as I'm scared of loving you. And you hurting me now will only prove that.'

She dared to delve that deep. She dared to look him in the eyes. He found her sex easily, pushed an inch into her ready heat, into her slickness, the temptation to thrust almost too much to bear. And as she swallowed hard and clenched her hands, he gritted his teeth behind closed lips, forcing himself to keep it contained for just a few seconds longer. But there was no panic in her eyes, no second thoughts.

She was his for the taking. This was her, without any fear of the consequences. She wanted him. Wanted him for exactly who he was. No compromise.

But one thrust would damn her. Could damn them both. Because the act would be more than sexual. For a long time it had been more than sexual. He felt too much, too deep for it to be anything other than fused with love.

He needed to end it. One lethal bite. Or one swift painless twist of her neck. A simple selfless act within his control.

'I love you, Kane,' she whispered, her gaze locked on his. 'I don't want to, but I do. I want you to know that.'

She may as well have put her hand on his heart and jump-started it from the power and quiet resolve behind her eyes.

Words that saved him. Words that condemned him.

She held his gaze expectantly and he knew she was on the verge of breaking.

He withdrew and lowered her to the floor. He pulled up his shorts and jeans and refastened them as he stepped away, stared back out into the darkness. He leaned against the arch as he watched the rain bounce on the cobbles.

'Why does this have to be so complicated?' he asked, partly to himself. 'Why couldn't you just walk away and get yourself a decent life somewhere?'

'Is that really what you want? For me to leave?'

He glanced across his shoulder at where she still stood against the wall. He looked back out at the cobbles. 'For your sake, yes.'

'And for your sake?'

'I'm trying to protect you.'

'Why?'

Just because he'd said it once didn't mean he was going to say it again. Letting those words slip the first time had been hard enough. He'd shocked even himself at how easily they had spilled out, Caitlin staring at him so defiantly, potentially ruining his plans, the soul ripper breathing down their necks. It had hardly been the most romantic of moments. But back in that warehouse he'd had no choice – here he did.

'You have no idea of the danger you're putting yourself in,' he said.

'I told you: I can look after myself. And I can make my own decisions. I know what's good for me. You're good for me. And I'm good for you. We're good together.'

Her footsteps were light and hesitant as she stepped out from his blind spot.

'Tell me if you were planning to kill me,' she said, her tone wary.

'Now who's talking in the past tense? Very presumptuous.'

'Were you?'

He pulled himself from his leaning position and turned to face her. 'Better than letting someone else do it for me.'

He could see from her startled expression that it wasn't the response she was wanting or expecting. But she'd demanded honesty. She'd cornered him for the truth and the truth was what he'd give her.

She took a guarded step back despite the resolution in her eyes. Her shock was obvious; it poured from her as transparently as her love for him. And what he did to deserve the love of someone so warm, so passionate, so giving and so beautiful both inside and out as Caitlin, he could never, and probably would never, understand.

'You wanted the truth,' he declared with a shrug.

Those vulnerable coffee eyes narrowed slightly. 'You love me that much?'

That certainly wasn't the response he was expecting. He stared at her dumbfounded. 'Only you would see it that way.'

'See you for what you are, you mean?'

He laughed tersely as he lowered his gaze before looking back at her, but his solemnity quickly mirrored hers.

She drew level, tilted her head up to his despite her three-inch heels, and kissed him gently, tenderly on the lips.

It was a fleeting but sincere kiss. It was all it took. After every intimate moment they'd shared, that one simple kiss told him he could no more survive without her than she could without him. Losing her wasn't an option. Losing her had never been an option.

He lifted her with ease, spread her thighs around him again as he gently pressed her back against the wall. As his lips met hers, he didn't thrust inside her – he pushed. Slowly. Deeply. Feeling every inch of her, watching every tiny reaction that her eyes betrayed. She gasped and trembled as he filled her to the hilt, as he withdrew inch by inch only to push deep into her again. She needed to know this was more than sex – it was a claiming.

He closed his lips over hers again, tasting her warmth, toying with her tongue and teeth in a way that made her clench around him. He bit her lip and she gasped again, her eyes flashing open to stare at him.

He smiled before sucking on her lip, her blood mingling in both their mouths as he kissed her more hungrily.

He released her hands to grab her thighs and spread them further as Caitlin wrapped her arms around his shoulders, buried her head against his neck, her nails digging into his back as his pace increased.

He felt her tears against his neck but she didn't ask him to stop. Her body only accepted him more willingly. It was the sign he needed.

He bit into her neck, his incisors penetrating her deep, breaking through her fragile skin with ease. She tasted divine – hot, sweet, intoxicating.

Seconds later he came hard and he came fast, just as her muscles clenched around him, just as he felt the first shudders of orgasm burst through her. Spilling inside her that time wasn't just release, it was a sealing.

Withdrawing his incisors, he clutched the back of her head, entwined his fingers through her soft, tousled hair and held her as both their orgasms gradually dissipated.

Head nestled against hers, he held her tighter. There was no going back. She was his now and all that went with it. 'I love you more than

I ever thought I could love again, Caitlin,' he whispered against her ear. 'How did you do it?'

She didn't say anything. She just tightened her hold around him and held him, the silence fractured by the pouring rain.

Minutes passed but it didn't feel long enough. He withdrew and lowered her gently to the floor.

Clothing adjusted, he eased her to the floor with him as he sat behind her. He wrapped his arms around her, his thighs either side of hers as they gazed out at the retreating rain.

'We sure don't make things easy for ourselves, do we?'

She rested her head back against his shoulder as she looked up at him. 'Is it really going to be that bad?'

'Yes, Caitlin. That bad.'

'But we can handle it, right?'

He wasn't sure. Not now he knew Feinith was involved. She was his first visit as soon as this died down.

'If you learn to do as you're told,' he said, lightening his tone to divert from the line of conversation he needed them to avoid. 'Maybe.'

'If I learn to do as I'm told?' She pulled forwards a little to look across her shoulder at him. 'Who put you in charge?'

Smiling, he pulled her tight against him again. 'I'm always in charge. Always have been. Always will be.'

She smiled back. It was fleeting but was still a smile. It was the first one he'd evoked in her. It made him love her to the point of being painful. 'You may have been around the block a few times, Kane, but you've still got a lot to learn.'

'So have you,' he said, brushing his lips over her ear. 'All sorts of dark, depraved, sinful little things that I'm going to inflict on you if you don't learn to be a good, compliant girl.'

'I told you – I don't do submissive.'

He laughed lightly. 'Oh, yes you do,' he said, nipping her lightly on the ear. 'And as soon as I get you back to my haven, I'll prove it further.'

'Is that where we're going?'

'For the time being.'

'And then what?'

He rested his head against hers as he stared back out into the darkness. He hadn't sighed in a long time, but he sighed then.

'I don't know, Caitlin,' he said, kissing her affectionately on the temple before resting his head against hers again. 'But you're going to be okay with me. I promise.'

'And you're going to be okay with me, Kane.'

As the darkest hour of Blackthorn crept along the empty street outside, he could only hope they were both right. That she'd still feel that way when she knew the whole truth.

The darkness out there was going to deepen.

It was only a matter of time.

# LETTER FROM
# LINDSAY J. PRYOR

Dear Reader,

When I started writing many years ago, it was with an aim – to entertain myself. As Blackthorn developed, I lived in hope that it would one day be out there to entertain others. That dream came true.

I really hope you enjoyed your journey into Blackthorn and sharing Kane and Caitlin's story with me. I'd love to hear what you think of Blood Shadows – I always check reader reviews and you can find me online at www.lindsayjpryor.com

I'll also be posting exclusive news about the next Blackthorn episode – Blood Roses – on my website.

Blood Shadows is just the start of the Blackthorn story. There's much more to unravel about the tensions between third species and humans, more to discover about Blackthorn itself and, of course, the vampire prophecies.

Piece by piece, I'll be revealing the integral role these forbidden love stories are going to play in the future of characters that I hope you'll come to love as much as I do.

Be assured that you've not heard the last from Kane and Caitlin.

Thank you so much for reading, and I hope you'll join me again as the mysteries of Blackthorn continue to unfold.

Lindsay

P.S. Read on for a sneak peek at the first chapter of Blood Roses. I have another very bad vampire I'd like to introduce you to...

# BLOOD ROSES

# CHAPTER ONE

It was the last place on earth Leila should have been. The thought of what she was about to do sickened her to her soul. She was supposed to kill vampires, not save them. Those were the rules. That was the lore.

But then again, the lore never accounted for wayward younger sisters.

Leila stepped out of the car and into the darkness of the dank alleyway. The breeze swept her hair from her shoulders, wafted the hem of her dress against her thighs. If she'd had time to go home and change, she would have put something more suitable on – something that may have at least made her feel a fraction less vulnerable.

Clutching the straps of her rucksack, she scanned the several stories looming above, rain trickling down the dreary walls. Yells echoed down from the road, suppressed by the low monotonous beat of trance music vibrating through the open fire-exit doors ahead. The air in Blackthorn felt alien in its density, its toxicity. Her head buzzed as if she'd just taken off on the runway but hadn't yet reached that comfortable height. She couldn't just see the darkness – she could feel it.

It was the final confirmation that she was making the worst mistake of her life.

A mistake she'd had no choice in making.

Alisha had been missing for days but, based on her track record, it still wasn't long enough for the authorities to act.

Sleep-deprived, sick with worry and brimming with fury at the possibility of her younger sister's ongoing nonchalance towards her feelings,

Leila had planned another late night at work rather than face the flat alone. But as soon as darkness had arrived in Summerton, so had the call.

'Lei, it's me.'

'Alisha? Where the hell are you? I've been going out of my mind! Four days! Four days and not a single call! You know how it's been. Have you any idea—'

'Leila, just shut up for a minute. Please. I need you to listen to me.'

In that instant she'd known something was horribly wrong. Whether it had been the uncharacteristic strain in Alisha's tone or that gravel effect she only got after crying, one thing was for certain – this was not like the other times.

'I need your help,' Alisha had said, seemingly biting back the tears – tears of desperation that had been verging on panic. And Alisha never panicked. Ever.

Her chest had clenched. 'Okay,' she'd said, softening her tone. 'Take it easy, Alisha. What is it? What's wrong? Are you hurt?'

'No. No, I'm okay.'

Leila had held her breath at her sister's hesitation.

'But I need you to do something for me,' Alisha had added. 'You know the Purification Book – the one grandfather gave you?'

Tendrils of unease had squeezed. 'What about it?'

'I need it.'

'What do you mean you need it? For what?'

'I'm in serious trouble, Lei.'

Something heavy had formed in the pit of her stomach. Every tiny hair on the back of her neck had stood on end. Already two steps ahead, she'd backed out of earshot into the depths of the library's storeroom. 'Where are you?'

'I'm in Blackthorn.'

It had been the equivalent to a punch in the chest. The same feeling of sickness had encompassed her as when she'd been told the search for Sophie had been abandoned – that their sister had been gone too long

Her voice had instinctively dropped to a tense whisper. 'What the hell are you doing there?'

'I'll explain later, but I need you to come here and bring the book with you.'

In the dense silence of the storeroom, Leila had slumped into a nearby chair before her legs had given way.

'Leila? Lei, are you there?'

'What on earth have you got yourself into this time, Alisha?'

'Tell me you're coming. Please.'

'I want to know what's going on.'

There had been an excruciating moment of silence. 'Someone needs a purification.'

Leila had already known the answer, but still she'd asked the question. 'Someone?'

'A consang. He's taken dead blood.'

Consangs, short for the consanguineous, was a term adopted by vampires who'd resolved that the representation of a kinship, an affinity by blood, would create a more positive image than the negative images of well-established clichés. To Leila they'd always be vampires – every last parasitic, deceitful, devious and manipulative one of them.

And her little sister was amongst them.

'How do they know about the book, Alisha?'

'I can't explain over the phone. You have to come here. Now.'

'But you know I can't bring the book there. If that book—'

'Please! If you don't, they'll kill me!'

Her stomach had flipped. 'I'm going to call the Intervention Unit—'

'No! No, if you do that you'll never see me again. Leila, listen, you have to get to the top border of Lowtown and wait at the café on the corner. Someone will meet you there in a couple of hours.'

'A couple of hours? Alisha, I've got to get across three districts, through two border offices—'

'There isn't much time. When you get there someone called Hade will meet you. He'll escort you through Lowtown, get you across the border and bring you into Blackthorn.'

'Who the hell is Hade?'

'Please, Lei. Please tell me you'll do it?'

Leila had tried to convince herself that it wasn't happening. That it couldn't be happening. But it was. Her worst nightmare had finally beckoned, just as she'd dreaded all her life. The vampire-infested Blackthorn district wasn't safe for any human. For Leila, it was deadly.

'Promise me they haven't hurt you.'

'They haven't. Not yet. They said I'll be fine if you bring the book. Leila, please, you've got to help me.'

Leila had closed her eyes. Swallowed hard. 'Just do as they say until I get there. I'm on my way.'

They'd been waiting when she'd arrived at the café a little over two hours later. She'd assumed the one who'd greeted her to be Hade – a tall, blond twenty-something with piercing grey eyes and a crew cut that was as harsh as his chiselled and stubbly face. Two silent bulks had accompanied him. All three, to her relief, were human. None of them would answer any of her questions, the two bulks refraining even from eye contact with her. Their orders had clearly been to collect her with maximum speed and minimal explanation. Minimal explanation being a flash of wallet-sized, photographic evidence to confirm they had Alisha.

It had been a reality made even more painful by the fact it was Alisha's favourite snapshot. It was six years old now, Alisha just nineteen back then. She was hugging her two big sisters like there was no tomorrow, each of them grinning inanely at the camera. Sophie was doing her best cross-eyed look, irreverent Alisha had her tongue poking out and Leila, the eldest and standing out from her fairer sisters with her russet hair, was laughing at them both.

They'd been driven to the border of Blackthorn. A far cry from the sophisticated and flawless high-security control of Summerton int

Midtown, the lesser but still effective security from Midtown into Low-town, Lowtown to Blackthorn had been a law unto itself.

The border office into the notorious vampire district had resembled a cattle market – people busily sweeping through the barriers, no one recording the movements, security officers marking the perimeter more as a deterrent against trouble rather than active involvement.

The mass of milling bodies had been overwhelming, the air dense with the alien scents of everything from smoke to sweat. She'd tried to hold her breath, desperate not to let any of the intoxicating substances into her lungs as Hade and the bulks had escorted her through the crowds, their presence ironically reassuring amidst the swarms of both humans and vampires.

A black Mercedes had been waiting for them out on the street on the other side of the turnstiles.

Removing her rucksack and clutching it to her chest, she'd gazed out of the back-seat window as she'd been driven even further from all she'd ever known.

Blackthorn was everything she'd imagined it to be and worse. Driven through the dark dismal streets, her beloved vibrant-green spaces and sporadically spaced houses had been replaced with a sprawling mass of compacted, characterless buildings. Noise boomed out from neon lit base-ments and shop fronts. Pollution merged with the stagnant smell of street-sold food. The over-filled streets were chaotic with people milling and par-tying, queues stretching back along the streets. People laughed, tussled and argued as noise poured from every open window, alley and recess.

She'd tried not to stare at the people lingering in doorways and on corners, something she never witnessed in Summerton. People back there had pleasant homes to go to, purposes. Now the sanctuary of home felt a million miles away and the phone call from Alisha like a dissipating nightmare.

The minute the Mercedes had slowed outside a nightclub, the crowds having parted to reveal an alleyway, fear had consumed her.

As she'd stepped out, Hade at least having the manners to open the door for her, her legs had nearly given way. Pulling her rucksack back on, she'd taken a deep steadying breath, a cold spray of rain hitting her upturned face as she'd told herself for the fiftieth time that she could do this.

Now, still clenching the straps of her rucksack, her attention switched from the dreary stories above back to Hade.

He cocked his head towards the open fire-exit doors and she followed him inside.

They stepped into a dimly lit corridor, the bulks behind keeping so close that she was virtually frogmarched along the concrete tunnel.

She followed Hade down one corridor then another, through double doors after double doors, Hade only stopping to key in security codes. Keeping a firm grip on her rucksack straps, the weight of the book and her Kit Box starting to tug, her five-foot-six-inch strides were no match for the swift and purposeful march of the six-footers escorting her.

The music gradually evaporated into the distance, the density of the corridors making her ears thrum. As Hade led her into a stone stairwell, they finally hit a wall of silence. He nodded to the bulks, both of who promptly turned back the way they came, leaving Leila and him alone.

She glanced anxiously into the darkness above before following Hade up the steps, the low square heels of her boots scuffing against stone as they climbed three floors.

Passing through a final door and stepping out into another dim corridor, Hade stopped outside the lone elevator and keyed in a code.

Entering first, Leila backed up and clutched the handrail behind her. Despite taking slow, steady breaths as they ascended, her breathing involuntarily became shallow again as the doors slid open.

'Is this it?' she asked, still clutching the handrail as Hade stepped out into a broad hallway.

'Sure is.'

'And my sister's here?'

He gave her a single nod.

'I'll want to see her before I do anything,' she said.

'That's up to Caleb.'

'Is that who I'm meeting – Caleb? Is he the one who has my sister?'

'He's also the one who doesn't like to be kept waiting. And tonight less than ever, so I suggest you move.'

Reluctantly, she uncoiled her damp palms and stepped out.

The hallway was surprisingly luxurious. The richness of the dark cream walls was deepened by the soft glow of the elegant, cast-iron wall lights. The dark floorboards were highly polished, the blue and gold runners plump and soft under foot.

Hade stopped at the ornate, mahogany double doors at the end and keyed in another code. As the doors clicked open, her tension surged as she followed him inside.

The extensive open-plan room was immaculate. Four broad oak steps led down to three black leather sofas positioned in a horseshoe central to the expanse. A low glass coffee table segregated the sofas, a large flat-screen television marking the opening. Mid-way on each wall to her left and right were hallways that mirrored each other – seemingly wings to opposite sides of the building. Dominating the top right-hand corner of the room was a highly polished mahogany bar. Straight ahead, glass doors opened out onto a generous stone terrace, the late night breeze inciting the voile to momentarily mask the otherwise unspoiled view across the district.

Hade led the way down the steps into the dimly lit surroundings. 'Wait here,' he said before taking the hallway to the left, marching down to the door at the end.

Leila wrapped her cardigan and jacket tight around herself. Folding her arms, she took a couple of steps forward. She glanced down the silent corridor where Hade had disappeared, peered out onto the terrace before turning to the hallway to her right as she searched for any sign of her sister.

She felt him before she saw him, the physical presence behind striking her sixth sense. The sudden chill was encapsulating, the tension excruciating. She had to turn around – like a tiny mammal knowing the bird of prey was looming above, Leila had to look.

From the way her hackles had risen, she would have pitched him at over seven-foot tall with the physique of a heavyweight wrestler, but the male that stood behind her was maybe just short of six foot. Absent of bulk, his lithe body was nonetheless clearly honed and powerful beneath his fitted, short-sleeved grey shirt.

Her attention was immediately drawn to his perfectly toned forearms and biceps by the black tattoo scrolling out from beneath his left sleeve, another coiling up around the right side of his neck. His handsome face was framed by dark hair cut close around his neck and ears. Loose bangs scraped his low straight eyebrows and emphasised his intoxicating dark-framed eyes. If he was human she would have guessed him to be in his mid-thirties.

Leila caught her breath, a warm flush engulfing her as his vibrant green eyes fixed pointedly on hers – eyes encased by thick, dark lashes that only exacerbated their intensity – eyes that were sharp, intelligent, astute and merciless.

The eyes of a vampire.

She could feel it as clearly as if she were holding a white-hot coal.

As those vampire eyes assessed her slowly and purposefully from toes up to eyes, she instinctively took a step back and clutched the straps of her rucksack again.

His sullen gaze pinned her to the spot as their eyes met again, the flush of trepidation and excitement flooding her. Amidst the dim surroundings, the breeze from the open doors stirring his hair, he looked utterly preternatural to the point of being hypnotic. He was every inch the vampire and every inch the last thing that should be considering remotely appealing.

Leila forcibly snapped herself from her daze, berating herself as she

minded herself of where she was and why she was there. More to the
oint, of what he was and that it was him who was clearly holding Ali-
1a for ransom. 'Where's my sister?'

'Show me the book,' Caleb said, a sexy rasp exacerbating his surly tone.

'Tell me she's all right.'

'Alisha's fine.'

'Prove it.'

'The book first.'

Leila tightened her grip on her shoulder straps. 'If you want it, you
t me see her.'

The tension in the room nearly squeezed the life-breath out of her
s Caleb narrowed his eyes. She took another wary step back, dropping
er hands from her rucksack ready to defend herself.

He held his penetrating gaze on her for an uncomfortable second
onger than was necessary before he looked across at Hade and cocked
is head towards the hallway behind.

Hade nodded then disappeared from sight, reappearing seconds
ter with a small figure.

She looked tired, worn and tearful, with no characteristic mischie-
ous bounce in her brown eyes. Alisha stayed perfectly still a few feet
way, her gaze on Leila hesitant.

Leila heaved with relief but as she stepped forward to greet her, Ca-
eb caught her by the upper arm with a grip that was powerful, com-
anding. Electricity pulsated through her, the impact of his touch staring her to stillness.

'Do what you came here to do,' he said. 'Reunion later.'

Leila's gaze snapped to his as she instinctively tried to pull her arm
rom his steady grip. 'And then what?'

Alisha broke the silence. 'Just do as he says, Leila. Please.'

Leila glanced across to her.

'Please,' Alisha pleaded more quietly, her wide eyes reddened from
rying.

Leila wavered for only a moment longer before pulling away from Caleb. She slipped her rucksack from her shoulders and unzipped the main compartment. She slid out the book and tentatively, grudgingly held it out for him.

Caleb flicked through the pages then looked back at her. 'You can read this, right?'

She didn't dare tell him she was a little out of practice nor that she had never, technically, carried out any of the spells at all. But she nodded. 'Yes.'

Handing the book to Hade, he stepped up to her.

Leila instinctively backed up against the sofa, her heel catching the base as she grasped the soft leather. Warily holding his gaze, she knew she'd strike back if she had to, but she wasn't stupid enough to instigate it. And she wasn't stupid enough to jeopardise Alisha. A little bit of humility had to be the order of the day, the rest she'd work out from there.

'And you can perform the spell?' he asked.

'Yes.'

He grabbed her wrist, holding up her protest rings – one gracing her thumb, the other her little finger – engraved silver bands that danced in the artificial light. Bands that were the ultimate sign of defiance against the social acceptance of his kind.

He barely looked at them as his eyes narrowed on hers. 'Your sister assures me you're smart, but you coming here with these makes me think otherwise.'

Leila tried to pull her wrist away but he held it fast, his closeness exacerbating the subtle scent of alcohol and smoke that mingled intoxicatingly with the musky woody undertones of his aftershave. 'I'm not going to hide how I feel just because I'm here.'

There was a hint of an amusement in his eyes, but it never reached his lips. 'I hear you're not our biggest fan.'

Her unease escalated as he searched her eyes. A light perspiration swept over her. He couldn't know what she was – not just by looking.

She held her breath, her heart throbbing painfully. The flutter of excitement she felt in her chest disturbed her. But she forced herself with every iota of willpower not to look away from those intimidating green eyes. Worse still, behind the aesthetics there was something more than the emptiness she expected – something beyond soulless, heartless windows. Within those eyes that should have looked dead, there was something deep, poignant and entrancing.

Heat rushed between her legs She swallowed harder than she would have liked, hating the way her body responded immediately to his. She knew it was wrong – deeply and horribly wrong on too many levels. But she still found her gaze wandering down to the top two unfastened buttons of his shirt, a gap that revealed a tantalizing glimpse of smooth, honed chest. She lingered on his masculine bow lips, his strong jaw, before sliding back up over his perfectly formed nose to his eyes. Beautiful eyes that lingered coaxingly on hers for another uncomfortable couple of seconds before he finally pulled away.

'Let's do this,' he said, retrieving the book from Hade before leading the way back down the hallway.

Lightning Source UK Ltd.
Milton Keynes UK
UKOW051449271212

204109UK00009B/175/P